Major Evielynne Gastineau, in her Army Service Dress Uniform, sat on the stone bench watching the soft orange sun slowly sinking in the west. The Silver Star on her chest gleamed in the setting sun. This was the last day she'd wear this uniform as an active duty member of the US Army. Thirteen years was a long time to wear the same thing every day! But today, that all ended.

As she gazed across the waters of Suisun Bay, a gentle breeze kissed her cheeks and sent sparkling ripples across the surface. It was a magical time of day at the memorial, easy to relax and remember all the men and women who died, right where she sat, all those years ago. Easy to remember three years ago when she'd first set foot on the cement of this very same memorial, and her life had taken an extraordinary turn.

Other Books by Miriam Matthews

THE GHOST OF PORT CHICAGO
a prequel to *ON THE SIDE OF ANGELS*

On the Side of Angels

by

Miriam Matthews

This is a work of fiction. Names, characters, places, and incidents are either the product of the author's imagination or are used fictitiously, and any resemblance to actual persons living or dead, business establishments, events, or locales, is entirely coincidental.

On the Side of Angels

COPYRIGHT © 2019 by Miriam Matthews

All rights reserved. No part of this book may be used or reproduced in any manner whatsoever without written permission of the author or The Wild Rose Press, Inc. except in the case of brief quotations embodied in critical articles or reviews.
Contact Information: info@thewildrosepress.com

Cover Art by *Abigail Owen*

The Wild Rose Press, Inc.
PO Box 708
Adams Basin, NY 14410-0708
Visit us at www.thewildrosepress.com

Publishing History
First Fantasy Rose Edition, 2019
Print ISBN 978-1-5092-2823-2
Digital ISBN 978-1-5092-2824-9

Published in the United States of America

Dedication

To the men and women who serve their country and live to serve again

~*~

For my mother-in-law, an angel herself

Chapter 1

Major Evielynne Gastineau, in her Army Service Dress Uniform, sat on the stone bench watching the soft orange sun slowly sinking in the west. The Silver Star on her chest gleamed in the setting sun. This was the last day she'd wear this uniform as an active duty member of the US Army. Thirteen years was a long time to wear the same thing every day! But today, that all ended.

As she gazed across the waters of Suisun Bay, a gentle breeze kissed her cheeks and sent sparkling ripples across the surface. It was a magical time of day at the memorial, easy to relax and remember all the men and women who died, right where she sat, all those years ago. Easy to remember three years ago when she'd first set foot on the cement of this very same memorial, and her life had taken an extraordinary turn.

Evie smiled softly. An extraordinary turn? That was an understatement! Her own unique talents, her Cajun family heritage, and a very impatient ghost had been the combination that all started here, the catalyst that paved the way for one old, dying man to be reunited with his soul mate, for eternity. Evie had been the conduit.

The American flag clanged against the metal pole, chiming in the breeze. Evie looked up just in time to catch a wavering glimpse of a huge WWII sailor in his dress whites, holding hands with the cute, blonde love-of-his-life, just as the sun shot its green flare across the water and sank beneath the horizon. The sailor saluted and his girlfriend waved as their images disappeared with the day's light.

Amee and Grady.

Tears welled and Evie sniffed loudly.

The ghost of Port Chicago was only the beginning of her life after Iraq and the Taliban prison. Now there would be another beginning.

A civilian beginning.

The thought made her mind stagger.

"Sad about leaving the army, Major?" Evie felt Conrad McIntyre take a seat next to her. "This is a beautiful place to contemplate the rest of your life, Evie."

"It sure is." She wiped away the tiny tear clinging to her dark lashes. "Did you ever think, when we were there, in Iraq, in that hell hole, that someday we'd be sitting here, watching the sunset, me and you?"

"Frankly, I didn't think any of us would be walking out of that place. Correction, carried out of that place." He patted Evie's arm, just below the long scar, that was slowly fading. "Had the ever-tenacious Captain Gastineau not appeared in our private abyss of torture and starvation, I'm sure Pete and I wouldn't have survived another week. We owe you our lives. Some fancy metal star will never be enough thanks for what you did."

Evie saw the emotion in Conrad's face. "Yeah," She tried for a lighter tone. Today had been emotional enough for a lifetime. "Those were the days, weren't they?"

Conrad cleared his throat. "And then some."

They sat in silence for a while before either could speak.

"Andrea sends her love and this." Conrad fished in his pocket and withdrew a locket. The cover was silver, flourished, and engraved with the initials E and G. He opened it and inside was a picture of himself and Andrea behind their wedding cake. Evie stood next to Conrad, and Pete Newcastle stood behind the bride. Their smiles were infectious, and the happiness of that day was clearly apparent on everyone's face. "It was our happiest day and she wanted you to have it to remember…and possibly find your…" Conrad cleared his throat again, "…happiest day."

"Oh, that is so sweet. I'll have to give her a call later and thank her." Evie took the locket and peered at the tiny picture. "That was such a hideous dress and my feet were killing me in those heels." She laughed. "But it was worth it. You two were meant for each other."

Conrad visibly blushed. He was a guy's guy under the suit and tie. She'd spent enough time in rehab with him to know. He was at home in cargo pants and a sweaty T-shirt, not Valentino or Marc Jacobs. "Thanks, Evie. She really is something, isn't she?" He pointed to his bride in the picture. "I'm the luckiest guy on the face of the planet. Speaking of which," Conrad looked intently at his friend. "Who was that lucky guy you were dancing with?"

"You mean Simon? A guy I met when I first came here. He's a friend." Evie felt the warmth spread across her face, and she couldn't keep the girlish giggle out of her voice. "And, soon he will be my boss. He offered me a job at his company…as the Security Director.

He's amazing. He made VP of the company before he was thirty-four."

"Ooooh, sleeping with the enemy, huh?"

Evie slugged Conrad in the shoulder. "No sleeping. Just friends. We met under very unusual circumstances. His great-uncle passed away here, at the memorial. I had to deal with it. We sort of bonded in a really strange way."

Conrad was intrigued. "The Port Chicago 50 guy? I remember that."

"The very same. Grandville O'Sullivan was his name. Simon is his great nephew. Grady raised him, mostly. Grady was an incredible man and I was honored to meet him, if only a day before he passed."

"Got in good with the family, huh?" Conrad raised his eyebrows and grinned like an attorney chasing an ambulance.

"What? No! I had some, ah, interesting stuff to deal with." That was putting it mildly! She'd been haunted by Grady's dead girlfriend from 1944, and pestered, until she actually got Grady to come back to the base before he died. It was an entire long story, in and of itself. It was one that only she and Simon really understood. Evie wanted to keep it that way. The military docs didn't need to know she could talk to ghosts. They'd stick her in the looney bin and throw away the key, for sure. "Why all the questions?"

"Since Andrea couldn't be here, she promised me something very special if I came back with some juicy intel." Conrad made a kissy face then grinned.

"You're kidding! Wait till I talk to her." Evie had to laugh. Andrea had found such complete love with Conrad, she was always looking for a partner for Evie and Conrad's buddy, Pete. "She is incorrigible. You know that, right?"

"Oh yeah! That's one of the many things I love about her." Conrad's smile turned into a bit of a leer as he watched the water sparkle while dusk descended around them.

"Simon is VP of Digital Mystery and Mastery. He programs games. I guess it's fairly lucrative." Evie watched a family of ducks swimming around the black pilings, the only things left after the historic explosion that blew away two huge ships filled with ammunition bound for Asia in WWII. Hundreds of people died in the tragic accident, her little ghost being one of them.

"That Simon O'Sullivan? The creator of Ghost Wars?" Conrad seemed intrigued. She knew he didn't have time in his life to play a lot of video games. "Pete is a huge fan. He plays that game in some kind of international league and then has to tell me how high of a score he got and how he wiped the competition, worldwide! Your Simon made that game? Wow!"

"That'd be the one. He finished the game just after his great-uncle passed away." What she didn't say was the main character in the game was fashioned after her little ghost, one notorious Amee McGee, the Ghost of Port Chicago.

"Hang onto that one. He's got to have a pretty decent income, not to mention a permanent job if he's the VP."

"You make me sound like I'm a gold digger. It's not like that. Simon and I went through the loss of his great-uncle together. It makes for a kind of bond, ya know." Evie didn't like the direction of the conversation. She didn't date Simon because of his money, or his fame as a game developer. She was comfortable with the guy who had shared his great-uncle's love with her, if only for a few days. But it was more than that. She was a broken soldier, suffering from horrible PTSD and still recovering from her wounds as an unwilling guest in a Taliban prison, when she first came to MOTCO as the Provost Marshal. Simon was a hurt, little boy who'd had a tough life with an addict mom and the Oakland streets for a home. Until Uncle Grady and her little ghost happened along. Amee took away Evie's nightmares and Grady gave Simon a home. They'd both witnessed the miracle of Grady and Amee's reunion and path to heaven. That was a connection that could never be broken. It was also one of those life-changing events that was never far from her mind.

"Well, hold onto that guy. You looked great dancing together. Like you fit." Conrad continued to contemplate the water. "For better, for worse. For richer, for poorer. But richer is better. That should have been written into the original vows!" While Evie had remained with the US Army, Conrad had started a company with Pete, once they had recovered and separated from the military service. Their company hit pay dirt with several government contracts. Now Global Systems Technology employed over two hundred people and was an up and coming Fortune 500 company in Texas. Evie got regular updates from Conrad and Pete both, and loved being an arm-chair witness to their success after sharing the worst together, in Iraq.

"Money isn't everything." Evie mused. "But it helps. He got me an apartment in Oakland as one of the perks of my job. It's in a high rise but I'm actually starting to move in and enjoy the place."

"Wow. Moving on rapidly, girl."

"Well, I've lived in military housing for the last thirteen years. It's about time for something other than tan and green." Evie laid her head on Conrad's shoulder. "I always thought I wanted a little place with flowers and green grass, but I've come to realize high security tops the list of desirable attributes in living accommodations these days."

"Nightmares still?" Conrad shifted uncomfortably. He'd seen the aftereffects of torture and imprisonment. Evie knew he'd felt them up front and personal.

"Actually, no. Things sorta changed after Grady died…right here." She pointed to the seat where they sat.

Conrad got up quickly. "Right," He pointed to the cement bench. "Here?"

Evie laughed. She'd never considered the bench a *death seat*. "Yep. Right here. Right next to me."

"And that doesn't bother you. Right there, huh?" Conrad peered at the seat and decided to stand. "Well, Major Gastineau, you have one more duty before taking that uniform off forever."

"And what's that?" She couldn't remember anything else required before she left the base for good.

"Get drunk with your two buddies. Of course." He pointed to the civilian car he was driving. "Simon can drive." He held out his hand and pulled Evie from the bench.

"You want Simon to come with us?" She was a little taken aback. They didn't usually speak freely around civilians. Most folks hadn't the slightest idea what hideous things the Taliban was capable of, and the things soldiers had experienced and seen in the sandbox. Simon was a sweet man. She had no idea how he'd respond to what might come out of their mouths with the addition of a little alcohol. "You think that's a good idea?"

"Looks to me like he might end up family." Evie knew Conrad was watching her for some tell-tale sign of budding love. She schooled her features to try and look innocent.

"Like it or not, he might as well get used to us and our ways." Conrad pulled Evie toward his car. "And if he runs, you'll know he's not the one."

Chapter 2

Eight months later…

Simon pushed the buzzer and waited. It took a minute or so, but soon he heard Evie's voice.

"Simon?" The voice paused.

"It's me. The only Simon in your charmed life, my dear." He smiled into the video camera. The building where Evielynne Gastineau now lived was wired for sound and entry. No one got past the doorman or the security system without permission. He'd set this place up for his new Director of Security when she hired on several months ago. He'd never regretted it, even though it was a little heavy handed on his part. He had a vested interest in his new Director's security and Oakland was a tough town. He grew up there and so had his mother. Until it took her life. Simon corrected himself. *It* hadn't taken his mother away. She took her own life by the choices she made, time after time. If it wasn't a wonderful new guy who turned out to be an abusive dealer, then it was the newest drug on the underground market. If it produced a high, she'd eat it, snort it, or shoot it up her arm. Simon reminded himself, negative rumination did no good. His life was what he'd made it. His great-uncle had taught him that. Uncle Grady had always been full of little sayings and good advice for the lonely boy with no father and a dead mother.

"Come on up." A buzzer sounded and the elevator doors opened.

Simon got in and punched the fifteenth floor. It wasn't a penthouse, but it was stylish and secure.

Evie had been Digital Mystery and Mastery's new Security Director since she walked off the base called Marine Ocean Terminal Concord (MOTCO), eight months back. Simon was proud of the way she adjusted to not only a civilian job, but also their growing friendship. Their relationship was easy and warm, but every time Simon entertained the idea of taking it to the next step, all he could see was his mother in her coffin at the Baptist Church. All dressed up in her Sunday best and ready to go away, forever. The funeral home had done their best, but even their funeral technicians and talented Director couldn't quite cover up her last binge, and the beating that ultimately ended her miserable life. Simon never wanted to hurt a woman, physically or mentally. The fear of doing exactly that kept him from testing the romantic waters and kept Evie at arm's length. It was better that way, considering what he knew she'd gone through in her army career. He never wanted to add insult to injury. Simon had seen some of the scars and heard the banter at her separation party. He knew she'd been awarded the Silver Star for bravery above and beyond the call of duty. He also knew she'd been seriously wounded but managed to escape her Taliban captors, dragging two other soldiers with her. But the night those two guys had gotten drunk with her after her ceremony was more than he could handle.

After about five or six shots they started playing a game called *Top This*. One would show a scar with the accompanying explanation for the wound, then the next would have to top that. The looser had to buy a round. Simon ended up buying all of the rounds. The only thing that marred his body in the least, was a two-inch faded appendectomy scar from when he was fourteen. Still, what he saw and heard made him sick for days. Or maybe it was the worst hangover he'd ever had in his life. It didn't matter. Simon held his own and was now an ex-facto member of the Iraq Trauma in-circle.

Evie met him at the elevator door. There were six apartment homes on the fifteenth floor, all spacious with views of some form of water. All very nice and clean. New appliances and rugs all around. All very secure. Simon waved to the hall camera as he walked under the surveillance equipment.

Evie took his arm as they walked the fifty feet to her apartment door. "Why do you do that?" She giggled at him. He never understood why she was always so happy, after so much pain. Maybe it was true that you had to know pain to really recognize happiness and the gifts in your life.

"Habit. My building has a two-way and the guy waves back. I like having people I can trust around me, and I always make sure they get recognition." He followed her inside. "I may have a bunch of money, a great condo, and a jet, but I come from the hood. Neighbors is neighbors. You wave."

"So where's dinner tonight? I have a couple things I want to discuss before I'm off the clock."

"You're way too efficient, Ms. Gastineau." He shook his head. "I still want to call you Captain Gastineau."

"That was a while back. When you hated the

military. Just for your information, Mr. O'Sullivan, I got a promotion, remember? I believe you were there, remember. When I separated, I was a Major." She tapped one shoulder with her finger.

Simon and Evie'd talked about her promotion several times. He knew she was very proud of the fact that she was promoted in her last position as Provost Marshal. It was still hard for women in the army to climb the rank ladder, and the move from silver bars to a gold oak leaf made an impression on most of the men she worked with. Not the promotion, but the recognition for a job done superbly well.

"But you can call me Captain if you want. You sign my paychecks now." She handed him a glass of wine. "I have a report over here that may stir up a hornet's nest at the office." She indicated two manila folders on the dining room table, grabbed her own glass and joined Simon.

"Do we have to work? I'm burned out." Simon whined a little. He really was tired, but mostly he had some exciting news he wanted to share with Evie over sautéed scallops and mushrooms with seasoned wild rice at Obedi's down the street. It was one of their favorite restaurants and Evie often mentioned how she loved the quaint atmosphere. "Let's go to Obedi's."

"I was just trying to be efficient, boss." Simon caught Evie's frown immediately.

"You're not in the army anymore. I like efficiency to a point. But not when I'm hungry. Let's go."

As they walked a half a block to the restaurant, Simon's bodyguard fell in behind them. His name was Bull for a good reason. He was as big as a bull and twice as strong. He was also Simon's childhood friend from the old neighborhood.

As they entered the restaurant, Salvatore ushered them to their favorite table and Bull took up residence at the table next to them, blocking potential fans or uninvited guests. He had to stick his legs out and around the small table to actually fit.

As they ordered and settled in with their favorite soft drinks, Simon fidgeted, waiting for the right time to present his news.

His behavior did not go unnoticed by his Director of Security and finally Evie had to ask. "Okay, Simon, what's eating at you?"

Bull chuckled behind them.

"Well, *Gaming Industry Report Magazine* came out with the game ratings for one hundred international game competitions. And guess what was in first place?" His smile was as wide as his face and brilliant as a shining star.

Simon had devoured the article as soon as it hit his desk and wondered if Evie knew. He felt like an idiot, but he could not resist the smile that stretched across his face. The rumor mill at the office was more like a freeway and word moved without restraint, at a high rate of speed. He figured Evie had to know.

"Ah, would that be Ghost Wars?" She smiled sweetly and toasted her boss.

"So you heard? Ah man..." Simon sat back.

She knew.

"I suspected. Why would you ask me that question if it wasn't your game?" She giggled. "After all, I am your Security Director. I know everything." She really didn't after only eight months on the job, but to her credit, she was working on it. Simon mentally congratulated himself on snagging this incredible woman, right out of the military.

"I should have known. I guess it was a kind of non-surprise then, huh?"

"Did you read the rest of the report, Mr. O'Sullivan?"

"No. Just saw the numbers. Numbers don't lie! What was in the article?" Their dinner arrived and Simon dug in.

"Well, you're right about the numbers. The dollar numbers." She picked delicately at the scallops while she talked. "Apparently, in the gaming world, your game has reached over five million players and your company has grossed more than that. Digital Mystery and Mastery is now the third highest rated digital gaming company in the world. You even beat out that new anime game, Dragon's Breath. That's impressive."

Simon's jaw dropped despite the food it contained. "No way! Holy cow!" He mumbled around rice and scallops.

Evie gave him time to clear his mouth as she laughed.

Mouth empty, Simon had one more surprise. "But did you know that next week's Digital Game Development World Conference will be in Cupertino? And I have a special ticket? Because…"

Now it was Evie's turn to show teeth and tongue. "No! Really?"

"Yes, really. And it is rumored that Simon O'Sullivan, master coder and game developer, is up for a big award and a company bonus." He twirled his fork in the air. He hated crowds and didn't like being touched by people he didn't know, but this conference was by invitation only. Astute marketing skills told him it was necessary.

"You're going? How are you going to handle all those people? That conference is by invitation only! You hate crowds."

They'd shared so much since Uncle Grady's passing, he could clearly read the surprise on Evie's face. "Of course I'm going, plus one?" He added the last as a question.

"Me?" She squeaked out. "You want me to go?"

"Sure. Why not? If I have to go stand up in front of all those people, you could at least be in the audience for moral support. Or standing next to me so no one would look at anybody but you!" Simon went back to his dinner and kept his eyes on his rice. He was very nervous about asking Evie to be his date. Their close relationship was common knowledge around the office, but going public? That was a challenge for the man who liked his privacy and kept his social life separate from the job.

"It's the movers and shakers in the gaming world. What would I wear?" She was reaching for an excuse to stay behind. Simon knew she hated crowds as much or more than he did... "I can't afford that kind of get-up yet. And the dinner is what? Twelve hundred dollars? I'm a new employee. I can't—"

"Say yes and I can make the rest happen. My treat. What you did for Uncle Grady and Amee is worth so much more." The memories of what she'd done for his uncle were still fresh in his mind. He felt the beginnings of a tear. He couldn't face his uncle's passing with any amount of coherent thought back then. At least for a couple days, Evie had taken the reins and done what had to be done, then helped Simon clean up Grady's estate. Simon sorta followed Evie's lead, like a puppy just separated from its litter. He was lost, but the good Captain Gastineau had found him and led him home.

"I don't know. I really can't..." Evie didn't know what to say. Simon was aware this conference was the gaming world's closest thing to the Oscars or the Emmys. Simon knew he'd blind-sided her with his question.

"You really can." It was a simple statement, and when Evie didn't respond, Simon jumped at the opportunity. "I take it that's a yes, then?"

Evie couldn't talk. She just nodded yes and took a huge bite of rice and scallops—and darn near choked!

Chapter 3

They're gonna be late.

Don't be silly, Grady, my love. It's Simon's big day! She sat, holding the hand of the man she'd waited an eternity for, as clouds pillowed around them.

Yep. They're gonna be late.

God was in his heaven and all was right with their world, but Simon? That boy was gonna be late!

****

Oakland, California

"Evie, we gotta go! Are you ready?" She could hear Simon hollering down the hallway from his seat in the living room. She'd left him sitting patiently, checking his email and letting the social media time-suck calm his nerves. This was his event and he was already sweating through his shirt. It probably made him feel clammy in his own skin.

Evie stared into the full-length mirror of her closet door. What was she doing? She took a deep breath and tried to quell the shaking of her spray-tanned legs, balancing on four-inch spiky heels that sparkled like a million stars in her reflection. Why had she told Simon she'd be his *plus-one* for this…this what? Coming out thing? Game party? She was dressed to the nines and it made her want to vomit.

She was a soldier. No. Strike that. She *used* to be a soldier. Give her a full complement of terrorists armed to the teeth and she knew what to do. She knew how to dress for that; desert camo-boots, ACUs, Tactical Banshee body armor, a forty-pound pack on her back, and she was ready to meet and greet. But an award party for some fancy video game with cute 3-D glasses and a buzzing glove? Really?

"Evie!" The tone indicated he was losing patience. "The guest of honor is going to be late for his own introduction. Can you move it a little, babe? It's a long drive to Cupertino and there might be traffic."

She took one more deep breath, or tried to, tucked her full breasts a little more down into the gown that almost covered her chest, and turned toward the doorway. Immediately her heel caught in the soft plush rug of her bedroom. She still wasn't used to soft and comfortable after years of *military acceptable.* She grabbed the edge of the dresser to balance. "Slow and sophisticated, Evie girl. Slow and easy. You can do this mission."

Simon had helped her pick out her dress for the evening's celebration, since her idea of formal wear was black Dockers and a clean T-shirt. He even insisted on paying for it as well! Simon wouldn't let her see the tag, he said he just liked the color, and how it fit so snugly. It didn't matter that the strapless burgundy satin hugged like a second skin, well, partial skin anyway, and felt like Clingwrap. It sure didn't cover much, showing her rich honey shoulders and one long, shapely leg, almost up to her hip. Every time she saw herself in the dress, she felt the need to take cover! The salon downstairs had sent a make-up artist up to do her war paint and now her shimmery lips could be seen miles away. Her hair was plastered with so much hairspray it would take a week of shampooing to get it out, and her scars were covered with some sort of paint-on plastic and airbrushed to invisibility. She hadn't looked this good since her high school prom. She hadn't shown so much skin since surgery at Walter Reed!

She looked almost normal. Almost. "Coming, Simon. But I'm not sure I'll be able to make it down the hall." Evie put both hands on the door jams and successfully eased out of the room. The hardwood flooring of the hall presented another challenge as she wobbled and clicked the way toward her man-of-the-hour. As Simon stood to take her arm, his phone dropped along with his jaw…nearly all the way to the floor and he stood there like a statue, frozen in space and time. He was acting as if Evie was the most incredibly luscious woman he'd ever seen. Like she was some angel from heaven wrapped in silky satin. It was evident his genius mind had stalled at the sight, but his body sure didn't. Evie couldn't help noticing one particular part rose to the occasion with a good deal of speed and precision, tenting the front of his slacks with a sure fire Howdy Duty salute that couldn't be missed by anyone, let alone the woman who'd caused it!

Evie teetered a foot away. "This is tougher than a recon mission in Mosul." She moved her feet back and forth in place. "And harder! Simon? Simon close your mouth, please. You look like you just saw an eighteen-ounce slab of prime rib." She chuckled in her soft Cajun manner.

Which did nothing to help Simon with his problem. He bent to adjust and cover his intense reaction and to retrieve his phone. "Ah…" His mouth wouldn't work. "Ah…"

"You're stuttering, genius programmer and creator of the hottest new game on the multimillion-dollar market." She reached out and smacked his shoulder.

The typical Evie snap-out-of-it smack brought Simon to his senses, which only did more to exacerbate his problem. Her get-ready *team* had applied all sorts of jells, creams and other unidentifiable stuff to her skin and now she smelled of honeysuckle and sugar rum, and molasses. It almost reminded her of home, but without the dress and heels. Her face shone with light sparkles and rich tones that were strategically intended to capture a man's eye. When his gaze settled on her lips, he had to sit down to catch his breath once again. Evie laughed at Simon's reaction. It was clear he was having trouble standing, speaking, just remaining upright.

"Holy cow." Simon licked his lips and Evie laughed again.

"I squeeze myself into this tight, red gunnysack, paint myself up like a trollop, and all you can say is holy cow? Do you know how much work went into this?" Evie did a slow, sexy spin on her tippy toes, motioning from hair to heels like Vanna White with a riddle. "Really? It took an entire tactical team of specialists to accomplish this."

"I, ah...I..." A grin played across Simon's face. "If I said you had a beautiful body would you hold it against me?" Heaven only knew why that particular saying came to his mind, but it did, and crawled right out his gaping mouth.

"My body or the song?" Evie had him, and knew it. It'd been a long time since she'd seen a reaction like this. Never because of her.

Simon choked and dropped his phone into his lap, just missing his body's standing ovation.

Evie laughed. She was enjoying the effect her appearance had on Simon. It was almost worth the hours she and an entire team of make-up artists and clothiers had spent on her get-up. "I thought you were in a big hurry, Mr. O'Sullivan? Stand up, man."

The apartment intercom interrupted her enjoyment. "Your limo is here, Mr. O'Sullivan."

"Limo? Ah, Simon, you shouldn't have." Evie pulled her matching wrap from the couch, grabbed a small clutch and opened the door. "Vamanos, baby." She motioned toward the driver who stood in the open doorway.

The mirror next to her door showed it all. The purposeful picture of her backside had obviously sent Simon's mind into overdrive and she got another quiet chuckle out of his attempt to stand and follow the procession, without hurting himself. It was still hard to believe, in about two hours, she'd be standing next to him as he received the industry's highest accolade. In front of millions of people. Simon followed Bull, and Evie into the elevator. It was nineteen floors to the basement, and about twenty steps to the car. She was sure he could do this. Sitting next to a satin-clad gift from heaven she looked to be? Maybe not. At least, maybe not without a good amount of mental manipulation and a significant dose of saltpeter!

"You're staring, Simon." Her sultry comment had Simon studying the floor and blushing to his roots.

Bull's huge frame shook as he chuckled. "That be cuz my man here never been with a sweet sista. He be all bunched up." Bull grabbed his crotch and moved it up and down.

That got Simon's attention. "Oh, for the love of Jesus, Bull. Can you please clean it up?" Ever since Simon had been dating Evie, or whatever it was they did together, Bull had been part of their life. One such sorta-date night, Simon's childhood history overflowed his mouth with a little too much fruity rum and chips. Evie learned a lot about her sensitive geek. Bull was a gang thug from the Oakland hood where Simon grew up. They'd been friends since second grade, when a bully from the other side of the tracks tried to steal Simon's lunch money. Bull beat the kid down and took everything he had, including his bright new tennis shoes. Like a self-appointed Robin Hood, Bull handed out what little money he took from the kid to his buds, then gave Simon the tennis shoes. After that, no one fooled with the scrawny genius who had a tattooed guardian angel with his own private army.

Bull straightened, as much as he could, for a six-foot, eight-inch, three-hundred-pound man in a small elevator. "Of course, Mr. O'Sullivan. Right-oh, chap." Bull affected a British accent and snapped a sharp salute. For a fellow raised in the inner city of Oakland, Bull's quick sense of humor and keen observational skills had served him well and kept him alive in some tight situations. His ability to mimic just about any accent lent the huge man a kind of comical timing that often drove anger to comedy, and deadly to survivable. That was until Simon pulled him out of the sewer and dressed him up as a bodyguard and driver. They were close, like brothers from a different mother, and Bull still protected his sibling. Now he just had a better set of duds and more expensive resources.

A quiet ding announced their arrival in the underground garage of the apartment complex. "Showtime." She placed a restraining hand on Simon's arm. "I hope I don't embarrass you, Simon. I'm not used to this kind of get-up. I..." She stalled.

He kissed her on the cheek. Her perfect shiny, glossed lips were off limits until after the Kodak moments on the green carpet of the gaming industry's celebratory evening. In fact, he'd only once kissed her lips ever, when he was drunk.

Simon tried a flirty comment to ease the tension. "We could ditch this circus and go back upstairs." His smile widened as her very exposed cleavage drew his eyes like a precious new toy at Christmas. He pulled at the collar of his ruffled shirt. The bow tie was way too tight and Evie understood his discomfort. It was hot and muggy in the garage and the tuxedo he wore probably felt like a straight jacket from Hell.

"No can do, boss. Mathers said I was to get you there at any cost." Bull opened the door and waved them into the spacious limo.

One more reassuring peck on the cheek and Simon straightened She was well aware of what they both knew would come. "I'm more worried about me embarrassing myself, Evie. You will do fine. Me? Not so sure." He helped her into the back seat. "Bull, sometimes..." Simon made a fist and punched his palm in a warning gesture.

"Uh huh, boss. Only in those fantasy games you make." Bull laughed.

"Really!" Once, back in high school, according to Simon's alcoholic historical, he had lost his temper. He seldom allowed that to happen and when it did, he was ashamed. He'd actually hit the wall of his uncle's living room. That had required a trip to the Emergency Room. The wall went unscathed. Bull was right about his physical acumen.

"Get in the car, Simon." Bull turned the man by his tailored tuxedo and gave a gentle shove, Evie played catcher and sent a subtle wink Bull's way. Once, during and unexpected heart-to-heart, Bull told Evie just how precious his relationship with Simon was. He'd also weighed in on Evie with admiration. He understood her scars and respected her military career. He thought she played straight with his brother and appreciated her no-nonsense approach to life!

He also thought they made a great couple! Bull said Simon was the geeky genius with more money than God, and Evie was the gorgeous war hero with medals and skills to kill. He knew they both had issues and promised to keep that confidential.

Settled in the back of the limo, Simon took Evie's hand. "We'll both do just fine." His cock-eyed grin said it all. He didn't even need to add, "I hope."

She was a soldier. She could do this. "Just one more mission. A little different uniform. No weapons. No forty-pound pack. Just forty pounds of make-up—" She smacked her lips and made a sucking sound. "—and half a gallon of petroleum jelly."

"Ah, honey, you're going to slay 'em with satin and half a gallon of petroleum jelly." For the first time in her life, she felt like perfection, holding her man's hand and watched as he licked his lips, again. She imagined what trickle of romantic thoughts slid through Simon's mind. *Maybe...Nah!*

"Yeah, right! If only Amee could see me now.

She'd have a fit. Probably turn the fire alarms on all over MOTCO!"

"They'd both be proud as heck. They are watching. I know they are." Simon's eyes watered a touch. Simon would hold back the tears if it was the last thing he did.

Evie squeezed his hand and gave a soft smile. "Yeah."

It brought Evie back to the beginning. It was a beginning they'd discussed many times and she knew he still found it hard to accept, in his concrete world of computer coding and marketing statistics. Yet, Amee, the infamous ghost of Port Chicago, was why and how Evie connected with Simon almost four years previous. Army Captain Evielynne Gastineau, the Provost Marshal of Military Ocean Terminal Concord, at the time, was the only living person who could hear and see the pesky ghost. Tormented, Evie helped the little ghost find her lost love, none other than Grandville O'Sullivan, Uncle Grady. Between the machinations of Simon and the dedication of Evie, Grady and Amee were able to spend their last minutes on earth together, one as a trapped ghost who'd died on that hot July night in 1944, the other a dying old man who'd lost his only love to the historic explosion. Thinking back to that evening at the Port Chicago Naval Magazine National Memorial still made them both understand real love through the eyes of the doomed couple. That night they actually got a glimpse of heaven, and felt the intense love that transcended time and life itself. They saw Grady as a young black sailor, full of life and adoration for his forbidden love. They saw Amee, the white daughter of a Naval captain, a ghost since her death in the explosion of Port Chicago, take her lover's hand as they both departed for the next life, together. As the reunited couple waved goodbye to a stunned audience of two, they both saw a flash in the sunset and knew Amyrillis Marie McGee finally wore the silver ring Seaman Grandville O'Sullivan made for her from his lucky nickel, in 1944.

It seemed like a millennium ago. Evie was still on active duty and charged with the safety of Military Ocean Terminal Concord, or MOTCO. A cheesy assignment for a Silver Star awardee, she was still recovering from her imprisonment and torture in Iraq when Amee's appearance slammed her back into the Louisiana swamps and the Cajun roots that blessed her with the ability to see and speak with ghosts. While her wounds continued to heal, her family's legacy reared its head and Evie was introduced to a love story that never ended…and a haunting that never would, if Amee could not confess her love for the man she was to meet on the night of her death. Simon was the belligerent nephew who protected his dying great-uncle with everything he had. Which was considerable, since he'd made vice president of Digital Mystery and Mastery, the leading digital game producer in the world. His hatred for the United States military was a brick, steel and titanium wall he built to insulate his uncle from the past and the disgrace of the Port Chicago 50 conviction. But that all changed with Evie, and the ghost of Port Chicago. Ultimately, Simon's love for the surrogate father his uncle had become, was the salve for his soul. Witnessing his uncle's passing in the arms of a love the old man had waited over sixty years for, was an epiphany that completely changed his life, and hers. It had also changed their view of not only the disaster in

1944, but love itself.

Evie found Simon to be an incredible crucible of warmth and, dare she say, love, in her structured and concrete military life. In the last few months, since Evie had gone to work for his company, she extended her fledgling civilian wings and gained the respect of her peers. Most of the nightmares that tortured her mind had ceased. All because of Amee and Grady's great love. She had to admit the little ghost brought something incredible into their lives and left a stamp on their hearts. She found Simon to be a man who understood her, someone she could trust with her scarred life. Someone who didn't look at her as broken goods, as a crazy woman who heard ghosts and had twenty cats at home!

"Ya know, when I separated from the army, I didn't think civilian life would be quite this difficult." Evie shifted precariously, tugging on the clingy satin as she tried for a more comfortable position on the wide seat.

"It's worth it, babe. You are the most beautiful woman in the world! Right Bull?" Simon yelled at his driver.

"Ah...huh! Yes, sir." Bull's huge smile could be seen in the rearview mirror.

"Oh great. Not helpful, Simon." Evie wiggled and yanked the bodice of her dress higher. "Not helpful at all." Her cell phone buzzed inside the sequined clutch on the seat next to her. "Probably Tootie wanting pictures."

Chapter 4

Evie opened her cute little clutch and viewed the buzzing cell phone screen. "Unknown number. Hmm. Probably a telemarketer." She hit the end button and closed her purse. Almost immediately the phone buzzed again.

"Someone wants to talk to you, hon." Simon nodded toward the purse between them.

"Oh, fine." Evie removed her phone and slid the bar. "Hello?"

"Major Evielynne Gastineau? I hope this is still the correct number. Please don't hang up."

"Who is this?" Evie had been a civilian for almost nine months now. Very few people used her rank anymore.

"Conrad McIntyre. Master Sergeant McIntyre. Is this Evie?" The voice on the other end of the line was not familiar and had a somewhat desperate tone.

"Rad? Is that you? How the hell are you, buddy?" Evie was pleasantly surprised. "Hey, it's been months and we barely caught up at my separation. You in California? Is this a new number for you?"

"Yeah, I know but it's not every day a hero leaves the army. Everybody wanted a piece of you." Never one to mince words, Conrad cut right to the chase. "This is my work number. Evie I've got a problem. I need help. Andrea's gone." His voice broke at the last sentence.

"She left you? Oh my God! What happened, Rad?" Evie put her phone on speaker, motioning to Simon to remain silent.

"No. *No!* She didn't leave me! She was taken, kidnapped. They left a note, then called threatening to kill her." Evie could hear the tense emotion in Conrad's voice. "They want codes to my program. Peter doesn't know yet."

Simon could hear most of the conversation clearly and was manically scribbling on the back of his VIP program. *That's CM? What's wrong? Kidnapped? Where? When? Surveillance cameras?* Evie had no doubt Simon knew exactly who was on the other end of the phone by her huge smile and the nickname she'd used. It was her army buddy from the horrible days that had gotten Simon soused with her and Pete.

Simon handed the paper to her, pointing at the questions.

At Conrad's words, her mind immediately kicked into mission mode. "Okay. Got it. Where was she taken? When? Any cameras around?" The questions were rapid fire as Evie scribbled answers on Simon's program. "Why haven't you told Pete?" She knew they were as tight as brothers after their last tour in Iraq. They started their business together after leaving the army. They lived in each other's pockets, for heaven sakes. The last answer took her by surprise.

"No, long story. I'm leaving the company after my project is done. No problem with Peter; it's me and Andrea. We're…" The conversation died on the vine.

Evie motioned to Simon to be silent. "Rad, I can hear the particulars later. Got the kidnap. Got the ransom demand. I…"

Simon interrupted, "We'll be there in a few hours. With reinforcements." He wasn't good at following directions!

"Evie, who was that?" Conrad's confusion was as clear, as was his suspicion.

"My…" She looked at Simon. What was he?

"Boyfriend. I'm Simon O'Sullivan. The one with the transportation. Text the nearest airport to Evie and we'll be there as soon as we can. Evie can keep you up to date as we go." Simon moved toward the front of the limo and spoke quietly to Bull as Evie finished the quick conversation.

"Rad, I'm not sure what we can do or how we can help, but apparently we are on our way. And Rad…" Evie blew a kiss to her boyfriend, "Simon has some unique talents. He'll be an asset. Text me the info. I'll get back to you. And tell Pete about this. You two are tight. He'll understand." She punched the end button.

"Bull, how long to Oakland International?" Simon asked his driver.

"Mathers is gonna kill my ass, boss. Twenty-one minutes according to the GPS." Bull was shaking his head as he swung the massive limo off the road in preparation for a U-turn. "I may need a new identity after this. You sure you wanna miss your shindig?"

"Yep. Didn't really want to go in the first place. Dress me up and trot me out? Not my style. But I could see Evie this way every day." Evie watched Simon punching the number for his private pilot. "Zackary, would you ready the plane for a cross country flight, please? Texas coast. We'll be there in about twenty minutes. Can you make that?" He really didn't have to ask. Zack was always ready and so was Simon's private jet. Evie'd seen it before and knew enough money could make all kinds of things immediately available. "And Zack, can you load my ACC? Thanks. Be there soon."

Simon sat back and took Evie's hand with a gentle squeeze. "He's *the* Rad? I mean the ex-Rad the Impaler? The one I met a few months back?"

"Yeah. His real name is Conrad McIntyre. I introduced you all before the alcohol started to flow. He started his tech company with Peter Newcastle when they got out of the army after..." Her voice trailed off as she turned her face toward the window. It had been a while, but the memories came flooding back. It didn't happen as often as it used to, but the power of those memories could still send shock waves through her system and paralyze her mind...if only for a moment...now.

"So, these are the two guys you pulled out of a Taliban cell and dragged to safety?" Evie's history and the story behind the scars on her body, and her Medal of Honor were not a secret. At her *private* party after the ceremonious separation, the four had gone drinking. Much to Evie's distress, Simon had seen way too much, and heard more than any man should have. The upshot was, he knew most everything, and still cared.

"Uh huh. Simon, you don't have to do this. Tonight is the biggest night of your life. You should be up on that stage, not chasing after me and my messed-up life. You earned this award." She looked back toward Simon as a little tear formed at the edge of her heavily mascaraed eyelashes. "I can handle this."

"No doubt. If you can handle an entire army of

terrorists chasing your cute butt a hundred miles through the desert, dragging two half-dead soldiers, you can handle anything the world, or otherworld, can throw at you." He kissed the tear's path on her cheek. "Amee knew that. And so did Uncle Grady," Simon whispered. "And it sounds like Rad needs saving one more time. What does his company do again?"

"It's high tech," she responded quietly.

"Competition?" Anything that contained the word *tech* was of interest to Simon.

Evie let out a half-snort, half-giggle. "Not unless you've decided to give up games for missile systems. He's VP for Global Systems Technology. He's also head engineer on GST's new targeting system project under contract to the Pentagon. All highly classified stuff. All stuff someone might want in return for his wife." Evie's jaw clenched at the idea.

"She's some kind of journalist, right?"

"Was. A combat photojournalist. Now she's just a wife." Evie shook her head apologetically. "I didn't mean that the way it sounded. She gave up taking pictures in some of the most dangerous places in the world after they got married. Last I talked to Andi a couple months ago, she was struggling with it." Evie tugged on her fancy dress and stretched her painted toes encased in leather and sparkly crystal. The parallel was a little too close for comfort.

"I can't understand why a woman would want to walk into battle with a camera. Crazy."

"Same reason a man would. It's the excitement. The desire to do what no one else can. Just because she's a woman doesn't make her incapable or unable." There was a certain tightness to Evie's retort. "Andrea is a hell of a photographer and cool as a cucumber under fire."

"I didn't mean to put her down because of her gender, Major Evielynne Gastineau." Evie felt Simon's fingers on her chin as he gently turned her face toward him. "I would never do that. You'd shoot me or something really dangerous and painful." He smiled sweetly at her. "I just wonder why she wanted to take pictures of combat. All that blood. The violence…"

"Exactly, Simon. She wanted to show the world how grisly and violent conflict is. How in a world of all kinds of people, one religious sect can gain such control through war and combat, not to mention terrorism. She wanted to put a face on it. Show the real truth behind the constant war in the Middle East. She wanted to shine a light on the devastation and pain it brings to those who must live in the midst of such desolation and destruction."

"A worthy cause, to be sure, but dodging bullets? Not so sure about that for anyone." Simon shook his head. His protective nature was endearing to Evie, but she knew Simon still thought of her as a kind of victim of the war. Someday she hoped he would see through the bumps and bruises to the real person she was. Her real ability. Amee took away the nightmares. Grady gave her back her belief in love and God. Simon, he was a work in progress. One that Evie was willing to wait for. At least for now.

"Everyone has a cause, a goal to shoot for. Sometimes the goal shoots back, Simon. You never know what you're capable of, until you're tested." Evie kissed her man. "Boyfriend, huh? Conrad is probably chuckling about that right now."

"What's so funny about having a boyfriend?" Simon looked a little incensed.

"Silly teeny-boppers have boyfriends. Women have relationships."

"So I'm your what…relationship?" Simon sat up straight in his seat extending his hand to some invisible individual. "Hi, I'm Simon O'Sullivan, Evielynne's *relationshipee*. Glad to meet you." Simon grinned and shook the invisible hand with vigor.

"Simon, quit!" Evie smacked her *relationshipee* in the shoulder.

"Knock that stuff off, kids. We're here," Bull announced from the front seat. "ID?"

Both Simon and Evie dug out their identification and passed it to Bull. "We used to just drive right on through to the hangar. Now it's all, ID and security." Simon waved at the guard.

"Sign of the times. Oakland isn't what it used to be, boss." Bull passed their IDs back after displaying them to the guard.

"Sometimes these are. Not so sure about that anymore," Evie caught Simon's soft comment.

"You're sounding more and more like your uncle all the time." Evie laughed and squirmed in her satin cling-wrap. "Simon, I can't show up in Texas like this." She tugged at the bodice for the tenth time. "Conrad won't recognize me! And I can't hardly move without falling out the top of this thing."

"Okay." Simon grinned at her cleavage. "I won't mind. Promise!" His grin widened as he crossed his heart. Evie was about to offer another shoulder smack at his statement.

Bull howled in the front seat. "Dangerous ground,

my boy. Dangerous ground." He took a deep breath to end the laughing-out-loud response. "Evie, don't leave any blood on the seat, girl. My boss is par-tic-u-lar about his wheels."

"Roger that, Bull." She grabbed Simon's arm and executed a playful twist and shackle movement.

Simon squeaked

"All right, you two. We be here. Zack has the plane out." Bull swung the limo up next to the aircraft's stairway. "Out ya go."

"Wait, wait, wait. I can't go like this." Evie was trying to scoot across the seat in a tangle of tight satin. One spiky heel was caught in the hem of her very spendy dress.

"Not to worry, Major. The ACC is onboard." Simon stood by the door at attention with a crisp salute.

Bull got out and came around the side of the limo. "Gonna be blood tonight, boss. Yours." He helped Evie to a standing position next to the car.

"What's an ACC?" Evie felt the beginnings of suspicion forming in her mind.

"My Alternate Command Center. My version of a go-bag for three." Simon was obviously proud of his pre-planning. "Got the idea from the major here. Clothes, food, moola, high tech resources. All packed and ready to go at twenty minutes notice." Simon took a bow. "Shall we?" He took Evie's arm to escort her up the steps of his private Embraer Phenom 300. The light jet could seat up to nine and could fly at an impressive five hundred and eighteen miles per hour. It had the largest windows of any private jet and even had a window in the head. Simon had purchased the jet after his second game went viral and the company gave him a bonus check for six million dollars. Not bad for three year's work and a video game that hit the number one spot on *Video Game Trader* nine months in a row. To date, it had made his company over a billion dollars. He'd given Evie a very in-depth tour when the plane had been delivered and she'd logged the endless list of facts and figures somewhere in her memory. After all, it wasn't everyday a gal from the Louisiana swamps got to sit in baby ostrich leather seats in a private jet that could cross the country in about six hours.

"Simon, wait. What do you mean a go-bag for three?" Evie pulled away at the bottom of the stairs.

"Me, you, Bull. Zack takes care of his own stuff. He actually lives in an apartment over the hangar right there." Simon pointed to a set of windows above the main part of the hangar and chuckled. "Like taking the car out of the garage and going for a spin. He cooks, too. We have a dinner of steak and salad waiting."

"And…" Evie did her Vanna White motion, highlighting her evening attire again. Her dress almost glowed in the afternoon sun.

"Oh yeah. Clothes too. In your size. I checked the labels in your closet." She watched Simon's chest swelled with pride. Apparently, he had considered everything…

Well, *not* everything.

"You did *what?*" Evie's eyes narrowed and her beautifully sculpted face scrunched into what could only be called the Perfect Storm. She squinted her eyes, clenched those Vaselined lips and drew her eyebrows together.

"Oh oh. Gonna be blood fer sure." Bull moved around Simon giving him lots of space. "Com'on, Miss

Evie. Get ya onboard before I gots ta report a murder." He took Evie's arm and moved her up the stairs gently, but with purpose, and a little enjoyment.

"Oh, murder is way too good for that boy." She smiled sweetly down at Simon following at a respectable distance. "Did you forget I have personal experience with torture?"

Evie watched him carefully ascended the stairway. She figured Simon's brain probably kicked in as he kept his eyes glued to the steps. He may have just figured out delving into a woman's closet was no-man's land. No man was allowed. Simon had just admitted to the biggest personal trespass in the universe. He'd encroached on sacred land and admitted it out loud to her.

"No, ma'am. I did not." Bull chuckled. "Let's get you settled, and I'll get the car stowed. No real bad stuff till I get back, ya hear? I don't wanna miss anything." Bull passed Simon at the doorway. "Best not say a word, boss," he whispered.

Zack stood in the tiny galley with a smirk on his face. Evie heard the pilot's comment clear as day. "Told him not to."

That started Bull's second round of laughter as he trotted down the stairs. "Be back in a few." He hollered to the pilot.

"Take your time. Flight plan's in the system. Waiting for release." Zack stirred the sautéing mushrooms and onions. He was not only the pilot, but the chief cook *and* bottle washer for O'Sullivan Airways. After the short exchange he'd heard, Evie suspected he knew his boss would be in dire need of a bottle on this flight, but not the kind with warm milk.

She eyed the wine rack pointing to a familiar red, and winked at Zach.

Simon sat down in the seat across the aisle from Evie, still looking at the floor. In his best little-boy-in-trouble voice, he asked, "You're mad at me, aren't you?"

Evie took a deep breath and let it out slowly. "There are just some things that are sacrosanct. A woman's closet is one. Did Uncle Grady never teach you anything about women when you were growing up?" She tried to keep the exasperation out of her voice, and failed. "I'm not mad. I'm just…feeling a little violated."

By the horrified look on his face, Evie knew Simon was stunned. He turned to her in abject fear. "Evie, I didn't mean to do anything that…"

Evie burst out laughing. "I'm just kidding, Simon. Yeah I'm a little taken aback that you sneaked into my closet, but what the heck. At least you did it for a sweet reason. And think about it—" She moved to the seat next to him and took his hand. "—in a minute's notice, we are on our way to Texas to bail out one of my old buddies. And you are missing out on a personal recognition that you have worked for all of your life. Ghost War is a fantastic game and you deserve to be getting your award and bonus. A huge bonus, I might add." Evie opened her arms wide as if the bonus was bigger than her stretch, which it was. It also presented a delicately perfumed wrist to Simon's lips. She giggled.

His lips traced their perfectly placed kiss to the tips of her fingers, then rotated her wrist and kissed his way back up. "Still *relationshipees* then, hon?" Simon deepened his voice, attempting a seductive tone.

That worked for Evie. It made her tingle through and through. Once again, her heart tugged at her mind, wanting to take things to the next step. She pushed it away with a gentle shove. This was not the time, or the place. "I guess." She sighed with a dreamy smile. Then the storm was back as she pulled away. "Just don't go messin' in my closet again, buster." The gelled and painted nail on her index finger poked at Simon's nose.

"No, ma'am. Never again." Simon flipped the arm of his seat up and pulled Evie into his arms. "No need, I already know your sizes."

She whacked his chest with her free hand before snuggling in and pressing her head to his shoulder. "Didn't Uncle Grady teach you anything?"

Simon settled back and relaxed. Evie could feel the tension drain from him as she cuddled deeper. "Of course he did. He taught me to stand on my own two feet. To get the best education I could. He always said, Simon, you are in charge of your life. Make it what you want. And I did." He rubbed the soft exfoliated, creamed, and massaged skin of Evie's arm up and down as he spoke. "He worked hard all his life and took in my mamma, even when he knew she wouldn't change. She'd get cleaned up and I'd get fed for a few weeks. Then off she'd go to find another needle and another guy to beat her up. There wasn't even a question of where I'd go when she lay down in that gutter, and finally gave up on everything, including me."

"That's so sad, Simon. At least you had Grady to love and support you. He was a wonderful man. It was an honor to meet him at the end." Evie's heart was breaking for the things Simon had endured in childhood. His uncle had been a Godsend for the boy.

She had been a Godsend for Simon's uncle, and the love the old man thought he'd lost.

"Yeah. He got a raw deal, but never complained about it. His belief in the good Lord saw him through and gave him back his love in the end." Simon raised Evie's palm to his lips and kissed it once again. "Thanks to you and Amee. That little ghost sure was something."

"And still is. Thanks to your game. I still can't believe you designed her before ever seeing the ghost in real life. Or unreal life…or whatever it was." Evie snuggled closer and closed her eyes.

Before Evie's run-in with the little pesky ghost on her military base, she didn't know anything about the old Port Chicago or the historical Port Chicago 50 legal case. She'd never experienced any kind of paranormal *thing*. That was her sister's gig, her mother's sham. Or so she thought. Maybe it was her time in Iraq. Maybe it was just some intergalactic coincidence. Something had switched on her extra sensory perception at MOTCO and shoved her head long into the ghost's story. There was no backing out. "Doesn't it make you wonder," Evie's voice had a dreamy tone as she lay comfortably in Simon's arms, "before the infamous explosion at Port Chicago, what might have been? Seaman Grandville O'Sullivan loved his Amee McGee, that's for sure. When she was killed at the Joe Meyers Theater, her ghost was trapped." Evie sat up and watched the busy workers on the tarmac outside their window. "What if Amee had survived? What if I'd taken a different assignment?"

Simon played with a crispy curl on her forehead. "Back in the forties, it was unacceptable for Grady, a black sailor, to as much as look at the white daughter of the base Commander. So they met when they could, and kept their love secret. What did they put on your hair?" Evie could feel the curl snap back into place when Simon let go. "Uncle Grady told me the night he was to meet Amee after her shift at the theater, he was going to give her his ring. The explosion separated them forever. Or at least that's what he thought. Then along came the trial of the Port Chicago Fifty and his conviction. Uncle Grady lived with his disgrace and a love he could never let go of. Until his dying day, he wore that simple silver band he would have given to Amee that night." He tugged at the curl again, watching it snap back like a spring.

"Simon, quit. I don't want my hair to crack off, or something." Evie settled against his chest and held his hand for self-protection.

"I still have trouble believing what I saw with my own two eyes. Uncle Grady so young, so strong. And Amee, sweet and..." She could feel his chest heave as Simon's voice cracked with emotion.

"They're together, the way they always should have been, Simon." She sat up again to look at her boyfriend. "And I have a new respect for my own heritage." She snorted and gazed out the big windows on the Brazilian jet. "Had I never taken the position at MOTCO, maybe my *family talent* would never have surfaced. Maybe Grady would never have gone back and Amee would still be haunting the base. But like my *maman* always says, things happen for a reason. Guess it was meant to be. And look," She pointed toward heaven. "They're finally together"

As if somewhere the two lovebirds listened, the

thin clouds parted and a beam of sunlight enveloped the plane, for just a few seconds.

"I think it's pretty cool. I have a *relationshipee* that can see and talk to ghosts." Simon pulled her back into his arms. "I don't know many people who can say that."

"Not many people admit it because they don't want to end up in the looney bin. And it was only one ghost. One particular pesky, annoying blonde ghost." She hugged Simon back and cuddled into his embrace. "Nothing like that ever happened to me before. I used to think my *maman* and Tootie were just fakes, taking money from dumb strangers and swamp tourists. You gotta admit there is a God and Heaven though, Simon. Because we saw it, didn't we?" She closed her eyes again and smiled at the memory.

"That we did." Simon agreed. It would always be a clear and ever-present memory for them both. The love they saw in the young couple still made Simon want to bawl like a baby and Evie knew it. "The sight of Amee holding my uncle's hand, walking off together, is a gift I thank God, and you for every day."

The emotions of the moment were just a little too strong for her *relationshipee.*

"I know what you mean. I thank God every day that I don't have to sit next to Mrs. Paulson in church on Sunday. What with her singing at the top of her out-of-tune lungs and continual farting…"

It worked.

Simon cracked up and Evie giggled.

"You are so bad, Evie, my girl."

Just as she was about to offer Simon her gooey lips for a kiss, Bull came bounding through the door. "Car stowed, and another murder averted. Looks like to me."

He'd given up his black suit for a pair of blue Dockers and a Giants team shirt. His ball cap displayed a Nike symbol, like his bright orange running shoes.

"So Superman, found a phone booth, did he?" Zack motioned to the galley. "Take over for me while I get this boat in motion."

Bull's British accent was back in place. "You, my good man, are the pilot. And this is not a boat, but a very nicely appointed aircraft. I"—he pointed both thumbs at himself—"am the bodyguard and driver. Not a cook. I do the heavy lifting, chap." Bull pulled the door up and locked it in place. "But yum, yum, that smell damn good, flyboy.

"Everything's in the warmer and ready to serve. All you have to do is dish it out after takeoff." Zack pointed to the fridge. "Cold drinks are chilling. Wine is breathing. I'm pre-flighting. Buckle up, everyone. We just got our clearance." Zack disappeared into the cockpit of the jet. He hollered back at Bull. "Seat belt extender's in the closet, big guy."

"Now that be cold, man."

Both Evie and Simon chuckled and buckled.

Chapter 5

Almost two thousand miles away, Conrad was on the phone again. "Yo, Pete, call me back." He ended his third call still in his car. Where was Pete? He was never without his cell phone. The guy never knew when some luscious babe would call, offering a deal he couldn't refuse. He was probably still pissed at Conrad for opting out of their very lucrative business.

Pete had a string of gals he kept sniffing around, but at arm's length emotionally. He and Conrad were working on the *multi* in multi-millionaire and money was a hot ticket with women. It wasn't that Peter Newcastle didn't care…he just didn't care enough about any one of them, yet. His focus was on the challenge. The contract. The design. But mostly he'd play the field until he could figure out trust again. He'd had that once, with a young woman in a red hijab. His unit paid the price for his overactive libido, and the flaming affair he had with the Taliban spy that occupied his bed for a month. The reward was an ambush and months in a dark, dank cell Pete shared with the only other survivor. Conrad. It was a stupid affair that cost the lives of eight good men. If Captain Evielynne Gastineau hadn't ended up in the same prison with her indomitable desire to escape, there may never have been a Pete and Conrad, no Global Systems Technology, and definitely no Iron Shield project.

Conrad punched the redial button on his phone. "Come on, Pete! Pick up."

His pleading must have been heard. Pete's slurred voice answered. "What do you want, traitor?"

"Pete, where are you, buddy?" Conrad could tell Pete was soused...again.

"I'm not your buddy and why would you care where I am?" The hurt in the man's voice was clear, and as apparent as an incoming missile. The target was Conrad's heart, and it found its mark.

"You alone?" Conrad needed his battle buddy sober and alone for what he had to say.

"What da you wan, Con-Rad?" Pete's voice was drifting.

"Are. You. Alone?" Conrad practically shouted the steely words.

"Nah. Havin' my own liddle party, man." Pete giggled like a little boy on the other end of the cell. Conrad could also hear a soft moan in the background and the squeaking of a bed frame.

"Listen, we have a problem. Get your head out of your ass."

"No problem at all on my en..." Pete's voice trailed off and more squeaking could be heard...along with louder moaning.

"Sorry to interrupt your...whatever. We got a serious problem with IS." They never talked about their highly classified project around others, but when the need arose, initials were the identifiers.

Conrad heard a loud thump and more squeaking. Obviously, someone hit the floor and Pete was now sitting up. "I'll call you back in three."

The line went dead. Nothing like pouring a bucket

of cold water on the scene to deflate the situation. Conrad sat in his mustang. He had to do something, anything. He needed action. But there was nothing to be done but wait. Conrad was not a patient man. He hit the seat with his fist.

The leather rebounded without a scratch. "Damn it to hell." His cell phone chirped. "Pete?"

"Yeah. Where's the fire, Conrad?" Pete sounded clear-headed…and angry.

"You alone?" Conrad didn't really need to ask the question, but he wanted confirmation in his own mind. The *situation* was too dangerous and important.

"Yes. Now, what is it? You got some other bombshell to drop, *Buddy*?" Pete's emphasis on the word buddy spoke volumes. He was hurt. He was angry. He was really pissed…and Conrad's coitus interruptus was the icing on Pete's pity party cake. "I was having some—"

"Pete, Andrea's gone."

"Yeah…so?" Pete huffed. So was his hard-on and Sandra. "She finally got tired of playing eye candy for Rad the Impaler?"

"No, Pete. She's been taken. They want the backdoor codes to IS." Conrad stopped. Their cell phones weren't secure. Anyone could be listening in.

"No shit! Where are you? At home? I'll be there in ten." All anger fled from his voice. Conrad could feel Pete's reaction as his friend came to the realization that Conrad's wife was in trouble, and so was the business they'd established and worked for years to develop.

"Okay. But are you sober enough to…" The line went dead. Pete was on his way and Conrad just hoped there were no cops between Pete and him. Emergencies had a way of sobering a guy real fast, but alcohol still impaired judgment and reaction time. He didn't need two emergencies on his hands.

His phone chirped once. Text message.

He grabbed the phone and read:—*KCRP @3.75 hrs. N696EP*—

It was from Evie's cell phone number. They'd be landing at Corpus Christi in about four hours. In an Embraer Phenom? Where the hell did she get that jet? And who was flying it?

More questions.

No answers.

He texted back:—*Roger*—

Conrad was five minutes from the house and would be there long before Pete. He turned the Mustang for home and gunned it. The traffic gods had him in their sights and he pulled into the driveway in short order. It took him a minute to gather the strength to enter the empty house though. His thoughts were all on Andrea. Where was she? Was she hurt? Did she know he would search heaven and hell to find her? Or had she given up on them? On him?

Conrad shook himself. Andrea was tough. She'd proven that time and again. Even under fire she kept her cool and constantly evaluated the situation, responding appropriately. If there was a way to help herself, she'd find it. He just needed to remind himself how strong and independent his wife truly was.

Guilt overcame his ability to move. She was so smart and brave and beautiful...he'd lost that picture when he founded GST and their IS project. Four years of focused concentration, incredible contracts worth millions and he'd lost sight of the one thing that mattered most in his life. His wife.

Conrad passed through the kitchen and headed straight for the one thing that would deaden the pain in his chest. He poured himself a straight shot from the antique Waterford crystal decanter that sat on their bar. It had been a wedding gift from his brother Keith and Keith's wife, Marianne. The note attached to the gift, said the couple had picked up the beautiful decanter in Scotland on vacation. It was a Longford Ships design and priceless, according to Keith. But then everything Keith possessed was priceless, according to Keith. Including Marianne. Next to the decanter was a framed picture of the four of them, at Conrad's wedding. Everyone was smiling and dressed to the nines. Andrea looked like an angel in white satin and a sparkly tulle veil. She glowed with love and happiness. Conrad finally understood Keith. Andrea was priceless to him as well, and she needed to know that.

He hoped it wasn't too late now.

He didn't realize how long he held their picture, mesmerized by his wife's beauty, as the bourbon slid its way down his esophagus. Screeching tires alerted him to the arrival of his partner and friend.

The kitchen door slammed the wall as Conrad heard Pete's voice hollering, "Conrad, where are you?"

"Living room." Conrad turned to see his buddy slide across the polished dining room floor and vault the two steps into the living room, then freeze. He was aware of the picture he presented. There he stood Pete's lifelong friend, a drink in one hand, a picture of his wedding day in the other. Tears streamed down Conrad's face. The rock-hard soldier who survived his horrific wounds and made it through the desert, was crying? Pete probably loved that! The steady, focused man who had painstakingly scratched a tick mark on the side of their cell for every one of the hundred and thirty-five days of incarceration, now stood helpless and shaken to the core.

Peter crossed the room in a flash, took the picture and drink from Conrad's hands, and grabbed the man in an intense bear hug. "It'll be okay, Rad. We'll figure this out."

Conrad was lost.

No.

He wasn't lost.

Andrea was lost.

But Pete was there, and Evie was on her way. They could figure this thing out. Hope cleared the tears and Conrad came back to life.

"I was just thinking…" Pete released Conrad. They were both a little embarrassed at the length of the mutual man-hug.

"What were you thinking, Rad? Sit. Bring me up to speed." Conrad let Pete steer him to the sofa as his friend took a seat across the coffee table. This was bad. Conrad knew Pete had never seen him so desolate. Not even in their cage in the sand box.

"I was just thinking about our wedding. She was so…" Conrad stopped and wiped the tears away. "We gotta get her back, Pete. She's my life."

Pete was silent for a moment. Conrad saw the wheels begin to turn in his buddy's mind. Finally, Pete was becoming aware of how much this woman, this intruder in their bromance, actually meant to Conrad. "Start at the beginning, buddy. One step at a time."

"I left the office after we had that fight…"

"Yeah, I know that part. Move on."

Conrad brushed the memory away with a wave. "I was late getting home. I called from the car about a million times. But she didn't answer. I kept calling. No answer. When I got home, there was no one here." Conrad wiped his face with his sleeve. "But this was." He pointed to the instruction note that still lay on the coffee table, right where the kidnappers had left it.

Pete reached for the note. "No!" Conrad stayed his friend's hand. "Prints."

"Right." Pete settled back into his chair. "Then what?" He craned his neck to read the note.

"A couple years ago, when we had that fire scare, I put a CDF tile in all of her purses. I never told her." Conrad smiled sheepishly. "Man, would she be mad if she knew. Anyway, they're all registered on my location app. So I activated the one she was currently carrying." Conrad went back to the bar to retrieve his drink. "Want some?"

"Nah. Had enough tonight. I need a clear head, and so do you."

Conrad nodded, left his drink on the bar, and returned to his seat. The nervous energy was building, and he had to do something. "The tile popped up at her gym. I couldn't figure out why she'd be at the gym on the evening of our anniversary, unless she was really mad at me or something." His voice softened. "She usually goes to the gym early in the morning."

"Okay. At the gym." Pete spun his fingers in a circular motion. "And…"

"I went to the gym. Long story short, her stuff was there. She wasn't. Her car was outside. She'd checked in a little after I'd left for work this morning. Never checked out."

"So, what did the gym staff say?"

"Guess I wasn't too nice about asking. They called the cops. The screaming queen who runs the place, gave me her things and that was it. He couldn't explain where she was or how she'd left without checking out. But she wasn't there. They looked everywhere." Conrad threw up his hands. "That's it. Then I got the call."

"On your cell? How'd they get the number?" Pete was well into the mystery now, and Conrad was dragging him along the timeline.

"Probably from Andrea's phone. I don't know. A digital voice said they had her and wanted the backdoor codes to Iron Shield. If I called the police, they'd kill her."

"So no one knows, but us?" Pete motioned to his friend and business partner, then back to himself.

It took a second, but Conrad finally responded. "I called Evie. She knows and…" Tears welled up in his eyes again. What was wrong with him? All of a sudden, he was a two-year-old cry baby.

"And…?" He could tell Pete was a little taken aback that Conrad had called the major first.

"Believe it or not, she's already on her way." Conrad grinned. "In a private jet." He shook his head in amazement. "With her boyfriend. That computer guy in California. Guess they are a little tighter than we figured back at her separation party. You remember him. The guy with the little appendectomy blemish?"

"Our Evie has a boyfriend? The geeky guy who makes games? How did we miss that?" Conrad watched Pete's eyebrows raise in surprise. His partner was so easy to read.

Pete, Conrad, and Evie had spent several months at Walter Reed hospital together, rehabbing their physical and psychological wounds. Conrad had stayed connected and close after they were released and separated from the US Army. Or at least he'd thought they'd stayed close over the intervening years, but he was still a little surprised by the boyfriend thing. He and Pete knew there was something holding Evie in California after her separation from the army, but not the particulars of what. They knew she'd walked into some kind of job at this Simon's place of business, and figured it was a pretty flush situation. A grand opportunity for a retiring military soldier. But a boyfriend? A Geek? His Evie had enough wounds for a lifetime. She sure didn't need one in her heart.

"Good for our Evie. Hope the guy is a stand-up fellow. She deserves the best this world can give her. He's the one that offered her a security job, right?"

"Yep. And her paycheck is pretty stand up, too. Anyway, apparently he has access to a jet, and they are on their way." Conrad stood and paced over to the bar and back, leaving his drink where it was.

"All right, Rad, let's get down to business." Pete motioned to the French doors on the other side of the living room. The doors led to Conrad's home office.

Inside sat a computer wired to the entire world's resources and a plethora of stacked magazines and papers. Files were scattered over most of the tabletops and the trashcan was overflowing with paper and old McDonald's soft drink cups. The housemaid was not allowed to touch anything in Conrad's office, hence the mess and garbage, as well as the hideous lack of organization. In the middle of the room was a round table used for impromptu meetings, and less often these days, a fast-paced card game or two.

Conrad chuckled. Peter was such a neat-freak, and just passing through the portal to Conrad's man cave probably made his friend's skin itch. No wonder Andrea had painstakingly covered each glass pane with fake stain glass sheets. That way she didn't have to look at Conrad's crazy-smart mind layered on every surface in the room.

"Jeez, Rad...ever think of emptying the garbage?" Pete pulled a huge tablet from behind the piled trash. They often used the large sheets to create basic code designs in flow-chart form, over late night beers. Half of the Iron Shield project could be attributed to Corona Gold and jalapeño roasted pecans. Pete called it the *beer and burn brainstorm*. Conrad considered it *furk*, short for fun work. Conrad's wife was convinced it was bromance at its best, and gave them the room to create the world's most intricate and strategic missile targeting system yet.

Pete flopped the chart paper onto the top of the round table. "Let's start from the beginning." He grabbed a large marker from off a pile of file folders on a side table. Writing Andrea's name at the top, he drew a line down, splitting it into horizontal boxes. Then he wrote *club* in one, *car* in another, *phone* in another and *purse* in the last one, leaving room to add more on each side.

"Shit, Pete, this isn't some project. It's Andrea's life!" Conrad was back to pacing.

"Yeah, but we think better on paper like this." Pete pointed to Conrad with the purple marker. "You know that and so do I, so get your head out of your ass and start using that remarkable brain of yours." Conrad had been part of Pete's *thinking* process many a time. It really was the way they thought and worked best. Two heads were definitely better than one.

Conrad nodded and grinned. "Roger that." He sat down at the table. "Andrea checked into the gym right after I left for work."

In the box labeled club, Pete wrote an approximate time. "Who does she usually work out with at the club? Do you know her trainer? Maybe a girlfriend or instructor?"

The blank look on Conrad's face told the entire story before he opened his mouth. "I don't know. She trains with some German guy and his girlfriend, I think. She's mentioned them before, but I have no idea who they are." Conrad found himself stunned as realization dawned. He really didn't know much about what his wife did at the gym, or anywhere else for that matter. "She meets her friend, Margaret for lunch sometimes."

"Good. Keep thinking. Margaret who?" Pete added another box to the line up and added the name, Margaret.

"What do you mean, Margaret who?"

"What's Margaret's last name? Come on Rad, get it together." Pete spun the marker in his fingers.

The blank look was back. "Ah? No idea."

"Okay, move on." It was Pete's favorite saying. "What about Andrea's car? Where is it now?"

"Ah…"

After fifteen minutes of grilling, Conrad realized he knew very little about what his wife did during the day, where she went, and who she met.

"Do you and Andrea talk about anything together?" Pete had always told Conrad, he envied Conrad's perfect marriage. Truth be told, Conrad realized Pete had nothing to envy. Their marriage was turning out to be a surprisingly blank page for him.

"Of course, Pete. I tell her about everything. The project, everybody's stuff at work, all the drama, you know. Our plans for the next year. Everything."

"Everything but her." Pete remarked quietly. Conrad, too, was beginning to see the real *perfect marriage* he always boasted about. It was perfectly all about him. If it hadn't been for the note and the call, it might have seemed that Andrea was the one leaving the scene, not being dragged away by kidnappers.

"This is all my fault, Pete." Conrad wiped his hands across his darkening five o'clock shadow. "It's been kind of bad for a while now. We used to be so…" He paused, looking for the word to describe the white-hot romance that had fizzled to lukewarm acceptance. "Today is five years. Nothing is the same. Andrea used to be so—" He couldn't continue.

"Got that. So let's find Andi and you can have the chance to make things right." Pete pointed with his marker again. "Or you can sit there blaming yourself and playing that mini-poor-me violin until the strings break, and your wife is gone for good."

"I'm not…"

"Yes, you are. Move on."

Conrad threw his partner a middle finger salute, grabbed his own marker, and set to work.

After a grueling hour of questions and few answers, Conrad had contacted the bank across the street from Andrea's Club to procure any video imagery they might have from the entry and front of the bank. He'd called his old friend at the security firm that handled GST security and enlisted his aid in checking and towing Andrea's car. Pete was combing through Andrea's address book and calendar for names and dates, as well as anything that might jump out at him as evidence they could use. Pizza was on its way from D'Pizza joint on Padre Boulevard and the small fridge in Conrad's office was stocked with beer.

"So, what do we know?" Pete cracked a can and handed it to Conrad, then opened one for himself. It was good to be back in the saddle with Pete, even if the circumstances were dire and the need was personal for Conrad, not GST business and government contracts.

"Andrea works out with some guy named Wilmer and his friend Callista. They are trainers at the South Padre Island Athletic Club. She clocked in a little after 6 a.m. and never clocked out. They have no record of her leaving. Her car was left across the street from the club. Her things were in her locker. Cell phone is missing, which is probably how her kidnappers got my number. It's encrypted and password protected, but not un-hackable if you know what you're doing. They obviously got into our house to leave this note." He motioned to the note that now resided in a plastic bag awaiting forensic analysis. "Morehead said her garage door opener was missing. Damn!" Conrad smacked his forehead. "I was going to program the opener in her car, and I never got around to it."

"Move on. Keep going." Pete was the one pacing now, with his beer and marker in hand. "Did Carl find anything?" Carl Morehead had served his hitch in the army as an MP and now headed up Tactical Security and Surveillance. "You trust him to keep this confidential and not make a big show of helping out?"

"Of course. I would stake my life on it. He's ex-army and a straight shooter." Conrad gazed out of the tall living room windows to the sculpted lawn beyond. "I'm staking Andrea's life on it." As Vice President of their company, it had been up to Conrad to set up their security protocols and hire whomever he needed. He kept critical personnel in the family, so to speak. The military family. "He should be here with the car and a sit-rep in about half an hour. Evie's ride is due to touch down at the Corpus Christi Airport in about three hours. I'm not sure what she can do, but another set of really keen eyes is more than welcome. And she's got skills."

"Why Corpus Christi? Why not Harlingen? Closer. Private stuff always coming and going. Good cover." Pete paused, then resumed his pacing. "Can you contact them and have them change their destination?"

"Yep. On it." Conrad pulled out his cell and texted Evie. He was sure this tech guru she was dating would have a satellite uplink and Internet onboard. She'd get the message.

He was correct! Almost immediately his cell chimed.

—*Roger that, amending flight plan. ETA 2104. E.*—

That was his Major Evielynne Gastineau. Ready at a moment's notice, and flexible. Thank God. "Semper, Mint Julep!" Conrad smacked the table and sent his marker flying.

"Excuse me?" Pete wasn't following and looked a bit bewildered at Conrad's comment.

"Harlingen used to be the home of the Confederate

Air Force. That's their rally cry, like Semper Fi." He grinned. Pete wasn't into aircraft and aviation. He didn't even like getting in the company helicopter with Conrad.

"They'll be landing a little after ten tonight. You want to go get her and this guy and bring them back here? I've got plenty of room at my place if the house is under surveillance, the less coming and going the better. We can work out of here or there. Your call." Pete had purchased an empty warehouse a couple years back and made the top floor into his home. Conrad also knew Pete had Carl Morehead install a security system that made Fort Knox look like Disneyland. He didn't care for walls after months in a tiny cell. Conrad didn't blame him. The only walls in Pete's place surrounded the luxurious bathroom, and even that had a glass door. Pete had never gotten around to doing anything with the other nine floors which remained empty or filled with left over building supplies and old discarded furniture or items abandoned from the last owner. The main floor was a high-security parking garage with forty spaces. Pete only needed one, but when he drove in and parked, he could see the entire place. Conrad had often asked his friend about development, but the answer was always the same; I'm thinking on it. No one would surprise Pete, or take him prisoner, ever again. It was a feeling they shared, and Conrad didn't blame his friend at all.

Conrad's phone rang. The display flashed *unknown number*. "Better get that. It could be the kidnappers." Pete moved close as Conrad punched the green button and put the call on speakerphone.

A metallic voice began talking without any social

platitudes. "Who took your wife's car? I told you not to notify the authorities or she would be killed. You had better take me seriously. She's real pretty. Shame to mess that up. Maybe send you some proof of life, eh?"

Conrad had already thought of his options to respond to a ransom call. "I ordered her car towed back to the house. I couldn't find the extra keys. I didn't tell anyone except my partner. He'd have found out sooner or later. Please don't hurt Andrea. She doesn't know anything about the project. She can't help you. Only me. If you hurt her, I won't give you anything." Conrad had the sense to record the call on the auto memo function of his cell phone.

Pete motioned to keep the caller talking. He was timing the call. If they had the time and duration of the phone call, maybe the cell company could give them a number. Then they could ping the phone and determine a location. It was a long shot, but more than they had a moment ago.

"Get me the codes and her nice face shall remain so." The line went dead. Right under thirty seconds. Too short.

"Well, that answers the question of whether or not we're being watched." Pete moved to the tall windows and closed the blinds, then made the rounds of the room, checking out nick-knacks, pictures, and bookshelves. He stood with his back to the wall and placed a finger across his lips, motioning to Conrad.

When they first had moved into their house on South Padre Island, Conrad purchased one of Coolidge's famous paintings of Dogs Playing Cards for his man cave. It wasn't a real Coolidge. Conrad was sure the real artist did not work on velvet. Andrea hated the picture, but Conrad hung it as a joke for the Saturday night poker guys. They all liked it. At some point, one of his notorious friends had cut out a Corona label and taped it over one of the bottles in the painting. Now Pete pointed to the loose label, mouthing *bug*. Obviously, the kidnappers left something behind when they took Andrea. He should have thought about that right off. But now, the kidnappers had tipped their own hand with that call!

Conrad rolled his eyes. If there was a listening device in his office, there were probably more. And possibly cameras as well. That would make sense, since Conrad often held meetings at his home and worked late at night in his office/man cave. Now everything in the house was suspect and he had no idea how much of their conversation had been overheard or seen. Surveillance devices were common, cheap, and easy in this day and age. You could purchase them at Best Buy all over the country!

Well, being bugged could be a bad thing…or it could be a tool. Conrad wrinkled his forehead and added a desperate sound to his voice. "Pete, what are we going to do? Evie's on her way for a two-week visit. They have my wife." He took a long drink of his beer. "Maybe I should give them the codes and this thing will be over. We haven't completed the project and the government would never know."

He spoke clearly toward the painting. The little story he made up on the fly was a ploy but could explain the addition of his friend and her man. He wanted the kidnappers to think he would cooperate and was desperate enough to compromise national security. He'd also immediately figured out the kidnappers weren't too bright, at least not techno-savvy. Anything he provided to get his wife back, could be changed after the fact. It dawned on him with the crushing weight of a ten-ton truck; they never intended to release Andrea alive!

Pete got it right away and winked at Conrad. They were playing a dangerous game.

With an anguished cry, Conrad cleared their worktable with one arm and threw his beer across the room. He picked up a potted plant from the coffee table and flung it at the opposite wall. He then tossed a bowl of nuts at the third wall with an angry yell. A desperate man would do something like that.

"Rad, calm down, man. Destroying your office won't help." Pete took a towel from the bar. "Look, you go out to the porch and wait for Morehead. I'll clean up this mess. And look, man, we can't give up our backdoor to anyone. It's only a tool for the company in case of some malfunction, or disaster with the system, no matter how farfetched that may be, accidents happen." Pete proceeded to the wall and furniture now splashed with beer. "Outside, buddy. No more thinking about the codes. Absolutely not. I know your wife is important to you, but so is the security of the country. The country we almost died for. Remember that." Pete continued to wipe the wall and furniture searching for more listening devices. It was good-cop, bad-cop now and Pete was doing his part just as Conrad had hoped when he began the overcome husband show.

Conrad left the room with a parting shot. "You never liked her anyway. You've been trying to break us up for years, admit it."

Pete couldn't admit anything. Conrad was already

out the door and on his way to the front gate of the property. He could hear Morehead honking for access.

"Damn bleeding heart." Pete said, just loud enough to be picked up by the tiny bug on the painting.

Chapter 6

"You never really told me the whole story about these two guys." Simon now sat with his feet up on the bulkhead, consuming the last bit of gravy with a piece of sourdough bread. The comment brought Evie out of her own thoughts. He'd changed into jeans and one of his gaming T-shirts that publicized Ghost Wars. A caricature of Amee in black leather holding some kind of sci-fi gun showed her leaning against one of the many rooms she was responsible for clearing on some far-away planet. It gave Evie a bit of a tickle. The ghost of Port Chicago would be with them forever in Simon's hugely popular computer game, and in her heart.

"Yum. Chow was amazing." Evie licked some butter off her bottom lip. "You have to make Zack your full-time chef." Evie was avoiding the tale behind her Silver Star and the months she'd been a guest of the Taliban. She slumped in her seat, legs hooked over Simon's. She'd changed as well, and now relaxed in comfortable sweats and tennis shoes. Her hair was still glued in place and her face resembled some heavily made-up Hollywood starlet, out for a stroll on the red carpet, but she knew Simon found the look charming…and just a tad exciting. He'd only said so a hundred times since Oakland. The last little swipe of cheesecake had been magnificent, and Evie now felt for the smear her fork had left on her chin.

Simon wiped the cake off with a finger, then licked it clean. "He orders in. Now what about this Conrad? And his friend Peter? I have vague memories of scars and lots of alcohol, but..."

"It's a long story, Simon." Evie put her legs down and sat up. "I was on a convoy mission. We were ambushed. My unit was hit hard. We had the security detail and that's who the warlords go after first. They know the drivers won't lift a finger to defend the load. And why would they?" She took a sip of the clear sparkling wine Zack had provided along with the sumptuous dinner. "Iraqi drivers drive. It doesn't matter where or to whom. They get paid to drive and survive. Anyway..." She took another sip. "We got hit. We were outnumbered five to one. Two out of the six of us survived. Max and I got captured. Max was really badly wounded. We ended up in an old bombed-out castle about a hundred miles away from the original attack. Max survived a couple days, but eventually, without medical attention, he died in my lap." Evie stretched her legs then curled them beneath her. The rest of the story was uncomfortable to verbalize, let alone revisit in the retelling. "It was okay. He was in terrible pain. I was held for several months, along with some other soldiers. I never really saw them, just heard their screams and swear words. Our captors loved learning new swear words in English, so—"

"You don't have to tell me anymore, if you don't want to." Simon pulled her into his arms.

"Nah. It helps. And you need to know who you are dealing with. Conrad is a real tough cookie. Pete, on the other hand, is a? I don't know. He's just Pete." Evie smiled.

How did you explain a guy who would never give up, even when he was in hideous pain, and barely able to move? Yet he'd refused her steadying arm and any water they'd scrounged, as he tried to carry Conrad in the beginning. It hadn't been long before he had to let Evie do the heavy lifting, then he stumbled along behind her, never complaining, just stumbling.

"Anyway, after a few months, I befriended the woman who brought our food. Let me correct that statement. We ate some kind of gruel. I wouldn't call it food by any stretch of the imagination." She used her finger to wipe the remnants of her dinner off the plate, then licked the finger clean. "She was a prisoner as well, but she was Muslim, so they didn't lock her up, just chained her feet."

"I can't imagine what you went through," Simon commented softly as he kissed her wet finger.

"Yes, you can. You've seen my back." After another sip of the bubbly wine, she continued. "The Allied forces were close. We could hear the bombing and gunfire. Asheefa came to my cell one night. She didn't speak English, but I could tell something was up. She gave me the key to my chains and pushed me out of the cell. I wouldn't leave without the two other American soldiers, so she helped me find them and then ran away. As I got the door unlocked, two Taliban fighters came down the passage. I realized even before they ran at me, it would be a fight to the death. I was up for it. Heck, another couple weeks with those guys and I would have been dead anyway."

"So Conrad and Pete were the two guys in that cell?" Simon kissed his way up her hand to her wrist.

"Yep. Pete was in a bad way, but he rallied. Conrad

was a little better off and got into the fight with me. We subdued the fighters and took their weapons, but Conrad was wounded. One of the fighters had a knife. He sliced Conrad up pretty good. There wasn't any time to fix his wounds. I hauled him over my shoulder, and we ran…or stumbled out of the ruins. There was an old truck we procured that took us aways, but not far, before its radiator blew. About ten clicks away, we stopped, and I ripped up what was left of my shirt and tied up Conrad's worst wounds. Pete used his bootlaces to tie up a particularly vicious wound on Conrad's leg, and on we went. After that, it was carry Conrad, or let him die in the desert. I wasn't gonna leave a man behind."

"Wow. I know'd you a badass sista, but fuckin' aye, you be some kinda hero badass sista." Bull lounged across the aisle from the couple, his long muscular leg draped across the arm of the seat. Despite the language, Bull's comment registered as a compliment in Evie's mind. Bull was pretty badass himself.

"Yeah, that'd be me. Badass to the bone, and just about dead, when we stumbled on a scout group the third day out. Not sure if I'd have made another day carrying Conrad and dragging Pete. But all's well, that ends well, right?" Evie's laugh was tight and raw. "The guys called in a medevac and pretty soon we were dining on MREs in a make-shift hospital, and awaiting a flight to Rhein Mein. End of that chapter. We hung out for a while there and eventually ended up at Bethesda. Rad, Pete and I have been tight ever since. They even showed up for my separation ceremony. All the way from Texas. The media made it kind of a circus and I didn't get to spend much time with them, but it was touching that they came. We did tie one on, huh, Simon?" She smiled, remembering the soused Simon trying to talk and walk. They'd all taken a taxi home.

"And now they have a business together, some kind of military technical stuff?" Simon needed a better picture of the here and now.

"Yeah. Turns out Pete was a hell of a businessman, and Conrad was like you, a techy-type. They started GST, Global Systems Technology. It specializes in government contracts for all kinds of goodies. Conrad's wife, Andrea, was a combat photojournalist. That's how they met. Talk about a badass sister, that girl has it goin' on. She runs into a firefight, just for a picture. She and Conrad make a great pair." Evie leaned over and pretended to take a picture of Bull.

"Hey, no photo ops here. I'm in the witness protection program." Bull's huge smile glowed as he waved off the invisible paparazzi.

Evie chuckled. "Right, I forgot." It was amazing how Bull could go from an inner-city hoodlum to a sophisticated man-about-town in the blink of an eye. "Their marriage didn't sit well with Peter, but he got used to it. And he seemed happy for his buddy, most of the time. They were like Mutt and Jeff at my separation party. 'Course Andrea was back in Texas, and it was just the two guys again."

"That's got to be hard for Pete. Being so close. Surviving a near death experience. Combat buddies and all. Then wham, an interloper jumps in." Simon mused, as he finished his wine.

Evie sat up and looked at Simon. "You think a wife is an interloper?"

"Nah, that's not what I meant. It's just, okay, I give...and retract every upsetting statement I've ever made." He looked like a whipped puppy, on purpose.

"Oh no, mister. You're not getting out of it as easy as that." Evie play-punched Simon's shoulder.

"You done it now, boss. You better be a little more careful with dat girl. She dangerous. Beat the bad guys down, all on her own." Bull shook his head in mock horror.

Simon gave Bull a dirty look. "You're not helping, Mr. Cheddar."

Bull raised his hands in surrender which made Evie break out in giggles. "Bull Cheddar? That's your name? Bull Cheddar?"

"Uncle Grady wouldn't let anyone in the house swear. Bull's gang name was Bull Shit, cause he was so full of it! And anyone who disagreed with him got the shit beat out of them." Simon's smug statement made Bull frown. "So, we called him Bull Cheddar around my uncle. I think Uncle Grady knew his real nickname all along." Simon's face softened as the memories seemed to wash over him. Evie's heart did a little flip in her chest. Simon was such a sweet guy.

"Everybody done respected Mr. O'Sullivan. He be nice to everyone, no matter where you be from, or who your folks be." Bull bowed his head and crossed himself.

"Bull, you're Catholic?" Evie was surprised.

"Nah. One of my foster parents was. Made me go to church with 'em. I just got the habit, and it stayed with me when I got shoved onto the next family." Simon had told Evie about Bull's background and the many foster homes he'd been in, before he just decided to give up on adults and live on the streets. From the stories, she knew there was always a good hardy meal and a helping hand at the O'Sullivan household. Uncle Grady never judged and always listened to the kids Simon brought home, and tried to give helpful advice, no matter their circumstances. "Never thought much about God, or any of that stuff. Didn't apply to me. I was too busy survivin'." Bull turned his face to the window.

"Well, I'm definitely a believer. Amee did that to me." Simon thumbed his chest. "I hope they're happy, wherever they are." He kissed Evie on the cheek.

"I'm sure they are, Simon. You saw." Evie whispered to her boyfriend then kissed him soundly. "The good Lord made sure of that."

Simon closed his eyes. Evie watched the soft smile appear then slowly fade as Simon relaxed into that space between asleep and awake.

Her tale done, Evie relaxed as well. Life was good. She had Simon, sort of. At least she'd given him an excuse to cuddle and be close for a while. They were headed to help her friend with an emergency. It was also a good enough excuse to stay away from a big stage, bright lights and a thousand people, yelling and grabbing at Simon, which he hated more than anything. Mathers would just have to understand. Simon would get his bonus either way.

She wondered if Simon had visions of her in her red satin evening gown and strappy heels, carrying a bleeding soldier over her shoulder? That would be something his strange and imaginative brain would come up with. Maybe it would be in the next version of his game.

Not more than a second later, Zack interrupted Evie's dozing. "Landing in about thirty minutes. Bull, clean up. Boss, buckle up. Beautiful lady, make sure they comply!"

Simon yawned. "Man, I just got to sleep."

"Really, Simon? How about three hours ago!" Evie yawned in response as she checked her watch and stretched her long limbs. "Bull, need a hand?"

"Nope. Got it, beautiful lady." Bull whispered on his way by, "I think Zack is in love."

Evie laughed and straightened up around their seats. "And so it begins. You ready for this, Simon? It might get messy."

"I can do messy." Simon flexed.

From the galley, Bull commented under his breath, but loud enough for Evie to hear. "Come on, boss. You whine if your mac and cheese isn't warm enough." He punctuated his statement with a slam of the garbage bin door. "Evie, you're gonna have to keep an eye on my man. He's not cut out for heavy lifting."

"Roger that, Mr. Cheddar." She giggled at the name again. "Ya know, Bull Cheddar isn't a very intimidating name for a big guy like yourself. Maybe you should consider changing it."

"I'm kinda used to it now. It grows on you, like a fine wine. A good strong cheddar is precious. Like me." Bull wiggled his butt and winked.

Evie cracked up. The huge man stood in the small galley, his head cranked to one side, pressing against the top hull of the plane. His lopsided wink looked a little pained, but sweet at the same time, while he tried to see what he was doing in the tiny sink. Giving up, he locked all of the bins and bent over to scrunch-walk back to his seat.

Evie began humming the *Jaws* theme song. "Da dum, da dum, da dum. Boss, we need a bigger plane!" She bent over laughing as Bull's knees cracked. "Maybe we should call you Bull Cheeto with all that crunching going on. I'll get the dishes."

"Thanks." Bull collapsed into his seat. "A bigger seat would be nice, too."

Chapter 7

Carl Morehead had towed Andrea's car to Conrad's home as requested. Using it as an excuse to be outside and free of any listening devices, Conrad met his old friend at their gate. Hopping into the cab of the tow truck, he quickly explained the situation to Carl, as they continued up the long drive.

"That's a pile of dog shit, Conrad. Sorry about Andrea. Any idea what the tangos want?"

"I've got a pretty good idea. It's about our company's new project. Classified. Heads up, the house is bugged so watch what you say. Keep it professional. I have no idea if the guys know me well enough to connect us, or if they just think your company works for GST. Pete's inside."

"Right. I got nothing from the car. No prints, no evidence of use. Just Andrea's stuff. They either didn't touch her ride, or they were very good." Carl handed Conrad a billing statement with the tests he'd done, and the results with some scribbled notes. "Don't worry about the bill. I'll invoice you later. Let's get this thing unloaded." He pulled around and backed the tow truck up to the empty side of the garage.

"Pete is waiting for bank footage. The front camera location shows the club entrance and side. We should be able to see her car and a little of the side of the building. Maybe the dumpster in back."

"That may provide some idea of what happened, but I have a sneaking suspicion these guys are pros." Both men hopped out of the truck. Carl hit the button to lower the platform and Conrad released the chains that held the car in place. As the winch lowered the car, Carl spoke quietly to Conrad. "Text me if you need anything. I'm here for you."

"Will do, Carl. Thanks."

In a few minutes, Andrea's car was on the cement and secured. Conrad had an extra set of keys locked in his safe, but he'd already told the kidnappers he could not find them. He'd stop by the local locksmith tomorrow, just for looks, then put the car away, later.

The two men shook hands and Carl drove off to his next emergency tow.

In the meantime, Conrad had to set the stage for Evie's visit and let her know about the complication of the bugs. They could work out of Pete's house if need be, and if the kidnappers knew anything about him, they'd know about Evie, so that made her visit a little more believable, or coincidental at least.

"Pete, where ya at?" He hollered for his friend from the kitchen. "Evie lands in a couple hours. Let's grab the pizza and head over to the airport."

"Right on. Can't wait to see our guardian angel again. You say she's got a *boyfriend*?"

Conrad motioned for Pete to bring his laptop along as he continued the verbal set up. "That's what she said. It'll be interesting to see who this guy is and if he measures up." Conrad was setting the stage for not only her visit, but her boyfriend's as well. "What'll we tell her about Andrea? This isn't the best time for a boyfriend-introducing visit, but it'll look suspicious if we cancel a few hours before she arrives, especially since she's already in the air." He was hoping his previous conversation, before the bug discovery, fit with their current story.

"I don't know. Wait! How about telling them she's visiting her sister in the Hamptons. You can fake that for a few days. At least until Evie heads home. She's only staying a week, right?" Pete was following along with the game.

"Yeah, I guess that'll work."

"She'll figure Andrea is having fun with her sister. Or out chasing some rabbit with her camera. They have rabbits in the Hamptons, right?"

Conrad snorted. "How the hell should I know." He took the laptop from Pete. "Let's go."

Pete's Navigator was in the driveway already, so they took his car. Conrad was sure there would be no bugs to worry about in Pete's car. As they pulled out into traffic, Conrad opened his laptop, connected the wifi to his phone for a hot spot, and searched for the bank footage. The video had downloaded about five minutes before.

"Got the footage from the bank. Pull into a McDonald's up ahead. We can grab drinks and take a look."

As they viewed the time stamp on the video, Pete munched his cold pizza. Conrad's stomach was a tangled mess of acid and anxiety. He sipped a coke. "Look. Six forty-five her car pulls up. Six forty-eight she exits the car, bag in hand. Look! She locks and checks her remote."

With a mouth full of pepperoni and sausage, Pete mumbled, "Enters the club. That's it. Scan through at

X4 speed."

They sat there watching people come and go at four times the regular speed, but Andrea's face did not appear in any of the footage. When the time signature showed 5 p.m., the two men sat back.

"Damn! Nothing." Conrad slammed the dashboard.

"No. Not nothing. We know she didn't come out the front entrance after checking in. I say we go see this Wilmer fellow, her trainer. And talk to his girlfriend too. What's her name, Cal something or other."

"Good idea, but they won't be at the club until the morning. At least I don't think so. But the club won't want to be very cooperative after today." Conrad was glad Pete let his comment slip without explanation. He wasn't proud of his behavior at the club.

"Pull up their training schedule and see when the two have classes."

Conrad found the home page for the South Padre Island Athletic Club and scanned the class schedule. "Man, they're early risers. Says Wilmer Dembeck's first class is at five thirty in the morning. Callista Shapiro's yoga class begins at six. Better to catch them early. Guess where I'll be at zero-five fifteen tomorrow morning?" Conrad closed the laptop. "Take a slow drive by the club, Pete. Let's see if there are any more cameras around the area." Conrad took a swig of his soda pop. "I can't just sit here and do nothing."

"You can sit there and eat and have faith in your wife. She's tough and smart, Conrad. If there is something she can do to get herself away from her kidnappers, she'll sure as hell do it." Pete drove toward the club, munching on a crispy pizza crust. "You need to eat something. Listen to your mom, now."

"Really?" Conrad's response was dry and pointed.

"Really." Pete picked up the untouched slice and handed it to his friend. "Eat up, young man, before I ground you for a week."

During the months they'd shared a cell together, Pete had always made sure that Conrad had enough food, even if it meant giving up some of his own. Pete was not a large man and ran on much less than his tall, well-built, friend. Raised on much less food than a boy should have been, Pete was slender and wiry, but tough as nails. They didn't have much to do in their cell, so childhood stories kept them grounded in the real world while they survived in Hell. Conrad understood Pete's upbringing and knew why he could skip meals and not miss much. He'd had to as a child. Often, during their incarceration, Pete had told him, hunger pangs just meant he was alive and could eventually find something to satisfy the empty feeling, but food was never essential to him. Conrad, on the other hand, had muscles coming out his ass and got real pissy when he was hungry. Unfortunately, as hard as he tried to cover it, Pete had seen that in their cell. Going hungry was so much better than growly Conrad picking fights with the shadows and snapping at him every moment. Pete knew what Conrad needed and he provided without hesitation. His friend was amazing during that short sojourn in their lives. Conrad was well aware that Pete had developed some unique skills as a kid, a kind of survival instinct that served him well whenever his father started to sober up. It just wasn't worth the beatings and abuse handed out in his family. So Pete always appeared with a shot for his father and an ice pack for his mother, when he wasn't quick enough with the booze. He knew how to placate and provide. Conrad figured that was why Pete was such a good negotiator for their company. It was a tough way to grow up, but skills hard-won were well used as an adult.

"Look, Pete." Conrad pointed to a camera on the corner warehouse across the street from the back of the health club. "And over there." Again he pointed. This time to the sports shop on the same side of the street as the club. Two cameras, one on each side of the building pointed directly at the parking lot and the back exit and dumpsters behind the club. "If she was taken out the back, it'll be on that one. Pull in and let's see if the manager will let us have a look."

Pete whipped into the parking lot and pulled up close to the front door. They had fifteen minutes until the store would close. "Let's go. Time is of the essence, Rad."

A very fit young gal in a tight spandex exercise outfit stood surfing on her phone behind the counter. As the little bell above the door tinkled, announcing the arrival of prospective customers, the girl put down her phone and smiled brightly. "What can I help you with this evening, gentlemen?"

Conrad put on his most engaging smile and swaggered up to the counter. "Would you happen to be the manager?"

"Ah? Is there a problem, sir?" Her smile faded.

"Not at all. I just have a question. No problems." Conrad was beginning to think their short excursion would be a wild goose chase.

The clerk eyed Conrad's wedding ring. "My friend here lost his wallet this morning. Out back of the club after his workout." Pete leaned over the counter, his hands clearly showing no evidence of jewelry. "We were wondering if your security cameras have twenty-four/seven coverage. Maybe you could help this lost cause." He winked. "Ah…" He peered at the girl's left breast that sported a nametag. "Britney? Britney, that's a nice name."

Britney had the good grace to giggle. "Not sure. I can ask." She returned the breast stare. "Ah, Izog?"

"Pete. Peter Newcastle. At your service." He held out his hand over the counter.

She took his hand for a quick shake. "Well, Peter Newcastle, I'll see what I can figure out." Britney picked up the phone and pushed the intercom button. "Fred, can you come talk to these guys?" After a pause and a frown, she continued. "No, boss, no problem. This guy lost his—never mind. Please come talk to them, yeah. Thanks." She turned to Pete. "Fred Stanislaugh is the owner. He'll be out in a minute. It's almost closing time." She glanced at the clock.

Conrad was actually enjoying the little scene and Pete at his best.

"Look, we don't want to cause any trouble. It's just that my bud here carries everything in his wallet. Do you have any idea what a pain it is to replace all of the ID and credit cards, the licenses? His wife is a killer. He's doomed." Pete pouted like a puppy that peed on the carpet and got caught.

Britney leaned in close. "Don't tell him I told you this, but play up the wife thing. Fred's in the middle of a nasty divorce." She whispered with a snicker.

"Thanks, Britney." Pete's face was only inches from Britney's. He gave her a quick smooch on the cheek before straightening, and just before the owner came through the door from the office.

Fred strode toward the two men like he was on an assault mission. Conrad recognized the body language. This guy was under someone's gun, and ready for a full-frontal assault. Conrad stuck out his hand right away. "Hi. I'm Conrad. I lost my wallet out here somewhere." He pointed to the parking lot in front of the store. "I thought maybe with your security cameras, I could see what I did this morning. Maybe find it or whoever picked it up."

"Look, we're almost closed. Only one of the cameras works. The one on the south side. I don't have time to rerun the footage on the server tonight. Come back tomorrow after ten and I will see if I can do something for you." The store owner turned to leave.

"But by that time my entire identification could be in someone else's pocket, and I could be in debt over my head." Conrad added the appropriate amount of whine to his statement. "Man, if my credit gets screwed up, my wife'll kill me. She's Hell on wheels about money. You'd think I didn't make over five grand a month and kept her in rags." He wiped a frustrated hand across his face.

Pete commented off-handedly, "You're fucked, buddy."

"Hey, I don't mind staying a few minutes longer today, boss." Britney was obviously feeling the emotion of the moment. Not to mention the idea of a couple guys who have steady jobs that provide a good deal of disposable income. She was a store clerk, after all.

Conrad smiled at the clerk. This little play was turning out to be an Emmy Award winner.

Pete turned on his best appreciative sex appeal.

"That'd be very nice of you, Britney." He actually patted her hand on the counter!

"Ah, no. No way, Britney. I don't turn my server over to anyone." Fred was adamant.

Britney had other ideas, and skills. She stood right up to her boss. "Unless you need something fixed, or erased, Fred." She raised an eyebrow with one hand on her hip. Obviously, she had something on her boss. "No overtime. And no problem. Your system is 1900's technology, anyway. I used newer stuff when I was in high school."

It was a fight to the finish and Conrad immediately recognized Fred was on the losing end.

That's when Pete jumped in to close the deal. "Look, we just need to see the parking lot between six thirty and about what?" He turned to Conrad.

"...I think I left around ten or ten thirty. It shouldn't take long." He looked pleadingly at their co-conspirator.

"I can pick out the time signatures and run it on fast forward. Should only take a few minutes." She smiled waytoo sweetly at her boss. What in the heck did she know that good old Fred wanted kept quiet?

At that, Fred threw up his hands. "Fine, freakin' fine. Just don't break anything. And be sure everyone is gone before you lock up." He pointed to the back and front doors as he stomped off. "And don't accidently erase anything, Brit. Or it's your butt." He disappeared through the office door.

Both Conrad and Pete could see him through the glass window of the office, tossing his jacket over his arm. He grabbed his keys and headed out the back door.

"He's not always like that. Big court date

tomorrow." She frowned looking after her retreating boss. "If he'd been a regular human being in the beginning, Sheila wouldn't have gone for the jugular." She shook her head of long fluffy blonde hair. "Oh well. Not my circus. Not my monkeys. We can look at the camera footage after I lock up. God forbid anyone come in here to buy something." She paused halfway to the front door. "Neither one of you guys are axe murderers or anything, are you?"

Pete opened his arms wide and did a slow turn. "No axe." He accomplished a graceful bow.

Britney giggled. "Didn't figure as much." Completing her rounds, she stopped at the office door. "In here. It'll be tight..." Conrad watched her smile at Pete. This was getting better by the minute and he would let Pete drive this train to the station. "...but tight is good. Right?"

He trotted over. "Right. Tight."

Conrad followed shaking his head. Pete was such a player.

After about twenty minutes with two sets of eyes glued to the monitor, Conrad hit the space bar stopping the footage in play. "Look at that, Pete." He pointed to the screen.

Britney slid over closer to Pete. "What? What are those two doing?" She pointed at two figures on the screen. "What's that?"

"Looks like..." Pete peered at the small screen. "...two men carrying a rolled-up mat. A heavy mat." He looked pointedly at Conrad. "Guess we know what that means."

Completely forgetting that Britney sat close, he replied, "Guess we know how they took her."

Britney looked confused and Conrad realized the mistake he'd made. "Took her who?"

Pete stuttered. "Well, that would be a little hard to explain. We weren't exactly honest with you."

Britney jumped up, backing against the opposite wall of the tiny office. "So, you *are* an axe murderer!" She pulled out her phone and snapped their picture. "Out! I've got my finger on 911."

"Britney calm down. Listen…" Pete stood up.

"Stay away from me." She backed out of the office, ready to run at the least provocation.

"No, wait. Just give me a chance to explain. We're not going to hurt you, believe me."

"Oh yeah, believe you. And why would I do that? Huh?" She headed for the front of the store and unlocked the door. "Out. Both of you."

"Just give me a chance to explain. Come on Britney. Do I look like a villain?" Pete was stalling, giving Conrad time to zoom in and copy the data to a thumb drive. "Look, Conrad didn't lose his wallet, he lost his wife. She was kidnapped this morning. She was at the club next door. She checked in and never checked out. Now we know why." He looked at the floor, hoping Britney recognized his penance and the truth of their circumstances. "But you can't tell anyone. They said they'd kill her. That's why we're so keen on seeing this footage. We have to find her." He moved closer to Britney and the door she held open. "Please believe me. I would never hurt you."

Conrad buzzed by him and out the door. "Come on, Pete. I got it."

Pete moved through the doorway, taking great pains to stay as far away from Britney as possible.

"Sorry." He turned and ran to the SUV. "I owe you." He waved to the confused woman as she slammed the door and secured the lock, still holding her phone up.

"That didn't work out so well. Think she'll call the cops?" Pete really didn't feel good about how they'd left things.

"Nah. She'll just lump us with the non-human beings and call it good." Conrad was loading the data into his laptop. "Let's head out to the airport."

"Right." Pete headed down the avenue that led to the on-ramp and onto the mainland.

****

Peter and Conrad sat in Pete's pristine Navigator watching the sky. Evie would be landing any minute and her plane would taxi to the small terminal for private aircraft. They'd be there waiting. Pete surveyed the landscape and scanned the sky as Conrad scanned through the video footage, enlarging frames that might identify the kidnappers. He zoomed in on one particularly clear image and took a screen shot. Not ten seconds later he had a clear view of the second man.

"Got 'em. Now all we have to do is identify these two guys and we may have a lead."

"Oh, that's all…" Pete pointed to a slick jet taxiing toward the private terminal. "If that's Evie, she's come up in the world."

The Embraer Phenom taxied toward the chain link fence with a high-pitched whine, then powered down. As Pete and Conrad watched, the stairway deployed and a huge black man in an orange hat and shoes lumbered down the stairs, surveying the tarmac and terminal. He shook hands with the terminal agent who'd come out of the building to meet the plane, and pointed to a couple different things on the airport. After a quick conversation, the big black man spoke into a handheld radio, and waved at the jet doorway.

The first one down was definitely Evie. Definitely Evie! Except she looked like a starlet ready for the red carpet, not a soldier, or a military cop. Her movements were graceful and smooth, so unlike the woman he'd first met who could almost walk, and spent most of her time in a wheelchair. Emerald blue workout pants and a matching blue sweatshirt outlined her sleek and fit figure. The tennis shoes she wore virtually glowed pure white against the black tarmac, even in the dim light of the late night. Conrad hopped out of the Navigator and hollered, waving wildly.

"Pete, will ya look at that!" Conrad hardly saw the man descending the stairs after his heroine and savior.

"I don't think I've ever seen her in civvies. Wow!" Pete followed Conrad to the man-gate.

Evie was already on her way at a run. Conrad barely had time to open the gate, before one hundred sixty pounds of six-foot gorgeousness jumped into his arms. Hands wound around his neck and gooey lips slid across his cheek, smearing lipstick and gel from his nose to his ear.

"Whoa. Hang on there, Evie." Conrad glanced in the direction of her boyfriend. Simon was moving toward the group followed by the big fellow in bright garb. "Which one is your guy? I want my head to stay attached to my shoulders."

Evie laughed and moved on to maul Pete in a fierce hug. "Guys, I want you to meet Simon, again." She motioned to the smaller of the two men. "And his personal assistant, Bull Cheddar."

Both men responded at the same time. "Bull Cheddar?"

"Long story. Simon is my main squeeze. Bull watches out for him."

Bull stepped forward and shook hands with Conrad first. "Nice to meet you. Evie done told me about your jaunt at summer camp." Conrad's hand disappeared in Bull's as if he was a young child shaking hands with an adult.

Pete stepped back a little. "I'm good." He put his hands up in mock surrender. "Welcome to our mess."

It was Simon's turn. "Remember me?" He pointed to his tummy where the little appendectomy scar was. "I'm Simon O'Sullivan, Evie's *relationshipee*." He motioned to his bodyguard. "Sorry about the big guy. Bull can be a little intimidating, but he's harmless. Well, not harmless, but definitely a friendly."

"Ah man, boss. Always gotta spoil the image." Bull hung his head in mock dismay.

"Head up, Mister Cheddar. We have work to do." Evie patted Bull on the shoulder. Conrad was completely taken aback by the man's brilliant smile and a deep chuckle. He was a minor mountain, but when he smiled, his intimidating size and bulging muscles kind of faded into the background.

"Yes, we do. Thanks for coming so fast. I have to admit I am really surprised." Conrad looked past Evie at the Embraer Phenom jet. "Nice transport. Beats the heck out of a C-130 and a canvas bench seat."

"Hell yeah. Thanks to my *relationshipee*, here." She smiled at Simon who cringed at the word *relationshipee*. "Boyfriend, actually." She placed a quick, slimy kiss on Simon's cheek. "He is the famous creator of Ghost Wars, hence the great wheels, I mean wings and this…" She waved at her face and held up her bright nails. "We were on our way to a celebration. His game broke ten million players last month and grossed about a zillion for his company."

Pete stepped forward. "You? You designed Ghost Wars? Oh my God." He took Simon's hand and shook it vigorously. "I love that game. Amee and I have gone to level five together. She's like my teenage fantasy come to life! Where the hell'd you get that girl? God, I'd love to meet her."

"Down boy." Evie snickered, wondering what would happen if Pete really did meet Amee.

As with all of his fans, Simon pulled into his shell with a quiet, "Thanks."

"He's shy. Doesn't like people making a fuss, Pete." Evie jumped into the mission as if she'd never left the army. Conrad recognized the quick and easy transition. He'd done it a few times himself. It was only a problem with civilian types. They needed the social stuff. "We're here, so let's have a sit-rep."

Conrad had a fuzzy memory of Evie talking about Simon at their soused dinner party. He'd seen Simon's dislike of praise before. He didn't understand it, but apparently it was a big part of her boyfriend's shyness around crowds and admirers. Evie told Conrad, Simon could spin the heck out of computer code, and create amazing characters that took over the universe, but personal recognition was bad medicine in his mind.

All five piled into the Navigator and Pete started the engine to cool the SUV. Conrad provided the intel, including the information that the house was bugged. He also filled her in on her cover story. She was visiting to introduce her new man to her old army buddies.

"Well, information can be as valuable to the bad guys as misinformation can be for us. Think about it." Conrad could almost see the wheels turning in Evie's mind. This kind of thing was her forte. "In the meantime, we'll need to communicate in alternate ways, writing notes to each other, etc. You have a shredder at home, right?"

"Yes, in my office. We should be sure to shred everything. I don't know if the house is under surveillance and I know the tangos have access, otherwise I wouldn't have gotten a personalized note on my living room table."

"Maybe we should establish an FOB at my place. It's secure. I'd stake my life on it," Pete said. "I've got plenty of room. It's not the Hilton, but it's home."

"That might be an excellent idea, but we could bunk at Conrad's, just for looks. Then the bad guys"—Simon couldn't quite handle the military talk—"wouldn't think anything about going back and forth. What's an FOB?"

Evie, Conrad, and Pete all answered at the same time. "Forward Operating Base." Evie added, "A kind of command center for the mission."

Bull chuckled and poked at his boss. "I kinda like this military stuff. Maybe I should'a enlisted."

Conrad smiled. "Nice idea, Mr. Cheddar, but you'd make a pretty big target."

"Wouldn't last an hour in the sand box," Pete added under his breath.

"Yeah, I don't really like gettin' told what to do all the time, anyway. Too much like a foster home." Bull's smile faded a touch, and Conrad got the idea there was a lot more to the enormous black man in the backseat than Bull showed. He immediately said a little prayer of thanks that Bull was on their side. Conrad was sure the man could do a lot of damage if he wanted to. That bright T-shirt certainly didn't stretch much tighter and the bulges it covered certainly weren't flab. "I got my own way about me, Mr. McIntyre."

Conrad smiled. "Call me Conrad and he's just Pete. I have a feeling we will be working very closely together for the next couple days. We've gotta get Andrea back sooner, rather than later."

"Here, here!" Everyone chimed in.

On the way back to Conrad's house on South Padre Island, they sculpted a loose plan. Conrad and Evie would hit the gym early with Pete, Simon, and Bull outside, in case anyone tried to run. They'd have a camera for gym members coming and going. Evie and Conrad would join Wilmer's class for a little intel round up, and they would go from there. Carl Morehead would provide the comm equipment in the morning and everyone would be wired for sound to keep up with the ongoing operation. By the time Pete dropped the guests off at Conrad's bugged home, everyone knew their part, and it was time to get some shut-eye.

"So, let me show you around the place." Conrad gave the short version of a guest tour and settled Evie and Simon in the guest suite, with Bull Cheddar in the third bedroom across the hall. "The maid knew you were coming for a visit, but if you need anything else, just pillage around. We have at least one of everything you could want." He opened cabinets, pointing to extra towels, pillows, guest robes, etc. "You're welcome to work out at Andrea's club. We have a family membership, and I know you are still working on that leg of yours." Conrad set the plan in action in case anyone was listening to their casual conversation.

"Sounds good, Rad." She hugged her battle buddy. "But first, I'm gonna take a long shower and scrape this goop out of my hair so I won't hurt Simon when we hit the rack!" She pretended to knock on the side of her hairdo. "And wash my face. Then maybe I'll feel human again, instead of like some painted up hoochie-mama in a whorehouse."

Simon quietly commented, "I like your hair, Evie."

"Then I will leave you two to the shower and family beauty discussion. For the record—" Conrad poked the side of Evie's hair. "—it could stop any incoming!"

"Right. Both of you need to just leave me to the hot water, then I'll be fine, in about three hours and a gallon of soap." Evie smacked her gelled lips. "Provided my lips don't slide right off my face first."

Bull left the two bags from the ACC kit next to the door, yawned, and pronounced, "I'm dead tired. I'm turning in. You have no idea how much energy it takes to watch after these two." He slapped Conrad on the back and headed for his own room and a king-sized bed. "Later."

"Good idea. It's almost midnight here so I think I'll turn in also. See you both in the morning." He extended a hand to Simon. "Good to finally get to spend some time with you, Simon. Sober anyway!" Both men chuckled. The last time they'd been together, Conrad and Simon were both very inebriated. He knew neither one had very straight memories of that event. Then he was back in Texas and didn't think about Evie's friend much after that. Now here he was as her boyfriend. Good for his Evie!

"Likewise." Simon shook Conrad's hand and closed the door behind his host.

****

Simon looked at Evie. "There's only one bed. Is that okay…?"

"Alone at last!" Evie jumped into Simon's arms. She kissed him soundly and then released him abruptly. "Now the shower…"

"Wait. What do you mean a shower? After that kiss? Wait…" Simon followed Evie into the bathroom. He had other things on his mind rather than a shower and wondered if he wanted to make that step. Wondered if *she* wanted to take that step. What would happen to their easy relationship if they ended up in bed together? It was what he'd wanted for ages, what he dreamed about. But he just couldn't do casual sex. Not with Evie. There had to be more. "Do you want to…" Simon couldn't really put his wish into words.

"No way, Mister. Not until I'm back to myself and can smile without the risk of cracking my face." She pushed him back out into the bedroom. "But hold that thought." She blew him a seductive kiss with her shiny lips.

"But I like you that way…" Simon stood outside the bathroom, fixated on the beautiful vision in the doorway. He could hear the water start. Was she ready for this step? His mind spun in circles, just considering making love to the beauty he'd begun to cherish in so many ways.

****

"I'll make it up to you, babe." Evie shoved the

door closed and slipped out of her sweats, then stepped into the steamy water. "Ahhhhh! I love it." She pumped about half a cup of shampoo into her hand and lathered her stiff hair. "I will never get this stuff out." She commented to herself as she scrubbed and scratched her scalp. A mound of lather topped her head as she worked the soap. So, Simon had finally gotten to the point, and they were about to hit the rack together?

Evie had thought long and hard about their relationship for a long time, but wanted Simon to make the first move. She knew he had reservations about commitment, relationships, and trust. She had no intention of scaring off the man she'd come to love. It *was* love, she realized. Simon had been through the wringer, after his uncle died, but through it all, he'd remained caring, generous, and supportive, if a bit confused and needy himself. On the other hand, she'd needed time to understand the whole ghost-talking thing, and he'd just gone right along with her need, accepting everything she tried to understand about her new family gift. For a while they'd stayed at arm's length, but through the three years, they'd grown close over memories, meals and finally a job offer. The pent-up need in both of them was beginning to wear on their relationship. Maybe it was time…

"So you need a hand?" Simon stepped into the shower.

"Eeek, Simon! You scared me."

"Good Lord!" He stared at the foot-tall mound of lather. "You look like the Bride of Frankenstein from that old movie with Gene Wilder." He chuckled and worked his fingers into the shampoo.

"Oh my God, that feels wonderful. I'll give you a

week to stop it." Apparently, her boyfriend had finally decided—

"It might just take a week." Simon's fingers tangled in the long curls that had been glued together with hairspray. "What did they put in here? Marine Varathane?"

Evie chuckled. "I told you it took an entire team and some very top-secret chemical formulas." She unwound his fingers and threw her arms around him, sliding some lather between them. As she wiggled and rubbed, Simon's manhood came to life. She leaned back to rinse her hair, which only displayed her perfect breasts to him, complete with rivulets of soap streaming down her body.

"God, you kill me, girl." Simon kissed her collarbone just beneath a jagged scar that showed deep red in the heat of the shower. "I truly love you, Captain Gastineau." He licked across her shoulder and down her arm, kissing and nipping as he went.

Simon said the "L" word?

He said the "L" word!

Evie pulled his head away from her arm. "Major…again, please."

"Okay…" Simon bent to continue his ministrations to her arm.

"No, silly. The hair. It's still as stiff as a board, and it feels like straw." She handed him the shampoo bottle and stuck out her hand. "Please?"

Simon let out a very long, very tired sigh. "Okay. But then can we?" He looked into her eyes. "Holy shit!"

The make-up on Evie's face had begun to run with the hot water. Black streaks lined her cheeks and tan globs had sunk to her chin. Catching a view of her face in the shaving mirror, mounted on the side of the shower, she had to laugh. "That's the price you pay for wanting me all painted up." She grabbed a washcloth off the rack just outside the shower and scrubbed her face. Soon the old Evie looked out from behind a gray and brown stained cloth. "How's this?" Her face was rosy and clean. Even the gel from her lips was gone, and her natural, healthy beauty was back. She felt more like herself and ready to take *her* next step.

"I kinda like the painted-up version..." Simon shrugged. "Call me shallow, I can't help it, I'm just a guy."

"That's a Brad Paisley song, and the painted-up version is way too high maintenance. Do you know what that make-up job cost you?" Evie laughed.

"Make-up or no, you are still the most gorgeous woman I've ever washed." He pumped a pool of soap into his hand and began scrubbing her hair again. He massaged her scalp and pulled shampoo through her long, tight curls. "I love your hair, glued up or not!"

Evie was squirming and enjoying Simon's attention. When he got to the base of her neck and began to rub gently, she moaned and leaned back against him. It felt heavenly. He'd decided and now it was up to her to carry on!

"You keep that up, and we'll never get out of this shower." Simon murmured in her ear.

Evie reached up and scooped a handful of lather from her head. Applying it to his swollen member, she tentatively stroked, long and slow.

Simon froze. He grabbed for the wall as his knees buckled. "Evie..." She watched him struggle to find the next word. It wouldn't come, but he would. She was blowing his mind and knew it. "Evie, stop. You'll make me…"

It was too late. Simon exploded into her hand, grabbing for anything to keep himself upright. His muscles clenched and everything in his body convulsed with the power of his orgasm. "Ahhhhh."

"Make you what, baby?" She giggled and held him close. Her lips found his, and she drank in his sweet taste. As their kiss deepened, she felt his body tighten once again. "Whoa, Simon. I don't want to have to carry you to the bedroom." She spoke around his hungry tongue, as she held him against the side of the shower, steadying his shaky body.

Simon's legs were soft as putty, and Evie knew that genius mind of his wouldn't work. He was everything she wanted, everything she needed. She loved every inch of his geeky mind and body. He didn't seem to mind her battle-scarred body and tarnished soul. His hands wound around her neck and he pulled her even closer, massaging her neck and shoulders. "Give me a minute here, would ya. I can barely stand." Slowly his hands returned to their primary job and Evie's hair began to soften. He rubbed and separated the curls, while she stood luxuriating in the simple task of being bathed, loved.

Evie enjoyed the attention to her neck and shoulders as she waited for Simon's breathing to return to normal. Finally, he stood, leaning against the shower wall. "Feels better."

"I'm sure you do." Evie's sly look made Simon wiggle his toes, anyway, she hoped it was her comment. Evie rinsed her hair one more time and added conditioner. "I think someone's ready for bed."

Simon's eyes were drooping, and he slumped precariously. "But, what about you, babe?"

She rinsed the conditioner out. "Clean hair. Clean face. Satisfied boyfriend." She gently poked him in the stomach. "I'm happy for the moment." Reaching behind her back, she turned the shower off, grabbed a towel from the bar, and handed it to Simon. "Sleep will be good for both of us. And I want to snuggle. Just sleep for twenty-four. It's been a hell of a day."

Within moments of his head hitting the pillow, Simon was asleep. Evie lay next to him, cuddled in the hollow of his arm, watching the gentle rise and fall of his chest as he breathed in sleep. There was something so warm and loving about being in his arms as he slept. He held her like she belonged right where she was, forever, cherished, adored and secure. She wondered if that was the way it was with Conrad and Andrea. She'd only met Andrea a handful of times, but it always seemed like Conrad held his wife like he would never let her go. Would she ever willingly let Simon go?

"Why would you want to do that, Evie?" The thought popped into her head in the voice of a ghost she knew well. "Amee?" She whispered.

"Of course, Evie. Did you think we would desert you and Simon just because we found our happiness? Now I'm not stuck at Port Chicago anymore. Isn't that wonderful?" Amee giggled her high-pitched teen giggle.

"Ah…possibly." Evie kept her whisper low and quiet as Simon stirred in his sleep. Her Ghost of Port Chicago was back? Or never really gone?

And keeping watch?

Her face heated as she began to blush, considering what she and Simon had just done in the shower.

"Go to sleep now, dear. Tomorrow will be a big day."

Evie felt a calmness invade her being, as she slipped off to sleep to the sound of a childhood lullaby, sung by the sweetest voice she'd ever heard.

Chapter 8

Evie woke to the soft chiming of her phone alarm. She'd slept all night with no dreams at all! Just restive, comfortable sleep, next to the man she loved! She hadn't had that kind of night since- she couldn't remember when. Evie stretched and felt the tight skin bind near the scar on her arm. It had gotten better in the subsequent years, but still plagued her if she relaxed her daily routine of exercise and stretching.

"At least you have an arm to stretch, Evie."

Amee was back in her life, after how long? Three years? But now instead of fear that she was hearing voices and going crazy, Evie relaxed into the sound and let it flow, even responding in her mind. *"And for that I am grateful every day, Amee!"*

A sweet tinkling, like a chime mixed with a girlish giggle, tickled Evie's brain. *"You and Simon have work to do today. No more lazing around. Up, up, girl! Andrea needs you."*

Evie startled.

What?

Amee knew about Andrea's predicament?

"Amee, can you tell me where Andrea is?" Evie sat up and spoke to the ghost, as if Amee was there in the bedroom with them.

There was no response, except a quiet sigh. Of course, finding Andrea wouldn't be that simple, even with Amee's help.

She rolled over and poked Simon.

He didn't move.

"Time to get up and do some sleuthing, babe." She yawned and poked Simon again.

He still didn't move.

"Come on. I know you're not asleep, buster."

Simon grabbed Evie and in the blink of an eye, rolled them over in the tangled sheets. Plastering kisses down her cheek, he chuckled then yawned. "Guess I didn't sleep fast enough." Flopping onto his back, he groaned. "Really, not fast enough. Or long enough."

Evie slid from under the covers and dumped the contents of her ACC bag on top of the stretched-out Simon. "Let's see what your male mind thinks my female body should be wearing."

Simon lunged for her and missed. "Nothing would be good." He smiled slyly as he watched Evie forage through his choice of clothes and accessories.

Evie held up a pair of hot pink string bikini panties, if that's what a person called two strings and a tiny piece of lace. "Honestly?" She sling-shotted the panties at his head. "Now this is a little better." She pulled a tie dyed pair of leggings and a spandex T-shirt with a built in bra, from the small pile. She found a matching scrunchy for her wild mass of hair and a pair of athletic socks near the foot of the bed. "Guess I'm good to go. Come on sleepyhead, we've gotta be at the club in forty minutes if we want to catch that skank-o."

"Noooo." Simon whined.

"Yessss." Evie countered. "This is serious shit. Now come on." She jerked the covers onto the floor leaving Simon free as a bird, then spun and departed with a skip.

Conrad was already in the kitchen with a cup of very black coffee and a bowl of flaky cereal covered in whipped cream. Some of the white stuff was smeared across his upper lip. "Morning." He didn't look like he'd slept a wink. His face was haggard and his five o'clock shadow was working toward midnight.

"It's always a good morning when I'm vertical." It was a saying they'd often exchanged during the oh-dark-thirty PT sessions at Walter Reed, once she was back on her feet and on the way to physical healing.

"Roger that. Coffee's in the pot. Raid the fridge for whatever you want. Cereal's left of the stove. Whipping cream is in the wine cooler."

"Are you really eating cereal with whipped cream?" Evie surveyed his soup bowl of frothy mess.

"It's just another form of milk, right?" He toasted her with a spoonful. Around the crunch, he mumbled, "And it makes the flakes stick together. I don't have to chase them down." As he munched, he drew a small bug on a sheet of paper on the kitchen counter and tapped it with his pen, then pointed to the small ceramic frog on the windowsill above the sink.

Evie nodded in response. She took one look at the black stuff in the automatic coffee maker and grimaced. "Think I'll skip the tar this morning. Have any juice?" Checking out the refrigerator, she grabbed a carton of orange and poured herself a large glass full. "How about hitting the club this morning? I like to keep up the routine. Docs say it's good for my scar tissue. Keeps it flexible and soft." She poked at a couple places on her leg and arm. All of the temporary cosmetic skin applied by Simon's experts had come off in the shower, and her normal scars were once again apparent.

"Not a problem. I can take you. Simon sleeping in?" Conrad wrote on the paper, *with Pete later*?

As if he was somehow magically summoned, Simon came bounding down the stairs and slid into the kitchen. "Did I hear my name taken in vain?" He slid by Evie with a passing air-smooch, grabbed a cup off the counter and poured himself a cup of coffee. One slurp and it went into the sink. "What the heck is this? It's not coffee for sure." He made a face and spit into the sink. "That's almost as bad as what my mama used to make. When we had a kitchen, that is." He wrote on the paper; *Pete's picking me up after you and Evie leave*. "Juice it is."

Evie handed him a glass and poured it full. "Want any breakfast? I'm not hungry. Last night's in-flight catering is still right here." She patted her flat stomach.

"I'm not a breakfast kind of guy. I much prefer brunch. When it's brunch time, of course." Simon downed the glass and set it in the sink next to the half-cup of black liquid. "Burrrr. That don't even look right."

"I can't figure out what you two are talking about." Conrad finished his cup and poured another. "I'm kinda fond of a rich black coffee. Straight out of the pot. Evie, you ready to go?"

"Roger that, Rad." She finished her juice and they headed for the car. "Did you ever get that Mustang you were drooling about? Holy Jesus, Joseph, and Mary, will ya look at that!" Evie was impressed. Conrad's Stang was a heck of a set of wheels. "That's a teenage boy's wet dream on four wheels. Andrea doesn't mind if you drive around in a chick magnet?"

"If she does, she never mentioned it."

Immediately Evie knew that was the wrong thing to say. Andrea was gone. Kidnapped. Possibly already dead. It showed all over Conrad.

"Let's go." It was a soft statement. Conrad placed his mug of coffee in the holder between the seats and off they went to 'work out'.

It was close to five fifteen when they parked across from the front door of the club. Wilmer Dembeck would probably already be inside getting ready for his class. "I hope the manager is a late riser. I don't think he'll remember me fondly. I sort of caused a ruckus yesterday." Conrad quickly explained his visit to the club, and the little visit with the South Padre Police officers.

"I can always do recon on my own and give you a heads up if anything comes of it. Will they let me in with your family pass if you or Andrea are not with me?" Conrad had shown Evie the picture of Wilmer and Callista late last night. She would be able to spot the two without any trouble.

"Should be fine. Andrea's niece used it a couple months ago when she was visiting. Had no problem at all." He handed her the pass. At the bottom of her bag were two blurry pictures; one of the first guy carrying the mysterious rolled up rug, and the second was the guy on the other end. It may not have been the way Andrea was removed from the club, but it certainly was suspicious.

"All right, Conrad. You hang out here for a little while and I'll see what I can find out." Evie placed the listening device deep in her ear. She would be able to speak to and hear her team. Pete had already picked up Simon. Evie could hear them talking about Ghost Wars and a quick McDonald's breakfast. Her stomach grumbled. She actually was hungry but didn't want to take the time to eat. There were more important things to do, like find Andrea and the sleaze-bags that took her.

"Good morning." She swiped her pass and smiled brightly at the gal behind the counter.

"Welcome to the South Padre Island Athletic Club. The McIntyre family guest pass entitles you to use any of the services and equipment. Please feel free to talk to any of our staff about an exercise program tailored strictly to you." The cute girl pushed a button beneath the counter and the gate swung open to admit Evie.

As Evie walked by, she casually mentioned, "I've heard there's a guy that does a great five-thirty class. Cardio, kickboxing, that kind of stuff."

"Sure. That would be Wilmer's class. It's tough, but he's a great trainer. If you like a hard workout with no holds barred, that's the class for you. She glanced at the clock. "It starts in about six minutes. Wilmer is always on time. It's a German thing." She leaned over the counter and pointed down the hall. "Lady's locker room is down there."

"Thanks. I think I'll try it out. Andrea said she loved it."

The girl had the good graces to blanch at the mention of Andrea's name. Evie almost snickered. So, word about Conrad's visit had gotten round, huh?

The lady's locker room was state of the art and shiny as a new dime. The tile work was haut-Mexican and resembled a modern temple ruin. Wall waterfalls kept the place cool and hydrated while lending a certain sophisticated ambiance. Evie wondered what a year's membership cost in a place like this. It probably didn't even dent Andrea's pocketbook. If Conrad never lifted another finger, his and Pete's company had already made several comfortable livings for the two of them.

Rounding a mirrored corner, Evie paused. She immediately recognized the petite, well-built woman stretching her hamstrings against the bench. "Morning. Come on in. We're open for business."

Callista's cheery manner seemed appropriate and honest. For more months than she wanted to remember, Evie had nothing to do but study her captors. She'd gotten very good at judging character and body language. This woman didn't seem to be guarded, or covering up a kidnapping.

"I haven't met you, yet." She stuck her hand out. "I'm Callista Shapiro, one of the personal trainers here at the club. Are you new?"

It was the perfect opening for a test. "Yes, I'm a friend of Andrea's." She held up the family pass Conrad gave her.

Callista smiled, shaking her head. "So, you're the reason she skipped lunch with us yesterday!" Then the young woman thought the better of what she had just said. "Not that that's a bad thing. Really! I didn't mean it to sound so..." She lifted her hands. "It's just that Andrea didn't say she was leaving yesterday, and we usually meet for lunch. She's been training with my boyfriend for a couple years now. We sorta have a standing lunch. Did she come with you?" Callista looked around Evie as if to automatically see Andrea behind her.

"No, she's up north with her sister. Some kind of family thing." Evie tried for an off-handed attitude. "I just got here yesterday." While she spoke, Evie observed Callista's expressions and movements. She saw no evidence of subterfuge "I need to work out though." She pointed to a long scar on her shoulder. "Doctor's orders."

Callista blinked. "Oh my God! You're Conrad's friend. The woman who saved his life." Callista took Evie in a fierce hug. "Oh my God, I am so glad to meet you. Andrea told me so much about you. You're a war hero!" One more tight hug and Callista took Evie's hand again, shaking it vigorously. "Very pleased to meet you, ma'am."

After a moment, Evie retrieved her hand with a giggle. "Well, I see my reputation has preceded me. Please call me Evie. I'm not in the army anymore." If this woman had anything to do with Andrea's disappearance, it must have been unwittingly. Liars kept their distance and didn't wiggle with excitement when meeting a potential opponent. They didn't make happy eye contact, or honest physical contact.

"Wait till I tell Wilmer. He'll be amazed to meet you. Andrea has told us so much about you. How you rescued Pete and Conrad from the Taliban. How you got shot but got them out anyway. It's just amazing. So amazing. I don't even have a better word for it." Callista tentatively touched the scar on Evie's arm. "So amazing." she commented softly.

"Okay, hang on there a minute. I like to keep a low profile these days. I'm a civilian now, so if you don't mind—"

"Oh, of course. I'll keep it quiet. But I have to tell

Wilmer. He'll just be out of his mind. He loves all the American military stuff. He'd probably enlist, if he was American." She put a finger to her lips. "But I won't say anything to anyone else. Promise." She held up a pinky finger to shake on it.

"Pinky promise. Does it for me." Evie laughed as they pinky-shook to seal the promise. "I heard from Andrea that Wilmer does a fantastic class. Mind if I join in? Just for today. I may not be able to handle the entire thing."

"Sure! I'll show you. He hasn't started yet. Mind if I introduce you...quietly of course." Callista took Evie's hand. "Come on. This is gonna be so great!"

Evie remembered Andrea mentioning her pal at the club and how she was always so cheery and upbeat, but this was almost over the top. This woman was one big smiley face in spandex and Nikes. She was in perfect shape, literally, and her smile could light up a stadium. No wonder Andrea had been so drawn to her.

Callista dragged Evie across the gym toward a series of glassed-in classrooms. The middle class already held several women in all shapes and sizes, waiting for their trainer. A very handsome, blond man stood at the door greeting each participant as they entered. "Stretch a little. Varm up, ladies." His demeanor and accent screamed German, along with his close-cropped and spiked blond hair and crystal blue eyes.

"Wilmer, come here." Callista motioned from a few feet away.

"Vat iz up, Calli?" Wilmer approached with a welcoming smile.

"Wilmer, you'll never guess who this is!" Callista

didn't even give him time to respond. "This is Andrea's friend, Evie. You know, the army hero who saved Conrad."

Evie chuckled. She'd long ago given up trying to mitigate her impact on people, once they learned of her activities in the Middle East, and the fact that she'd received the Silver Star and a Purple Heart for her efforts. She stuck out her hand.

Wilmer took it with the gusto of a fan meeting his favorite rock star for the first time. "I am honored to meet you." He looked around. "Vere iz Andrea. Iz she not vit you?" His face showed honest interest. His clear pupils did nothing at all, a sure sign of truthfulness.

"She's at her sister's in New York. But Evie came in to exercise. Doctor's orders." Callista pointed to Evie's scarred arm.

"Vell, den, velcome. I promise to vork you hard!" He hooked Evie's arm in his and escorted her into the class. "Varm up, please." Wilmer resumed his place by the door, welcoming each participant with a warm smile and words of encouragement. No wonder his classes were so popular and full. By the time the class began, there were at least thirty worshiping women sweating to the oldies and ogling Wilmer's fit, handsome body, as he took them through the paces.

As fit as Evie was, halfway through the hour, she excused herself. She was drenched and panting. Finding a bench outside the classroom, she sank to the richly stained wood and sat, just breathing. She had maybe five seconds to herself before Callista appeared.

"You okay?" Again, her concern was genuine and sincere.

"Yeah. I've slacked off since separating from the

army. Guess I better get back into the routine." Evie slapped her thigh. "I used to run every morning with the MPs. Now I get up, take an elevator to the first floor, and drive to work. Not good for the love handles." She tried to pinch a love handle, but there wasn't one to be found, yet.

"You are in great shape." Callista smiled warmly. "I know these things. You should see Andrea work it. Man, she's a killer to keep up with." Callista leaned in conspiratorially, "But don't tell her I told you that." The young trainer giggled. "We usually get together for lunch after she works out all morning, hard. You'd think the Devil himself was chasing her." She looked down at the floor. "Or she was running from something."

Evie picked up on the girl-talk invitation right away. "Running? Maybe after the picture of the year, but her life is perfect. What could she be running from? Something I should know?" Evie put her hand on Callista's knee. Personal contact often encouraged divulging secrets.

"I don't know. It just seems she hasn't been so happy lately. She didn't go to her sister's, like permanently? Did she?" Callista turned toward Evie and moved closer. "If it's none of my business, just say so. But Andrea leaves abruptly. Then you show up. I mean." She stopped mid-sentence.

"Nah. The problem was with her sister. Some kind of family issue. I was already on my way for a visit with Simon. You know, introducing my guy to my family-by-choice." Evie winked and tried to plaster a sexy smirk on her face.

Callista giggled. "Well, I hope everything works

out. I know her sister has four daughters. Must be a zoo at their house. I can't imagine four girls at home and a working mom."

"Yep." Evie commented, shaking her head in agreement. She actually had no idea what a big family was like. She'd only had Tootie and Maman until she joined the army family. Then she had thousands, but it wasn't the same.

"I know what you need." Callista brightened, leaving the worry behind as her perpetual exuberance took over. "You need a good massage. I'll introduce you to Master Moto. He's fantastic with his hands, if you know what I mean." She squeezed her hands open and closed as if to massage a perspective client. "Andrea swears by his work." Callista took Evie's hand and dragged her toward the hallway that led to the spa rooms.

"Ah, I'm not crazy about massages, Callista." She was trying to stall. She still had serious recon to attend to.

"Ah, you'll love it. He is soooo good." Callista winked. "Just for a half hour. You'll see." At the third door, Callista paused and knocked softly. "I hope he's free. Usually is this time of the morning."

As the door swung open to reveal a small room with a massage table and a shelf full of various treatments, Evie froze.

She knew this man!

She'd already seen a picture of him.

At the end of a rolled-up rug!

"Master Moto, this is a friend of Andrea McIntyre. She needs some of your magic touch." Callista stepped back, motioning to Evie.

This was not going to happen!

"Ah, I'm sorry. I don't think I'm up for this yet, Callista." She pointed to three scars on her arms. "Sorry, I still don't like to be..." She hung her head in mock fear, "touched."

Immediately Callista threw her hands to her mouth. "Oh God, I am so sorry. I didn't think." Her eyes began to tear. "I just thought. I am so sorry." She hugged Evie once again. "I guess today is my brain-dead day. Please forgive me. I really didn't think before just rushing off like some crazed—"

Evie took the shorter woman by her shoulders. "Callista, stop. It's okay. I'm still a little uncomfortable with male touch. It's not your fault."

"I completely understand." Master Moto was very gracious beneath his bushy brows that seemed to hide secrets in his dark eyes. He bowed slightly, "If you change your mind, I am always at your service." He slowly closed the door.

"Maybe a hot shower would be better?" Callista was trying to smooth over her blunder.

"You know..." Evie pretended to consider her options carefully, "I think I'll just head home and shower. That way if I want to collapse afterwards, I'll have a cozy bed a few feet away." She rubbed her thighs. "Wilmer really is a task master. Please tell him I really enjoyed myself."

"Sure. No problem. You're sure you're all right to get home?" Callista was truly concerned. There was no subterfuge in her at all.

"Of course. Conrad and Andrea only live a few minutes from here. Rad's home so I should be fine. Trust me, I've felt a lot worse and made it home before." Evie went for the soft arm pat and reassurance-between-women smile.

It worked.

Callista followed Evie into the locker room. "Well, if you should need help," she pulled a card from a small holder on the wall next to the mirrored dressing room. "Just whistle." Affecting a sexy pose, she added, "You know how to whistle, don't you, Evie? You just put your lips together, and blow." Callista giggled her way back out of the locker room leaving a somewhat confused Evie alone.

"What in the world...?"

"It's a line from an old Humphrey Bogart and Lauren Bacall movie." Evie heard Rad's voice in her ear. "What's with the Master?"

"He's one end of the rug." She spoke very quietly as she headed for the exit. "Pete, I think you need a massage. And I know the perfect guy for the job."

In the car, Simon was already dialing the number to make a massage reservation for Pete. "Already on it, Evie, my love."

"Out in two seconds, guys," Evie whispered, as she swiped her family pass and walked into the brilliant morning sunshine of Padre Island. "So, what do we do next?" She got into the Mustang next to Conrad.

"I think we need to play a little question and answer game with the good Master Moto."

The growl in Conrad's voice actually scared Evie.

Chapter 9

Pete used his killer smile on the woman at the front desk. She lit up in response. "No, a friend made the appointment for me. It's a birthday gift, really." He perched on the side of her desk leaning in. "I know he has this surprise planned right after I get inside." He put his fingers to his lips. "Shhhh. Don't tell him I told you so! I'll save you a piece of cake, okay?"

Cassy, or Sally, or Halley, whatever her name was, bought into their planned intrigue right away. That immediately left Peter wondering how much intelligence it took to sit at a desk and push a little button every time the computer screen in front of you said *approved.* "So, it's okay if I go in?"

"I guess." The young woman hesitated for show. "But since it's your birthday, I guess it will be fine." Cassy, or Sally, or Halley pushed the button, her entire job, and Peter threw her a kiss, as he disappeared down the hall toward the locker rooms. "Happy, um, birthday, Mister…"

Peter moved into the men's locker room, talking softly on his comm. "In. Heading to the loading dock now." He wore designer sweats and tennis shoes, so he fit right in with the local clientele, except for the bulbous muscles and straining veins he saw all around him.

The loading dock was on the east side of the

building, and it took seconds to slip through the Staff Only door. It occurred to him that a club catering to the elite clientele of South Padre Island should have better security. He'd walked right into the loading and supply area without being challenged, or even noticed. There were no cameras in the staff area. Maybe that was on purpose. His mind was winding around a conspiracy theory that included the entire staff of this club. A seeming dumb bell at the front desk? A German war god for a trainer and a sweet cheerleader to lend enthusiasm? A muscle-man masseur for the dirty work? It all fit in Pete's mind. This was a snake pit and he was strolling on in like nobody's business.

He eased the door to the loading dock open admitting Conrad, Evie, and Bull Cheddar. "I have a date with Master Moto. But I may need a chaperone. Care to accompany me?" He grinned at his friends and said a prayer of thanks for the cheesy guy with the bright shoes.

"Simon's watching the cars. He's on comm in my rig. You knock and go on in. We'll follow. I want to know what this guy did with my wife." Pete could hear the angry snarl in his friend's voice. This was not going to be pretty.

"Right." Pete waved them past. "Hang back. I'll leave the door open a crack. We all ready?"

The small group answered in unison, "Ready."

Pete trotted down the hall and the rest followed. Outside Moto's room, he paused motioning to his team before knocking loudly. "Master Moto?"

The door swung open to reveal a short, stocky man of Asian descent. "I am Master Moto. You are my seven o'clock?" The masseur stuck out his hand in greeting.

"Yep. That'd be me. I'm John." Pete shook his hand and followed Moto into the massage room, leaving the door just a touch ajar. Enough for someone to enter, if the door locked upon closure.

"Have you ever experienced a massage before, John?" Moto stood against the back wall between two tall shelving units that held jars and tins, a stack of sheets and towels, a fleece blanket and several candles. Soft music played in the background. It was a pleasing room, decorated in muted colors and smelling of some sort of witch hazel or camphor.

"Ah, yeah, sure." With his comment, the team came through the door.

"What is this? What are you people doing in…" Obviously startled, Moto pressed his back against the wall and eased toward the door.

Bull put a stop to his movement. "Where you think you're goin' there, shorty?"

"You cannot be in here. You must leave. This is not…" As Moto tried to threaten his way out of the precarious position, Bull reached into his cargo pants and pulled out a roll of duct tape, slapping a piece over the masseur's mouth. Bull's huge hand clamped around the man's throat, stilling further movement. His fingers actually wrapped all the way around as Moto's eyes settled on Conrad. Recognition dawned and fear replaced recognition.

Conrad leaned close in the small room. "What the hell did you do with my wife?" Spittle sprayed Moto's face. "Let's go have this conversation somewhere else. Somewhere quiet."

Conrad led the way as Bull dragged Moto through

the hall. Pete followed with Evie behind the group. "Simon, bring Conrad's rig around to the back." Pete spoke through the comm.

"Okay. I mean, roger that!" Everyone heard Simon's snicker following the military type response.

Pete thought Evie's boyfriend was having a little too much fun and this was a critical mission. "Okay is fine, Simon. Just get the SUV as close to the door as possible. Less for the casual observer to see."

As they left the club through the loading dock exit, Bull taped Moto's hands and feet. Lifting the masseur into Conrad's SUV, Bull got in beside him. Through the window Pete could see Bull staring at their captive, an evil smile plastered across his face. It was a very intimidating look, and very effective. Moto sat immobile and did not struggle at all.

Conrad got into the front passenger seat. "Drive, Simon. Back to Pete's place."

"Roger that!" Simon chuckled over the comm. "I love this military stuff."

"Yeah, my sista here be real proud, bro." Pete heard Bull comment over the comm link. Pete's car was on the street and as Conrad's SUV pulled out of the parking lot behind the club, Pete caught sight of Brittney, the salesclerk in the athletic store next door. She was locking the front door and glaring directly at him. Pete smiled and waved. He got a middle finger for his efforts. And a Kodak moment, as she raised her phone and obviously caught their actions on her camera.

"Our little adventure is now recorded for posterity, guys. We need to move fast. The clerk next door got it all and probably, so did the security camera." Pete waved at Britney for no reason than he kind of liked her and he'd already been caught. Maybe it would help him if they were found out and cops got involved. She'd liked him before their cover was blown. Maybe… He trotted around the corner, and ran for his ride.

If Brittney called the police, all they'd have to do is check Conrad's license plate for identification and residence. It wouldn't be long before the Padre Island's finest put two and two together and came looking for Pete. He pulled a U-turn in the road to avoid exposing his own license plate to the girl and the store's one functioning security camera. "Hang on, Evie. See you at my place." He stepped on the gas and followed his team in the SUV ahead of him.

Conrad just grunted in reply. The comm was quiet as Pete followed. There would be consequences for their part in this caper, but Andrea's life was at stake. Hopefully it would be worth it.

Close to his place, Pete pulled in front of the little convoy. Since he owned the entire building and, as of yet, there were no other tenants; they had the underground parking lot to themselves. He pressed the button on his rearview mirror to open the gate and sat drumming the steering wheel as it slowly inched up. "Damn, I should have upgraded that gate." As soon as there was clearance, he sped through.

Pete could see Conrad's SUV was right behind him, Simon at the wheel. The man's huge smile could be seen a mile away let alone one car length. Hoping they got through the gate before someone, someone in blue with a badge and a gun, drove by looking for a group of kidnappers in fancy cars, Pete led the way to the central freight elevator and parked right in front. No one else would need to use the handicapped spot anyway.

As everyone got out, Bull tossed the bound Moto out onto the pavement and Conrad dragged the mumbling and flailing man into the spacious and padded elevator.

Pete punched the button for the third floor. He actually lived on the tenth floor, but number three was a complete mess of construction debris and tarps. "Three's got a bunch of old tarps in case we need a body bag." He tried to leer at their captive, but his total good looks and pretty-boy image just made him seem like a three-year-old that had stolen his sister's cookie. Some men had that hard, committed look that said *don't fuck with me.* Peter Newcastle's serious look was more like, *hey babe, wanna take a shower together, and then I'll cook us something vegan?*

The third floor was intimidating. Old tarps and rolls of dusty plastic lay scattered everywhere. Pipes and discarded lumber littered one corner, and the windows were blacked out with centuries of grime and weather. Loose wires hung from various timbers holding up a warped ceiling. Nails, screws, and wooden pegs were scattered all over. Several of the wall bricks were lose, having lost their mortar in the last millennium. It was dim and smelled of rust and mold. It was perfect.

Conrad threw Moto against a sack of some kind of dirt and ripped the duct tape from his mouth. Pete winced as part of the man's scraggly beard came away on the tape. "Go ahead. Scream. No one will hear you here."

Moto looked around at the circle of serious, threatening faces, except for Pete, who looked like he was impatiently waiting in line for a skinny, mocha, van-cher delight coffee from the Human Bean Delight coffee house downtown.

"What do you want?" Moto choked out. Tiny beads of blood appeared around his mouth where the tape tore out hairs. He looked like he was sweating blood.

Conrad stormed over and punched the man in the jaw sending his head swiveling. "My wife. I want her back."

"I don't know your wife, mister. I don't know you." Moto whined pathetically. "Please, there is some mistake here. Let me go and I won't say a word. I promise."

"You're trying to tell me you don't know Andrea McIntyre? Bullshit. She's been going to you for massages for over a year now, and you don't know who she is? Pure bullshit." Conrad punched the man again.

Each strike made Pete a little more queasy as memories of his own torture came flooding back in bright flashes. Conrad wasn't a small man. The punch accompanied a sick crunching noise as blood spewed from Moto's nose. "I don't know the fucking bitch. I tell you. I don't know what this is all about."

None of the people on floor three believed what Moto was saying, including Master Moto. But he realized that just a second too late for his own good. Bull stepped up and placed one very orange tennis shoe on Moto's ankle and applied pressure. "Man, tell me when you remember."

Moto screamed in pain, as Bull levied his weight on the bone. Pete had to look away. He was feeling everything as if it was happening to him. It had, once upon a very different time and in a very different place.

In between screams and cursing, Moto ground out. "Kill me and you'll never find the fucking cunt."

Bull stepped back with a big evil grin. "Man, I forgot how much I liked that."

Pete was amazed how quickly Moto had given it up. What a wuss that tough guy turned out to be. He saw Evie shake her head. This was nothing compared to what they'd been through. Pete giggled like a little kid watching some kind of prank. It just slipped out unexpectedly and the nausea disappeared. This man was a fake from the word go, a marshmallow in kidnapper's clothing.

"So now that we understand each other, let me set you straight. Give me my wife and I won't kill you, Moto. Where is she?" Conrad squatted next to the masseur, old rusty pipe in hand. "Where. The. Hell. Is. She?" He punctuated each word with a strike to some portion of Moto's body that caused incredible pain. "You see, I consider myself a master at torture. Granted, I was an unwilling student, but I learned all the tricks of the trade in the months I was taught by the Taliban's experts." He squinted at Moto. "For example, see this little bone on the side of your wrist here? Did you know it could turn to jelly with enough hits?" He smacked Moto's wrist.

Moto screamed and tried to struggle away from the crazed Conrad. Pete saw realization dawn in Moto's eyes. He'd seen the same look on faces of some of the rebels they'd roomed with in their Taliban Motel 6. Moto thought he was never going to get out of this alive. That was a plus for their team. Pete was sure

Moto was right where Conrad wanted him, afraid and not thinking, just reacting. The man believed he had to give up the location of Andrea to save himself.

"Stop, stop please." Moto finally whimpered. "I'll tell you."

"I'm listening." Conrad dragged a cement foundation block over and sat in front of Moto.

Chapter 10

Twenty-eight hours earlier...

"Sure, see you at six." Andrea's droll statement slogged through the air.

"That's it? No *love you, babe*? No goodbye kiss for the hard-working hubby? It's our anniversary." Conrad's light tone was only a cover. His heart curled in his chest. He knew Andrea was lost, and he was at a loss to help her.

But tonight would be different. Tonight he had plans to change all that.

"Love you, babe." It was a flat statement without a lick of emotion followed by a perfunctory peck on the chin. "Six."

He watched his wife's figure ascend the steps to their second-floor bedroom. The clingy white satin robe she wore left nothing to his imagination. Her long wavy chestnut hair flowed down her back and swayed with the rhythm of her hips. When had this incredibly talented, amazingly hot woman become a- what? Housewife? Still, her statuesque figure commanded his undivided attention for the moment.

The words rattled in his brain, bouncing from one cell to another then settled behind his throat. He almost gagged. Guilt rose and he swallowed it back like so much bile before the vomit. Tonight, he would find that woman he married five years ago. Tonight, he would fix their lives. Tonight, everything would be different. The knots in his chest loosened a touch.

He took a deep breath.

Tonight.

Conrad grabbed his security pass card, GST ID tag and wallet from the kitchen table. Tonight, everything would be different. He fingered the pass card lightly rubbing the gold metal square that was imprinted with his identity, iris pattern and fingerprints. It was reassuring, like a zoo cage to which the captive tiger returns every night. The cage that is a safe place where everything is provided. There is food, water...and keepers.

Keepers? He smiled to himself. This tiger was about to be set free. That old soundtrack emerged from some lone memory cache in his brain. "Born free...as free as the wind blows. As free as the grass grows. Born free to follow your heart."

His heart disappeared around the end of the staircase and into their upstairs bedroom. His heart, his life, his dream of happily ever after. His wife of five years.

Where had the time gone? Five years seemed like yesterday.

Wasn't he just out of the military and heading into a new life with a gorgeous, talented wife? A future all lined up to be the top military contractor for missile guidance systems and digital targeting programs? Global Systems Technology was his baby—his and Peter's. But the baby had grown up and unlike the normal parent scenario, he was the one who needed to be pushed out of the nest. Rather, he was the one who needed to jump out of the nest.

And jump back into his life, more so, into his wife's life.

Conrad stuffed the slim wallet into his front pant pocket and walked out the front door, into the southern sunshine of the early morning. Not o'dark thirty, but early enough to beat the heat and traffic into Corpus Christi. Today was the road trip. Conrad split his commute between his new tricked out Mustang Shelby GT 6500, and the company's Schweizer S-434. The nasty little S-434 chopper had a souped up Rolls-Royce engine, and a ceiling of twelve thousand five-hundred feet. His office at Global Systems Technology was only three blocks from the Corpus Christi International Airport. Considered a commercial service 'small hub' airport, it made the perfect low-footprint launching pad for GST and an easy commute for its Vice President.

But not this morning.

Today it was the monster "Stang" and I-77 North. Conrad smiled to himself as the garage door swung closed behind his car. How many limits could he push today?

****

Andrea flounced onto their rumpled bed with a deep, guilt-ridden sigh. She loved Conrad. She'd made him the center of her world when she'd given up her fast-paced career. To be with him was all she wanted. This morning, five years to the day later, was the first time she'd questioned that decision. She couldn't even bring herself to kiss his lips. A small peck was all she could muster. A memory of passionate embraces flashed through her mind, bringing a stab of heat she hadn't felt in a long while. She used to make him late for work on a regular basis. Now she couldn't wait for him to leave. Generally she waved, but these days he didn't even look back to see the wave, or her.

"Come on, girl, you're listening to that biological clock a little too much these days." She rolled over and hit the "on" button for their security system. The little red light blinked green, and she was in lock-down.

What a great way to live! Safe and secure behind a million-dollar security system and iron bars. Granted, they were beautifully sculpted bars, but bars none-the-less.

At thirty-three she'd made it all the way to high-priced eye-candy. What an accomplishment for the woman once voted Best New Photojournalist of the Year. That was a long time ago. Now she lived in a huge house behind locked doors and windows, drove a new Beemer, belonged to the best clubs and the newest high-tech gym in Texas. Her handsome, successful husband was the envy of her small group of gal pals, had a Platinum card with no limit, and shopped in the best boutiques on both sides of the border. Everyone was fond of telling her, on regular basis, that she was so lucky to have it all.

Then why did she feel so empty? So entirely unbalanced? Unhappy?

Andrea rolled off the bed and headed for the closet.

A good workout was what she needed.

Some endorphins and sweat would make things better, maybe yank her out of the malaise that descended with the garage door, behind her husband's departing car. It was 6 a.m., but Callista would be there and so would her yummy partner, Wilmer.

The blond God of War was Callista's main

squeeze, and together they trained most of the upper crust from the Mexican border to Galveston. Wilmer had several clients in Ciudad Monterey as well. Between the two of them, they made a more than comfortable living, but it was Callista's effervescent nature and positive outlook that drew Andrea to the professional trainer in the first place.

Andrea patted her tight abs and pulled on the neon orange spandex top. Callista's training wasn't bad either. Now that Andrea wasn't chasing after the perfect photo in some war-torn corner of a third world country, regular exercise was the only thing that warded off middle age spread, and kept her size eight body fit. Lately it'd become an obsession that plugged the empty holes in her life, and provided what little excitement was left to her.

She stretched and flexed a thigh, pulling on her black yoga pants. If she'd become only eye candy, at least she was great eye candy.

The gym was a short drive from the house and Andrea arrived early enough to grab a parking spot just a half-block away from the building. Later in the day, parking on South Padre Island would become impossible to find. Another good reason to work out early in the morning. She grabbed her bag from the passenger seat and headed for the posh entry with its toned, tanned security staff. One swipe of her membership card, a quick nod from some bulked-out, but dull clerk, and she was buzzed through. The buzzer sounded and she was on her way to stretches, crunches and a few miles of going absolutely nowhere.

"Hey girl, how you doin' this wonderful morning?" Callista stood primping in the full-length mirror of the woman's locker room. She was muscle and curves, all in the right places. Her tanned, toned body was her business, and she was a complete package-compact, five foot four inches of money on the hoof. She was a combination of three very different ethnic cultures, and could blend in to almost any group of people, except possibly Sweden or one of the far northern European countries where white and blond was the limit of color variation on the streets. Her tanned skin and dark curly hair was a compliment to her dark eyes and full lips. There were days Andrea envied Calli her height and seductive looks.

"I'm doin'. As usual." Somehow Andrea couldn't muster much enthusiasm in the light of Callista's perpetual optimism and sunny disposition.

"Better to be doin' than not, honey." Callista slapped Andrea on the shoulder and hung a small white towel around her neck. A companionable tug came next. "Any time you need inspiration, just check out that nasty-ass website called Walmart People. It'll keep you moving your buns for sure."

Andrea watched Callista grab a handful of gluteus maximus and wiggle it. "I just need to work out some of the stress, Calli. And you have nothing to complain about. Your nasty ass is as hard as a rock." They'd known each other since Andrea moved to Laguna Vista five years before and it wasn't long before the trainer relationship developed into real friendship.

"Stress? What stress do you have in your perfect life? Really, Andi, hunky husband? Beautiful home with a view of the bay? No financial worries? And you don't have to get up every day and listen to people complain about their love handles, while stuffing their faces with fast food and fat pills. Honestly, what I wouldn't give to be in your Massimo Doganna CFM shoes."

Andrea pulled the towel from around her neck and playfully snapped at the anatomical part Calli was pinching and wiggling. "Yep, grass is always greener. And ya know why? Manure. Lots and lots of manure."

"Bullshit." Calli grabbed the towel and tossed it back to her friend.

"Exactly." Andrea slid past. "I'm going to go stretch out and watch that guy who you seem to adore, and who seems to adore you." Andrea ducked through the door to the exercise floor before her friend could see the envy in her eyes. Calli thought Andrea's life was perfect, but Conrad didn't look at her the way Wilmer looked at Calli. He used to, but that was a long time ago. It was before Global Systems Technology. Before Vice President and palatial mansion on the bay.

"I Need a Hero" blared over the loudspeaker system as she caught sight of the tight-clad Wilmer putting a small group of women through their paces in the private instruction room. She'd never, *ever* see Conrad in tights. He was way too macho for anything other than jeans or tactical pants. He condescended to wear Dockers to work, but that was as far as his fashion aplomb décor would allow him. He was definitely a man's man, and perfectly comfortable in muddy tactical pants and a Kevlar vest. That was her guy, male to the nth degree and proud of it.

She used to like that.

Andrea sank into a split stretch and tried to center her mind. Moving through a set group of stretches without thinking was good. Unfortunately, her mind wandered as her body acted on autopilot.

She'd fallen in love with her man's man in a dirt hole in Afghanistan on a photo shoot for *Combat Soldier Magazine*. He'd saved her life, but more importantly, he'd saved her camera. She knew he was the one when he calmly asked her if she had a wide-angle lens for the upcoming firefight. Back then, he never treated her like a helpless woman, only the competent photojournalist she was. Their relationship was based on respect and admiration. She admired his tactical skills and he respected her ability to capture it on film. They made a good team, each excelling at what they did. It wasn't until a year later when Conrad's team was pinned down in the mountains that he actually figured it out. Out of the eight members of the team, Peter and Conrad were the only two to come out alive, after months in a hellhole as guests of the Taliban. He'd called her from the hospital, just to hear her voice, so he said. She'd flown to Reihmstad to be there when he came out of surgery. Six months later they were married.

Five years later she was wondering why.

Andrea collapsed onto the mat and took a deep breath.

Wondering why?

Really?

She still loved Conrad with all her heart but...things had become so...complicated? Different? Wrong.

So wrong.

"Mein lipshkin!" Wilmer plopped down next to her. "Vut make da frown on such a pretty face?" His German accent had not faded much with the years he'd spent in the States. It was part of his charm. Like his muscular build, sculpted blond hair that didn't even move with exercise, and his startling, crystal blue eyes. He and Calli made a great couple; dark and light, ebony and ivory, yin and yang.

"Ah Wilmer, I'm just in a blue funk today." She bent one leg in and lay flat across the mat to grab her ankle.

He pulled her up by the back of her spandex. "Vut for da blue funk on such beautiful day?"

Andrea flopped to her back and lay there looking at clear, ice-blue eyes in a handsome Arian face. "I don't know." It was a simple lie that came easily to her lips.

They both knew it.

"Zen to da feet and move. It vill clear da head and make da brain tink straight." He jerked her to her feet and pushed her toward the first station on her regular workout regiment. "Scoot. Svet more, tink less."

She grabbed the hand weights and stood facing a full-length wall mirror. Her face wore the dull reflection of a less than enthusiastic outlook on life. From across the mats she heard him begin to count. "Vun, two, tree, come on, vork it, baby."

She had to smile at that. Work it she did, counting in her mind to the beat of the music. Soon her blue funk began to fade, as her pulse increased, and her muscles worked. By the time she hit the elliptical, there was no more blue or funk. She was wet, pumped, and ready to run across the Himalayan Mountains. Some fast-paced music blared through the main gym. She attacked the digital program on her elliptical with a vengeance. The machine's wide screen showed a mountain trail zigzagging through green hills dotted with wildflowers and small bushes. The machine gaged the terrain and adjusted to the incline automatically. A spritzer periodically released pure oxygen mixed with the appropriate scents of the digitally created flowers on the screen, from concealed ports near both her hands. If she never took her eyes off the screen, she could almost believe she was running through some lovely pass in the hills of Switzerland. It sure beat the hell out of some places she'd run through. And spandex was a lot lighter than Kevlar.

By nine-thirty she'd beaten up the free weights, raced through the hills of paradise, climbed the Matterhorn three times, soaked in the restoring pool of Bian Lia and baked her skin in the Amethyst Room. Now it was time for a massage, then brunch with her favorite trainers.

Three days a week she submitted her tissue to an hour of heavenly manipulation, then met Callista and Wilmer for brunch at Bilar de Vida. After her workout and their morning clients, they'd meet up at the club's private little eatery. The gym's café made the best egg-white habanero omelet in Texas. Andrea loved the morning scorch of the spicy breakfast. Spice made her feel alive and exotic again. And it gave her a good reason to drench her thirst with hand-squeezed tropical juices from the gym's new juice bar. Since Jiame Vargas came to work at the Juicy Delights, Andrea had developed a taste for his amazing concoctions, all made with hand-squeezed fruit juices, mixed with a limitless variety of unusual flavored sprinkles. He was truly a liquid artist and Andrea was addicted to his work.

She lay on her stomach reveling in the feel of the deep massaging hands of the gym's Shiatsu specialist.

Calli introduced her to Master Moto just a year before and Andrea never looked back. Used to a very active and physically challenging lifestyle, there were days when his hands were the only thing that kept her sane in her skin. She lay there under the working hands of Master Moto, wondering what mixture Jaime would come up with to surprise her today.

Just to surprise her? Was life all about her?

Andrea mentally slapped herself. It used to be all about the cause, the perfect photo, the story to tell. Now it was juice surprises, massage and endless miles on an elliptical. And a husband who didn't even look back to see if she waved.

She sighed as Master Moto squeezed and pummeled her tired muscles. It felt like heaven. She didn't even feel the little prick, just before everything went black.

Chapter 11

"Come on, Peter, I have to go. It's our anniversary and I can't be late." Conrad paced in front of the company President's desk. He and Peter were battle buddies overseas, but lately their relationship had taken on a certain tenseness.

"She can wait. This is business, Rad. I never thought you'd bail on me." He looked up from the legal documents he'd been reviewing. The papers that would separate Conrad and his best friend. "I'll have to have Legal go over this stuff. I have questions..." Peter let the statement trail off.

"It's cut and dried, Peter. I want out. I'll finish the Iron Shield project, then I need to take some me time. Us time. Andrea is slipping away, Peter. I can feel it more and more." Conrad wiped a hand across his clean, shaven face in frustration. "I love her more than..." He was at a loss for words as his heart twisted.

"More than me, buddy?" Peter brought both hands to his heart. "You're killing me, Rad."

Conrad knew it was meant to be a joke, but there was just a little too much reality in Peter's tone. "I can't let her just drift away. I love her. I need her. Let's face it, Peter. After we complete Iron Shield and close the contract, you'll be sitting pretty. The company will be set, and you'll be very wealthy. You won't need me around."

"That's not the point, Conrad." Peter shoved the

papers across his desk in disgust. "We signed up together. We fought together. Almost died together." He gestured at the empty file folder. "We made the dream and lived it. Together. Everything we worked for is right here." His fist slammed the folder on his desk. "And you want to dump it? Dump me?"

Conrad looked at his lifelong friend. The tortured look was more than he could handle. "Peter, it's not like that, man. Andrea's my wife."

"And I'm your best friend. Or I used to be." He gathered up the papers, stuffed them in the file folder and headed for the door. "I'll drop this off at Legal. Go celebrate with the little lady."

"Peter, don't be like that. You and I have been buds for—" Conrad's voice fell on absent ears.

Peter was gone.

"Shit!" Conrad checked his watch: 5:40 p.m.

He was going to be late.

Not a great start to a romantic anniversary celebration.

"Mr. McIntyre? Sir, you asked me to remind you to get flowers on the way home." Rita, his executive assistant poked her head inside the door.

"Damn, now I'm going to really be late." Conrad checked his watch again. When he looked up, Rita stood full on in the doorway, a beautiful bouquet of pink lilies and white roses in her hands.

"Maybe not, sir." She passed him the boxed and wrapped bouquet, along with a pink envelope. "I took the liberty, sir."

"What would I do without you, Rita!" Conrad grabbed Rita's offering, bussed her cheek, and ran for the garage and his car. He would be late, but not by much. He just barely heard her retort before the elevator doors closed behind him.

"Be late, of course, sir." The doors closed on Rita's calm smile. As he rode the elevator to the garage, he thanked his lucky stars, or whatever it was that brought Rita into his life and company. She was the gatekeeper of the castle for Conrad, and took her job seriously. More than that, she took him and all of his complexities seriously. Unlike her cohort next door.

Conrad had never warmed to Rose, Mr. Newcastle's administrative assistant. She was a piece of work. That woman was trouble in a rolling chair. Rose Cohen had only been with GST for about a year, and already she was ordering people around like she sat in Pete's chair, not outside his office.

I-77 was packed, bumper to bumper. Conrad swore and punched the button on his GPS to select an alternate route.

"Recalculating. Take ramp right then turn left." The map switched views showing a winding route through the coastal area. The off-ramp was still two miles away.

"No good." He smacked the wheel and picked up his cell phone. He hit the icon for voice commands. "Call Andrea."

The phone automatically dialed Andrea's cell phone. After six rings, he heard her voice.

"Andrea, honey, I'm sorry…"

"You have reached the person to whom you dialed. Leave me a message and I might return your call." The giggle at the end definitely belonged to his wife.

"Honey, I'm stuck in traffic, but I am on my way home. It's six-o-five. Should be there in about fifteen.

I've got a big surprise just for you, babe. Love you." Conrad hit the end button. "Shit! Big surprise? Right Conrad."

He did have a big surprise, but his message sounded so lame, even to him. He eyed the flowers. The envelope lay in the sun on the seat. Sitting behind a large delivery truck going absolutely nowhere, he opened it. Rita had picked out a beautiful and heart-warming card with a sweet message. Very romantic. Very *not* him, but Andrea would love it.

He grabbed a pen and signed it, *love always, your Soldier.*

Now that was him!

Opposite the signature, he drew a box and wrote inside the lines: *Good for one Best New Photojournalist of the Year award. Or forever, whichever comes first.* Then he drew three xs and three ohs and one smiley face with a tongue hanging out. That was definitely him!

The traffic crawled and by quarter to seven, he was pulling into the garage, ready to meet his wife on their fifth anniversary. Immediately, he noticed her car was not in the garage.

Had she gotten his message and left in anger?

Run out to get something at the last minute?

He took the flowers and card into the kitchen and checked the refrigerator door, the place they always left notes for each other.

Nothing.

Touching the familiar icon on his phone, he said, "Call Andrea."

The phone dialed his wife's number. It went directly to voice mail and he heard her giggle again.

"Andrea, I'm home. Where are you, hon?" He hit the end button.

Where was she?

Why didn't she call him or leave a note?

"Andrea?" He yelled through the house.

No response.

He checked the back yard.

Nothing.

Across the fence he saw the neighbor lady. "Mrs. Chambers, have you seen my wife today?"

Cathy Chambers and her husband lived next door. The lady of the house spent most of her time in the chaise lounge next to the pool, tanning herself and smoking cigarettes. At forty-six, she looked like a mummy.

"I saw her leave this morning, Mr. McIntyre, when I was getting Donald out the door to work. I don't think I've seen her car all day." She waved a glowing cigarette at him.

"Thanks, Mrs. Chambers." Conrad waved as he headed back inside.

"Is anything wrong…?" Conrad ignored the question.

He dialed Andrea's number again. "Andrea, call me." And hung up.

This was not funny.

Obviously, the maid had been in. The dishes were done. The bed was made. Clean towels hung from the bars in the bathroom.

Nothing was amiss.

Except his wife.

After a quick search of the house, Conrad returned to the kitchen. He unpacked the flower arrangement, added water and placed the vase on the dining room table with the card.

Pouring himself a drink, he wandered into the living room and flopped onto the couch.

Everything was in its place. The mantel was dust-free. The fireplace had been set...

That's when he noticed it.

A single piece of paper lay in the middle of the coffee table. On it was a message written in large letters with some kind of ink marker. He reached to pick it up, but something told him to wait.

He twisted around to read the script and his heart skipped a beat. Several beats.

We have your wife. Wait for our call.

So now he knew! Andrea was gone. Someone had taken her.

Someone had his wife!

He ran for his study and computer. He'd installed a tracking device in her handbag, when he and Peter began the Iron Shield project two years before. In fact, he'd installed one in every handbag she owned. They'd had a small fire in their garage and Conrad couldn't find Andrea. She wasn't answering her cell phone and he panicked. After that, Conrad insured he could always find her if he needed to. His fear of losing her was a breathing, hunting animal that lived just outside his realm of sanity. Now it stalked him as prey and the only thing he could rely on was a tiny electronic device and a special frequency dedicated to her safety. Conrad punched the button on his computer and banged his fist as the system began to load. It was not a slow computer, in fact, it was about as high tech as a computer could be. But it wasn't fast enough for

Conrad, when Andrea was missing.

The screen came up and Conrad touched the track pad loading the app that would fine Andrea and her handbag. The planet appeared on his screen and began to spin, narrowing down the search area, and finally zooming in on one point with a bright yellow arrow indicating the position of the tracking device. Indicating the position of Andrea, he hoped.

There it was, downtown South Padre Island. The bag was at Andrea's gym.

Conrad race to the Stang, hit the garage door opener and almost backed out before the door was completely up. He spun the Mustang in their driveway and laid on the gas. All of those evasive driving classes he taken as a special operations soldier had to be good for something.

Within minutes he was screeching in front of the gymnasium. He slammed the car up onto the curb, parking halfway in the street and halfway on the sidewalk. Jumping out, he didn't even bother to lock the classic car's doors. Nothing in his life was more important than Andrea. Conrad crashed through the double glass doors, following the little blip on his cell phone screen. Once the program had locked on the location of Andrea's handbag, he'd transferred the location automatically to his phone.

Vaulting the front counter, much to the surprise of the clerk, he tore off down the hall following the blip. As he neared the women's locker room, the frequency of blips increased and so did the noise behind him. Obviously, the clerk had alerted the security guards. The gym catered to some very wealthy health nuts and prided themselves on the security and privacy of their clients.

"Sir, stop!" Some nebulous guard shouted. "Stop now!"

Conrad slammed through the locker room door amid shrieks and half-clad women running for cover. He followed the signal right up to a locker and froze. Andrea's bright green lock lay immobile against the handle. The sensor screamed and so did some of the female patrons. He dialed the combination with expertise. He'd set it to her birthday, the day they bought the garish lock.

As the locker door popped open, he heard the obvious sound of a round being chambered. "Freeze, mister. This thing is loaded, and I know how to use it. Get down on the floor." The portly guard pointed his nine-millimeter Glock at Conrad's head.

In a split second the guard was on the floor, and Conrad held the man's gun. "Don't be stupid. I just need to find my wife. This is her purse. Where is she?" He waved the gun at the full locker then at the guard. "I need an answer, buddy."

"Then, perhaps I can be of assistance, Mr. McIntyre." The club's manager sauntered into the locker room, ignoring more shrieking women. His workout attire matched perfectly, tailored to fit a muscular body, and he wore the latest Nike Lebron X shoes.

"Where's my wife? This is her stuff." The club manager reached into the locker only to be restrained by an iron grip. "Don't touch anything."

"Mr. McIntyre, I assure you, if these are your wife's belongings, she is in the club somewhere. But not in this locker room at the moment. This is the women's locker room, and men are not allowed in here. For obvious reasons." He motioned for the guard to get up and leave. "Please give Officer Wilson his gun back, and leave this room at once."

"Not until I know what happened to Andrea." Conrad took a step back and raised the gun.

"Then come with me and we will check the login at the front desk. And do not aim that gun at me, or you will be searching for your wife inside of a cell at the Corpus Christi jail." The manager was losing his temper.

Conrad slammed the locker door with the nose of the gun and replaced the lock. "No one touches this locker. It may have evidence." He handed the gun back to the guard who had heaved himself off the floor.

"Out, McIntyre. Now." He led the way with a purposeful stride. "My utmost apologies, ladies. Please forgive the intrusion and feel free to register your complaints at the desk on your way out. I am sure we can provide some compensation for your distress." His parting feminine wave left distaste in Conrad's mouth.

"Where are we going?" Conrad refrained from calling the man *fairy*.

"The front desk. You know as well as I do, that every client logs in and logs out with their club card. We can check the record and see when your wife arrived and if she has left. Then, sir, we will discuss how you will make this club whole again." The obvious hint at a monetary settlement was not lost on Conrad.

"First we find my wife."

"Of course, Mr. McIntyre."

Two police officers in crisp tan uniforms stood at the front desk eyeing the manager and the guard as they escorted Conrad to the front of the club.

"William, could you please pull up Mrs. McIntyre's club record for her distraught husband. He seems to think she has gone missing." The manager slid his hand across William's back as he sauntered on by.

William smiled at the touch. "Of course, sir. Mr. McIntyre, come around this way." He opened the counter and ushered Conrad behind the desk to see the computer screen. "She checked in at six twenty-two and checked out at…" William looked up. "She has not checked out yet, sir." He pointed to the screen. "She is still here, according to our records."

"William, please have Mrs. McIntyre paged." The club manager moved to stand next to the police officers. "If she is here, she will hear the page. It even sounds in the spa areas."

"Mrs. McIntyre, please come to the front desk. Mrs. Andrea McIntyre, you are needed at the front desk." True to his word, the page could be heard down the hallway and even in the front lobby. The manager smiled solicitously at Conrad.

Conrad crossed his arms on his chest and waited. Five minutes passed. It was the longest five minutes of his life. "She should be here by now." Conrad moved toward the hallway.

One of the officers stepped forward to block his way. "Patience. Give her time. She may be in the shower, or getting one of those wrap things. My wife gets 'em. Then she smells like rotten fish for a week." The officer chuckled at his own joke.

Another five minutes passed before the manager moved. "William, would you go check the spa areas. Ask Marie to search the women's locker room and sauna." He took the microphone. "Mrs. McIntyre, please see the manager at the front desk." The page echoed down the hallway.

When William returned with no news, and Andrea did not show up at the front desk, Conrad had had enough. "Look, you little ferret, my wife is not here. Her belongings are in her locker. And she is not in this club. We have established that. Her car is parked outside. Where—"

"Hold on there, son. I'm sure this is just a misunderstanding. Have you and the little lady had a squabble recently?"

Conrad ignored the officer. "Look—" He peered at the manager's nametag. "—Pierre? Look, Pierre, you must have security footage. I want to see it. Now." He moved toward the manager.

Pierre stepped behind the two officers. "That will not be possible. This club is known for its valued privacy. Our clientele—"

Conrad reached between the two officers and grabbed Pierre by his expensive and matching athletic outfit. "Look, the only clientele I care about is my wife. She checked in here, and never checked out. What does that tell you, Pierre, huh?"

"Now just hold on a second." The larger of the two officers grabbed Conrad, intent on separating him from the manager. "How do you feel about an assault charge, mister?"

Conrad's cell phone rang.

"Shit." He let go of Pierre and stepped back. "I'm listening." Conrad held the phone to his ear.

A metallic voice responded. "We have what you want. You have what we want."

"Yeah, and what's that?" Conrad turned his back on the officers and the club manager.

"The backdoor to Iron Shield."

Conrad froze. "There isn't one."

Iron Shield was ultra-top secret. No one, outside a handful of Pentagon pukes, knew GST was working on the high-tech missile guidance program. Only essential staff at GST knew about the project. In fact, Conrad could count on one hand, the people involved in the evolutionary process of developing the program.

"Then make one. You have twenty-four hours. Tell no one, or she dies." The line went dead.

His cell phone screen showed *unknown caller*. "Shit!" Conrad turned around to face four inquisitive faces. "That was my wife. She's at home." He tried to look sheepish. "She forgot her stuff." He shrugged and tried to play the dumb, overly possessive husband. "I'm really sorry. Would you mind getting her things for me?"

Both officers shook their heads and snickered. "Man, you and the little lady better have a talk. Get some things straight. Before you end up in real trouble."

"William, please have Marie retrieve Mrs. McIntyre's things from the locker." He handed Conrad a sticky note and pen. "If you would, Mr. McIntyre."

Conrad scribbled the combination on the little square of pink paper. "Sure. Look, Pierre, I'm real sorry, it's just that I worry about her. Ya know."

"No, I do not know. And I do not want to know. But there will not be a repeat of this behavior in the future. This you know, correct?" Pierre handed the combination to William who scuttled off to find Marie.

"Understood." Conrad turned to the officers. "Ah, thanks guys."

Neither officer responded. They simply stood there waiting for Conrad to leave.

In no time at all, William returned with Andrea's things in a white plastic garbage bag, tied with a red piece of ribbon. William placed the bag on the front counter and stepped back a couple paces.

Conrad grabbed the bag, saluted the two police officers, and exited through the glass doors. As soon as he hit the sidewalk, he ran for his car. He had no idea what was going on, or where Andrea was, but he was about to find out.

Throwing the bag into the back seat, Conrad revved the motor, pulled onto the street and took off.

He needed to think.

He needed to plan.

He needed his wife.

Chapter 12

Andrea's lids felt like lead as she tried to pull herself from the groggy, all-consuming sleep. Man, Moto must have done a great job. She didn't even remember falling asleep on his table. She rolled her eyeballs around beneath her lids and tried once again. One opened a bit, but the other one seemed to be glued shut.

Shit!

She was going to be late for lunch with Wilmer and Calli.

Andrea moved her arms to hoist herself off the massage table. Or tried to.

Why wouldn't her arms move?

She lay on her stomach, drifting for a few moments before her mind cleared enough to remember she needed to move.

"Come on, girl. Lunch is waiting." Her own muffled encouragement set the wheels spinning in her brain. "Up you go."

Andrea tried to move her arms again and found it was useless. Not because she was so relaxed. She was confined!

What?

Her eyes flew open this time, despite their dry, gritty feeling. Her nose kicked into play as well.

She craned her neck, looking around the small

room. She was lying on a filthy mat on the floor. Her hands were obviously tied behind her back because they were numb and confined.

She tried to move her legs. They worked, but her feet were somehow restrained too.

Andrea peeked around the room, enough to know she was alone, then carefully rolled on her side.

How?

Why?

The two questions surfaced through the mental fog.

Drugged.

Her mind was wading through the last vestiges of some kind of chemical agent.

Drugged.

Tied up.

In a very small room.

On the floor.

A grease-stained cargo blanket covered her naked body.

Naked?

Yep. Buck naked.

She lay still and listened for any sound that would identify where she was, or provide a clue as to what was going on.

Muffled words could be heard but nothing made sense. Maybe she was still suffering from the effects of whatever drug they'd given her.

Andrea curled into a ball and eased her hands beneath her, bringing them to the front of her body. Thank God for exercise and flexibility!

Two neat tie-wraps encircle her wrists and a third connected them within an inch of each other.

No help there. Can't undo tie-wraps.

The pins and needles of neurological wake-up tortured her hands for a few moments before easing to a dull ache. She rubbed her hands against the cargo blanket until feeling returned, then wiggled into a sitting position.

Her ankles were in the same condition. The tie-wraps were not tight enough to cut off circulation, but closed to the point she could not slip out of them either.

Efficient.

A bottle of water sat on the floor next to the mat. Her mouth felt like the entire Fifth Regiment had marched over her tongue in mud-caked boots.

Water would help.

She reached for the bottle at the same time her brain screamed *drugged*! She froze.

It was now clear to her, she'd been kidnapped. Would they want her unconscious?

She grabbed the bottle and felt the cap.

Tight. Still sealed.

Maybe.

Maybe not.

Her brain screamed, *no!*

Her body argued, *need!*

Her body won.

It would do no good to become dehydrated and senseless.

Andrea removed the cap. At least her kidnappers had allowed her wiggle room with her hands. And given her water. Clothes would have been nice.

She downed the bottle in greedy delight. With the first gulp, the tepid liquid brought life back to her body. How long had she been out?

There was no window in her room. No furniture.

Only wooden walls and a rusty steel door. No door handle. So where was the light coming from?

She looked up. A light, or skylight. Which one? Her vision blurred...

There was no switch on the wall, so she figured it must be a skylight.

It would be day then. That was about all she could determine from the bright square in the ceiling that hurt her still-sensitive eyes.

Her *cell* was about eight feet wide and about ten feet long.

Andrea wiggled her feet. Stretched her legs. Moved her bound hands and arms.

Everything seemed to be in order.

Except the smell, and the heat.

The placed stunk of old oil and grease. The cargo blanket she'd tossed off was a hundred years old with rips and tears on both sides. The batting inside hung in glops from the original blue fabric quilting. Dark stain splotches were everywhere and the binding on one side had separated long ago.

Andrea set the bottle down next to her mat and stood, stretching her arms and legs as best she could, considering her confinement.

She needed to figure out what was going on and formulate a plan to get out of the mess she was in. Her anniversary was tonight. Or was it?

What day was it?

Was she still on South Padre Island?

Questions banged around in her head as the light in the room began to fade. Definitely a skylight up there. It was getting dark.

She moved to the door and pressed an ear to the

crack.

She couldn't understand a thing she heard. Not because the voices were so muffled, but because they were not speaking English!

She listened carefully and picked out a loud "*nein.*"

German. They were speaking German.

German?

She identified another common word. It sounded like "dun-kah." German for *thank you*. Definitely German.

Immediately her thoughts jumped to Wilmer. He was German.

She heard a chair scrape and hurried back to the mat, sat, and covered herself with the cargo blanket despite the hot mugginess of the room.

Something rattled outside her door, then it opened slowly with a rusty screech and some difficulty in moving. She wouldn't be sneaking out that door without the entire county knowing it.

There stood a rather portly man with longish blond hair and sea-blue eyes. Even in the soft light of the setting sun, they almost glowed. He was clean-shaven, except for the square patch of dark hair above his lip. The man sported a Hitler mustache! And wore a khaki uniform of some sort. The wide black belt dipped below his pendulous belly.

"So you are a-vake, Mrs. McIntyre. Goo-t." He threw two more bottles of water at her and turned to leave.

"Wait! Who are you? What do you want with me?"

"Who I am vill remain a healthy mystery. Better for you to not know. Vut I vant you for is bait. Be goot.

Stay alive." He pulled the door closed behind him with a grunt. Andrea could hear the rattle and click of a lock outside her door.

Bait?

She took one of the bottles and unscrewed the top. It was cold. She held the bottle to her forehead for a moment, thinking. What was the last thing she remembered?

She'd been at the club. Working out, then a sauna and massage...then, nothing.

A muffled whistle interrupted her thoughts.

A Train? A boat?

Shadows crept across the room of her dimming cell as she finished off the bottle of water. Her stomach growled, protesting only liquid.

Tears welled up and threatened to spill down her hot cheeks. She should be enjoying a delicious prime rib dinner and a glass of wine with her husband right now, celebrating their anniversary. Not naked, locked up who-knows-where, with a bottle of water and a filthy mat. The fat man said she was bait.

Bait for what?

For whom?

She wiped away the tears. Tears weren't her style. Well, didn't used to be her style...before. That was a while back, before Conrad's metamorphosis from kick-ass soldier to Mr. Vice President. She used to be his world. Now the company was his main focus and she was a sideline interest.

Conrad? Was she the bait for Conrad?

Holy shit!

The new targeting program he was working on?

The wheels in her mind spun at warp speed.

She literally had nothing anyone would want. Lots of material stuff, but nothing truly important. Not like when she actually had a career. It had to be something about Conrad. Something about his projects, probably for the government.

Global Systems Technology had several government contracts. Everything from some little gadget that enhanced the speed and accuracy of bullets, to their most lucrative program called Iron Shield. The multi-million dollar targeting system was supposed to be un-hackable, globally synchronized, and able to control a mass missile strike from a single point of contact. It had to be Iron Shield.

But if the project was compromised, the company would just alter the coding and anything gained, would be useless. How could she be bait for something potentially useless? It didn't make sense.

She allowed one more pity-me tear to slide down her cheek before the old Andrea kicked, in and her survival instincts rose to meet the stubborn and single-minded determination that had kept her alive as a combat journalist.

With the last few rays of light, she studied her cell.

Nothing on the walls. Check.

No door handle. Already checked.

No furniture. Just a few half-pulled nails where something had been attached to the walls. Che…

Nails?

Andrea scrambled over to the wall and felt the nails, looking for a sharp edge. The tie-wraps were plastic and strong, but…

She found one nail with a half-smashed head. Working the nail back and forth, it loosened but would not come out of the wood. *Damn.* Andrea hooked the right tie-wrap over the nail head and pulled. The plastic cut into her wrist, but did not break. *Double damn!* That wasn't going to work.

The heat was stifling, and Andrea could feel sweat slick her body. At this rate she'd lose the liquid she'd just drunk in no time at all. She took a deep, breath and tasted a hint of grease. Where the hell was she, anyway?

Crawling back to the mat, she continued to study her cell. Environmental weapons bounced around her brain. Environmental tools...the concept had been drilled into her head during a pre-embedding survival class she attended with other journalists headed for the sand box. There were five journalists in the class. She was the only woman. It was a tough class with personal self-defense training, and mental preparation for a world she'd never even imagined. And well worth the five days of sweat, bruises and brainteasers. They studied the culture, posed problems, practiced basic self-defense and familiarized themselves with typical weapons used in the war, both enemy and friendly. *Always look for tools in your environment to survive in case of being separated or captured while on assignment.* Environmental tools and situational opportunity. It was the mantra that put her to sleep at night in the one-hundred-and-thirty-degree desert. It was the song she woke up to in the twenty-degree mornings. It was the theme she'd lived by and survived a handful of skirmishes with, back when she had a career and a mission.

Naked.

In an empty cell with no windows and no door

handle.

One incredibly stinky and dirty mat.

A torn and well-used cargo blanket.

Three plastic bottles.

A handful of bent and stuck nails.

The twilight crept from her cell through the skylight above, and her tiny world went dark.

So did her mind.

Just as the second tear made its way down her nose, Andrea heard commotion outside her cell. Chairs were scraping on a floor. Loud low voices were raised in, argument? More movement was heard then a loud thump against her door. Andrea hastily wiped the tears away and pulled the cargo blanket up to cover herself. Another loud thump and more yelling. This time right next to her door.

Andrea flinched when a gunshot rang out, obviously impacting her door. She hit the floor and lay flat, listening.

More yelling.

Another shot.

This time it must have been in another direction because there was no metallic sound and no new dent.

Then silence.

Was someone outside to liberate her? Police? Conrad? Andrea lay flat and listened for several seconds.

Nothing.

"Hello?" She yelled from her position on the floor. "Anyone out there?"

She stayed low and crawled to the door. Andrea banged on the metal door close to the floor. "Help! Anyone out there?" She screamed, "Help me!"

The lock rattled and Andrea had just enough time to slide out of the way before the door scraped open with a loud screech. "I tell you, behave." The fat man crossed the floor and kicked Andrea with a heavy boot. His face was screwed up in anger and his eyes burned with hatred.

Pain exploded in her shoulder. Andrea slammed into the wall. She was able to block the next kick a little, but the fat man was spitting and screaming at her in German, as he kicked, again and again. Andrea could smell alcohol on his breath as he screamed and kicked. He held a half empty bottle in one hand and an ancient revolver in the other.

Andrea blocked the kicks as best she could, but they still continued. The fat man was out of control and was taking out his frustration on his victim. Her survival class instructor had taught her, sometimes the only way to survive was to feign unconsciousness. Captors often found it useless and not very satisfying to beat an unconscious person who didn't respond. She flopped over on her stomach and lay there, steeling herself to be unresponsive. One more vicious kick to her side and he was done.

The fat man was obviously furious at her lack of response, and threw the now-empty booze bottle against the wall. It shattered, and the smell of whiskey mixed with grease and ancient oil was about all Andrea could take, but she remained still and unresponsive. The door screeched once again, and she was alone.

Still she remained on the floor, eyes closed, not moving an inch.

Every bit of her body hurt like the devil and she was sure one eye was swelling shut. Her right side was on fire and the fat man's boot had opened a gash on her arm. She could feel blood trickling down to her elbow.

Slowly, with great pain and careful movements, Andrea rolled over. She pulled some of the less filthy stuffing from the cargo blanket and daubed at her arm. Moving her fingers and arm, she was sure the kick had not broken any bones. The gash was about three inches long and superficial. She tenderly pulled the torn flap of flesh back into place and patted it down. Moving various parts of her body, she assessed what damage he'd done. She probably had a couple broken ribs. Definitely a black and swollen eye, possibly a broken nose. Her lip was split, but had already stopped bleeding. Legs were fine. One hip was sore and swelling but it functioned the way it should, and the pain was receding with movement. Her left ankle was swelling, but it seemed to move correctly. The inside of her foot burned, but in the dark, it was hard to tell what was going on. Andrea lightly touched the area. Her fingers came away dry, but even the slightest touch sent licks of fire up her leg. That was not good.

Andrea pushed herself to a sitting position and winced. Her hand came off the floor with more blood, a piece of broken glass embedded in her palm.

Glass?

Broken glass?

Sharp broken glass!

She pulled the piece from her hand, ignoring the sting and small puncture wound. The piece was too small to be of any use. But where there was one, there would be more!

Andrea eased herself onto her knees and cautiously felt for more. She quickly found more broken glass, but nothing of the size she could use to cut her ties. It was a slow, arduous task, since her body screamed with every move, and she had to be careful not to miss a chunk that would add more insult to injury. Just as her hand contacted the broken neck of the bottle, the moon added its full light to her cell, illuminating the floor with a silvery glow.

"Hah!" Andrea took the broken neck with its sharp edge. "Now we're cooking with gas." She carefully retraced her crawl and sat with her back to the wall. The mat she'd found herself on when she woke, provided little padding, but it didn't matter. Her body ached so much from the beating she'd suffered, a Lazy Boy recliner wouldn't have mattered.

Andrea studied the glass bottleneck to find the best and sharpest side, then began to cut at the tie-wraps. All she really needed to be free was to cut the connecting tie-wrap between the ones on her hands and feet. She'd worry about the ones around her ankles and wrists when she was free of this tiny room from Hell, and the fat man with his temper and gun. The tie-wrap between her ankles popped free and she stretched her arms and legs. Pain exploded in her side and she tried not to scream. Screaming required a deep breath and more pain.

She stood up, testing her legs. So far, so good. Her side was pure agony on top of torturous pain, and the left instep reminded her to check it, now that light was available. Andrea sat back down and pulled her foot up to see the instep. In the moonlight she could see angry red skin and the beginning of some serious bruising, but it didn't look or feel like anything was broken, except blood vessels. She pressed her hand to the area and applied pressure. The human body was an amazing thing. It could take a great deal of insult before it actually broke down and needed the kind of medical help one only found in a hospital.

The one last bottle of water sat next to her on the floor. It was still cool to the touch. It wasn't ice, but it would help. She held the bottle to her foot, closed her eyes and tried to figure out what just happened.

Obviously, the fat man won whatever battle had gone on, but by his temper and anger, everything wasn't going his way. Did that mean her life was in more danger now? Was there more than one guy involved and it wasn't working out? Did someone disagree with the fat man? Was he even the boss? She'd seen his face. Did that mean he would kill her, no matter what?

Probably…

Her pain was taking over and it was too much. Andrea drifted on flaming red clouds, until Mother Nature took her away and she succumbed to fitful sleep.

Chapter 13

Andrea dreamed she was swimming in a vat of pure pain. It swirled around her entire body, submerging her in agony, touching every nerve, every single cell. She was suffocating in complete torment as the world dimmed to an infinitesimal black hole somewhere beyond her reach.

"Conrad..." She whimpered, opening her only functioning eye.

She couldn't even gasp at what she saw.

It hurt like hell just to see, let alone try to breathe.

The world came back into view with the stench of her own vomit.

She was lying crumpled, on a filthy mat, her face stuck to the fabric encrusted barf.

In a cell.

In the dark.

Alone.

Afghanistan? Had she been captured?

Sierra Leone? No, that was jungle. And a long time ago.

Her mind turned in sluggish circles.

Conrad?

Her anniversary?

"Ahhhhh." Andrea tried a shallow breath. Her side burned as if someone applied a branding iron to every rib on her right side. Another shallow breath. More burning.

"At least I'm not dead." she commented to herself, since there was no one else around. "Dead people don't hurt this much, right?" She licked a swollen lip.

"Of course you're not dead, or you would be here with us." A sweet little voice out of nowhere, came to her.

Startled, Andrea jerked then groaned in pain. "Insane, though, right? Cause I'm hearing someone who's not there." Andrea glanced around to reassure herself of her insanity. The room was empty except for her.

"Not at all, Andrea. A friend sent me to help."

"Right." Andrea snorted. How could insanity help her? And why did it talk back? She was imprisoned in a tiny room with a door that had no knob. Her body was beaten and broken to the point she could barely move, and now she was hearing voices. Maybe it was some strange after effect of the drug she'd been given. "Great."

"Thank you. I plan to be."

Well, if she was going to lose her mind, then what the heck. "Okay, I'll bite. Thanks for what? And what do you plan to be?"

"Great, of course. Now listen, you've got to get up."

"Why?" Andrea was sure she couldn't crawl, let alone stand up.

"Because that ugly, mean, fat man out there is drunk and asleep. You need to get out of this room."

"Right." Andrea moved a foot and murmured a foul word.

"Yes. Before he wakes. I do not believe he will let

you live, and then Evie will be mad at me."

"Right." She moved the other foot and felt a burn sizzle through her ankle. "Not good."

"But workable. Now get up. You must do this on your own. I cannot physically help."

"Of course not. How would a voice help me stand?" Andrea was acting along in a bizarre play of her own deranged imagination. How would she escape this room, even if she could stand? There was no handle or lock from the inside. It was a steel door. There was no way to climb to the ceiling and leave through the skylight. Andrea rolled over and gasped in horrendous pain.

"But I can help that."

Andrea felt a cool, peaceful calm wash over her body and the intense pain began to fade. "What the hell…"

"No, not Hell. Heaven. No matter. Can you stand now?"

Andrea pushed herself up to a sitting position expecting the worst. It never came. A slight burning sensation emanated from her ribs and her foot tingled like it was waking up from a sleep. She tested her left eye. It opened, but still felt heavy and thick. "Oh, my God. What did you do? I can move. I can see out of my eye."

"Just what I promised." A melodious giggle tickled Andrea's heart, prompting energy and hope. *"Now you must go. Quickly. The other man will return soon. He is even more evil."*

"But, how?" As she asked the question, Andrea could hear the lock on the door click. The heavy steel drifted open a crack. "Never mind."

Andrea rose to her feet. Her pain was there, in the back of her mind, but not immediately in her body. In one swift movement, she was at the door, pulling gently at its substantial weight.

A not-so-subtle scraping sounded like rending metal. Andrea froze, peeking through the widened crack.

A few feet away, her assailant slumped in an old office chair. His ample belly rose and fell with each loud snore, and his arms hung off his sides. His chin sat solidly on his chest, eyes closed, his open mouth and drool attesting to the number of empty beer bottles on the table.

That's what you get for mixing your alcohol, you bastard, Andrea thought.

"Move the door slowly, Andrea. Then run. I can open a lock, but I cannot stop a bullet."

Andrea jumped, looking behind her. There was no one there. "What the…"

"Shhhhhh. Out through that open garage door. Look, over there."

Suddenly infused with energy, Andrea eased the door open a tiny bit. To her, the screeching sounded like a full orchestra belting out a warmup exercise, but it didn't seem to stir the fat man. Keeping an eye on the sleeping goon, she moved the door a fraction of an inch at a time. It seemed like hours, but finally there was enough room to slip through.

The fat man was still snoring away in his chair as Andrea shimmied through the crack and headed for the garage door.

"The shirt, Andrea!"

An old work shirt hung on a peg near a line of

lockers next to the far wall. Andrea tiptoed to the locker and slid into the shirt. It was long sleeved denim and almost hung to her knees.

Good. After all, she was naked. Running around South Padre Island naked was sure to stir up some interest, and interest was not what she needed. Until she was safely away from her captors.

Turning back toward her exit, she stumbled over an empty gas can. The metal can clambered across the cement floor with a racket that would wake the Devil.

And it did.

The fat man came out of his chair as if he'd been shot, gun in hand. He first turned toward the steel door, but seeing it half open, he spun to draw down on whatever had caused the noise.

But Andrea was gone. Flying out the big door, she ran for all she was worth.

Right into the arms of Master Moto.

Her masseur?

What was he doing here?

Contained by the strong grip of a professional masseur, Andrea could not move. However, her mind was not a prisoner, and she immediately recalled her hand-to-hand combat training. A fast knee to the groin had Moto releasing his iron grip enough for Andrea to twist away and run.

And run she did.

As fast and as far as she could.

Away...

She cut across the grass and marsh near the Queen Isabella Memorial Bridge, gaining the highway in a short scramble. It must have been the middle of the night since the moon was high and there was no traffic to be seen. No help to solicit, and she was a perfect silhouetted target.

Crouching as she ran on bleeding feet, Andrea stayed low, trying to cross the Laguna Madre as fast as she could. If Master Moto was part of her kidnapping and this nefarious plot, whatever it was, she now understood how they'd taken her out of the club.

A lethargic garbage barge drifted below the bridge on its way to be dumped out at sea with the dawn. A half rotted carcass of a small fishing boat crowned the foul load as it passed beneath her.

"Duck!"

The warning voice came too late.

Andrea felt the bullet crease her forehead, knocking her off her feet and completely off the bridge. The last thing she remembered was falling, then the smell of decaying fish and rotting wood.

Chapter 14

"You fucking idiot!" Moto grabbed the gun from his partner. "What do you think you're doing? She's our insurance."

Keizer Dembeck bent and vomited over Moto's shoes.

"Son of a fucking bitch." Moto kicked Keizer to the ground. "Dembeck, you moronic fucking faggot. You killed the bitch. Now what are we gonna do?"

Dembeck rolled to his back, wiping his mouth and lay there.

Moto wasn't done with his partner. Another kick to the gut ended with, "Asshole, how did I ever get hooked up with your worthless hide? Get the fuck up!" He pulled Dembeck to his feet, surveying the area for unwanted observers. "Anybody see you, shitface?"

"I don't know. I vuz asleep. Den she escape and run." He lumbered to his feet, swaying, still unsteady as he wiped the mess from his face. "She vuz asleep and hurt. How do I know she could escape through locked door?"

Moto backhanded the fat man, almost knocking him to the ground once again. "You drink too much, you piece of shit. You probably left the door unlocked in your drunken stupor."

Sobering quickly, Dembeck held his ground. "No! Dah door vuz locked. I do not understand. If Vilmer finds out about dis, he vill kick me out for sure. Vhere vill I go? Vut vill I do?" Wringing his chubby hands, he continued to sway as he lamented. "I have no family but Vilmer. I have novhere to be. I cannot go back to Germany. There are people, bad people, there who vill kill me, for sure."

"Like me?" Moto leveled the gun at his partner's head.

"No! No, please. I vill do vatever it takes to get vut vee need. The voman's body vill never be found, vunce the barge dumps at sea. But vee can still get the codes. Vee don't have to have the voman in hand, so to speak." Keizer Dembeck may have been a drunk and a societal leech, but he had a very diabolical mind when threatened. "Vee can still do this, Moto, I tell you, vee can still do dis." His arms flapped about his rotund body. "Vee don't need da vooman."

Moto lowered the gun, glowering at his partner. "No more screw ups, you hear me?" He headed toward the old warehouse they used as their hideout, with Dembeck waddling behind.

"For sure, Moto. For sure."

Inside the cavernous building, Dembeck fell into his broken chair. "I am not feeling so vell." He reached for a beer bottle from the cooler on the floor.

"No more drinking." Moto smacked the bottle from his hand. "None. Nich, nill. I see you take a drink, I end your fucking worthless life. Wilmer will probably thank me. How many years have you been mooching off your brother now?" Moto crossed to the steel door only to find it closed and solidly locked. "Now how the hell..." he turned to see Dembeck slipping a bottle beneath his billowing shirt. "...you locked this door when I went after the girl? Put that beer back, Keizer. I don't make idle threats." He punctuated his statement with the barrel of his gun.

"No. I followed you." He placed the beer back in the cooler and slammed the lid. "One von't hurt. My head aches, for sure."

"So explain this, dumb fuck." Moto pointed to the locked door.

****

"Andrea, wake up. You must wake up now!" The sweet, almost childish voice floated just beyond awareness as Andrea lay in a pile of putrid fishnet atop the pile of garbage and construction debris on the barge. It was all she could do for the moment. Her body was broken and torn. Her brain was pounding against her skull like a sledgehammer as blood oozed down her forehead and into her good eye. She couldn't even reach up to feel the wound.

The stars twinkled in beautiful patterns above as Andrea closed her eye and drifted away from the pain and the irritating voice. The barge continued to make its way to some unknown destination where it would deposit its rubbish into the depths of the briny.

Along with Andrea's lifeless body.

Chapter 15

I must be developing hot flashes prematurely, she thought as she lay in bed damp and sweaty. She resisted saying; *man, I'm hot,* out loud. Her husband would just make some kind of crude joke and start peeling her nightgown off.

Foreplay was more a pain than a pleasure these days.

As it was, he kept flicking at her earlobe. She lay still, trying to ignore his little game. If she feigned sleep long enough, he would give up, get up and get ready for work. She could escape his attentions this morning, at least.

"Ouch! Stop." He bit her ear hard enough to make it sting. She tried to swat him away, but her hand wouldn't move. It was caught in the sheets. "Damn it, I was sleeping so good, why couldn't you just let me be?" She pulled at the covers. They were rough and scratched at her skin. She would have to remember to tell the maid to use more fabric softener.

He did it again.

"I *said* ouch. Isn't that good enough? Or you want a full-fledged fight before coffee?" She cracked an eyelid to see if he was moving away after the half-hearted attempt at getting him to back off. She really had been sleeping so good.

Sun flamed in, burning her vision and causing tears

to well up. She licked cracked lips and tried again with the other eye. Why hadn't that damn maid closed the curtains before leaving last night?

Searing sunlight pierced her brain and she squeezed her eyes shut tight. Man, what a morning.

She sat up...

Or tried to.

Why couldn't she sit up?

What was scratching her skin and burning?

She tried to lift a hand to rub her eyes. Her hand was securely stuck to her body.

What the hell?

She scrunched onto her side and opened one eyelid just a bit. Through the thick dark eyelashes, she saw nothing.

Nothing?

She opened both eyes a little, squinting in the hellaciously bright light.

Nothing.

Well, not quite nothing.

Blue.

Vast amounts of blue everywhere.

Her cheek stung.

Her eyes stung.

Her skin stung.

"God damn it. This is not a fun game." A name was missing. Like someone had erased part of her mental sentence.

Who?

Who was she blaming for the love nips?

Who was...she?

"Oh my God, oh my God, oh my..." She struggled against the bonds that held her secure and felt her skin slice.

Where was she?

Who was she?

She opened both eyes despite the glaring sun. Pain exploded in her head and drove out through her eye sockets.

What she saw turned her overheated blood to ice.

Blue. Miles and miles of blue.

Carefully glancing about, she assessed the situation. She lay tangled in a filthy, salt-crusted fishing net on the rotten, broken deck of a small sinking boat in the middle of nothing but blue.

The crab pinched her ear again.

This time she didn't even flinch.

Chapter 16

The pesky crab pinched at her leg, this time she moved, then regretted it. Pain exploded in her side. Her foot lay in the cool water of the ocean, mitigating the burning around the bottom of her heel. But there was something definitely wrong with the foot. She chanced a glance. "Damn!" The entire side of her foot was a blackish purple, and a small slice was open from her heel to the ankle bone.

The crab pinched again, winning him a flying trip back to the ocean from whence he crawled. "Damn it. Is everyone after me?" With every movement her head pounded and drummed a rock concert against her skull. She felt her forehead. It was hot and crusty, and swollen. She took a handful of seawater and rinsed it across her wound. The tiniest movement made her world spin and she felt like vomiting.

Struggling to sit up, she collapsed in hideous pain. "Well, that's not gonna work, girl." Using her eye and nothing more, she glanced around. The sun was low on the horizon. It was either getting dark or getting light, but which one? Garbage bags and plastic containers surrounded the rotten sinking boat on which she lay. "Okay…damn." She struggled to remember something, anything.

Her name was gone.

The reason for her predicament and pain was gone.

Everything was gone...

Except her survival instinct, and that was setting off all of the alarms in the universe.

Obviously, someone had beaten her, then dumped her body on this boat.

She glanced around again. This time with purpose.

Get up. You must get up. The voice of reason spoke loudly in her mind and some of the pounding decreased.

She struggled amid the incredible stabbing pain in her side. It took a few minutes, but soon she was sitting, holding her side with a scraped and bruised hand.

"Oh my God! I'm adrift!" Tears welled and spilled to join the saltwater she sat in.

No time for tears. You have to survive. Figure it out. Fight.

She felt a kind of energy infuse her body and she struggled to stand on the tippy surface. The boat was sinking faster than she realized. When she'd awakened, only her feet were in the water. She had to find a way to stay afloat. Surveying the mess floating about her, she spied a red plastic gas can a few feet away next to a broken Styrofoam cooler, its lid floating separately. Those combined with the fishing net would make a small raft that would float. "You go, girl."

She jumped into the water without hesitation. The ocean cooled her pounding head. It did not even occur to the woman that she might not be able to swim. She just did it. And she could swim, of sorts. Her right side burned fiercely, but her left stroked toward what she needed. Eventually she captured the gas can and began her way back to the boat. Now the fishing net floated in what was left of the cabin. She grabbed the net and piled it on the plastic can, then set out stroking for the cooler and lid. A loud gurgling sound made her turn around to look. The last of the boat cabin disappeared beneath the surface, and now only the bow stuck up. Soon it would be submerged as well.

"Don't look back. It will not help," her inner voice warned her.

"Ahhhhhhhhh! I'm alone. In the water. Get the cooler—I need a name for myself. If I'm the only one I have to talk to, I want a name!" She struggled toward the white chest and its detached lid. "Jane Doe will have to do. Swim, Jane, swim!" She cheered herself on.

Soon her struggles paid off and she lay atop the scratchy net which held the gas can, cooler and lid beneath her in its tangles. "Made it, Jane. Good girl. Now what?"

She had no water. The only thing she wore was a long man's denim shirt.

The sun had moved higher into the sky. So, it was day.

That presented another problem.

The sun.

Did she sunburn? She pulled a hunk of hair in front of her eye. It was dark. She surveyed the skin of her arm that held the hair. It was passably tan. But she would still burn if she didn't have cover of some sort.

"Think, Jane."

The clouds on the horizon were dark and built like cotton candy, all poofy. A quick thought flashed crossed her mind. That scene would make a great photo. Why was she worried about photos at a time like this? When she was stranded in the middle of the ocean on a gas can and a cooler?

She leaned on her good elbow. The wind was

coming from the direction of the clouds. That could mean trouble. Since the sun had risen from that direction, it must be east. The little ditty every child learns, rang through her head: The sun rises in the east and sets in the west. It's the way the good Lord made it, all for the best. Unfortunately, she did not know where she was, or even who she was, so direction meant nothing.

Environmental and situational awareness. Remember your training.

She closed her eyes. What training?

Her feet trailed in the water as she let go of the pain and descended into the welcoming velvet fingers of unconsciousness.

Respite from pain.

Respite from fear.

"Respite from life if you don't wake up! Now!" The voice in her head shouted.

She grabbed the fishing net just as her body began to slide off the make-shift raft. Her good eye flew open, only to meet a crashing wave blotting out her vision and stinging her face. She grabbed the netting and held on for dear life as the wind howled, and the clouds sped across the sky.

It seemed like years as she clung to the raft. Her hands ached and bled as the fishing net cut into her skin, and still she hung on. Occasionally the sun would blast through, adding insult to injury. It was high in the sky and the direct impact of the heat only made her hands burn in the saltwater. When she thought she could take no more, the waves calmed, and the squall seemed to turn into a gentle caress. Exhausted and parched, she curled up on top of the raft as best she could, and lay there. She was too dehydrated to cry and too spent to move.

Somewhere, in the back of her mind, a man stood, tall and dark. His silhouette was familiar. He held a gun aimed directly at her. Was her memory coming back? Was this the man who had hurt her? As she tried to concentrate on the picture, it shattered and disappeared into the water that surrounded her. "Nooooooo!" she screamed to the heavens that looked down upon her with such disregard. She held an arm out to nothing in particular. "Help me! Please."

"Then look up. Look to the horizon. You have to fight for your life. No one can help you, but you."

She contemplated the voice in her head and glanced to the horizon. Even turning her head hurt after the storm, and her last-ditch effort at survival.

Then she saw it.

Sitting up too fast, her vision swam, and her head pounded viciously.

"Am I seeing things? Am I dying?" She wailed to the water and wind.

"No silly, it's an island."

And she was drifting closer. Energy she had never known she possessed, came to life and she started to paddle, adding momentum to the current and wind. "You go, Jane."

****

Master Moto, the infamous masseur of the South Padre Island Athletic Club, sat on an old hard bag of soil, thinking as fast as he could. There was still that dumb fuck, Keizer. That piece of shit could be his way out. "Water? Can I have some water?"

"Talk." Conrad's voice was steel.

"It wasn't me. I swear. This guy made me do it." Sweat dripped from his round forehead making him blink rapidly.

"This guy, go on." Conrad was as still as a cobra, ready to strike. Cold eyes looked on Moto with complete contempt.

"This guy, Wilmer's brother, he made me do it. Said he'd tell my boss about…" Moto added a touch of tremble to his voice.

"Tell your boss what?" The story was taking too long. Moto thought Conrad doubted any of what he was saying and he began to concoct a plan of sorts.

"Tell my boss that I did time. I'd lose my job and go back to jail. I skipped out on probation." Moto pleaded with his words and his hands.

"So, someone else cooked up this thing? You just carried your end, huh?"

"Yes, I swear!" Moto blinked several times. "Water?"

"So where is my wife?" Conrad grabbed the man by his throat.

"I don't know." Moto choked out. And it was kind of the truth. He had no idea where the barge had gone or where Andrea's body ended up.

****

Conrad got up and walked to the other side of the building. He motioned to the group, as they huddled away from Moto's hearing. "What do you guys think?"

Simon was the first to comment. "Lying. I know a liar when I see one."

"I second that." Evie commented quietly. "I watched my torturers when they made up stories to taunt me. I recognize the look."

"I third that." Bull chuckled.

"I'm in agreement with the gang. He didn't even make up a viable story. I can check on him in a heartbeat." Pete crossed the room and took a water bottle from his bag. He handed it to Moto who downed the entire contents immediately.

"Thank you. You are the kind one." Moto handed the bottle back.

"Nope. Thank *you*." Pete took the bottle with two fingers on the bottom. "Now I have your prints, sucker." He turned to his group. "Back in a few. I'll check that story with our security team."

Pete departed down the stairwell as Conrad turned to Evie, "Pete is a genius. So now what?"

"I say we talk to the fabulous-looking trainer, the German guy. See what he has to say for himself and his brother. This could be some kind of spy ring after government secrets." She waved toward Moto. "He can stay here, but let's get some better restraints. No sense letting the chicken out of the hen house before he lays the eggs we want."

"Good idea. Andrea used to meet this Wilmer and his gal pal for lunch after her workout. I saw their names in her calendar. His classes are probably over by now." Conrad sent Bull and Simon upstairs for better tape, or rope, or whatever. Back in front of Moto, Conrad was up for one more try. "Sticking to your story? One last chance, Moto. Where is my wife?" Conrad poured on the intimidating attitude and tried adding a scowl to his menacing look.

"I told you, I don't know. I'm just a masseur, a nobody. I didn't know there was anyone in the rug. Honest." By the looks of his body language, Moto was beginning to relax. "You can't keep me here. That's against the law."

"Who said anything about a rug, you son of a bitch?" Conrad kicked Moto in the gut as hard as he could.

Moto bent and vomited across his legs.

"Jesus, what a mess." Conrad leaned down. "And it's only illegal to hold someone if they are alive. Get it?" He was stretching the law a might, but it was a decent threat.

Evie laughed. "Nah, Rad, it's still illegal, but the cops would have to find the body to charge you with anything." A wicked smile split her lips. "They're still pouring cement over by the airport." Evie could be very naughty when she wanted to be and right now, Conrad seriously appreciated her naughty side.

Now Moto was trembling. "You can't kill me. You'll never get your wife back." Moto realized his mistake the second the words left his lips.

Conrad rounded on the man. "You said you didn't know where Andrea was, you lying son-of-a-bitch!" Conrad smashed a fist into Moto's jaw and heard more crunching. Blood pooled between the man's lips and dribbled down his chin.

Bull returned with rope and more duct tape. "Got what we need." He held out an international-safety-orange roll of duct tape and a coil of hemp rope. "I'll do the honors. One of my many skills."

Bull set to securing Moto with gusto and a lot of the vibrant tape. He ended with the rope securing both Moto's hands and feet. Moto was trussed up like a steer in a 'rope and ride' rodeo contest.

"A little ambitious there, Mr. Cheddar. I don't

think he's going anywhere." Simon snickered. He lounged on a stack of burlap bags filled with who knew what, his back against one of the ancient scarred timbers that held up the roof.

"Damn right, boss. Watch TV, ya learn something." Bull grinned. "Uncle Grady used to let me watch the National Rodeo Finals at his house. Always wanted to rope me an animal and hog-tie it up."

Conrad and Evie both smiled. Bull Cheddar definitely had a unique set of skills.

Conrad's cell phone buzzed. "It's Pete." He hit the green button. "Yeah?"

"I'm at Morehead's office. You're gonna love this. Our friendly masseur is none other than Henry Mikamoto, the New Orleans cop killer. Remember last year during that big tropical storm? Took out the power for a couple days and the gangs went nuts looting in the city? The Asian gang hit Silverstein Diamond Exchange, got into a firefight with the cops? Apparently Mikamoto was the head slime ball. Shot three cops before it was done. Two died. Your wife's masseur is on the FBI's most wanted list."

"That's just rich. Thanks, Pete. Later." Conrad ended the call. He turned to Moto. "Well now, Henry..."

Moto's eyes grew huge, and he shook his head back and forth. Behind the orange tape high-pitched mumbling could be heard. It was more than apparent the jig was up, and Moto knew it.

"Game's over, chum. Tell me where my wife is or I'll kill you right here, right now. Nobody'd blink twice and I'd probably get an award from the New Orleans Police Department. They don't cotton to losing their own." Conrad's voice was low and vicious. His hate for this man was shining through in every word he uttered.

It was clear to Conrad, Moto did the only thing he could, considering the situation. He threw Dembeck under the bus.

Moto blinked toward the tape on his mouth and winced as Bull ripped the tape, and more facial hair, off his face. "Keizer Dembeck has her. He stashed her somewhere, man. I don't know where. He's a crazy German. He'll kill her if you don't let me go."

"Really..."

"He's waiting for the codes, man. I'm supposed to meet him at noon. We were going to move the woman. The island is too small, too risky." Moto turned his head and spit blood across the floor. "You want her, you give me the codes. I tell Dembeck. He'll give you the woman. Easy as that." Conrad figured Moto knew he was negotiating from a very weak position. He also knew Moto figured Conrad was consumed by his own emotions. Emotional men were often desperate. Moto's plan might work if he kept talking, or so Moto thought. "Dembeck wouldn't tell me where. He's a devil. He'll kill her, I tell you."

"Where's this meeting supposed to be?" Conrad ground out. He was consumed with emotion, but he was also a professional soldier, or had been. He was in complete control, only showing Moto what the man expected to see in an angry husband with a kidnapped wife.

Moto whispered, "Sea Ranch Marina. On State Park Road." He hung his head as if he'd just ratted out a diabolical mastermind and knew his life was forfeit. "At Dirty Al's. I'm a dead man, and so is your woman if this goes south. You know that, right?" Conrad recognized the game.

"And that's supposed to bother me?"

"Look, I helped you. Give me a break. Dembeck's the one you want." Moto pleaded pathetically.

"Sit tight there, Henry." Conrad slapped a new piece of orange tape across the man's mouth and patted it into place a little more briskly than needed. "We'll be back."

Conrad headed for the elevator along with the rest of his team. "Let's take this upstairs. I need to think."

Evie followed him into the freight elevator, patting Conrad on the back. "We'll find her, Rad."

Bull pulled the old wrought iron gate down and hit the button with a half visible number ten on it. The freight elevator lurched and ground its way up. "Your pal ever think about upgrading this thing?" Bull held onto the straps hanging from the roof of the elevator car as it lurched to a stop a few inches short of the tenth floor. Never one to be without a sense of humor in the worst of situations, Bull affected his British accent. "Lady's sportswear, shoes and feminine sundries. Watch your step, ladies and gentlemen." He hefted the gate and waved the group into Pete's loft.

"It's eight thirty. This supposed meeting is at twelve." Conrad moved to Pete's massive computer against the only interior wall in the place. He logged in with a few quick strokes on the keyboard. Google Earth appeared and began to zoom into Texas as he typed in the name of the marina. "This is the spot." Pointing to the screen, he continued. "I looked at this place when Andrea and I were thinking about getting a boat. Lots of places to hide. Lots of opportunity for escape."

Conrad zoomed in closer and moved the map around showing most of the area in detail.

Simon scrutinized the map. "Lots of room to run."

"Yeah, that guy'll rabbit for sure, boss." Bull pointed to several open spaces and a couple docks. "Hard to set up surveillance. Moto's not stupid. His partner picked a great place to meet, if you swallow his story."

Evie paced back and forth in the warm sunshine of the enormous front window. "If I've got the story correct, Mr. War God's brother is the head dude in this caper. Moto is the hired help." She paused and stretched in her workout wear. Three pairs of eyes were immediately drawn to the magnificent silhouette in the window.

Out the side of his eye, Conrad watched Evie's boyfriend. The man was in pure worship mode. Simon just about swallowed his tongue. Conrad held back a chuckle. *Relationshipee*? Absolutely not!

"Do any of these people seem like they would know about backdoor codes, to you?" She turned to the three men who stood staring at her. Their jaws slack. "Guys?"

"Baby girl, you need to take a step back." Bull shifted his stance to cover his reaction to her innocent stretch.

"Oh, for heaven's sake! You guys need to get your head in the game." She charged at Bull with a double chest shove. It broke the spell. Conrad heard Simon clear his throat as he tapped a button and the map disappeared.

Bull mumbled under his breath, "Not my fault if the boss hooked up with the queen of the Amazon in tights."

"Really?" Evie was exasperated. "The question, guys…"

"Right. I mean, no." Simon stuttered. "The answer to your question is, no."

"Pete told me Moto is a gang thug from New Orleans. He's wanted for a cop killing in a diamond heist, after tropical storm Nate took out the power last year. Seems there was a firefight resulting in two dead cops." Conrad typed in the name Henry Mikamoto as he briefed the team on Pete's intel. A long list of articles appeared with a mug shot of their prisoner downstairs. "He was the head of the No Wah Ching, the New Orleans version of the Wah Chings out of California. Says here they make MS 13 guys look like kindergarteners."

"That be some bad dudes, man." Bull Cheddar squinted at the big screen over Conrad's shoulder. "And we got one tied up downstairs. Shu-wee. This thing just gets better and better."

Simon moved to the keyboard, "May I?" Conrad moved and Simon took the hot seat. His fingers flew across the keys. Articles flashed by in a flurry.

"What's he…"

"Don't watch. It'll make you sick to your stomach." Evie turned Conrad's chin away with a bright tipped fingernail. "Trust me!"

The computer chimed five times in a row. "Here ya go." Simon sat back and pointed to five different documents on the screen.

The first one gave an overview of the storm. The second showed the Silverstein Diamond Exchange. The third was an article on the robbery, shootings and casualties. Police officers weren't the only ones who died. The fourth showed historical pictures of the No Wah Ching gang. And the last article covered the insurance companies that had gone bankrupt due to multiple insurance claims that couldn't be covered, including the largest claim from the Silverstein Diamond Exchange.

"I wrote a quick algorithm to show articles related to Moto and the gang, then prioritized the information with a greater than ninety percent validity of the conflag...never mind." He smiled at Conrad. As adept at research as he was, Conrad hardly followed Simon's explanation and knew he had a glazed look in his eyes. Once again, he reminded himself to heartedly thank his BFF for dragging her *relationshipee* into his private mess.

Evie slung an arm around her guy. "English, babe." She kissed his cheek.

"There is a big connection between your wife being kidnapped and these variables." He pointed at the documents tiled across the screen.

Conrad looked at the articles, then back at Simon. "What connection?"

"Well, I'm not sure, but the program says it's there. Algorithms don't lie."

"Unless your algorithms can tell us where my wife is, I don't see how this helps." Conrad grabbed a beer, popped the tab and guzzled half, then set the can down hard. "Our best bet is grabbing Moto's partner and beating the answers out of him."

"Yeah! That's my kind of algorithm." Bull smacked the table with his fist. The beer can jumped precariously.

"Down, big guy." Evie laughed, then sobered. "If Simon says there's a connection, then there's a connection. We just have to figure it out." She moved closer and pulled up a chair to read each document carefully.

The stairwell door opened on a panting Peter. "Hey, guys." He crossed to the industrial refrigerator and grabbed a carton of orange juice. "Give me a minute." He downed several gulps in between pants.

"You ran up ten flights? You got an elevator, ya know." Bull stared at the out-of-breath man.

"Good exercise." More juice. "I don't think that thing's safe." More panting. "Not serviced in a couple decades." Another long drink. "Shuuuu, it's getting hot."

Bull looked at the open elevator, then at Peter, then back at the elevator they'd just used.

Breathing normally now, Pete shrugged, "It's probably okay, though. What have we got?"

Evie did a quick brief for Pete, including Simon's revelation. "There is still a couple missing pieces." Conrad finished his beer and reached for another. "Conrad, sit! You need a clear head and your pacing is making me crazy. Sit." She pulled out a chair and pointed at it like a mother giving her child a time out. "Now, Mister."

Conrad flopped into the chair, slumping. "Fine." Conrad was ready to explode with this new information. He couldn't stay still. A second later he jumped up. "No. Not fine. I can't sit here and do nothing."

Evie grabbed his shoulders and forced him back into the seat. "Planning is not doing nothing. Cool your jets, Mister." Her command worked the second time.

Conrad sat.

He watched her take up his pacing as she set into a review and question briefing. "Moto says Wilmer, God-of-War-Handsome trainer's brother, is the mastermind behind Andrea's kidnapping. You think he and his perky gal could be in on it?" Evie rubbed her chin in thought. "I didn't get any bad vibes from them. Not even a blink of subterfuge. That takes a lot of talent, or they are honestly not involved. Or sociopaths." She shrugged and Conrad fidgeted. "I didn't feel that either."

Now completely recovered from his ten-flight climb, Pete threw in his two cents worth. "If they were, that would mean some very long-range planning. Doesn't fit their image in my book."

"Nothing fits, damn it!" Conrad's rage welled up inside as he crumpled his empty beer can and tossed it near the trashcan. "We got a masseur at one of the highest priced clubs in Texas who is an accomplice to a kidnapping, and also wanted in Louisiana for murdering two police officers. This German trainer's brother supposedly set this thing up and what else? How would any of these people know anything about backdoor codes for Iron Shield? They knew it by name, when they called me."

Simon played the bad guy. "Maybe Andrea mentioned…"

Conrad cut him off. "She knows better than to talk about classified shit to friends. Even close friends, definitely not some couple at her gym."

"Maybe she didn't have a choice." Evie jumped in with a supportive arm squeeze for her lover.

"They kidnapped her *for* the codes," Pete added. "They had to have known about the project ahead of time to set this all up." The very unhealthy theory Pete was developing made Conrad's skin itch. "Could we have a leak at GST?" Pete immediately discounted his theory. "Our people are so well vetted, Morehead knows the size underwear they wear and their blood type. It can't be one of our own."

Now it was Bull's turn to weigh in. "How much would these codes be worth, if they got into the wrong hands?"

Both Pete and Conrad replied at the same time. "Millions."

"That'd do it for me. People'd sell their folks for a lot less." The group all looked toward the ex-gang member turned butler, personal bodyguard, and all-around intimidating fellow for one of the richest game developers in the country. "I'm just saying..." He shrugged at Conrad.

"No. He's right. Money's a hell of an incentive." Conrad was going over their employee roster in his head, looking for any connection. "Pete, can you get Morehead on it? Immediately, Pete picked up his cell phone and moved away to make the call.

"And, I'm gonna go back to the club and talk to the girlfriend. She seemed so...open and caring. If she's faking it, I'll know." Conrad nodded his agreement.

Pete hollered from across the room, "I'll drop ya on my way to Morehead's office."

"Bull, stay with Simon. He's out of his depth here." Evie whispered to Bull as she grabbed her bag.

"Roger that, my Amazon Queen. Your wish is my command." Bull bowed.

"And stop that nonsense, right now." She shook a fist at him with a laugh. "Men!"

"If you don't make it back by noon, you can meet us at the marina." Bull hollered after the two heading down the stairs.

Bull's glance at the elevator with some trepidation had Simon asking, "How long has your friend been living here?"

"About three years." Conrad answered absently, watching Simon on the computer. "Is that a government satellite site, Simon?"

Simon grinned up at the hovering Conrad. "Of course not. I would never hack into a secure government satellite data site. That would be illegal, Mr. McIntyre."

"Can that be traced back here?" Conrad recognized the data stream. It was a secure site and it was definitely government owned.

"Please, I'm not that clumsy. And how can anyone trace anything back to us? We were never there." As one of the world's best developers giggled to himself maniacally, Conrad shook his head and stepped away. Plausible deniability was a good thing.

****

Andrea's legs felt like blocks of cement, but she continued to kick as hard as she could. Her little raft was making progress, helped by a stiff current heading right toward an island with a sizeable hill in the middle. Her tongue was parched, and she couldn't avoid swallowing saltwater as she paddled and kicked. She heard the crashing of waves just about the same time a triangle shaped fin broke the surface in front of her.

Shark.

"Oh shit!" She scrambled up on the tiny raft, pulling as much of her body out of the water as she could. Her feet still dangled beneath the surface as the fin circled her raft. "You didn't paddle all this way to feed a damn fish, Jane Doe!" She scrunched a little higher. The raft dipped and tilted precariously with each tiny move. "No, God. Please don't let this happen. I don't want to die as fish bait!" She shook her fist toward the sky. "I don't know who I am, but I don't think I deserve this."

"Come, little fish. Come play with me." An enticing voice drifted across the waves and sank beneath the surface. *"You wouldn't like the taste of those dirty, nasty human feet. Come, and I'll show you a lovely school of squirrelfish all sweet and tender. Waiting just for you."*

Jane could hear the voice but couldn't believe it. "I'm losing my mind." She whispered as she watched the fin move away. "Nope. I've already lost it." She crouched on her raft a reasonable amount of time before she returned to paddling and kicking. The waves pulled at her arms and legs, crashing just a few yards ahead. But it wasn't a beach; it was a reef. "Death by shark attack, or torn up on a reef? Neither one is very appealing."

Jane crawled up as high as she could on her gas tank. There was a break in the waves to her left. Try to ride over the reef on her raft, or swim for it and hope she could make the opening?

A voice in her mind shouted, *"swim for it. You can make it."* She felt a gentle shove and slid into the water as the current separated her and the raft. "No choice now." Jane put her head down and swam for all she was worth, praying the shark would not come back before she made the shore.

The rate at which she sped through the water was a complete surprise. Her long, strong strokes and fluid motion said competitive swimmer. A picture of a skinny girl standing on a block wearing a speedo and a first-place medal flashed through her mind as she burst through the gap in the reef. The water was warmer and less turbulent inside the reef and soon her feet were touching sand. Exhausted, Jane climbed above the waterline and fell to the sand, panting and completely spent. Sleep overwhelmed her before she could even tell her silly mind thanks for the decision.

****

"She'll be fine from here, my love."

"Of course, Grady, dear. She's stronger than she knows, and she's a survivor. Just like you." Amee leaned close to the love of her life, and death, placing a sweet kiss on the smooth cheek of the man she would spend eternity with.

Above the sleeping figure on the beach, a tiny lightning bolt zinged across the heavens. Instead of thunder, a high-pitched giggle could be heard for miles.

Chapter 17

"Hey, Callista, right? Callista?" Evie trotted down the hall toward the perky trainer and girlfriend of Wilmer Dembeck. "Thanks for turning me on to your friend's class. But I couldn't hack all of it." She shrugged apologetically.

Callista impulsively hugged Evie. "Quite all right. He understands. He has a devout following. Those gals torture themselves regularly with my Wilmer. They're used to it. They love him. Everybody loves Wilmer." She leaned in close and whispered in Evie's ear. "Especially me."

Evie scrunched up her nose and giggled conspiratorially. "Andrea might have mentioned that a time or fifty. How long have you two known each other?"

"Come on, I'll buy you a juice delight and we can girl talk." Callista led Evie to the quaint restaurant near the front of the gym. "Andrea loves these crazy concoctions our new juicer makes." She ordered two fruity drinks and sat at a small table near the window. "You back for more?"

Evie pretended to take a sip of the drink. "This is heavenly." She smiled and watched Callista take a long drink. Their glasses were poured from the same blender so it must be safe to drink. "Nope." Evie pointed to the floor. "Forgot my bag. I was a little rattled about the massage thing."

Callista frowned. "I am soooo sorry about that. I just didn't think."

Evie patted the girl's arm. "No worries. It's my baggage. You couldn't have known." She smiled warmly at Callista. "So how long have you known Wilmer, the handsome-beyond-real man of yours?"

"Call me Calli. He is, isn't he?" She squirmed in her chair and giggled. "We met about six years ago in Austria. He was guiding climbers, and I was one of the women in his group. We hit it off right out of the gate. My mom gave me and my sister a trip to Europe for Sarah's college graduation present. She got her degree, and I got to be the chaperone. We had a blast. When I got home, Wilmer friended me on social media, and it just got better from there. It's all legal and stuff. He got his work permit and everything." Calli's smile chilled a touch and Evie caught it right away.

"And then what? What's the frown for?" Evie mirrored Calli's physical movements and expressions to build rapport. She'd learned that trick from her captors as well.

"Nothing, really. Except…" Calli leaned in. "Wilmer's brother came over a couple months ago. Keizer's such a slob, and he doesn't have any money of his own. Wilmer pays for everything." Calli took another drink for strength.

Evie did too.

"And he's fat! Oh my God, is he fat. Wilmer makes excuses for his older brother cause he thinks he owes Keizer. His brother quit university to take care of Wilmer when their parents were killed in an avalanche while skiing in the mountains. Wilmer was still in school." She drew back. Evie figured Calli realized she was sharing very personal information with a woman she'd just met.

Evie sat back as well purposefully instilling relaxation into the situation. She took a long drink savoring the sweet pulpy liquid. "You're right. This is delicious. Amazing." She took another drink. "Your secret is safe with me, Calli. I have a really weird sister I don't tell people about, too." Again, Evie tried for the let's-share-confidences air. "She's a Marie LaVoe convert. Lives in a swamp and tells fortunes." Evie leaned in close. "Hair all nasty. You know the type. *Call me now!*" Evie impersonated the famous fortuneteller who'd run amuck with the law a few years back.

That set Calli to giggling, and back in the sharing mode. "Well, Keizer doesn't have a job and can't work in the States, but he keeps talking about this big deal and some chunk of money that will be coming in any day now. Then he says he's going to Argentina and buy a ranch." Calli finished her drink. "That'll be the day. He'd never be able to get his fat butt on a horse. Wilmer is so fed up. His brother sits around eating our food and drinking anything he can get his hands on. Wilmer would kick him out, but he doesn't think Keizer has anywhere to go."

"I'm so sorry you have to put up with that. My sister is always begging for money. She just spends it on dead mice, dried frogs, and voodoo stuff." Evie gave a visible shudder. "That's why I joined the army. Got me out of the swamp." Evie shook her head sadly.

"Maybe Keizer's not so bad." Calli giggled and squeezed Evie's hand.

"Ladies." Wilmer appeared with a glass of something green and frothy. "May I join you?" He planted a chaste kiss on his girlfriend's forehead.

Calli smiled and squeezed his hand. "Of course, Wilmer. Evie and I were just girl talking." She smiled sweetly.

"Ut oh. Am I in trouble?" Wilmer smiled and the lights got brighter. The table vibrated with anticipation and Calli giggled outrageously. The Prince of Personality was in spectacular form.

"Not at all, Wilmer. I came back for my bag and Calli introduced me to these juice delights. They are incredible. She was telling me about how you guys met. So romantic." Evie fanned her face. She still had her ear bug in, so everything said was heard by her team. "And you have family here. How nice."

Wilmer snorted. "Not for long." He turned toward Calli. "I gave him two veeks. Hiz visa expires den. I cannot have an illegal in my house. I have too much to lose." He slid a finger down the side of Calli's cheek. "Dis voman means the vorld to me."

Calli giggled and blushed appropriately. Nothing in his body language or verbal communication gave Evie pause to think he was not completely honest and forthcoming with the truth. He was definitely in love with the cute little Calli.

"I believe you. Calli, you're one lucky woman."

Calli took Wilmer's hand under the table. "Yes, I am."

"Darling, have you seen Moto today? He had a massage scheduled vith Mrs. Ortega and did not show." Wilmer frowned. "Dat man's character is questionable. Mrs. Ortega is not a voman to be stood up."

"Does he do that often? Just not show up?" It was the opening Evie jumped into.

"Not really. And he's a good masseur. Strong hands. But sometimes I get a creepy feeling around him." Calli shuddered and Wilmer put an arm around her.

"Dare is somtink strange in here." Wilmer pointed to his head. He guzzled the last of his revolting looking drink. "Back to vork vit me." He kissed the top of Calli's head. "Two veeks, darling."

That made Calli's smile even bigger.

After Wilmer was out of hearing range, Calli leaned in closely. "Two weeks can't come soon enough for me. Wilmer won't do anything to compromise his visa. He won't even speed. He loves this country, and his position here. We make good money and Wilmer wants to become a citizen."

"Sounds like you two have a great life planned. I can see why he wouldn't do anything to hurt his chances, and you. You're such a lucky lady. And nice." Evie smiled at the effervescent trainer.

"This fall we're both starting a fitness science program at Texas A & M. The gym is paying. I already have an Associates in physical education."

"A real go-getter, huh? Now I know why Andrea speaks so highly of you two." Evie held out a fist for a congratulatory bump.

"I could never have done all this without Wilmer. He really set me straight about education and setting goals. Eventually we want to open a franchise of high-class gyms, and a line of health drinks. Together we can do it. I'm glad he's getting rid of that leech of a brother." She paused to take a breath. Calli was obviously excited about her future and bounced in her chair while describing their plans. "We'll probably have to pay for his ticket back to Germany." A little frown peeked out from behind all her exuberance. "It'll be worth it."

Evie nodded in silent agreement. "I wonder what happened to your masseur?" She pulled her bag from the floor as if to leave.

"No idea. He's only been with the club about a year and sometimes he's a very secretive guy. I keep my distance." The young woman shrugged. "How's Andrea? Have you talked to her? She's really okay, isn't she? I mean, I don't want to pry, but I really do consider her a friend. If there's anything I could do for her, or Conrad, you'd let me know, right?"

"That's very sweet, Calli. I'll let her know you're concerned. Maybe she'll give you a jingle. She's having a great time with her nieces." Evie hated lying to Calli after sharing such personal confidences, but it was necessary for the moment. "I gotta go. Thanks for the, what was this again?"

Calli jumped up and spontaneously hugged Evie. "Orange cran-raz banana flip. It's Andrea's favorite."

Evie laughed. "There's no way I'm going to remember that, but it was fabulous. Gotta go."

Evie checked out of the club with a swipe of Conrad's family pass and headed down the street toward a little taco stand a block away. "Guys, need a ride. Meet you at Chacko's Tacos."

She heard Conrad's response in her ear. "Be there in five. Bull's babysitting. Simon's doing whatever Simon does. You know he hacked into a government satellite data file?"

"This is an open frequency. And no, I didn't. I was never there." Simon spoke absently, obviously engrossed in pulling data from somewhere he never was.

Evie chuckled. "That's my guy."

"*Relationshipee*, I believe is the correct term." Simon's response was dry and low. His focus was obviously split between their communication and the computer and was working overtime, but he had to get his little dig in.

"Roger that, baby." Evie responded as she spotted Conrad's SUV down the street. The ear bug system was an open forum and she could identify several chuckles.

****

Her tongue was stuck to the roof of her mouth and her lips were cracked in several places. She wiggled her legs to shoo the biting sand fleas away. Gritty sand caked the side of her face along with the remnants of dried blood from the gash on her forehead. Her hands stung from a million small cuts and her foot was a lovely shade of purplish-black. She still had no name for herself, but flashes of a tall man in a uniform with a gun, persisted. From what little she could retain in her pounding head, she knew he was a soldier, a fighter of some kind. His dark, tanned face showed white patches and lines around his dark brown eyes from sunglasses and hours of squinting in the bright light of some far-off battlefield. He was tall and dripped masculinity. The soldier carried his AR like a father carries a young child; protectively and with purpose. His muscular arms bulged beneath a camo shirt and Kevlar vest, while long legs sported a tactical style holster trapping a handgun against his thigh.

Was he the one who shot at her?

Was he the one who saved her? Saved her?

Her mangled neurons couldn't quite figure it out.

What had she done to become a target?

A victim.

Random thoughts buzzed with painful vibration across her gray matter, but nothing substantial remained to take hold as a solid memory.

"Damn!" She swatted at a mosquito on her cheek. Fire burned through her rib cage. She swore she could hear the pest laughing at her, as it hovered just beyond reach.

Slowly, inch by painful inch, she pushed into a sitting position. Her head hung and her arms cradled her fiery, throbbing middle.

Broken ribs.

She placed her foot in the sand and felt a twinge of tenderness. The purple was only a bruise then.

Her hip ached. But only as much as it had the last time she'd taken a hard fall, trying to catch her tipping tripod.

Tripod?

Where had that come from?

"Well…Jane, time to bite the bullet." Her first attempt at standing produced so much pain, she almost passed out. After a few minutes of shallow panting, she tried again, but it was no good. Her sorely abused core muscles screamed at their host. "Ahhh!"

The edge of the water was a little closer, but if she waited for the tide to reach her, it would probably be too late. She needed to cool off and find fresh water.

She glanced at the sun. It was high in the sky.

Noon.

Only Englishmen and fools go out in the midday sun. The colloquial saying danced in her mind.

A piece of caked sand fell from her forehead. It was rusty colored from dried blood.

Her blood.

"Lord, help me! Heaven knows I need it." A sense of calm washed across her tortured body. Like that first drink of really cold water on a hot day, the feeling began in her chest and spread outward. Grasping a white limb of driftwood for a crutch, she summoned as much strength as she could, and fought her way to her feet. Stumbling and limping, Jane waded into the tide pool, relishing the cool water that lapped about her waist. "At least you know you can swim, Jane."

There was no current behind the reef's barrier and the pool was not very deep. She sank into the water letting herself float, easing her pain and cleaning some of the garbage smell from her shirt and body. She closed her eyes to the bright sun and floated, dipping her head beneath the water occasionally to rinse her hair and soak the sand and dirt from her head wound.

This time when she stood, there was less pain and she felt refreshed, almost clean.

She knew her island was small since she'd seen the entire thing from the ocean as she'd paddled her makeshift raft with all her might.

Small islands had people, right?

At the moment, people weren't as important as water and food. Her mouth felt like a salty sewer, and her tongue was thick and dry.

"All right, Jane, my girl. Survival 101 says water first."

Survival 101? Where did that come from?

Wading ashore, Jane surveyed her stretch of beach.

The white sandy shore bordered heavy green vegetation. The reef protected the shore as far as she could see, from her position on the ground. Brightly colored birds flitted among the tall coconut trees that formed a canopy above tangled vines and flowering bushes. In any other circumstance, the scene would have come right out of some Caribbean travel advertisement for Paradise Lost and Found. The tangy sea air and humid jungle scents combined to create a heady aroma. The only thing missing was the sweet coconut smell of suntan lotion and a Dirty Margarita.

And her memory!

Limping down the beach with the help of her make-shift driftwood crutch, Jane breathed shallow gulps of the scented air and listened to the chatter of the island birds. She had no idea of what direction she went or where the beach might end, but still she trudged on. Doing something in pain was better than just sitting in pain.

A Bananaquit, rousted from a tree near her, squawked and fluttered its wings. "Little Banana-quit, you have a big mouth for such a small bird." Jane admonished the yellow and black bird as it flapped it wings and darted farther into the vegetation. "Bananaquit? Am I an ornithologist?" she considered out loud. Maybe that explained the camera memory. Maybe she photographed birds!

A sooty shearwater sailed low across the tidal pool which was turning into a lagoon the farther she limped. "I know these birds!" She would have patted herself on the back, had she been able to lift an arm that high. Looking around with renewed interest, she named more birds as she saw them. It helped ignore the pain of her stiff gait and awkward movements.

After what seemed to be hours, she paused. Was that the sound of rushing water?

She couldn't run, but she limped faster toward the sound. Rounding a small dune, she saw it and nearly fainted! A small stream tumbled down high rocks forming a little pool before emptying over more rocks into the lagoon.

Water!

She stumbled into the cold water laughing with glee.

Fresh water! Number one on the survival list.

Gulping handfuls, Jane splashed her face then sank into the sweet cold, up to her shoulders, lapping water like a puppy after a wild run.

For a while she just sat there…breathing, lapping and breathing some more. She took a mouthful and spit a stream through her teeth several feet into the pool. She followed that with a girlish giggle. A flash of memory saw her and another girl spitting great mouthfuls of water at each other in a plastic kiddie pool.

Family?

A sister?

Then it was gone, and her moment of clarity faded like ripples on the surface.

"Augggg! Why can't I remember?" Her anguished cry sent a pair of Monk parakeets into the air. She followed their flight path until they disappeared behind a dilapidated shed near the top of the waterfall.

A building! Food was number two on the survival list, but she would take shelter instead!

Careful to follow a barely recognizable trail through the twisted vines and overgrown bushes, Jane made her way toward the shelter.

It sat on the edge of the stream. Mostly covered in jungle vines and flowering bushes, it looked like a quaint summer cottage in an overgrown English garden gone wild, waiting for occupancy. Tiny Purple-throated Caribbean hummingbirds buzzed about, feeding from the many flowers. Zipping in and out, they ignored the human's approach. On closer inspection, it wasn't a structure at all, but an ancient Mosquito net strung between four trees, draping to the ground. Many years ago, the vegetation claimed the net as a trellis, and now the walls and roof consisted of woven vines and air roots so thick Jane had to push a hand through to even realize the composition.

"Will ya look at this! My own house of flowers. Just like a fairy princess in some far away land." She bent to peer through the hand hole she'd made, and winced. "A somewhat bruised and battered princess." Jane straightened, leaning heavily on her crutch. She carefully pulled at the base of the net. It was solidly attached to the ground by vines and roots. "Damn."

The trail led around the net house, so she followed the impressions in the grass.

Who had stayed here?

When?

Were they castaways like herself, or campers on holiday?

A few feet away she spied a grassy ring reminiscent of a fire ring. The stones were green lumps in the ground and a bougainvillea had grown up the three-sided frame where a pot must have hung. That pot now lay rusty and full of holes buried in the grass, the handle broken away from its attaching hinges.

Situational tools and weapons.

The words just popped into her head as the handle gleamed in the sun.

A rusty handle gleamed?

A deep chuckle seemed to emanate from the pit, beckoning her to grasp the handle.

"Take it girl. Use whatever you can to survive."

Jane looked around for the voice, but not a leaf moved. Not one blade of grass bent to a strange footfall.

"Who's there?"

There was no one to answer.

Jane's ears strained to hear anything. But the only noises she could detect were those of the island, and its inhabitants. Birds squawked, peeped, and sang their exotic songs. The stream babbled and fell to the pool below. A slight breeze rustled through the coconut trees. One large green coconut dropped into the stream and floated toward the falls, disappearing over the edge before Jane could rescue it. "Damn! Number two on the survival hit list." And she'd let it go without so much as a lifted finger. "Get your head together, Jane."

Where there was one, there would be more, she told herself. Retrieving the pot handle was a challenge. Like standing the first time, it took a couple tries. She leaned in and gasped. She tried to squat and almost passed out from the intense pain in her chest. She would have to figure out something else if she really wanted the rusty handle.

"Tools."

The irritating voice in her head was back. But this time it was low and rich, with a southern accent.

How strange...

"*Tools.*" The voice repeated.

"Yes! Yes. Yes, of course!" She balanced on one foot and used her driftwood crutch to pry the handle from the tangled grass and lift it to her hand. It took time and several attempts, but soon she held the rusty metal in one hand and her crutch in the other. "Ta da!" She congratulated herself on a task well done.

A task well done? "How about the first step of many, just to live."

"*Exactly.*" The high sweet voice was back.

She was hearing voices. More than one? With different accents and tones?

There was crazy. Then there was *really* crazy! Jane was beginning to accept really crazy. If it helped her remain among the living for one more day.

She shuffled back to the net house and picked at the vines and netting with the pot handle. The netting came apart with ease, but the vegetation had grown so thick, the semi-structure stood now on its own. She worked at separating a hole just big enough to skinny through. It took a great deal of time and her body ached with every move. She could feel the task draining what little energy she still had, but after a while, the vines parted just enough, and she stumbled through.

The interior was dim and fragrant in a humid sort of way. Small, maybe six feet square, a stick and rope platform sat against one edge. A filthy tarp from some long-ago contributor, lay covered in dry grass.

A bed!

Jane collapsed on the tarp and let the pain take her off into oblivion.

The sweet voice called to her just as her eyes

closed.
"Sweet dreams."

Chapter 18

"Everyone in place?" Conrad's voice came over the ear buds to each member of the team. It was close to noon.

Various voices stepped on each other's signals as everyone answered in unison. Bull was the last one with a rousing, "Ten-four, good buddy."

Conrad sat on the back of a luxury yacht tied to the mooring closest to Dirty Al's Seafood Bar supervising the mission. When Conrad hired Carl's company, he never thought he'd need personal attention. GST wasn't the only company Carl's security firm worked with. Carl Morehead also did security for several wealthy clients who just happened to keep their expensive toys tied up at the Sea Ranch Marina. When they finally found Andrea, he would owe Carl, big time. The man had come through like a trooper.

"I got my eyes on Henry." Bull reported from the passenger seat of Pete's SUV out in front of Dirty Al's.

"Roger that. Eyes on the perp, as well." Pete snapped pictures from a dockside bench by the back of the Breakaway Cruises building.

Conrad had placed Simon and Evie at a patio table for surveillance. They were holding hands and sharing a shrimp cocktail as they watched Moto, three tables away.

Conrad snickered a little. He heard Moto order ice

water. His face was beginning to turn a purplish blue in places where bruises emerged from his interrogation. He held a glass of ice to his jaw as Conrad watched from his position.

Pete had held Moto while Bull wired the man for sound, before bringing him to the meeting place. Conrad was sure Moto considered it a demeaning process, just as he was sure the masseur tolerated the wire job in hopes of stalling, to figure out an escape plan. Now the team could hear every groan and curse, as Moto pretended to wait for the meeting that might never happen. Keizer had no idea that the team was there, or that Conrad had put their kidnapping together and fingered Moto. However, Moto had been in their custody for a while and out of communication. The dumb bastard was probably in some low-life bar getting shitfaced as Moto sat, trying to figure a way out of his mess. Just about the time Conrad was ready to give up on the meeting, he heard Moto.

"The dumb ass." Moto murmured just loud enough for the others to hear over the mic. "Late as usual."

It was twelve twenty pm.

"Just stay in place. We'll give him another few minutes." Conrad ground out.

As Moto sat at his table, watching the team, who sat in their places watching him, two of south Padre Island's finest swung into the parking lot on their bicycles. Cruising by the back of Pete's Navigator, Conrad saw them peer through the smoked windows.

"Uh oh, boss. I be a black man in an expensive set of wheels. May be trouble if they run the plates." Conrad was well aware of what profiling could do and Bull's size was enough to evoke suspicion in some communities. "Shit. They be checking. I can see the big one on his radio." Bull's voice came over the comm loud and clear.

"Pete?" Conrad knew Pete had some kind of in with the South Padre Island cop shop but wasn't sure what.

"I'm on it. Leaving my position now." Pete slung the Nikon over his shoulder and headed for his Navigator and Bull.

Moto could not hear the team's communications, but he could see the officers parking their bikes near the road and walking toward Pete's car. Something was up! This might be an opportunity to lose the fellow if he made a stink. Conrad was ready to handle Moto, but not in front of the cops. The man already had a few too many bruises.

Pete rounded the corner of the restaurant just about the time the smaller of the two officers, slid along the side of the white SUV, while the taller lagged back, unstrapping his handgun.

"Officers, good afternoon. Did I park in the wrong spot?" Pete waved and addressed the policemen. Conrad listened and waited for the situation to turn into a goat fuck. He could hear most of what was being said and figured out the rest through the binoculars he brought along.

"This your vehicle?" The tall one called from behind. He stood ready to move or shoot at the slightest hint of trouble. "You know the guy inside?"

"The little guy? Hell yes. My brother-in-law. He plays for the NFL." Pete laughed as he approached with his hand out. Conrad was hoping Pete could schmooze his way through this without incident. They needed to get the police away from the meeting site. Keiser would never show up with all the blue shirts around.

The smaller officer yanked his shorts above his belly. "ID, sir?" He held his hands up to stop Pete's approach.

"Of course." He reached for his back pocket.

"Slowly, please. Two fingers, sir."

Bull lowered the driver side window and hollered past the officer. "Yo, bro, how long you gonna make your sister wait before she takes it out on me?" He smiled his huge white smile at the officer. "How ya doin', Officer?"

Pete retrieved his license from his wallet and handed it over. "Peter Newcastle. Photographer extraordinaire and late getting my sister's husband to his lunch date."

"Shit, he's running!" Conrad's voice cracked over the comm.

Conrad watched Moto leap out of his chair and head directly for the parking lot where the police were engaged in questioning Pete and Bull. For a guy who'd been pretty well roughed up, he ran like the wind. Evie was right behind him and Simon was right behind her. This was turning into that big goat fuck Conrad feared.

He jumped up on the dock and rounded the building in time to hear Pete swear and see Bull bail out of the passenger seat, heading after Moto. Evie crashed through Dirty Al's front door, sending the glass smashing against the doorjamb. Shattering glass flew everywhere as Simon joined the chase.

Moto was halfway across State Park Road, running hell-bent for election when the officers shouted "freeze!" and drew their guns on the team trying to follow him.

Conrad hoped Bull was street-wise enough to know *freeze* meant fuckin' freeze and don't move a hair unless you want a hail of bullets up your ass. Bull stopped mid-stride and slowly raised his hands. Conrad said a silent prayer for common sense.

Pete wasn't quite so familiar with police actions and hit the ground hard, as he tried to chase after Moto.

"SPI, Unit Two, ten-thirty-three, Dirty Al's. Requesting immediate back-up." Tall-Cop spoke into his radio as he kept his gun aimed at Bull's back. "Down on your knees. Hands behind your head," he shouted.

Tall-Cop's partner had Pete on his face and cuffed in a flash, then backed up and drew his gun on Conrad. "You too, buddy. On your knees. Hands behind your head."

Simon moved in front of Evie, pushing her behind him. "Wait. You don't understand."

"Shut up. On your knees." The outnumbered officer waved his gun back and forth between Conrad and Simon. The whole situation was out of control, and the two bicycle cops were nervous as hens in a lightning storm.

"Just do what he says, boss." Bull's low quiet voice floated across the hot pavement. The tall officer hovered over Bull, handcuffs open and ready.

That's when Conrad couldn't help the smile that spread across his face, even though he tried really hard to keep a straight face in light of the situation. He heard the smaller of the two cops and bit his tongue to squelch the laugh that threatened. They'd already lost Moto and this whole shit storm needed to be managed carefully. That did not include laughing at the bicycle cops.

"Ah, Gary? They won't fit." The tall cop was nervous and fidgety. Clearly his fear level was pegging as he held his cuffs in one hand and a set of keys in the other.

Conrad sank to his knees and Simon followed suit. On their knees, Conrad figured they were less of a threat.

"What won't fit, Bill?" The shorter of the two officers responded.

"The cuffs, you moron." Evie was the only one of the team still standing, her purse slung across her torso in preparation for the chase. "Didn't you see that guy's wrists? Look, you've made a huge mistake and now that thief just got away." She was making it up as she went, flapping her arms like a damsel in distress. "He stole my boyfriend's credit card right off the table and shot out of the restaurant." She pointed at Conrad and Pete. "These guys were just trying to help when I screamed." She leaned against the wall, fanning her face and panting as if she was about to faint. It looked real to anyone who'd never met the stalwart Major Evielynne Gastineau!

Conrad heard the sirens blaring before he saw the lights flashing. Two patrol cars careened into the parking lot, slamming on their brakes to avoid the group in various states of arrest. The officers in the first car slid out of their seats and took up positions behind their doors, guns trained on Bull. He was the biggest and most imposing target. The other two officers approached their peers, guns drawn at the ready. What had the bicycle cops called in? A terrorist assault on the island?

Evie took two steps forward and fainted into the held-up arms of her boyfriend, who promptly caught her as he knelt on the cement. "Call an ambulance, my fiancé has heat stroke. You have to help her." Simon wailed. Conrad found new respect for Simon's acting ability as his girlish scream cried medical crisis and boyfriend completely out of control.

Evie, on the other hand, faked the most realistic faint as Conrad watched her lips twitch, trying desperately not to laugh. Simon fanned her face and yelled at everyone. "Somebody get me water. She's burning up. Hurry."

"Pete? Peter Newcastle? What the hell…" One of the patrol officers holstered his gun and stooped to pull Pete to his feet. "What the hell is going on here?" He unlocked Pete's handcuffs and turned to the shorter bike cop. "Please tell me why you have one of South Padre Island's leading citizens on his face in the dirt, with his hands cuffed, Gary." He waved to the other officers who rose and stood their ground, but holstered their weapons.

"Bit of a misunderstanding, George." Pete smiled at his long-time handball partner. "You mind?" Pete motioned to the team members still on the ground.

"Get 'em up boys. And somebody, please explain this *situation*." Officer George Billings apparently knew Pete Newcastle fairly well. Conrad remembered Pete's generous contributions to the Policeman's Widows and Orphan's fund. There was some big to-do and the entire station knew the man was a wounded warrior and decorated veteran. Only a couple of the officers also knew Pete was well-off enough to live in a virtual fortress disguised as an old warehouse. Billings had probably seen Pete, Pete in shorts and a tank top and could only guess at what he'd given for his country. Conrad and Pete never talked about their tenure with the Taliban around *normal* folks.

Bull limped up behind Officer Billings rubbing his knees and wrists, where the officer had tried to close the handcuffs. Billings turned and jumped. "Jesus, you're a big guy!"

Bull smiled down on Billings from about a foot above the officer.

"He's harmless, George."

Billings opened his arms to encompass the group. "Anyone wanna start?"

Evie sat up, kissed Simon then gracefully got to her feet, "Thanks, babe. All better." She turned to the flabbergasted officers herding up next to the SUV to see the comedy of errors in progress. Evie was gorgeous on a bad day. When she wanted, due to a little support from the glam-squad, spray on tan enhancer and nail gel, she virtually glowed. She commanded attention when she simply moved her little finger. "The dirt ball that ran past Gary here, swiped Simon's credit card right off the bill. Before we paid, I might add." She did a sexy slow turn, indicating Conrad and company. "They saw what happened and jumped in to help. Then along comes Officer Gary and Officer Bill who decides we're the bad guys. End of story." She stepped up to Officer Billings. "Except the dirtball got away. I'm Evielynne Gastineau and this is my boyfriend, Simon O'Sullivan."

Conrad was itching to go after Moto, but common sense had already told him the man was long gone, and they were back to square one. He was the next to do an introduction. "Conrad McIntyre, Pete's—"

"Partner?" Officer Billings already knew the name. "Well, I can see we have a bit of a pickle on our hands." He hitched his utility belt up. "Ma'am, shall we get you something to drink, and I'll take a report on this incident." He wanted the politically charged incident just to go away. "Sid, call it in."

Evie took the officer's arm and daintily stepped through the broken glass, back into the restaurant. Conrad shook his head watching her act. When his Evie turned on the charm, she turned on and charmed!

"Phyllis, could we have a pitcher of ice water and some glasses, darlin'?" Did this officer know everyone on the island?

Conrad motioned to Pete, who knew what he needed to do immediately.

****

Pete and his killer smile followed Phyllis into the kitchen. "Ma'am, if you have a broom and a dustpan, I'll get that glass up for you."

Phyllis was probably in her early fifties, overworked and underappreciated, but she took one look at Pete and melted into a puddle of pudding. "That would be so nice of you, Mr.-?" Her big smile showed generous amounts of gum tissue and yellow stained teeth from years of smoking and no dental insurance. Not everyone on Padre Island counted as the beautiful people.

He gave her shoulder a friendly pat. "Peter Newcastle. Just call me Pete, darlin'." He added a touch of Texan drawl to the last word. "What's a jewel like you doing behind an apron?" He followed her through the back-storage room where the cleaning supplies were kept.

"Gotta pay my bills, like all the other respectable folk around here. Tips are good most days."

Dirty Al's was a seafood eat-in or take-out kinda place. Buyers could watch their fish and shellfish prepared right behind the iced-up glass case. And smell it too. The tables were small with plastic flowered table coverings and greasy old-style napkin holders.

"Thanks, ma'am." Pete touched the tip of his purple GST ball cap like a good Texas Ranger would, took the old straw broom and grodie plastic dustpan and left Phyllis to her kitchen.

****

As Pete cleaned up the door's broken glass, Evie, Simon and Conrad sat with Billings, providing what little concocted information they could without committing a federal crime by filing a false police report. The entire time, both bike cops lounged at the lunch counter munching on corn chips, listening. Conrad noticed Officer Bill kept cocking his head, looking at Simon as if he'd grown an extra set of hands.

"Mr. O'Sullivan, you should call your credit card company as soon as possible and cancel your card." Billings was providing the usual counsel he did with all tourists who ended up as victims of the local hoodlums. The island prided itself on its police protection and safety, but never lost track of the fact that they were only a few miles from the Mexican American border and a resort area, as well as a seaport. Almost anyone could come or go with ease and that was the thing that bothered Conrad. They were sitting there playing a part while Moto was probably heading for the border.

"Good idea. If you'll excuse me." Simon tip-toed through Pete's job and walked into the parking lot, already pretending to be on his cell phone. "Bull, where you at?"

A breathless response told Simon and the team, Bull was running. "At the water park, boss. Spotted Moto, but lost him in the crowd. Still looking. Cops done with you back there?" Each sentence came out clipped between heavy pants. Conrad monitored the conversation while trying to pay attention to the crime at hand and Officer Billings.

"Almost. Stay with it. We'll come to you."

As soon as Simon had gone outside, Officer Gary took the seat next to Evie. "Don't mean to pry, ma'am, but is your boyfriend, *the* Simon O'Sullivan? The gamer guy?" Conrad could tell the man had stars in his eyes. He'd seen the kind of crazed fan look on way too many faces while he and Pete had been celebrated and honored. Now, Conrad was introduced to the international wave of fame that engulfed Evie's man.

"As a matter of fact, he is. Do you play Ghost Wars or Evil Genius?"

His tall blond partner answered for him from the counter. "Play it? He lives it, ma'am." The officer laughed. "It's his wife, kids and job. He only patrols to support his habit." More chuckles followed.

"Wow! Wow. I just detained Simon O'Sullivan!" Officer Gary was in la-la land staring out the greasy window at Simon on his phone. Conrad swore he could see a little drool on the man's lip. His gaming habit explained a lot about the officer; the tummy paunch, the slight gamer slouch, the way his fingers twitched at the mention of Simon's games.

Evie chuckled. "Well then, maybe you could hit him up for a new copy of Ghost Wars 4.0. It fixes the planet rotation glitch in the previous versions. Just came out..." Evie looked at her watch, "three days ago."

"You play?" Officer Gary was in awe.

"Never." It was a dry answer that gained Evie a sad frown from the officer as Conrad watched the exchange. "But I do listen."

"All right Mutt and Jeff, back out there on your bikes. Go protect some teenager who needs sunscreen." Officer Billings waved the two bike cops toward the door. He returned his attention to Conrad and the complaint at hand. "When I get this written up, I'll give you and Mr. O'Sullivan a call. You can come down and sign the formal complaint. That way, if we should recover anything, or catch the guy, you can press formal charges. But, honestly, don't hold your breath. Credit card fraud is very common, especially if they can cross the border."

The small group watched the two bike cops retrieve their wheels. Officer Gary gave Simon a wide berth with a deep bow, his hands clasped together like a karate student greeting his sensei.

Officer Billings snorted. "There's a reason we don't give that guy a car."

Conrad was itching to go. "If we're done here?" He stood.

"Unfortunately, we are." Billings turned to Simon who'd just stepped through the door. "Please accept my most sincere apologies for this inconvenience on your holiday. Let the SPIP know if there is anything else we can do for you." He shook Simon's hand, then turned to

Evie. "Ma'am. Mr. McIntyre, nice to finally meet Pete's partner. Thanks for trying to help out." He yelled into the kitchen, "Pete, Thursday night?"

Pete's voice came out of the back. "Right, beat you again on Thursday night."

"Don't think so." Billings smirked as he exited through a now, glass free doorway.

****

In his patrol car, Officer Billings threw the paperwork on the back seat with a sigh.

"Not going to enter it now, George?" His partner asked in surprise.

"Nah. No point in wasting my time." George watched the players exit the restaurant with a good degree of suspicion. "I don't know what's going on here, but the story I just got is bullshit."

"What? What do you mean?"

"Never mind. Just roll."

Chapter 19

The second the police cleared the parking lot, Conrad was running to his vehicle, followed by Evie and Simon. "I'll take the north end of the water park. Pete, you take the south entrance. Shouldn't be too hard to spot Bull. He's a head taller than everyone else." He spoke through their comms. "We gotta get Moto back."

Schlitterbahn Water Park and Resort on South Padre Island had two sections—the actual outdoor park with rides and arcades, and indoor part that was the resort hotel. The entire park, inside and out, was connected by a man-made river flowing in a huge circle through and between both parts. What the resort called the transportainment system connected all of the attractions and beaches. You could enter the Rio Aventura River from one of several beaches or attractions and then choose your next water adventure from there. With the help of the aquaveyer, you never had to leave your air mattress or inner tube and could float the day away at Schlitterbahn, hitting just about everything at the park. It was one of the most popular places on the island, and packed with families and tourists seeking respite from the hot Texas sun. Cabanas and palapas dotted the park filled with people enjoying their friends, drinking, eating, and frolicking in the cool water. He and Andrea had taken her nieces there. The girls loved it and wanted to stay forever, floating around and around the park. It was the easiest babysitting job Conrad had ever had.

"Bull, location." Conrad tore out of the parking lot down State Park Road.

"By the castle thing. Lost Moto. He just melted into the crowd. Damn."

Pete's voice came over the comm. "Sand Castle Cove."

"He could be anywhere. This place is a madhouse." Bull's comment conveyed his discomfort in large crowds. In one of their quiet conversations, Evie told Conrad about Bull's early days in Oakland, a city where anyone could slide out of the crowd and slit a throat before you would notice.

"Head to the south entrance. Pete'll meet you there." Conrad sounded lost.

Evie, next to him in the front seat, patted Conrad on the shoulder. "I have an idea. If we can't get Moto, maybe we can get his pal. I have a feeling, a really good feeling, Callista and Wilmer can help." She spent the next few minutes recounting her friendly drink with Calli and the information she'd gleaned. "I have a sneaking suspicion Wilmer'd give up his brother in a heartbeat if he thought he'd stand a chance of losing his visa. That is, if he knows anything about what his brother is into, which I seriously doubt. He and Callista have a plan for their lives and I don't think he'd let anything mess it up." She looked at her boyfriend in the backseat. "Plans give you roots. They've enrolled in college classes next semester. Both of them."

Conrad didn't miss the jab. Evie must be serious about this boyfriend or she wouldn't be feeding him things that were important in her life. At Bethesda, she'd talked about someday having a real home, and roots. That was something she'd not had since she stepped out of the Cajun swamp and raised her right hand.

Conrad could see the wheels turning in Simon's brain. He wondered if they ever stopped. Plans give you roots, huh? So, Callista and Wilmer were more than *relationshipees*. They had plans.

Simon broke the silence. "If I can get back to Pete's Internet, I can do some more digging in places where I've never been. You know. Maybe I can get the time and date signature off the video you guys got and see what there is to see. From where I won't actually be, that anyone will see, that is." Simon was trying hard to talk around the serious hacking he was contemplating.

The comm crackled with laughter stepping on each other's signals. Evie grinned into the rearview mirror at Simon. "Good idea. Meet you guys back at the warehouse and we'll regroup."

Conrad added, "Then I think a visit to Callista and Wilmer's place will be in order."

****

"Look dip-wad, they know." Moto crouched beneath the skirting around the bottom of the giant water slide. Through a crack, he could see the enormous black man searching for him. "They've figured it out, I tell ya. Now go to ground and stay put. I'll snag some wheels and come to you." Moto ended the call, erased the number, and threw the phone farther under the slide. Some kid will miss his phone later, but too bad for him. Moto was free and he'd make sure he stayed that way. Rubbing his purple, sore jaw, he watched his pursuer move away as he buried the wire he'd been wearing, in the sand at his feet. A little longer and then all he had to do was jack a car, drive to the warehouse and get that dumb-fuck, Dembeck. He ought to just off the stupid shit, but the German was his connection to the money and the contact in Europe that would pay. His life depended on it.

Worse yet, his sister's life depended on it.

He shuddered.

He knew his life had not been lived by normal standards. He'd done things that would bring a grown man to his knees. And enjoyed it! But it wasn't his sister's fault. She was clean. She didn't approve of his life, or his gang activity. She shouldn't have to pay for his sins. He didn't care what other people thought of him. He didn't care that he had run one of the most notorious gangs in New Orleans. They ran ragged over the police and politicians, taking crime to a new level, and he was the leader, the one with the power. That was until a storm changed his neighborhood...and his life.

Moto still remembered the pictures of his guys, their bloated and mutilated corpses displayed like dolls sitting up against the sea wall. Six of the toughest, most loyal gang brothers had disappeared right after the botched diamond job in New Orleans. Three days later, someone dropped a package off at his sister's deli. It contained color glossies and the right hand of each of the missing guys. A note wrapped around a burn phone simply read; *Atonement. Wait for my call.*

That was a little more than a year ago.

However, it was just the beginning of this mess, and now Moto was facing enemies on all sides. For the first time in his life, he was running scared. It didn't sit well with him and he swallowed the genuine fear for his sister.

Moto grabbed an over-sized Hawaiian shirt from the back of a chair he passed, and a straw hat from a table of drunken Mexicans.

"*Oye, asiático—*" Moto didn't hang around to hear the rest. He jammed the hat low over his head and kept walking. Through the throngs toward the parking area where he could get some wheels, he kept track of the big guy ahead of him. It didn't take long before the fellow hopped into the white Navigator and the SUV sped away. Moto breathed a sigh of relief then wound through the cars, looking.

One beat up old pick-up sat near the exit, its windows rolled down against the heat. Moto reached in and dropped the sun visor. "Of course! I'll do you a favor and take this heap off your hands. Shouldn't be driving a piece of shit like this anyway." A set of keys dropped onto the seat along with a small sandwich bag of pot, with a couple joints ready for a light. "Damn. It must be my day." Then he reconsidered as he wiped a bloody drip from his nose. Well, maybe not all his day, but this part was looking up. All things considered, he'd been in worse situations before.

Out of the exit and on his way to the old garage, Moto considered his next move. It was getting late. Dembeck better be sober. He needed the man to sell the codes to the German contacts and get his share of the pay, as soon as they got them. He only had five more days to pay the piper, before he would end up in some morbid photo with his right hand missing. Damn! He wished he knew who the piper was. He'd kill him and be free.

A year ago, the diamond heist had seemed so simple. The storm was supposed to cover their handiwork. Who knew the old man would be sitting in his flooded store with a shotgun. When the gang stormed the building, Tyi didn't have to kill the old fart. Things just went sideways before anyone could stop it. Tyi took a full blast of birdshot to the gut, but got off two shots before he went down. The old man's head exploded as he went over backward in his wet plastic lawn chair. Stunned, the rest of the No Wah Ching gang stood staring at their dying brother. Moto grabbed a towel from the counter and pressed it to Tyi's gaping wound, but there was nothing to be done for the nineteen-year-old. He was gone before his blood soaked through the towel. The whole scene dissolved into a grisly mess in a split second. Silverstein Diamond Exchange was supposed to be a slick, easy job under the cover of rain and wind. It turned out to be so much more than diamonds, as well as a death sentence for most of the gang members. Moto didn't even know how, or why, or who.

Moto's memories replayed the scene in his mind. Tyi's sister, Kria, was so angry, she grabbed her brother's gun and filled the old man Silverstein's corpse with every last bullet in the magazine, screaming the entire time. Then the gang smashed the glass display cases and took everything in sight. Brodi searched the office and came up with three flats of unset gems, and a wad of cash, but the big haul was the small safe. Two of the bigger guys used a tire iron to pry it off the soaked floorboards of the ancient building. It wasn't until that night that they saw the contents. They'd just stolen three million dollars in bearer bonds! Back then, he didn't even know what a bearer bond was.

Then the nightmare started. The loot disappeared from the gang's hideaway when Moto was ducking the police around New Orleans. Kria's car was found at the bottom of Lake Pontchartrain, her six-month-old still strapped in the baby seat. Kria sat at the wheel, two bullets in her head. Brodi's mother found her son's body in the dumpster behind their tenement, but not his head. Moto had only seen pictures of Danny, Crawdad and his brother Minnow. And there were more members missing. Moto feared for his sister and her children, but had stayed away after the gruesome package was delivered. She had nothing to do with her brother's gang activity, and hadn't spoken to him in years. He needed to keep it that way.

What connected the diamond heist to Dembeck and GST's projects was a mystery to Moto, just as the how and why of his gang members' deaths. But his share of the take was the atonement required. The voice on his burn phone had been crystal clear. As he pulled into the warehouse, he could see Dembeck at the door, ready to slide the huge metal sheet across the opening. He'd never really put any pieces of the puzzle together, because he didn't have any puzzle pieces to begin with. Somehow, someone knew about these codes, whatever they did, and wanted them. He and Keizer were targeted by some unknown person on the phone with procuring the codes by kidnapping the head honcho's wife. His atonement would be made with his share of the money Dembeck got for the information.

"What happened to you?" Moto could smell alcohol on the fat man's breath.

"That bitch's husband and company, happened to

me, you dumb-fuck. Get me some ice and a beer." Moto needed to think. He'd ratted out Dembeck to his captors and it wouldn't be long before they went after Wilmer and his little cutie. "Does your brother know anything about this?" Moto held a dirty garage rag filled with ice to his jaw.

"*Mein* brother?" From the startled look on his face, the question hit Keizer out of the blue.

"Yes, ass-wipe, your beautiful-body brother. The German vunder-machine." Moto sneered. He'd often been jealous of Wilmer's success and patronizing way with the ladies. It made his stomach turn.

"No. He knows nothing. I swear I have told him nothing." Keizer began to wring his hands and pace back and forth. "He would send me back to Germany and then..." Keizer drew a finger across his throat.

"Serve you right." Moto mumbled. "Sit down. Stop pacing. I can't think." He rubbed his head which had begun to throb, and took a long gulp of beer. "Why the hell did you have to shoot the bitch? Huh? Don't answer that." Moto was disgusted with Keizer and anything the stupid shit said, at this point, would just make his head hurt worse.

Keizer plunked down in the broken chair and reached for his own beer.

"Not on your life, Dembeck."

Keizer folded his hands across his obese belly and waited.

The sun was sinking. Golden rays burned through the holes in the metal door, spreading across the greasy cement floor. Moto watched the patterns grow longer as he sat, thinking. Moto didn't know what to do or say. Soon it would be night and Wilmer would wonder where his brother was. He and that pitiful whore of his had given Keizer the marching orders. Keizer had two weeks to clear out of his brother's life. It was that little shrew's fault his brother was kicking him out. Moto had come to hate the popular young trainer. She was too bossy by far and had Wilmer wound around her little finger. No real man should tolerate that.

****

The late afternoon sun made a quilted pattern of bright and dark beneath the little net house Jane had crawled into. As she woke to her situation, she lifted a hand, moving it back and forth watching the patterns form and slide across her skin. As the patterns changed and moved, a foggy memory flashed across her mind. For a split second, she visualized a pattern of lace, similar to the light pattern, on her hand and arm. White lace, dainty, with tiny sparkles, reflecting in candlelight reminded her of—

"Damn! Why can't I remember!" she cried. But there was no one to hear.

The babbling stream called to her as she licked her cracked lips and tenderly felt her swollen cheek and eyelid. "Can't imagine how I look." The comment almost produced a laugh, but the pain in her midsection eliminated that idea rapidly. "Ow…"

Jane pulled her driftwood close and used it to prop herself up, then crawled to a standing position. Like the last time, it took a certain number of tries, some cursing, and a good deal of pain, but sleep and fresh water had done wonders for her wounds. She stumbled through the hole in the netting to the edge of the stream. The sky was turning orange over the island and the bird noises had increased. All over, sounds of coos, chirps, squawks, and lilting songs celebrated the coming evening. One last chance to speak, eat, find a mate to settle down with for the night. "So, who is there to give me comfort, little kestrel? Where is my mate?"

The big-eyed falcon sat high in a tree above the stream. Its easily identifiable *klee-klee-klee* marked the evening hunt. "So, you look for food too?" Jane watched the small falcon launch toward the beach. "Good hunting, little one." Its rufous coloring and black bars shimmered in the evening light as it soared over the stream and dove toward some target near the pool below the falls.

"Watch out! Watch out!" A voice screeched behind her and she almost fell into the stream. "Silly bird. Watch out!" A colorful green, red, and yellow macaw spread its wings and sailed to the top of Jane's shelter. "Silly bird. Silly bird. Drinks too much." It waddled back and forth across the limb where someone had attached one side of the netting. "Uh oh. Drunk bird." The macaw flapped clumsily to the ground and lay on its side in the grass. Within seconds Jane could hear a snoring sound coming from the bird as it watched her.

"Drunk bird?" Jane tried to suppress the giggle that rose inside her. It didn't work, despite the pain it caused.

"Drunk bird. Drunk bird. Silly bird." The macaw jumped to its feet, hopped around with each statement, then fell over and began to snore again.

Did this comedic bird belong to the person who built this shelter? Was its owner still around?

She knew macaws could live for decades, but someone had to have taught this bird to speak! "Hello! Anyone there?" She turned and hollered in several directions. "Hello? Help!"

The macaw struggled awkwardly to its feet and waddled toward her. "All gone. All gone. No more rum. Silly bird."

"Okay silly bird, where is your owner? Who taught you to talk?" Jane eased herself to the soft grass that grew next to the stream. She soaked her sleeve in the cold water and pressed it to her swollen face. "I could use some rum right now."

The bird repeated, "All gone. All gone. No more rum. Silly bird."

"You might be silly, but at least you're someone to talk to. Now I'm not all alone." Jane soaked her sleeve again and applied it to her forehead. It came away rusty and red. "Ouch."

The bird waddled closer. "Silly bird. Got rum? No more rum." It looked sideways at Jane with one eye. Then flapped away in a hurry. Jane looked around for whatever could have startled the bird.

There was nothing.

She spent the next few minutes washing her many wounds in the clear water and soaking her sore foot. Out of pure boredom, she counted the bruises and scrapes. "Seventeen bruises and five open wounds. Perfect…" She lay back on the green carpet and watched the sky darken.

Her stomach growled.

The sole of her foot throbbed.

Her head hurt, but not as much as when she'd first arrived on the island. A thought popped into her brain; *headache is one of the first signs of dehydration. Drink more water. You can live without food for a while, but not without water.*

The macaw flew to a tree above where she lay. "Back so soon, silly bird?"

It held something white in its beak. As the bird released the object, it floated through the bushes to land on the surface of the stream. Jane leveraged herself up in time to snag the thing from the flowing water.

"You're kidding!" It was a label from a bottle. "Tortuga Citrus," The next word was so faded she couldn't read it, but the last word was perfectly clear, "Rum!"

The macaw floated down to sit just beyond her reach, staring intently at her.

"Where did you get this?"

"Silly bird. All gone. Got rum? Silly bird."

Jane couldn't tell if the bird was laughing at her, or trying to tell her something. "Okay, Silly Bird, that will be your name, from now on. Silly Bird, where did you get this?" She held up the label and pointed to it. "Show me."

The macaw cocked its head, as if trying to understand the human's question.

"Silly Bird, Rum all gone? Where's the rum?" Jane studied Silly Bird carefully.

"Where's the rum? Where's the rum? Dead bird. Give me my rum."

Despite her wounds and bruises, Jane laughed out loud. It felt good and something she hadn't done in a while.

Silly Bird ruffled its feathers and waddled toward what looked to be an old path. At least there was an impression in the grass and an opening in the dense foliage. Silly Bird paused and looked back at her as if to say, "Well, come on."

"Coming. Just wait for me. I don't have wings."

Silly Bird squawked and waddled off into the bushes.

Jane worked her way to her feet and shuffled off down the path after the bird. "Wait!"

Following the rough path and Silly Bird's squawks, Jane did her best to follow the bird and keep up. Every once in a while, Silly Bird would pause and look back at her. "I'm coming. Slowly but surely." Jane reassured the bird as she hobbled along.

After what seemed like hours, Silly Bird let out a screech and took flight. "No! Don't leave me! Silly Bird, come back." Jane watched the colorful macaw fly off and disappear. Right into the hill ahead. "No..." She leaned heavily on her driftwood crutch. Tears filled her eyes. It was getting dark and she had used up most of her strength following that stupid bird, just to be abandoned at the last...

Silly Bird screeched angrily and reappeared a few yards ahead. Then disappeared into the hill again.

Where in the heck was the bird going?

Then it hit her. A cave! Silly Bird was flying into a cave!

"Hello? Anyone there?" She shuffled faster as Silly Bird flew in and out of the hill, screeching louder and louder.

Jane was standing in the opening before she saw it. Long vines hung from the top of the cave almost obliterating any view of the entrance. Where the vines touched the ground, other vegetation had grown up making a virtual living wall. Silly Bird entered and exited through a well-used hole at the top, about five feet above Jane. Agitated and impatient, the bird flew at the growth, pecking and tearing with its strong beak.

"Well, this must be it, then." She grabbed a handful of flowery curtain and pulled. Silly Bird flew about her head adding its beak to the job. Soon there was a spot in the vegetation where she could struggle through.

The sun was sitting low on the horizon, but the cave was a few feet above the jungle floor, the rays illuminating the interior with warm soft light patterns.

"Holy God in Heaven!" Jane surveyed Silly Bird's cave in the dimming light.

The macaw flew right to its perch with an echoing screech. On a shelf made of weathered old planking sat three bottles of Tortuga Citrus Honey Rum! One was missing a label.

"Silly Bird, I should rename you Smart Bird."

Silly Bird pecked at the nearest bottle. "Silly Bird. Give me my rum. Drunk bird. Drunk bird. Ha ha ha haha." The macaw looked directly at Jane, then right at the rusty pan sitting on the shelf next to the bottles.

"Well that's clear enough. And you deserve a reward." Jane carefully took one bottle down and studied the seal. With nothing to remove the wax and cork, how would she get it open without breaking the bottle?

Silly Bird set to squawking with such a racket, Jane shouted at the bird. "Quiet. Let me think."

Silly Bird flapped across the cave and returned, an ancient knife, rusted and black, clutched in its claw. The bird dropped it in the pan and landed back on its perch in style. The handle was made from wrapped cloth and leather straps. Whoever had lived in this cave must have had plenty of time on his hands. The blade had obviously been fashioned from a metal hinge of some kind, and crudely sharpened.

"Next time I need something, I'll just ask you." She worked the top from the rum bottle with the dull blade and poured a little rum into the bird's pan.

Silly Bird let out a half human, half avian whoop, and set to licking the rum as fast as it could.

"You're an alcoholic! Shame on you, Silly Bird."

The bird ignored her and stuck to guzzling its rum. How long had it been since Silly Bird had a drink? Jane shook her head. What a crazy thing to worry about. Once an alchy, always an alchy, so said her—who?

Another memory flashed behind her eyes; a rather portly man slept in a broken chair, beer bottles scattered around the floor. One bottle leaned precariously in his hand as he snored loudly. Then it was gone.

Just like Silly Bird's rum. The pan was dry.

Who was that man she glimpsed? He looked harmless. And drunk. A father? A brother? Jane's memory ran just ahead of her cognition. At least he didn't look dangerous or carried a big bad gun like the other man whose image she'd remembered, for an instant.

Her Swiss cheese memory was frustrating, but so was the growling of her stomach. With the last few rays of light, she surveyed the cave. Silly Bird had settled on its perch, and now sat with its eyes closed. Drunk already?

Apparently.

The bird's side of the cave held a couple shelves, on one of which sat the three rum bottles. The other was stacked with moldy and rusting pots. An old ceramic coffee pot lay on its side against the rock wall. Some of the blue coating could be seen through the gray-green mold.

On the other side, an old steamer trunk sat, belted closed. The leather belts had long since deteriorated or been nibbled away, and two of the wooden slats had worked loose. Jane judiciously opened the lid. Inside, an old Kelly Girl tin sat atop several oil-skin wrapped packages. One package near the corner with the loose boards was home to a young family of mice. The female mouse burrowed beneath the chewed nest, fluffing bits and pieces over her litter, in a vain attempt to protect her brood.

"It's okay, Mama Mouse. I won't hurt your babies." Jane removed the can. Inside was a flint and striker as well as a handful of steel wool. "Now we're getting somewhere!" Warmth was number four on the survival list that kept popping up in Jane's head. Water, food, shelter, and warmth. Warmth wasn't a big issue in the tropics, until the sun went down and the moist air turned cool and insidious. However, warmth meant fire. Fire meant light, and light was important to a lone survivor to keep animals away, and signal for help.

The cave ended in a fall of rocks and dirt closing off any further exploration for the night. The sun was almost down, and the cave was becoming darker by the minute. She rustled through the unoccupied end of the trunk and was surprised to find an old wool blanket at the bottom. Folded and wrapped in oilcloth, it was in remarkable condition, considering how long it must have been there. Carefully removing the blanket, she took the tin, knife, one of the better pans and one of the rum bottles, tied them up in the blanket and began her way back to the net shelter. It was twilight and slow going, but soon she heard the stream and recognized the tree where she'd first met Silly Bird. "Home, sweet home, Jane."

Exhausted by her short trek, she drank deeply of the sweet, fresh water in the stream. Shaking any dust or vermin from the blanket, she spread it out on the bedframe in her shelter and eased herself down. It was getting easier to move, but her ribcage still burned intensely with any exertion. She let her mind drift and soon her eyelids were too heavy to hold open. She sank into sleep. Her last thought brought a smile to her face; I hope Silly Bird doesn't wake up with a hangover.

Somewhere, off in the distance of her mind, she heard the soft words of the angels, "*Sleep. Sweet dreams.*"

Chapter 20

Evie knocked on Callista's door. Wilmer and Callista lived in a small quaint house in Port Isabel. It was well kept with potted palms and climbing bushes. Evie convinced Conrad and Pete to remain in the SUV and listen in, as she talked with the couple.

Callista opened the door and Evie got a whiff of spicy meat and baking bread. It was wonderful.

"Evie! What a surprise." Callista held a dishtowel, wiping her hands. "Come in." She opened the screen door wide.

"Sorry to interrupt your dinner, but...I have a problem."

Callista hollered toward the garage where heavy clinking of weights could be heard. "Wilmer, Evie's here!" She took a frying pan of bubbling meat and sauce off the burner, setting it on a trivet. "Is it Andrea?"

The anxious look on the woman's face only served to reinforce Evie's belief that Wilmer and Callista had no knowledge of Andrea's kidnapping, and they were not involved. Evie hung her head. She really felt bad about lying to them both. "Yes, I'm afraid it is. Can we sit?"

A sweaty and pumped Wilmer stepped through the door and pulled out a chair for Evie. "Vut is wrong?"

"I really don't know where to begin. First, I need to

apologize. I've not been honest with you." She studied the tablecloth. It matched the towel Callista still held. Her kitchen was so cute and sweet. It almost made Evie's eyes water. "Andrea is not with her sister in New York." She tried to look as apologetic as she could. She hoped they would believe her.

"I knew it!" Callista threw her towel across the kitchen. "She left him, didn't she? I knew something was wrong when she was working out."

"Da blue funk. Ya." Wilmer shook his head. "She vas not happy lately."

"How can we help? Where is she?" Callista was jumping in just like a good friend would.

"Is dat Conrad out dare?" Wilmer peered out the kitchen window through the lacy curtains.

"Yes. I asked him to wait outside until I could explain this mess. Please let me get through this..." Evie opened her arms in a pleading gesture. "You're not going to like it."

They both took a seat at the table and pushed the dinner settings aside.

"Okay. Go." Callista put both elbows on the table and leaned in. "He didn't hit her, did he? Cause I can have Wilmer—"

"No, no, no! For heaven's sake, no. Andrea didn't leave. She was kidnapped!" Evie waved away the idea that Conrad had abused his wife.

Calli jumped up. "What?"

Wilmer pulled his girlfriend back into her chair. "Let her talk, *meine liebling*." His face had taken on a serious expression, quieting his girlfriend immediately.

Evie started again. "She was taken out of the club in a rolled-up rug, unconscious." She paused to let the information sink in. "Yesterday morning."

"Dat is vhy she miss our lunch!" He took Callista's hand. "How do you know dis?"

"Security footage from the athletic store behind the club. Pete and Conrad got it from the store's camera." She nodded. "This is the part you won't like."

Wilmer encouraged her to go on with a wave. His face wore the expression of someone who already suspected something.

"Moto and your brother are involved. We have video of them carrying the rug." She stopped again.

"So that's why Moto disappeared. I knew something was up. And Keizer? He's involved? You're sure?" Innocent Callista was genuinely surprised. The shock on her face was real.

"I do not doubt vhat you say. My brother is not goot person." He was shaking his head as he spoke. "And I know Moto falsed his papers. Mr. Dornbecker asked me to keep eye on Moto just last veek. Ya. Dis is bad. And Keizer is in it, ya?"

"Can we come in now?" Pete's voice was buzzing in Evie's ear.

"So, I take it you are not part of this?" Evie looked directly at Wilmer, then at Callista.

Both shook their heads, then Wilmer spoke. "Dis is very bad for me as vell. Do da police know? Vill I lose my vork permit? Ya." Wilmer looked distraught, shaking his head sadly.

"No police. The kidnappers said they will kill Andrea if we contact the police. They want codes to Conrad's new government project."

Callista gasped and quickly covered her mouth. Tears welled in her beautiful chocolate eyes. "Oh no."

She squeaked out. "I bet Keizer heard me and Andrea talking about Conrad's company." Then her tears turned to confusion. "But we never talked about any project. She was very careful about what she said concerning his work. It was always *just government* stuff. I didn't really care, I just liked to train with Andrea. Oh, my God. This is so bad. Did I cause this?" The tears were back, and Wilmer pulled Callista close, rubbing her arm gently.

"No, Calli-*meine*. Do not so fret. Vee vill figure dis out, ya?" He looked speculatively at Evie and then glanced toward the car parked outside. "Ya?"

Evie pointed to her ear. "They are asking if they can come in now? Conrad and Pete. Is it okay?"

"Of course. We have to help!" Callista leaned toward Evie and spoke loudly, punctuating each word with a pause. "Please. Come. In. Now." Then she jumped up and went to the door.

Conrad, Pete, Wilmer, Evie and Callista wouldn't fit in the tiny kitchen, so they all took seats in the somewhat larger living room. Evie led the introductions.

"Wilmer, Callista, this is Peter Newcastle, Conrad's partner in the company. You all know Conrad." She turned to Wilmer. "They've heard everything we've said." She pointed to her ear bug again.

"Can you tell us anything about your brother, or Moto, that will help us find them, or Andrea?" Conrad sat on the edge of a flowery couch, his hands gripped together. The tension showed in the protruding veins and white knuckles of both hands. "We had Moto, but he got away after fingering your brother."

"Dis explain a lot. Keizer has been very secretive lately. Possibly because I have asked him to leave soon." Wilmer was thinking. "He spoke about big deal soon. Could dis be da ransom?"

"They don't want money. They want information about one of my projects." Conrad sat forward.

Pete pulled him back. "Down, boy. These two are helping."

"Yeah!" Callista chimed in. "Keizer kept saying he would soon have a chunk of money to buy a ranch in Argentina. He didn't want to go back to Germany." She looked into the kitchen where three place settings had been shoved to the side. "He didn't come back for dinner tonight, and Keizer never misses a meal."

"That makes sense." Pete snorted. "Moto got away and knows we are looking for him and Keizer. They're probably hiding somewhere with Andrea. We have to find them before…" He paused before saying the obvious. "Any ideas how to find your brother?"

"He goes to a bar up by the Holiday Inn and Suites. It's a German place. Serves really heavy beer." Callista looked toward Wilmer and he nodded her on. "Keizer's an alcoholic." She whispered, embarrassed as if she'd had something to do with his character foibles. "Wilmer pays his tab."

Evie, sitting next to Callista, gave her a tight hug. "It's okay, Calli. It's not your fault."

Both women knew that, but the confirmation hug between the two women was comforting anyway.

"Vait! Keizer has papers hidden under his bed. I find them looking for drink. I don't like him drunk around Calli. I don't trust him."

Calli look strangely at Wilmer. "He's never been

inappropriate, Wilmer."

"Goot. I would have to kill him. Brother or not." Wilmer got up and headed down a hallway. "Come, come."

Conrad and Pete followed Wilmer while Evie stayed with Callista.

"Evie, I swear Wilmer has nothing to do with Andrea's kidnapping." She whispered.

"I believe you, Calli. Really. And I felt so bad about lying to you. I hate that, but they threatened to kill Andrea if we told anyone." She hugged the perky trainer. "Cat's out of the bag now."

Calli's perpetual enthusiasm got a shot in the arm and she hugged Evie back.

"We have to rescue Andrea. The club wouldn't be the same without her." She frowned. "*I* wouldn't be the same without her. She was the one who convinced me to go for my dreams. Me and Wilmer. She talked business and gave us design ideas. She's so smart. I—"

"We'll figure this out. And protect Wilmer at the same time. He's a trooper." Evie reassured her. "And cute as the dickens!"

That comment brought a smile back to Calli's face.

"What about your *relationshipee*, huh?" Simon's voice came over the ear bug and Evie laughed.

"My boyfriend just made a joke." Evie pointed to her ear bug. "He's at Pete's, doing some checking on his mega-computer. He's a techy kind of guy."

Callista leaned close to Evie's ear. "Hello. How. Are. You?"

"Fine, thank you, Miss Callista."

Evie spoke the words for Simon out loud. Callista clapped her hands. "This is so James Bondish! Can I have one?"

"Don't have any more, or I'd give you one." Evie would never have given Calli an ear bug to follow all of their communications, but it didn't hurt to let her think it would have been a possibility.

Conrad and Pete emerged from the hallway, followed by Wilmer.

"Anything?" Evie was hopeful.

Pete held up a couple magazines. "Porno. Candy wrappers. Two empty bottles of some kind of German beer, and a couple receipts for…" Pete read the pale type. "a Shell gas station up island." Pete shrugged.

"I am sorry dere is not more. Keizer's clothes are gone." Wilmer sat next to Calli who leaned into his arms. "Vhat else can vee do?" Evie could clearly understand why Wilmer wanted this situation resolved as quickly and quietly as possible. He had a lot at stake.

"It's not your fault. You didn't know." Evie waved him off. "But we can check out the gas station before it gets too dark. Maybe the clerk will remember something. Keizer can leave an impression on people."

Callista had the ill graces to snicker. "Big impression. Big, big impression." She grabbed her belly and shook the imaginary fat.

Wilmer swatted her hands down but chuckled and kissed her ear.

They were so cute together.

"Sit tight. Let us know if Keizer comes back." Evie scribbled her phone number on a scrap of napkin. "Whatever you do, do not let on you know what is going on. Master Moto's real name is Henry Mikamoto, and he killed a couple cops in New Orleans last year. I have no idea how he got to Texas, or mixed up with this kidnapping, but he's extremely dangerous."

One more woman-comfort hug and the team was back out in the SUV.

"Once Moto gets to Wilmer's brother, I'm sure Keizer won't go back to the house. He'd know better." Conrad was on the comm. "Simon? Any chance you can find some connection, anything we can use?" He headed across the causeway to South Padre Island. "We're going to check out the Shell station."

"Already on it." Simons voice was neutral and flat.

Evie mouthed; *he's in the zone*.

Both men in the SUV smiled back at her.

****

Conrad couldn't believe his luck in bringing Major Gastineau on board, but her boyfriend was a gift from the Tech Gods. Evie was a wonder as an operative. She was smooth and calm as a cucumber. Simon was a cross between Abby Shuto, Cable McCrory and Bill Gates rolled into one. And he came with his own jet and Godzilla in orange sneakers!

The Shell gas station also hosted a convenience store that sold, among snacks; medical supplies, sunscreen and day-old, over cooked hotdogs, beer, and wine. The attendant for the station couldn't remember any particular customer, but the storeowner could, and did!

"Yeah, it's that fat German guy that comes in about every other day. Buys a couple six-packs and complains about American beer." She wiped her hands on a stained apron behind the hot food case. "Usually walks, but sometimes he gets gas in this old-fashioned Beemer. He was in here yesterday. Got two corndogs and two six-packs. Paid cash. Counted out the pennies right down to the last cent." She gulped black coffee out of a horribly stained ceramic cup.

"Do you remember which way he would walk?" Pete turned on the charm just like a pro. Conrad watched Pete play his role, thinking the entire time that he would have made a very successful con man, if he hadn't teamed up with Conrad and founded GST. He was slick. Again, for the hundredth time, he said a little prayer of thanks for such great and diversely talented friends.

The woman belched like a trucker and leaned toward the window. She pointed down the side street next to the station. "That-a way."

"You, my dear, are an angel of deliverance. Thank you." Pete slid a C note under the greasy napkin holder on top of the hot food case and winked at the woman. What? Did Pete just walk around the world with hundred-dollar bills in his pockets? Conrad smirked.

While the woman's face wore a certain stunned look, her hands deftly snatched the bill from under the holder and stuffed it in her back pocket, making sure the gas attendant did not see a thing.

Outside the store, and out of hearing, Conrad commented, "So how do we want to handle the surveillance on this street? Moto knows all of us now. If he happens to see us moving in, he'll take off. He'll dump Keizer for sure and possibly kill Andrea. I don't doubt he is capable of it in a heartbeat." Conrad leaned against the SUV, his head hanging like a beaten puppy.

"Guys, you there?" Simon's voice sounded excited over the comm.

"Yep, go ahead, Simon." Pete responded first.

"You guys are on the corner of West Kingfisher

and Padre Boulevard?"

"Yes, why?" Conrad touched his ear to listen more carefully.

"Cause I just found video footage of an industrial style van pulling into an old auto garage/warehouse at the end of West Kingfisher. Around the time Andrea would have been nabbed, two individuals unloaded a large long object. About ten minutes later, one individual emerged and drove the van back to the South Padre Athletic Club. If I was a betting person, I'd say I just saw Andrea's kidnapping. Thank you, Homeland Security and ICE."

"Wait, Simon? Are you on my computer?" Pete was wondering how many firewalls had been violated for Simon to come up with the footage, and if Homeland Security was already tracing the IP address, right back to Pete's computer.

"Not to worry, Peter-meister. A tracer has been activated and is on the fourteenth IP skip. They only have a hundred and," he paused letting the calculator on the screen catch up, "seventy-five to follow. Should take the government Peabodys another hour and a half to find my IP, which I bounced off the DQ free wi-fi. By then, I'll be long gone." Simon was chuckling as he spoke. "So down the block to your left. Toward the mainland. It should be on the right, tucked behind some over-priced condos. Looks like there is a metal fence around the place."

"Gotcha! Thanks Simon." Conrad got into the SUV. "I'll park around back of the station. Meet me back there for some insurance."

"Insurance?" Pete shrugged at Evie who aimed a finger at the pretty boy and pulled an invisible trigger.

"Bang, bang. Thanks, baby. You are the Wiz." She couldn't see Simon, but she knew he was smiling at her comment.

She'd started calling Simon, the Wiz, when Ghost Wars hit one million players. The main character in Simon's video game was fashioned after the real Ghost of Port Chicago, their Amee. Beautiful and blond, the heroine in the game, leads a planetary insurrection that expands across Simon's fictitious universe. The more planets she gets involved in the rebellion, the more points the player wins, and the more difficult the levels of the game become. Each level adds more challenges and characters, as well as weapons and resources. The real Amee McGee was killed in the horrible explosion of Port Chicago in 1944 while awaiting a rendezvous with her love, Seaman Grandville O'Sullivan, Simon's great-uncle. Stuck on the old naval base as a ghost, unable to move on, Amee haunted the place for decades, waiting for her rendezvous that never happened. Enter Evielynne Gastineau, Provost Marshall, latent medium, and army captain on her last assignment before separation from the military. Somehow, Amee activated Evie's hereditary ability to speak to the dead, just in time to reunite a dying Grady with his love, as they moved on to the hereafter together. Since then, more than once, Evie had felt their angelic hands in her life. She and Simon both accepted their divine meddling as a part of everyday life, and death. How could they not? On that dock, months ago, they'd both been given a glimpse of heaven, a gift they could neither deny, nor forget.

As Conrad and Pete snuck down one side of the street, Evie took the other. Conrad had provided some pretty sweet firepower from a special compartment in the back of his SUV. Once a spec ops guy, always armed and ready! Conrad carried an FN 5.7 X 28 close to his chest. The small caliber handgun fired a high-velocity rifle cartridge that did significant damage. It wasn't called the Cop-Killer for nothing. The round could pierce body armor and cinder block, yet it was light and incredibly accurate.

From Conrad's stash, Pete selected his favorite for hurt-locker equipment; a Ranger Crossbow tricked out with a multiline scope and carbon 18 arrows. After Afghanistan, he'd given up firearms all together. Conrad was well aware they made his stomach turn. It was a small part of what they both had to deal with on a daily basis, leftovers from the sand box. Pete wouldn't touch a gun, but he didn't have to. The crossbow was a silent killer, with three hundred feet-per-second power. He and Conrad used to shoot competitively on an archery range south of Reynosa, on the Mexican side. That was before Andrea and the unexpected growth of GST.

Evie carried a Walther PPQ tucked into the waistband of her sweats and a couple extra mags stuck in each side of her bra. Apparently, bras were good for more than one thing, after all!

"Let's get to it. Fifteen yards, to the right." Conrad motioned to his position and moved from shadow to shadow, whispering into his comm.

"I got the back, but there isn't much here. Couple of barrels and a port-a-potty. A really dirty port-a-potty." Pete slipped over the fence with ease and not a sound. It had been several years since they'd needed their covert skills, but it still amazed Conrad how fast they could slip right back into play.

"Roger that. I got Rad's six." Evie was back in the sand box on recon. For Conrad, it was a good and bad feeling, all at the same time. The exhilarating feeling of impending danger mixed with the knowledge that this may be the last thing you do in the world, lent a kind of adrenaline high to the whole operation. But the flip side was intense fear that this might be the last thing you do in life. Or in Andrea's life. Conrad swallowed his fear and focused. It was what a soldier did to survive, most of the time.

"Going in." Conrad found a break in the fencing where two massive sheets of corrugated metal had rusted and separated in the marine environment. He bent one side back just enough to skinny through. Evie followed, watching every step. Silent as ghosts, they crept up on the building.

The old cement and metal place had seen better days. None of the outside lights were functional, many missing bulbs altogether. The yard was a maze of old car bodies, parts and rusted, unidentifiable metal junk. Old cable coils and pans full of some kind of dark, thick liquid dotted the ground. Various car doors and bumpers stood against one wall, while a leaning scaffolding precariously propped up more large truck parts. A stack of tires provided the perfect staircase to an upper window.

Conrad motioned to Evie in the sign language soldiers were used to. He headed up the tire stack as she remained on the ground, providing cover from behind an old truck bed.

"In position." Conrad bobbed his head above the windowsill, then down again. The window was open, and apparently, he was in a good location. He raised his head for a longer period, motioning to Evie who translated the message to Pete.

"Rad says two people inside. One is Moto. He assumes the other is Keizer." Evie crouched behind the box whispering into her comm.

"Roger that. Back door is locked. No entry here. In position." Pete's quiet voice responded.

Conrad sent another set of signals.

"One handgun. One rifle." Evie suppressed a giggle. "Five empty beer bottles. This may be quicker than we think."

Conrad rejoined Evie on the ground and huddled behind the truck box. "Moto is in bad shape. Keizer is just sitting. Let's go on my three. You cover me from above." Conrad was personally aware of Evie's ability to shoot, and was confident she could handle the sniper duty tonight. "Pete, keep an eye on the back in case Keizer is a fast fat man."

Pete responded. "Roger that…"

Evie climbed into position atop the tire stack and motioned to Conrad. "In position."

Pete reassured. "In position. Still."

Conrad snuck across the dirt yard, careful not to step on anything that may alert the two inside of what they were about to face. When he was next to the mandoor, he slowly tried the handle.

It was not locked.

"One…two…three."

All hell broke loose.

Conrad threw the door open and rushed inside, gun drawn.

Keizer fell out of his chair and scrambled toward

the back door. Finally gaining his feet, he unlocked the heavy metal door to find Pete with an arrow pointed at his nose.

Moto dropped his ice pack and reached for the handgun on the table in front of him. It went flying across the room as a well-aimed bullet from above, hit its mark perfectly.

Keizer let out a piggy kind-of-squeal and fainted dead away. His rotund body hit the floor with a sort of splat noise.

Moto stood stock still, hands frozen over where his gun used to be.

"Move and you die." Conrad's voice was dead calm.

Evie scrambled down from her vantage point and came through the door as Pete was emptying a beer bottle over the unconscious Keizer's head. It had no effect. "Well, that went swimmingly."

Moto mumbled under his breath. "Fuckin' cunt."

"That is my least favorite word in the world, sucker." Evie cuffed Moto in the back of the head with her gun, sending him off his chair to the ground.

As soon as Moto was no longer a threat, Conrad ran in a frenzy looking for Andrea. "Andrea? Andrea? Where are you, honey?"

"I'll remember that, sweet thing. Everybody okay?" Simon's voice came over the comm. He'd been able to hear everything but had no visual on the situation.

"Roger that. Both down, thanks to your lady." Conrad smiled at Evie.

"That's my baby-girl!" Conrad could hear Bull, back at Pete's place with Simon, cheer over the comm.

Conrad ran through the filthy place calling for his wife. "Andrea? Andrea?"

Pete secured the unconscious Keizer with zip ties from the side pocket of his quiver, and relocked the door then joined in searching the building as well. "Clear." He announced as he checked the two rooms adjacent to the main shop. In the last small room, he paused. "Ah, Conrad, you might want to come here."

Rushing to his partner, thinking the worst by the tone of Pete's voice, Conrad froze at the doorway. The solid metal door stood open, but inside a bloody and tattered moving blanket lay crumpled on the floor next to two empty water bottles.

His heart stopped beating.

His lungs could draw no breath.

His gut twisted into one big knot.

Then the anger began to boil, and he came to life.

Dangerous life.

In four quick strides he was towering over a recovering Moto. "Where is she?" He viciously kicked the man on the floor. "What did you do with my wife?" He bent, shoving a fist into Moto's face. Conrad was out of patience.

"Keizer..." Moto mumbled as he tried to stand.

Keizer Dembeck still lay in a dead faint by the back door. Conrad grabbed the small ice chest from the table and emptied it onto the fat man: water, ice, bottles, cans and all. Keizer came awake immediately, squirming and wiggling away from the cold and wet puddle surrounding him. He reached for a bottle and Pete stepped on his zipped hands. "Nah ah, buddy."

Conrad grabbed him by the front of his shirt and hauled Keizer to his feet. "My wife? Where is she?"

Conrad punctuated the last question with a punch to the gut. The gurgling noise warned him just in time to step back, as Keizer emptied the contents of his stomach on the floor. The smell of rotten fish and alcohol permeated the air.

Pete covered his mouth and nose with his sleeve. "Jeeze-zuz Key-rist, what a pig." he mumbled behind the makeshift gas mask.

Evie, securing Moto to the only sturdy chair in the place, groaned.

Keizer heaved several times before he could stand up, then looked around at the situation. He looked lost and Conrad knew it. If the team didn't kill him, his brother would. Worse yet, Keizer's contact might even take care of the fat fellow when he didn't come through with the info. Conrad was sure Keizer had no way out.

Tears filled Keizer's eyes. "She got avay." He motioned to the tiny room where they'd kept Andrea. Or tried to.

"What do you mean, she got away? Where'd she go?" Conrad stomped into the room and dragged the bloody blanket out, shoving it in Keizer's face. "If this is her blood, you're a dead man."

"I am dead man either vay." Keizer hung his head, but looked sideways at Moto, who sat tied to a chair, his head hung low as well.

Keizer nodded toward his partner in crime and mouthed, "He shot her."

Conrad's head exploded! He raged at the man. "He shot her? Andrea?"

Keizer leaned against a metal pole, nodding pathetically toward Moto. "I try to stop him, but I am only..." he motioned to himself, as if to say; *I'm a tiny, insignificant person. What could I do?*

That got Moto's attention, as his head snapped up and he spit, "No. He lies! He shot the bitch."

Evie punched Moto in the mouth. "That's my second most un-favorite word in the world." Her right was a powerful comment on word usage.

Pete scratched his head. "He said, he said. I say we chain 'em both up in the yard with my pit bull. I get tired of buying all that dog food anyway." He finished the sentence with a maniacal smile.

"*Nein.* You have to believe me. Dis gink kill her." He made a gun with his fingers and placed it to his head. "Pooh in da head." Keizer begged, wiping the vomit from his chin. "I would never hurt a voman like dat."

"Gink?" Simon's voice questioned over the comm. "Is that a German thing?"

Evie answered in a hushed voice. "Combo; chink and gook. Like the n-word for Asians, only worse."

Bull's deep chuckle could be heard next. "Just when I thought I knew all them bad words…"

Moto screamed at his partner. "Shut up, you stupid fuck." He turned to Evie, pleading with the woman who might have a little more compassion than the men. Course, he couldn't have been more wrong, but he didn't know that. "That shithead was drunk. The woman got the door open somehow and ran. He shot her." He licked his bloody lip. "Up on the bridge." Moto nodded toward the channel.

Conrad grabbed Keizer by the neck, his big hand digging into the triple chin. "That right?"

Keizer nodded in the negative as Conrad began to squeeze.

"She fell off the bridge onto a garbage barge." Moto shook his head in mock sadness. "She's dead and so are we."

Keizer's face began to turn red and his hands flailed as his lungs burned for air that could not get past Conrad's tightening fingers.

"Hey, Rad. Don't kill the guy, yet." Pete gently stayed Conrad's hand, and Keizer fell to the floor, gasping for breath. "We need to know who's behind this. These two idiots can't have put this whole caper together."

Evie came to stand next to Conrad. "Between the two of them, they don't have a single brain to know about codes or your projects." She spoke softly, putting an arm around her pal.

Conrad crumbled.

His life was gone.

Nothing mattered but his wife, and their love.

And that was gone as well.

Tears welled in the seasoned soldier's eyes and he collapsed into Evie's arms.

****

Pete had never seen Conrad like that and didn't want to be an eyewitness any longer. It made him feel some way he didn't like. His friend, his battle-buddy, his partner, Rad the Impaler had an Achilles heel after all. He hadn't understood how tightly Conrad's world was wrapped around his wife. Until today, he'd never realized the woman he considered an interloper, was actually the lifeblood of his friend. He dragged Keizer away from the scene, giving Conrad and Evie their moment.

"Sit." Pete forced Keizer into the broken office

chair and secured his hands and feet with more zip ties. He took out a coin and flipped it. "Heads, you shot." He pointed at Moto. "Tails, you shot." He indicated Keizer. "Hmmmm." He took Evie's gun and held it to Moto's head.

A telltale smile crept over Keizer's face that told Pete the whole story. But there was more game to play.

Moto squeezed his eyes shut and mumbled something in a foreign language. Pete kept the gun at the man's temple. "Last rites, Moto?"

"I have done many things." His face seemed to relax a bit. "I shall be reborn as an insect to be punished for my transgressions in this world, and that which came before." He shook his head sadly. "I had thought a longer life to atone…"

"Really?" Pete was more entertained than shocked. Moto was a Buddhist! After everything he'd done, he worried about his Karma and rebirth? "You have to be kidding. Maybe you'll be reborn as gravel so people can walk on you daily, like you've walked on lives since you were old enough to take a step." Pete poked Moto's temple with the barrel of his gun.

"I do not practice as I should. My sister worries for my path to the Pure Land. And rightly so." Moto figured he was about to die.

Keizer interrupted the last confessions of his criminal partner. "He lies! All lies! You must believe me. He did all of dis. He told me I could have money if I help. Vilmer is sending me home to Germany. I cannot go. There are people who vould kill me dere."

Pete aimed the gun at Keizer's nose. "There are people right here, who will kill you, jackass. Shut up." He turned back to Moto. "So, how about some atonement right now. Tell me about this set-up. Who is behind the kidnapping and the request for classified information?"

Moto shrugged, all pretense gone. "I honestly don't know. I did a job last year with my guys. It went down bad. Me and a couple of the guys got out, but most didn't."

"Yeah, yeah. The jewelry store. The cops. We know." Pete kept the gun trained on Moto, but pulled a stool to the table, and perched on the edge.

"No, nobody knows." More head shaking. "Most of my guys and my girl got away. At first. Then they started disappearing. My sister…" Moto choked.

"Holy moly, guys. You won't believe this." Simon's excited voice was loud in all of their ears. "Henry Mikamoto's gang all turned up dead, or parts of them anyway. Even the girl and her kid. Oh my God!" They could all hear Bull's gasp as Simon continued. "Henry's sister got a very special present from some unknown perp: hands in a box! Crap, that's ugly."

"Boss, get rid of those pictures." Bull's deep voice was more a command. "Before I barf all over your computer."

Pete touched his ear bud. "That bad, huh?"

Bull's response was one word. "Worse."

Pete returned his attention to Moto as Evie and a recovering Conrad joined them at the table. "So, your guys got what they deserved and…"

"I got a burn phone. And a note. All of this," his head swiveled, "was set up for me. I got orders. I followed the orders." He nodded in the direction of Keizer. "He kept saying he needed money, so I got him to help. Bad idea, I guess."

Keizer chimed in. "He lies. All lies. I am innocent."

Conrad cuffed the German, knocking him into silence. "Go on." The deadly tone was back in his voice and Pete cringed.

"My sister was never in our gang. She has kids. They told me they'd do the same thing to her and my nieces, if I didn't do as instructed." He shrugged again. "So I moved to Texas, South Padre Island. Got the job they said to with fake papers they sent me, and followed instructions." He looked directly at Conrad. "Believe me, I've done some bad shit, but my sister and her family are innocent. They shouldn't have to pay. Not that way." Moto closed his eyes.

"Who shot my wife and why?" Conrad ground out between clenched teeth. His fingers worked the handle of his gun. Pete wondered if his buddy could maintain and not give in to his anger. Andrea was Conrad's world and his life. If she was gone, he might just be capable of anything, including murder.

"Keizer. That shit-for-brains was drunk. Again. I still can't figure out how she got that door open." Moto was in full atonement form and talking as if it were a casual conversation.

"I can."

Evie nearly jumped out of her skin. "Amee?"

Then she heard Simon's voice in her ear. "Ah, babe, we have a...visitor."

"Amee who, Evie? Who are you talking to? What visitor?" Pete was confused. One minute, Evie had been sitting still and quiet. The next she was jumping and talking about a woman named Amee?

****

"Ah, guys, I need a moment." Evie removed her ear bud and stepped away from the group. *"Amee?"*

"Of course! Do you talk to other ghosts?"

"I didn't know I could hear you anymore. I feel you sometimes." Evie just had to think her conversation, and Amee's words popped into her mind.

"I wouldn't leave you alone. Grady and I keep watch over all our people. You must know that." Amee's tone was a little petulant.

"You *helped Andrea get away?"* Evie was amazed. She knew the ghost could move things if she tried hard enough, but this was the first time since Simon's Uncle Grady joined her in heaven, that Amee had done something like open a door.

"It takes talent, and I seem to be talented." Amee's light-hearted giggle warmed Evie's soul. She'd kind of missed the little ghost in the past few months

"And humble. So is Andrea with you?" Evie was afraid to ask the question, but needed to know.

"Evie, live humans cannot be here with us. It's just for the ones who have passed. You know that. It's just me, and my Grady."

It struck her like a bolt out of the blue. "Andrea's alive! She's not with you!" Evie shouted out loud.

Three heads swiveled in her direction at the pronouncement.

Evie ran back to the table and shoved her ear bud back into her ear. "Simon, could you hear Amee?"

"Nope, but Uncle Grady gave me an earful. Andrea's alive, right?" Simon had a bit of a hitch in his voice.

"What are you two guys talking about?" By the look on their faces, Pete was now very confused, and

Conrad was right behind him.

"Evie?"

Simon came over the comm. "Hang on a minute, guys." Everyone could hear the rapid fire of the computer keys being assaulted by one fast typer. "Holy crap!"

"What?" Conrad looked at Evie then at the floor, touching his ear bud. "What's going on?"

It was Simon's turn to shock the hell out of Conrad and Pete. "Andrea is alive, folks."

Bull's cheer drowned out the rest of Simon's explanation.

"Wait. Come again..." It was Pete's turn to press his ear bud deeper into his ear. "Did I hear you say Andrea is alive?"

"Bull, shut up, man. Only one of us can be heard at a time." Simon was still punching the keys, but slower now.

"Sorry, boss. Look." Bull shouted through the comm again. "There she is!"

Without any kind of visual, Pete and Conrad were losing patience. "Where?" Conrad stood and began pacing. Evie was trying desperately to figure a way out of her little slip, without having to explain she could talk to ghosts who were feeding her intel. They would never believe it.

"On a garbage barge, crawling around. It's headed out to sea." They heard more tapping. "At 17:45 yesterday, Andrea was alive and moving."

"I gotta get back to Pete's. I gotta see this." Conrad was on his way out of the garage and headed for the car stashed behind the gas station at the end of the block.

"Evie, go with him. I'll take care of this mess."

Pete circled his head with his finger. "Go! Take care of our guy. He's messed up right now."

"What will you do..." Evie didn't want Pete to murder two men.

"Go. I got a handball friend who can help. Go!" Pete waved her off after Conrad.

"Roger that." She grabbed her gun, leaving Pete's bow behind, and sped out the door after Conrad. *"Thanks, Amee, Uncle Grady."* The only response she heard in her mind was a simple sigh and a deep chuckle, the one she remembered from the hospital where Grady lay dying, over a year ago.

She caught Conrad as he fired up the SUV. She hopped in and buckled up before the mad man at the wheel tore out of the station, and down the highway.

"Slow down, Conrad, or you'll spend the night in the stockade, not at Pete's place." She touched his shoulder.

"Who's Amee?" His eyes focused on the road, glancing right and left, watching for police cars.

"Amee?" Evie tried to play dumb. The interchange between her and her little ghost took seconds, but she truly couldn't remember what had happened in just her brain, and what she may have said out loud.

"You said, thanks, *Amee*. Who were you talking to?"

Evie let out a deep sigh. "Long story. Once we get Andrea, I'll explain everything. What we need to concentrate on now, is finding her. She is alive, Conrad. Believe me when I tell you that."

Conrad swung into the underground parking at Pete's warehouse. "Deal." He jumped out of the car and hit the elevator button. "Come on, you piece of junk."

The doors swung open almost immediately and there stood a smiling Bull. "Ready and waiting. Get in." As soon as Evie's feet crossed the threshold, Bull slammed the gate up, and hit the tenth button. "You are not going to believe what the boss found." He chuckled and clasped his huge hands in front of him.

"What Bull? What?" Now it was Evie's turn to be impatient.

Bull just stood there, a finger crossed his lips. "Lips zipped." He mumbled through closed lips. But immediately the smile returned. Bigger than ever.

Conrad was the first to burst out of the elevator as if he'd been ejected by a cannon. "Whatcha got, Simon?" Four strides and he stood next to the computer geek.

Simon turned the screen so Conrad had a better view of sixteen still photos. Evie caught up and stood just behind Conrad. A little grainy and pitted, the photos tiled the screen. Each one showed Andrea's progress from falling off the bridge to being dumped with the garbage, recovering, making a raft out of floating debris, swimming toward an island, going ashore and finally lying on the beach.

Conrad slammed his fist into the desktop, rattling the keyboard. "That's my girl!"

For the first time since they'd arrived, Evie felt a sense of relief and something close to success. Andrea was alive and now they just had to find her little island. She patted Conrad on the back as she watched tears fall from her friend's rugged face.

Chapter 21

Jane's dreams were not sweet at all. She slept fitfully, her mind filled with disjointed images of the past few days. She was at an athletic club in Germany. This incredibly handsome, Arian-looking man shouted orders in her face as she tried to keep up with the rest of the women who ran, as if the Hounds of Hell chased them. Through the Alps, up tall mountains, down into beautiful meadows that smelled of wildflowers. Jane wanted to stop and smell the fantastic scent, but the gaggle pushed her on. One petite, and very well-developed woman dragged her by the hand, through a swamp, across a bridge.

"Jump. It will be better," the sweet brunette shouted midway across the bridge.

"I can't! My feet are stuck in the cement." Jane tried to move her feet, consumed in terror.

The sweet brunette frowned, then rounded on Jane and punched her in the head.

Over the bridge Jane went, into a vast blue ocean with an ominous red sky. Her head went below the water and she could not breathe. A multi-colored parrot swam by, its wings propelling it through the water. "Help me, pretty bird." Jane begged.

"Silly Bird. Silly Bird. Got no rum." The bird began to swim circles around Jane, squawking and talking.

Jane tried to grasp ahold of the bird, to no avail. Each time she reached out, the bird swam farther away, laughing at her. After several tries Jane was almost out of air and weakening.

"Silly Bird. Rum all gone." The bird circled close and pecked viciously at Jane's floating hand.

She woke from the dream with a start. Silly Bird waddled across the ground inside her enclosure, squawking outrageously.

A wind had come up and rain pelted the tiny hut, running through the vines and netting, like a million rivers.

Lightning exploded overhead and Jane jumped. Silly Bird crouched and hopped behind her, burying its head beneath the drenched tarp. Close to her, a tree split and cracked as the electrical charge blew apart the trunk, dissipating into its roots and the surrounding ground.

"Silly Bird need rum. Rum all gone. Get me my rum." Silly Bird burrowed further beneath the covering.

"Good idea. Silly Bird." Jane pulled the tarp around her, grabbed Silly Bird, who did not object at all, and ran for the cave. "Let's go get some rum."

Silly Bird snuggled its head against Jane's neck and cooed quietly as Jane struggled for the cave as fast as she could in the wet foliage and mud.

It wasn't hard to find since lightning strikes lit the way with their brilliance and her previous steps had marked the grass. Silly Bird's feathers were wet and cold, but the bird remained close, not fighting the human contact. The humidity in the air was overwhelming and the rain came down in buckets as Jane trotted through the weeds and flowers that hung limp in the deluge.

In minutes, the cave entrance appeared, and Jane rushed through the vine doorway she'd made earlier. Inside she put Silly Bird on its perch and poured a little more rum into the dish. "There ya go, Silly Bird. Salute." She took a gulp of the rum for herself.

As the alcohol burned through her insides, warming her body and easing her pain, it occurred to Jane that she'd left everything at the little hut, including the flint. She reached out and slid her hand across the back of the macaw. "Thank you for waking me, my fine feathered friend."

The bird didn't seem to mind her touch. Or it was preoccupied with consuming the rum as fast as its little tongue would slurp! "Stay here, Silly Bird. I need to go secure my equipment."

Secure my equipment? Who talked like that?

The military!

That's who.

Was she a soldier then?

That might explain the scary guy with an AR clutched to him, in her flashes of memory.

Or maybe she'd been some kind of prisoner. The drunk fat man flashed before her eyes. He'd given her water. Maybe he was the jailor, or? "Ack!" Jane hit her head with her fist. "Why can't I remember? Damn it!"

She left the cave and crawled down to her hut. The scarce path was so thick with mud now, the going was rough and sloppy. Retrieving the few items she'd taken from the cave earlier, she was halfway back when a mighty bolt of pure white light hit a tree near the top of the nearest hill with a deafening crack. The rumble that followed had Jane on the run. How she associated the deafening sound with an avalanche, she would never know. But she ran. As fast as she could, away from her little hut, the streambed, and the beach.

Gaining the side of the hill where the cave began, she turned back, just in time to see half of the hill come sliding down in a volley of mud and rock. Trees were swept away, and the landscape turned from a wild Garden of Eden, to a mud slicked barren hillside in seconds. She crouched there in stunned silence. If Silly Bird had not awakened her…

The bird's slurred squawks pierced the quiet. "Andi, got rum? Rum all gone."

Andi?

Somehow that name was familiar.

Andi? Was that the previous owner of the bird, and this cave?

It must have been since the bird knew the name.

Andi? Andrew? Angelo? An…

Andi tickled her brain, but no other name seemed to fit.

Jane stood and walked into her new home. There was nothing left of the other. She unloaded the tarp and placed things next to the wall where she would not stumble over them in the dark. The moon had come out with the passing of the storm and the cave glowed with a silvery light that lay in intricate patterns across the cave floor. It was still night and Jane was exhausted, both physically and emotionally. She lay down next to the steamer trunk and pulled the tarp around her like a cocoon. Her stomach growled outrageously.

"Good night, Silly Bird." Tomorrow was another day and another challenge of survival. She said a silent prayer of thanks for her bird's warning and slipped off to sleep.

In her dreams, the scary man in camo and dark glasses was always behind her. Pushing her to move faster. Poking at her with the barrel of his gun. Yanking her arm when she veered to close to the edge, of what? At one point, he threw her a bulky bag to carry. It was heavy and dirty, having been picked up on the trail to somewhere? Her mind teetered on the brink of remembering. They walked until her feet were raw and bleeding, then continued on even farther. Every once in a while, the fat man would pop up like a practice target in some macabre arcade, drunk in his chair, snoring loudly, but hand extended with a bottle of water. Some bottles she drank. Some she poured on her feet. Still the scary man prodded her on.

As the morning sun shone through the mouth of the cave, Jane slipped into a lighter sleep and a different kind of dream. She sat on an immaculate lawn, her face to the warm morning sun. Children played near the azure pool and a perfect blonde woman served her lovely cucumber and shrimp sandwiches cut into two-inch squares. The children screamed and laughed with abandon.

In a soft, almost undetectable voice, the woman commented, "Andi went away. She is gone forever, I think." A glistening tear hung, quivering at the tip of full, mascaraed eyelashes. Her crystal blue eyes turned a deep sea-green as the tear cascaded down her powdered cheek, leaving an ugly trail through her flawless makeup. "The children will miss her." The woman spread her flowery skirt across the green grass and tucked her legs demurely beneath her, as the children, one after the other, came slipping down a bright shiny slide. As they hit the ground, each one lined up behind the other, heads hung low. When the line was complete, the children marched toward the woman on the grass. As they passed her, each one whispered, "I miss Andi." The woman held the rusty old pot Jane had found in her cave, and each child shed two tears into the pot before moving to the end of the line and repeating the sequence. Soon the pot was overflowing, and so was Jane's heart. Whoever this Andi was, she was truly loved and cherished by this woman and the children.

In her dream, Jane raised a heavy camera and snapped pictures as the children paid homage to their Andi. Silly Bird flew to the pot and perched on the edge, rocking back and forth precariously.

"Silly Bird. Got no tears." It ducked its head and drank from the pot, then flew to Jane's lap and settled close to her belly. There it sat, cooing and gurgling with pleasure.

Jane woke to the sound of her stomach growling amazingly loud. She was weak and tired, and just wanted to close her eyes and go back to sleep, but the dreams were worse than her reality, and she knew she had to find food soon. Her belly told her that. It growled again as if to say "Yep. We're hungry!"

She unrolled from her tarp cocoon and stretched carefully. Many of her wounds were closing and didn't seem to be infected. A scab had formed over her eye and was crusty and tender, but not too painful. Jane felt her rib cage and winced. Thanks to the rain deluge the night before, she was not quite as filthy as yesterday, but her hair was still crusted with sand and mud. She finger-combed the worst rat's nests out and wound it around a stick, then secured it at the back of her neck in an impromptu bun, of sorts.

She'd lost her driftwood crutch in the net hut, so she used the steamer trunk to clamber to her feet, then leaned on the wall of the cave as a wave of nausea and dizziness washed across her head and stomach. "Great, vomiting with nothing in your stomach is a totally useless effort." She chided herself as she held her breath and swallowed the saliva welling in her mouth.

"Number something on the survival list is food. Today it's number one." She chanced a step and found the dizziness had dissipated. "Well, Silly Bird, my guardian and savior, I need food."

The crazy macaw cocked its head. "Rum all gone. Got rum?"

Jane laughed. "Rum is not food. What do you eat when you are not drinking yourself into a stupor?"

To her amazement, Silly Bird flew to the mouth of the cave and looked back at her.

"Okay, I'm coming." Jane found that her foot was much better and she limped much less. As she followed the waddling macaw through the cave opening, a fantastical scene greeted her. Stunned, Jane gasped.

Half of the hill above her hut had slid into the ocean below, leaving a ginormous scar through the island. Trees and massive amounts of vegetation lay in a jumble at the bottom of the hill. A small trickle of water worked its way down the middle of the mess, to pool above the rubble, already creating the beginnings of a small pond.

The waterfall was gone. Her hut was nowhere to be seen. The trail ended at the mudslide just feet away.

"Looks like we find a different path, Silly Bird."

The macaw squawked and took to wing.

"Great for you, but I can't fly!" Jane surveyed the newly formed landscape. To one side lay the impassible slide. To the other, moss covered rocks and bushes hid a very faint pathway she'd not recognized before. "Ah ha!"

Jane worked her way along the path, taking great care to remain upright. There was very little to help her regain her feet if she fell. The path seemed to curve around the side of a rock outcropping, and slowly led toward the beach. Below, Jane could make out another lagoon. Or maybe an extension of the lagoon she'd first seen. The calm turquoise water looked inviting. "Well, I know I can swim just fine." She hurried toward the water.

The denim shirt she wore was one more enigma that teased her mind. It was *all* she wore. The sleeves were torn and full of holes. One cuff was missing. It hung to her knees like a billowing dress, but where was everything else? Panties? A bra? Shorts?

She slipped out of the shirt and waded out into the water and slowly submerged herself, letting her dirty hair go free. Saltwater wasn't necessarily good for a woman's hair, however; it beat sweat, mud and caked sand. The water restored some of her vigor and she just about gulped a mouthful of saltwater when something hard bumped into her head. She surfaced with a scream, flailing away from whatever had touched her, only to find a brown, hairy coconut floating a few inches away. Silly Bird flew circles above her head, screeching.

Jane looked into the clear blue sky and waved a thanks to the colorful spot above her. "Thanks for the warning, Silly Bird." She grasped the nut and waded ashore. "Food!"

Smashing the thing against a rock on her third try, Jane picked up a large piece of the husk and chewed the inside white meat away. "Yes! A feast at last!"

Silly Bird alighted next to her and began licking the coconut milk from the rock and chomping small pieces in its hard, sharp bill. "Got rum." It cooed enthusiastically, white specks of coconut dotting its dark beak.

"Oh yeah. Got rum!" Jane was beginning to speak Silly Bird's language.

Refreshed from her swim and a breakfast of coconut, Jane sat on the beach watching the ocean as the sunlight played on the water. Across the lagoon, to what she figured was the east, sat the remnants of a small boat. At some point, it had been tied to a tree, an old rope, now green with moss still clung to the trunk. A kind of rough table sat at the bottom of the tree made of lashed sticks. Jane watched the patterns on the water before deciding to swim across and explore the other side of the lagoon. Toward the ocean she could see an opening in the reef where the waves were smaller and did not crash onto coral heads. Farther toward the lagoon's end near the shore, a small river wound back into the jungle.

Would there be a dangerous current? Could she make it across without a problem? What about that shark?

Jane took a long palm frond and dragged it along the beach closer too the river's edge. She tossed the frond into the water, much to her rib's objection, and watched. It moved lazily toward the ocean.

So, there was a current.

The actual river was only about twenty feet across at that point and the spot she wanted to swim toward, was now several yards out toward the ocean. Silly Bird sat on a rock, watching her intently.

"Someone lived here, at least for a while. Was that Andi? Your person?" She queried the macaw.

Silly Bird cocked its head. "Yuck, yuck, yuck. Andi's here. Andi got rum?"

Jane laughed and then grabbed her rib cage again. It felt wonderful to laugh and painful at the same time, but not half as bad as yesterday. Her foot was so much better, Jane was amazed. And so were the wounds she'd received when-when what?

She pushed the thought of her malfunctioning mind away and waded into the water. The mixture of river and ocean water was a bit of a surprise. Flowing warm, then cold, then warm, Jane swam, prepared to fight any current that might wash her away. In the end she swam and drifted to almost the exact point where she wanted to be. Leveraging herself against the wrecked boat, Jane waded ashore to explore. Silly Bird flew to the old table and sat watching its new friend.

A red bougainvillea wound around the base of the tree where the table leaned, its flowers decorating the small structure, creating the appearance of a delicate hutch. The previous owner had constructed a shelf of long sticks below the tabletop. On the shelf lay a rusty machete with a carved wooden handle.

"Ah hah! One more tool." Jane reached for the handle only to draw back in a flash.

Silly Bird squawked and took wing. Landing on the prow of the wrecked boat, it screeched. "Watch out! Watch out. Spill the rum. Rum all gone."

Jane was learning to trust Silly Bird's warnings. Something moved next to the machete. She peered beneath the tabletop but saw only sticks.

"Spill the rum. Spill the rum. Rum all gone!" Silly Bird continued to squawk, as Jane looked closer. Stretched out like just one more stick, lay a long brown snake. Its black beady eyes watched the newcomer with little interest.

"Well, howdy, Mr. Boa." She recognized the Cook's Tree Boa from…from what? "And how do I know who you are, Mr. Boa? How'd you get here anyway?"

More puzzles and no answers. It was becoming a lifestyle.

A fleeting thought wound through her mind; he would make a great photo! She'd name it Boa's Bed and send it to…

Send a photo?

To somewhere?

Someone?

The thought was gone.

Rummaging through the bushes, Jane found a stick and carefully lifted the small boa off the table and tossed it into the bushes, reminding herself to step more carefully in the future and look before she reached.

"Once again, Silly Bird, I owe you a debt of thanks." She used the stick to clear away some of the greenery that had overgrown the back of the table. Boas weren't poisonous, but they had teeth. A heavily accented voice reminded her, *anything with teeth can bite!*

Heavily accented voice?

Whose voice?

What accent?

She poked and prodded with her stick, finally contacting something hard and solid sounding. Carefully pulling vines and leaves away, she saw a bit of blue. It was a can!

"Oh my God! Spam!" Jane pulled the small square can from the bushes and did a little victory dance. "Look, Silly Bird! It's Spam. And the key is still there!" The blue can was rusty around the edges, but the big yellow letters were almost clean and clearly spelled out its contents. She turned to her companion, "This stuff lasts forever." She rubbed the grime from the bottom of the can and searched for an expiration date.

Really? An expiration date?

On a Spam can?

What was she thinking...

She'd seen a lot of Spam cans in her life, and this one was probably older than she was. But as long as the can was intact and not bulging, it was probably okay. Especially if she cooked it. Using the wet sleeve of her shirt, Jane rubbed the can clean of most of the grime and inspected the rims. It looked fine. She set the can on the tabletop and rummaged through the vines again, but all she found was a moldy box of crackers that had already been found by some hungry animal, and a cake of some kind of soap. The wrapper was long gone, and the bar had half melted into the shelf. It was tan and smelled slightly antiseptic.

"Hmmm, dinner and a wash. My world is looking up."

Silly Bird watched with mild interest.

Jane took the machete and wacked at some of the clinging vegetation. Not much happened. The edge hadn't been sharpened in probably a hundred years, and the handle promptly split in two. The blade was rusty and gouged in several places.

After closer inspection, Jane found nothing more of use, so she crawled along the bank of the river into the jungle, using her stick to test the way and keeping the machete close, just in case she needed to beat off a marauding boa or an attacking hutia. The rodents were pervasive in the Caribbean and larger than rats, but generally docile.

Jane laughed at herself. How did she know that?

Was she some kind of biologist?

Or a wildlife specialist?

That could explain her desire to photograph everything.

She was beginning to add up the puzzle pieces, keeping them safe in the back of her mind. If she remembered enough, maybe they'd form her own photo, a picture of who she was. And maybe not. First, she'd have to survive, and now she had two more pieces of that puzzle.

She sat on a rock, cooling her sore feet in the river and watched the water. This place was beautiful, like the real Garden of Eden. It even had a snake!

A small fish jumped near the far shore. That's when she noticed a kind of path. It led into the jungle and back the way she'd come. Which path to take back to her cave? The beach with its safe scramble over rocks and across sand? Or the more risky road through new and unexplored territory?

She'd already chosen one path in life, and it must not have been a very good one, considering her current circumstances.

Jane headed back to the beach, her Spam can tucked in the big front pocket of her oversized shirt, a dull machete in one hand, a clearing stick in the other.

****

Simon rubbed his eyes. He'd been at his computer all night, searching. It was close to sunrise and Conrad was wearing a path in the floor of Pete's apartment. The crazed man had been pacing all night, pausing occasionally to lean over Simon's shoulder and grunt at what he did not understand. Simon briefly considered how many sites he'd been to, that he never should have, and how many federal laws he'd violated in the process of trying to locate Andrea. He'd covered his tracks, but he never knew when he'd come up against a smarter coder, a better hacker. It could happen, he reminded himself.

But not likely.

Evie curled in an overstuffed chair, dosing fitfully, mumbling every once in a while in her light sleep.

Pete and his handball buddy on the police force had returned around 3:00 a.m., and now they sat at the kitchen table across the room, talking quietly, concocting the story that would explain how Henry Mikamoto, Louisiana's most wanted man, had been efficiently apprehended by the South Padre Island Police department while investigating an anonymous breaking-and-entering complaint. In an attempt to escape, Mikamoto had been injured, but was taken alive and a bit worse for the wear. Mikamoto's accomplice was a legal alien on a tourist visa. He was immediately arrested and detained for deportation. Apparently, the German tourist had resisted arrest as well, and was being treated at an ICE detention center for his bad behavior.

Simon replaced the headphones he'd been wearing earlier to block out the noise of the others. He liked to work in silence, or while listening to hard rock. It was a curious anomaly in his character, but it worked for him. Before he could tune in to his music channel, a familiar voice came over the headphones.

"Check the weather, boy."

He jumped at the familiar voice. "Uncle Grady?" Simon whispered.

"Just check the weather and don't ask a lot of questions, son."

Uncle Grady was often frustrated with Simon's thousand-question-games as a child. Sometimes Simon used it as a way to get the older man off task and Simon out of a chore. But sometimes he was just hungry for knowledge, and wanted to know everything about everything. Many a time, his uncle would resort to the very same statement that put a lid on conversation, and got Simon to do what Grady wanted. Simon chuckled. His heart beat with a new warmth. "Roger that, Uncle Grady." Simon spoke quietly so others would not wonder if he was losing his marbles.

"Gettin' kinda cocky there, aren't ya, boy. Check that weather."

"Yes, sir." Simon pulled up the latest NOAA map of the Texas coastline out to Cuba. "Holy crap!"

Evie stirred and Conrad was at his shoulder in less than a heartbeat. "What? What's happening?"

"Simon, you find something?" Evie uncurled and leaned over the chair arm.

"I hope our girl's not on that island chain. Take a look at the weather." He pointed to a tiny island chain and a massive storm that swirled white and gray over the area. "These islands are right in the eye of the storm." He didn't want to finish the rest. He was waiting for a particular and very secret satellite, to reach the perfect place in its geosynchronous orbit. Then it could spy on the island he figured Andrea might have swum to, given a very sophisticated algorithm he'd developed to analyze the wind, currents, ocean traffic and garbage barge pattern of dumps. The combined data should pinpoint which tiny speck in the Caribbean would be the target island to search. Otherwise, they could spend a lifetime searching the area and never find Conrad's wife. The satellite would be in perfect position in three hours, forty-five minutes and six seconds. The countdown timer ticked down the seconds in the upper right corner of his screen.

"The storm hasn't been rated as a hurricane, yet. But look at the development. If it gathers more power and speed, it won't be long until we have a full-blown hurricane in our search area." Simon confirmed aloud what he saw on the screen.

Conrad looked desperately at the rest of the group.

Officer Billings and Pete grouped around Simon. "Shit." Pete patted Conrad's shoulder like a brother consoling his sibling on the receipt of bad news.

"Good thing about this," Officer Billings pointed to the storm's eye. "It's moving north and east. It'll crawl up the coast and lose power quickly. Louisiana doesn't need another Katrina." He hitched up his britches and utility belt. "Guess we're done here, Pete. See you Thursday afternoon? I gotta get some of my money back." He turned to Conrad, hand extended. "Nice to finally meet you, Mr. McIntyre, wish it was under better circumstances. We'll take care of your little problem for you." He winked at Conrad. "See you at the Policemen's Ball next month? It's a fundraiser. Pete never misses it." With another wink, Officer Billings headed for the stairs. Apparently, he'd done the elevator once, and thought the better of the stairs.

"Wait." Simon yelled after the officer. He rummaged around in his computer case and grabbed a CD. "Here, give this to that guy who plays Ghost Wars." Simon scribbled his name across the front of the case. "Tell him thanks for helping me and my girlfriend."

"I'm sure he'll have a heart attack when I hand it to him! Signed and everything. Thanks, Mr. O'Sullivan."

As Officer Billings took the stairs, Simon swore he could hear Bull murmur *relationshipee*, when the door closed on the retreating officer.

Simon turned to Conrad. "My eyes in the sky will be over the islands in about three hours. Then we should be able to see something, provided the cloud cover doesn't block the view." He pointed to the timer.

"What kind of eyes in the sky? A satellite? Plane?" Simon was sure Conrad hadn't slept for two days and his mind was fuzzy at best.

"Ah? Well, I guess you could call it a satellite." Simon's fingers twitched. He smiled sheepishly. "It's classified, sort of. If I tell ya, I have to shoot ya." He resorted to the famous saying that ended any more questions.

"Boss, you gonna get us arrested?" Bull had joined the group and hovered over Simon.

"Nope. They'll never find my IP address." Simon took his chair and put the headphones on.

****

"Famous last words." Pete shook his head. "Evie, how many people in the world can do what your friend here is doing?"

"Five." Evie curled up and closed her eyes.

"They'll find him...us." Conrad returned to his pacing and Pete wandered toward his bed on a raised platform across the room. Before collapsing onto the comforter, Pete queried his partner. "You want me to call the office and let Rose know we won't be in?"

Pete's executive secretary was Miss Efficiency and would usually send a text if Pete was not at his desk by nine in the morning. She had been with GST for about a year and was originally hired for her high-tech skills and expressed loyalty. She had a habit of tracking Pete like a dog, but made his life easy in so many unexpected ways. She'd even done background checks on his various liaisons. The ones she knew about. Just in case there was an implied threat to the company's lucrative government contracts. Rose Mayfield was also a stunning woman who always looked smart and classy. Everything matched from her shoes to her earrings, like she bounced off a fashion magazine ad every day.

"Nah. You'll get fifty questions. I'll call Rita and ask her to pass on a discreet word. She's the best, and can handle anything that comes up." Conrad ceased his pacing and whipped out his phone.

"What are you gonna tell her?" Pete came down the three steps from his *bedroom* area. His place had very few walls and he liked it that way. He could see what was coming and who was around at all times. Even his master bath had a glazed glass door.

"That I have a family problem and you are helping

me deal with it. She won't ask a personal question, so we're safe." Conrad stared at his phone for a second, then hit the autodial number for his office. "Although I don't know why it matters now."

Pete spun and returned to his bed, flopping on the mattress and kicking off his shoes. "Let me know when you have something." In seconds, a soft snore came from the bedroom area.

****

"Good morning Rita. Pete and I won't be in this morning. We're dealing with a family issue."

"Of course, sir. Is there anything I can help with?" The concern was immediately apparent in Rita's voice.

"No, but thank you for asking. I'll let you know how the day goes. Could you let Rose know without a lot of questions? Pete doesn't need a million text messages."

"My pleasure, sir." Rita was good at keeping things to herself and thoroughly disliked Rose's intrusions into Pete's life. She knew her job and did it with grace and efficiency. That's what Conrad appreciated about his administrative assistant.

"Thanks." Conrad hung up and stared at the walls. Evie had gone back to sleep in her ball in the chair. Simon was in the zone. Conrad could hear something from the Rock of Ages album playing faintly as he skirted the wiz at his computer. Bull was slumped on the kitchen chair, head hanging over a cup of very black coffee. Conrad resumed pacing. The amount of nervous energy coiled inside him precluded any sleep he might have tried to get.

Conrad poured himself his fifth cup of coffee.

Two hours and fifty-five minutes…

****

Evie twitched in her sleep. Something was eating at her pleasant dream. She was wandering through the jungle with a bird. It kept talking about rum. Pretty soon, she came upon a lagoon where a man was fishing with a kind of throwing net. His clothing was tattered, and he looked like he hadn't eaten a solid meal in months. In the distance Evie could see half of a small ship sitting above the coral reef. So, he was a castaway!

"Captain's got rum. Give me my rum. Captain Bob got rum." The bird continued to chatter.

In the distance Evie could hear a woman's voice. "Silly Bird, where are you? I have your rum."

Evie jerked awake.

It was Andrea's voice!

"Find Captain Bob and his bird and you'll find Andrea." Amee whispered to Evie over the various snores in the room.

Jumping out of the chair, a little too fast, Evie swayed as a wave of dizziness washed over her. She grabbed the arm of the chair. "Simon?"

Simon was truly in his zone, as music blasted over his headphones and his fingers flew over his keyboard. The newest revisions to Ghost Wars was under development while everyone waited for the satellite to move into place. Evie recognized the program immediately. She could hear the thump of the bass music Simon was listening to.

She stumbled to her boyfriend's side and tapped him on the shoulder. Her legs had gone to sleep, as she herself, slept in a ball.

Simon almost jumped out of his skin. "Evie, say something before you scare the living daylights out of me!" Simon removed his headphones and Evie could still hear the music.

"You're gonna go deaf with that volume up so high." She'd said it more than once and got the typical response she expected.

"Huh?" Simon teased.

"Right. Simon, would you look up, and I know this sounds crazy, but can you find anything on a Captain Bob who may have been wrecked on one of the islands we are looking at?"

"A castaway? Named Bob? Could you be a little more specific?" Simon looked at her as if she were out of her mind.

"Not really. But there has to be something." She leaned close to Simon's ear. "Amee said to find Captain Bob and we'd find Andrea."

"Amee talked to you?" Simon smiled and shook his head. "Uncle Grady's been bugging me too." He took his *relationshipee* in his arms and hugged her tightly. After a close moment, Simon turned to his computer. "Let's see what we can find out about Captain Bob."

Typing in all kinds of related data, Simon initiated his own special search engine and sat back. "Mirror, mirror, on the wall, where's Captain Bob after all?"

Evie giggled until the computer chimed with a list of topics. Scrolling through, Simon clicked the pages until he paused at the fifth one. "Hello! I think we have it!" He clicked on the title; *Captain Bob Fisher Found Alive After Seven Years on Pretoria Atoll*. A picture of a skinny, bearded man in tattered clothing, fishing with a net, opened.

"That's him!" Evie almost yelled in Simon's ear.

"That's who Amee was talking about. Captain Bob!" She leaned down and gave Simon a noisy wet kiss. "You, my love, are the Bomb!"

"What? What's going on?" Conrad was behind them in a flash and Bull sat up straight at the noise.

"I think we may have the name of the island where Andrea is." Evie was so excited, all weariness had fled.

"The satellite?" Conrad was hopeful.

"Well, no. Not really." How would she and Simon explain the heavenly help they'd been receiving? Ghostly messages in their sleep? Conversations with dead people?

Suddenly, the female character from Ghost Wars popped onto Simon's screen and Amee, in her black leather uniform, waved, then faded just as quickly.

Simon waved back like a child saying goodbye to his favorite cartoon character as the TV program ended. "Got it, Amee. Thanks."

"He calls his computer Amee?" Conrad was totally confused.

Simon looked at Evie, who looked back with a curious expression

Bull smiled from his seat at the table. "Best not ask, Mr. McIntyre. Best not ask." The big man leveraged himself up and grabbed someone's cup from the table, filled it with black tar-like coffee and joined the group. "The man always comes through."

"The man?" Conrad was losing it. "Are you guys talking in some kind of code, or something?"

"Simon, find Pretoria Atoll, would you?" Evie was so excited she was hopping from one foot to the next and blazed right over Conrad's questions.

Simon pulled up Google Earth and proceeded to

find the tiny atoll called Pretoria, almost a hundred miles east-south-east of their location. "And there ya go, my sweet Evie." He pointed to one of the larger shapes in a chain of tiny islands. "The leading edge of the storm has just passed this island's location and the eye sits right here." He pointed to the atoll. "If this is where Andrea is, she has beautiful weather, for the moment."

The eye of the storm was very well defined and clear. About sixty miles across, the clouds swirled around the island like a giant fence, encapsulating the speck of land.

Conrad had his phone out and was dialing Carl Morehead before anyone realized what he was about to do. "Carl? Yeah, sorry for the early morning call. Do you have any ships that can brave a tropical storm? I think we found my wife's location."

Evie motioned to Conrad to look at the screen's map. "Yes, I can give you coordinates." After a few moments, Conrad ended the call and turned to the rest of the group. "He'll have a 'substantial' ship ready at the Sea Ranch in two hours."

"All right!" Bull patted Conrad on the back, knocking the man a couple feet forward with the strength of his excitement. "Now we're cookin' with gas. I need me some friends like that."

"Look, you guys have been awesome, but I can't ask you to risk your lives like this." He pointed to the weather map. "I got it from here. This could turn into a goat fuck, or I could find my wife and bring her home."

"You're kidding, right?" Evie looked at her friend. "We're a team. It's a big island, even though it looks tiny. We have limited time. Cut the crap and let's get on it."

"I wouldn't miss this for the world." Bull held out his fist for a bump from Evie.

"I'm in." Pete had heard the commotion and joined the group.

Simon dug in his briefcase and came up with a small device that looked like a thumb drive with a stout antenna. "Have hot spot, will travel. The Bomb is ready." Simon took a deep breath. "Anybody got some Dramamine?"

Chapter 22

In the beautifully designed executive offices of Global Systems Technology, Rose Mayfield sat at her desk stewing.

Where was her boss?

What was going on with Pete and Conrad?

Rita, Conrad's little *makhasheyfe* had only said they would not be in the office today. Rita was always full of herself and the true definition of Yiddish witch. Rose resented the motherly woman who wore flat shoes and flowery prints that did nothing to improve her rotund figure or looks. Rita rarely wore any kind of makeup, except lipstick in bright red, and always brought her lunch in the same old plastic butter container. Today she was particularly secretive and preoccupied with herself. The same way she always was when she had information she didn't want to share. It chaffed Rose's cheeks and she focused her attention on searching for Pete's cell phone signal. If she could find out where he was, maybe she would have a hint, at least.

Information was power. Power was money, and influence, and everything Rose had lost in the last year. And everything she had gained! She tapped her acrylic nails on the edge of her desk. Something was up and she needed to know what it was. Now!

She dialed the burn phone number hidden on a note

card under her drawer.

No answer.

Rose dialed again, just to make sure she had the right number. She'd only purchased the phone a few months back and rarely called the number. "Come on, Henry, pick up." Rose tapped her keyboard with a shiny silver pen that held the inscription, Executive Assistant of the Year. She'd been given that award after her first nine months at GST, by her boss, himself. She'd stood at the head of the auditorium, calm and graceful, accepting an award that should have gone to Rita. Shoulda, coulda, woulda. That frump wasn't even at the dinner. She had a family to take care of. Big deal. Rose wiggled the fourth finger of her left hand. Her five-karat diamond engagement ring sparkled with the fire of the stars. The gold band next to it solidified her union with Zede and the *Tools of God*.

Checking and re-checking the number, she hit redial.

Nothing.

Something was definitely wrong.

Her next call was to Seth Cohen. His name meant *appointed by God* in Hebrew and he took his name seriously. He was the head of the group she'd engaged to punish those who had killed her father and destroyed her family. It was all about atonement in her Talmud.

Their plan had been perfectly crafted and executed. What could have gone wrong?

****

Jane sat close to her small campfire; a hunk of Spam on a long stick sizzled as it leaked fat into the flames. She'd opened the can carefully, listening to the hiss to make sure the can had not leaked or been punctured. The familiar smell of cooking pork products reached her nose and she considered eating it semi-raw.

Jane's stomach growled loud enough to spook Silly Bird. It sat complacently on its perch, the rum pan empty. When the outside of the meat was suitably dark and crispy, Jane ventured a bite. The salty meat was manna from heaven, and she took a bigger bite, promptly burning her tongue.

"Hah! That's what you get for being a pig, Jane." Talking to herself was better than silence, and Silly Bird wasn't speaking since its morning draught of rum. Did the bird actually eat, or just drink itself into a stupor? "You should taste this, Silly Bird. It's wonderful." She consumed the hunk and put another chunk on the stick to cook. "Better than hot dogs on Fourth of July."

As she cooked the can of meat and ate to her heart's delight, Jane sat watching the sky through the cave's bigger opening. She'd hacked at the vegetation with her newest tool to clear the cave mouth.

The sky was really weird. On the horizon to the west, she could see a wall of clouds. To the north and south as well. Strange indeed. The sky was a pretty shade of red and yellow hues above the cloud walls. The air was dead and humid beyond belief. It was as if Jane wore a lead overcoat in a sauna.

"What I wouldn't give for a little AC right now…"

"Red sky in morning, sailors take warning." Silly Bird ruffled its feathers and squawked. "Red sky at night, sailors delight."

"Well, Silly Bird, it's morning and there is red sky. But I'm not a sailor on a ship and I've already weathered my storm." She peered across the muddy gash in the hill near her cave. "And the avalanche, and almost drowning. Don't forget being shot at and falling onto a garbage barge, and being dumped into the ocean to die…

Holy mother of God!

She remembered!

She'd been shot at by…who?

The fat man's image appeared before her eyes. He aimed a gun at her and pulled the trigger. A searing pain exploded in her head and she fell backward over a bridge railing onto a…

Garbage barge?

The fat man in her visions wasn't some benevolent grandfather, some drunk dad on a bender. He was her attacker! And he was German! The voice manifested itself in her mind.

The cell.

The water bottles.

The beating!

Jane held her head and screamed.

Silly Bird jumped of its perch and flew out the cave entrance, disappearing into the dense jungle.

"I'm sorry, Silly Bird. I didn't mean to scare you." The tears began as Jane pulled the tarp around herself and curled into a ball next to the fire. It was hot and humid, and the tarp stunk, but it was security.

Jane didn't care.

She cried herself into oblivion and slept.

****

"You think you got everything?" Bull considered the pile of equipment and arms in the back of Pete's SUV. "Nope, wait! You forgot the kitchen sink…" Bull was sandwiched into the back seat next to Evie and

Simon. Conrad drove and Pete sat shotgun as they headed for the marina and the *substantial* ride that awaited.

There was no wind this beautiful morning and the sun shone with already building warmth. Evie closed her eyes and concentrated on a quick prayer. *Please, Lord, keep that storm in place until we find Andrea.*

"We're working on it, Evie. We'll do our best," came her answer.

Evie opened her eyes to Simon's bowed, smiling face. He grinned at her a little sideways. "They're working on it, babe."

*****

"Grady, like this. With your legs." Amee sat on the edge of a cloud wall, her legs dangling down, holding the storm back with sheer strength of will. She had a lot of strength of will for a dead woman!

"I ain't been here as long as you, honey. It don't work so good for me." Grady looked down on the earth below, trying to maintain his leg-hold on the edge of the clouds.

Amee pointed to her legs. *"It's not here."* She pointed to her heart. *"It's here. Pull from your heart."*

Grady considered the thought, then reached way down deep into his soul and gave a mighty tug. The storm began to stabilize, the eye remaining over the little island where Andrea and Silly Bird slept.

"That's the way, honey! I knew you could do it!" Amee's gleeful cry sparkled across the water with the early morning rays of the sun, now above the cloudbank.

Grady pointed to his heart. *"It ain't so hard, when you pull from here."*

He was rewarded with a cherubic giggle as he focused on the task at hand, and his love for the angel who sat next to him. The simple silver band he'd made in his younger days now graced the hand of Amee, where it was intended all those years ago. It mattered not a fig that he had to wait a lifetime and pass into the next to finally place it there. It caught the sunlight and twinkled, as if to wink at its maker.

The two sat together, holding the pressure system with their combined power and watching the ship below cruise toward the coral atoll where they would find Conrad's wife, and a very silly bird with an alcohol problem.

"You think they have Alcoholics Anonymous for birds?" Amee grinned at her love.

"I wouldn't be surprised, girl." Grady grinned back, consumed with love and emotion. It was always like that now, here with Amee. Reverend Summers, the holy rollin' preacher that used to make the rounds of his Arkansas hills home, was right. The love never ended with life, you simply carried it with you into the beyond.

Grady took Amee's hand and kissed her knuckles, one by one.

She giggled outrageously and kicked a hole in the cloudbank with her joy.

The Miss Bliss sailed right on through into the calm of the eye of the storm.

****

The grisly captain of the Miss Bliss stood scouring his map of the island chain. "This is Pretoria. Never been there myself. Looks like we can get through the reef, here." He pointed to a dotted line someone had drawn on the ancient map in marker. "The guy who used to own this tub, knew these waters like the back of his hand. Made all them scratch marks." The captain pointed to a cubby chest on the back wall of the ship's less than spacious bridge. Each little square box held several rolled-up maps. Some were tattered and stained, some new and curled tightly. The chart cabinet was a library archive of the waters of the Caribbean. "Left me all his charts when he sold her to me." The captain spit chew into an empty tuna can on the counter. "Wanna see what burrito sauce looked like from the fifties? Just pull the Cuba C-54 chart."

Pete winced and swallowed. He was a little green around the gills but holding his own.

Conrad chuckled.

This kind of junk heap was right up his alley. Rusty, solid steel everywhere, and a hull as thick as a cinder block. They could plow their way through the reef if necessary. The barge tender must have been built in the forties and still had the original upholstery and wheel. The brass was shiny with use, but the console had seen better days. Duct tape held the radio in place and a Garmin GPS, usually found in cars, sat in an old bicycle basket, screwed to the wall and plugged into a cigarette lighter outlet. From the stacked garbage can, it was obvious the captain lived onboard his boat. Conrad recognized trash from no less than six different fast food restaurants. A small fridge was cargo belted to the wall on one side, and dirty clothing was strewn about the cabin.

Simon sat on a bench behind the captain's chair, his computer on his lap, his *relationshipee* at his side. "Ah, Captain Ron, I just got an update from NOAA.

You are not going to believe this!" He swiveled his laptop toward the captain.

"Name's Cecil there, Matey." He spit again and Conrad watched Pete, behind Cecil, swallow hard.

"Right." Obviously, the captain didn't get the Kurt Russell joke. "See this." Simon pointed to the satellite picture on the screen. "The cloud bank has just opened up right there. Where we need to get in." Conrad rubbed his eyes as if he couldn't believe what he saw. "Right where we need it. Right now, when we need it."

"Ain't believin' that there sky picture, son. Just keep yer eyes on the water. Water never lies."

Evie commented quietly. "Divine intervention, I'd say." She shot Amee a mental note of thanks and opened the door to the walkway next to the bridge.

Pete and Conrad followed her out, taking great lungful's of fresh air. "A little of that guy goes a long way." He looked toward the island. It was a speck in the distance. "We'll be there soon. Cross your fingers." Pete held up both hands. "And watch the water. The water never lies." He imitated Captain Cecil and crossed his fingers with a grin.

As the island came into full view, Conrad gasped. The first and most prominent feature was a huge gash from the top of the island's one hill, clean down to the ocean. He grabbed binoculars to scan the area closer. "Will ya look at that." He leaned over the railing where Evie stood, holding Pete, who was intermittently feeding the fish. Handing the binoculars to Evie, Conrad pointed. "That's some avalanche. And fairly new by the look of the mud."

Evie focused the binoculars on the huge slide. "Man, looks like a big mess." She surveyed the surrounding area, slowly moving the binoculars back and forth. "Jungle, trees, birds, monkeys…Conrad! There's smoke. Look!" She handed the glasses back to Conrad and pointed to a place halfway up the hill on the east side of the slide.

Pete stood up, wiping his mouth with the tail of his shirt. "You sure?"

"Sure as rain." Conrad focused the binoculars and looked again. "Definitely smoke. Where there's smoke, there's fire. Where there's fire, I'll bet my wife is involved." His grin was almost bigger than his face. He could feel his cheeks stretch for the first time in days. It felt so good.

"Inside." Captain Cecil yelled out the open window. "We're slippin' the gap."

"I know that means something…" Simon grumbled as the group moved inside and Evie took the laptop from Simon, closing the lid. "Hey, that's my…"

"Sensitive instrument?" Evie plopped down on the bench next to him. "It'll live." She patted his upper thigh suggestively and grinned.

"Bad, bad girl." Bull mentioned in passing. He'd just come from below and still held a cup of coffee.

"Don't ya know that stuff'll stunt your growth, Bull?" Conrad chuckled.

Bull toasted Conrad with his metal cup. "Here's hoping."

"Hold on. I'm gonna run this channel." Captain Cecil shoved a lever forward and the engine roared as the boat lurched ahead with the combined force of the motors and wave action.

Simon grabbed Evie.

Pete threw up in the garbage can.

Conrad grabbed the counter rail and held on.

Bull stood there like a tree trunk, rooted in place. Sipping his coffee.

"Yee ha!" Cecil sat in his captain's chair, feet braced on the chart table. "Rollin', rollin', rollin'. Keep them doggies rollin'. Yee ha!" He sang. Well, Conrad wouldn't call it singing.

"What year is this again, babe?" Simon was watching the captain in disbelief. "I hope he knows what he's doing, cause there's no doggies here, and we're headed for a coral reef, not a corral."

It only lasted a couple minutes, and Conrad heard Pete swear. "This is like being back in high school! Holding on for dear life and vomiting, which was most of my senior year, But I survived." Pete hurled into the garbage can again. When the ship finally settled in the calmer waters of the lagoon, Pete's stomach had to be about as empty as Mother Hubbard's cupboard. With a pitiful groan, Conrad's lifelong buddy stepped outside to breathe as best he could. Leaning on the railing, Pete looked into the azure waters. A triangular fin slid by the hull beneath him.

Shark!

Pete slammed his back against the wall of the cabin and froze. Conrad hated sharks as much as Pete. They'd had an adrenaline-hyped interlude with the species once, diving off the coast of Texas. He never wanted to repeat that particular interaction again. The shark had been nosy. Pete had been terrified. Conrad was cautious and ready, but very uncomfortable with the size of the fish's teeth and strength. He watched as the fin dipped beneath the surface and disappeared.

I will lift up mine eyes unto the hills, from whence

cometh my help. My help cometh from the Lord.

The biblical saying just popped into his head and he looked up.

Overhead, making lazy circles in the sky, soared a beautifully colored macaw. Conrad swore it looked him straight in the eye before screeching.

"Got rum? Rum all gone. Give me my rum."

"Stupid bird. Where'd you come from?" Pete laughed. Now that the water was calmer and he was outside in the air, he was recovering. The humidity was oppressive, and Conrad wiped his face with the side of his shirt.

"Silly Bird. Silly Bird, got no rum."

The bird flew lower as if to land on the front of the ship.

At the bird's squawking, Evie rushed out of the cabin and onto the deck. "Did that bird say 'Silly Bird?'" She asked in disbelief.

"Yeah. I wonder who taught it to talk?" He considered approaching the macaw as it landed, but nixed the idea as the bird snapped its beak and eyed him dangerously, or what Conrad thought was dangerously, anyway.

"Simon, come out here." Evie shouted for her boyfriend. "That's Silly Bird. We have the right island."

Conrad stripped off his shirt and prepared to dive in and swim to the beach. It wasn't far or deep and he was a strong swimmer.

"Nah uh. No swimming in shark infested waters, Rad." Pete grabbed Conrad's belt from behind to keep his friend from diving in.

"What?" Conrad struggled to get loose. "Andrea's

on that island. I can feel it."

"Look." Pete pointed to the fin just above the water a few feet to the port side of the ship. "You'll feel something, all right! Triangle fin. Sharp teeth. Unquenchable appetite. All adds up to Conrad hors d'oeuvre. Did you miss the fact that your finned friend is still around and possibly hungry?" Pete held Conrad's belt, shaking his head. "No, no, no. Our project is not finished yet and I can't fulfill the contract alone. No swimming today, buddy. I fed the fish enough for both of us."

"Bunch of landlubbers." Captain Cecil mumbled as he strolled by, headed for the stern of the ship. "Ya think they'd look for a dinghy." He grumbled and spit into the ocean. "Back here."

The captain lowered the Miss Bliss's dinghy at the back of the boat and showed his passengers how to open the ship's hatch and lower the gangplank to form a docking platform.

Bull, whose brain was working overtime on caffeine and Ritz with Cheese Whiz, had already assembled a few necessities and handed them down as the group crawled into the dinghy.

****

Jane was hot as hell and climbing up some mountain pass behind a string of soldiers. Her pack must have weighed a hundred pounds and a fifty-pound camera dragged at her neck. Every time she looked up, the mountain got higher.

The ping of a bullet ricocheted off a rock by her left hand.

"Incoming!" The group scattered and hid behind rocks and in ditches.

The scary man with dark glasses yanked her down, just in time to miss a hail of well-aimed rounds.

He saved her?

See looked down. The camera was gone. "My camera!"

She tried to stand, but the man held her down. "I'll get your damn camera. Stay here. Stay down. I don't want to explain a dead journalist on my watch."

The man was angry and clearly resentful of Andrea.

Andrea?

Journalist?

Afghanistan?

Jane woke to a foreign sound outside her cave. She threw back the tarp and felt the assaulting, oppressive heat in the cave entrance where she'd fallen asleep. Her small fire now smoldered, and thin wisps of smoke drifted out the entrance.

"Silly Bird…" She surveyed the cave. The bird was gone. She had no one to share her revelation with.

"My name is Andrea and I was a photojournalist in Afghanistan!" She shook her head, reaching for more in her Swiss Cheese brain. There was nothing to grasp onto, but sunshine and smoke.

Stepping out into the open area in front of her cave, she almost fainted. Below in the large lagoon, floated a big tugboat. About to start waving and screaming, her survival instinct clicked in, as a hand went to the crusty wound on her forehead.

Friend or foe?

Her view from the side of the hill was perfect. She watched from behind some bushes while three men and a woman crawled into the dinghy and headed for the beach. The man who sat at the back steering the boat was enormous and the dinghy ran lopsided in the water. The other two guys looked like they were ready for war, and the woman wore bright yoga pants and a halter top. What a strange assortment of friends, or foes? Why couldn't she tell?

The slight smell of burned wood touched Andrea's nostrils.

The fire!

She crawled to the edge of the cave and covered the last few embers with dirt and gravel.

The visitors had probably seen the smoke.

Hiding in the undergrowth once again, Andrea watched the beach as the people piled out and the huge black man hauled the boat up onto the beach with one hand.

Silly Bird flew into the cave behind her, screeching then flew back out.

"Shut up, Silly Bird. You'll give us away. They may not be friendlies." Andrea shooed the bird away, but Silly Bird was having no part of it.

"Got rum! Rum's here. Get me my rum!" The bird screamed.

The group turned at once and Andrea saw the scary man in dark glasses.

And ran...

****

"Andrea! Wait." Conrad saw his wife's head pop out of the bushes and his heart nearly burst out of his chest.

She was alive!
She was here!
And she was running away from him?

Running...

From him?

What in the world was wrong with her?

Before anyone could figure it out, Pete took off through the bushes at a dead run. "Andi, wait!" He screamed.

Evie followed Pete into the jungle.

"Up the hill and to the right, guys." Simon was on the fly-bridge of the Miss Bliss watching the scene with binoculars and spoke through the comms they'd set up before leaving the ship.

Conrad stood in place on the beach, rubbing his neck. He'd found his wife, and she'd run from him. What was that about?

"Mr. McIntyre, sir? We should go along the beach and head them off." Bull pulled at Conrad's arm. "Sir?"

Still stunned by Andrea's behavior, Conrad didn't move.

Didn't breathe.

Didn't think.

Not getting a response, Bull jerked a little harder and Conrad flew into the side of the dinghy.

That got his attention. "What?" Conrad rubbed his shoulder and pushed himself off the rubber pontoon.

"We should go along the beach. I don't think she knew who we were. Her face was messed up." Bull looked as apologetic as he could. "Sorry."

"No, it's okay. You're right."

"Conrad, along the beach to your left, around the lagoon. The hill meets a small river. She has to come out of the jungle there, unless she decides to climb to the top of the hill." Simon reported from his lookout post in the lagoon.

Pete was a flash for about ten minutes, then his speed and vigor began to fade, and he slowed. It wasn't hard to follow Andrea's trail, between the ripped greenery and the squawking bird that flew above her.

A flash of blue denim ahead of them had Evie passing Pete in a blur. "Catch your breath. I've got this."

Evie scrambled past Pete and saw Andrea's back. "Andrea! Wait, Andi!" Evie pulled out all the stops and chased the fleeing woman. "Andi, stop. It's Evie." She yelled between pants."

****

Silly Bird dove at Andrea. "Silly Andi. Need to stop. Need to Stop."

Andrea froze mid-step. She was panting and dizzy from the scramble and the dense heat. Her side burned like the Devil. "What did you say, Silly Bird?"

The bird flew to perch on a limb next to her head, as the woman from the boat crested the hill Andrea had just climbed at break-neck speed. "Silly Andrea. Need to stop. Need to Stop. Got rum? Give me my rum."

"Andrea? Andi? It's Evie. Major Evielynne Gastineau, Conrad's friend from California." Evie held up her hands and approached slowly. Andrea stood to run, but something in her brain said stay. Conrad? Evie? Friend from California? Friend?

"It's all right now. You are safe and she is your friend." The voice was back. She still had no idea who this voice belonged to, but instinct, or insanity, whatever the voice was, told her to listen.

Evie sat down to catch her breath a few feet away.

Andrea put her hands to her head and the tears began. "I'm so confused. I can't remember…"

"It's okay, Andi. We found you, and you're safe now."

The searchers below heard it all and Conrad responded. "Evie, she's with you? Is she okay?"

"Holy crap! They're on the top of the hill. Evie's with Andrea." Simon reported through the comm. He was still on his observation platform on the boat.

"Roger that. Hold in place." Evie touched her ear and reported in. She turned her face back to Andrea and inched forward. "Honey, what happened to you?"

"I…I don't know. It's all so blurry. I can't remember…" Tears rolled down her face as she wiped at her nose.

"Andi, I'm your friend. Your husband is down there waiting for us. We came to rescue you." Evie chuckled at her comment. "But it looks like you are doing a fine job of surviving on your own. You are one hell of a strong woman." Evie inched forward again, peering at the wound on Andrea's head. "You got shot by the men who kidnapped you."

As she heard the words, Andrea gasped. It all came back in a rush of memory so strong and emotional, she started to fall over. In a flash, Evie caught her in a tight hug. "It's okay, Andi. It's okay." Andrea rocked sobbing on the shoulder of the woman who held her. "Guys, give us a minute." Evie commented into her comm.

"You can have all the time in the world. I'm still trying to catch my breath, and it's not letting me. There's too much stuff in the air here." Pete sat halfway up the hill, next to the cascading stream that joined the river below.

****

"Look Grady, they found her!" Amee clapped with glee and accidently sent a lightning bolt down toward the earth. She pulled Grady to his feet and they danced a little jig on cloud nine. Unfortunately, in their exuberance, Amee inadvertently released the edge of the storm.

"Uh oh, baby." He took Amee's hand and they peered over the edge of their cloud. *"They better get out of there on the double."* Grady paused in his celebration to watch Simon on the fly-bridge. *"Son, you better get a move on."* He directed his thoughts toward his great-nephew with all the strength he possessed.

****

They all saw the lightning hit the top of the hill, its bright light blinding Simon for a second. Then he heard his uncle's voice and swayed with emotion. It happened every time Uncle Grady spoke to him from heaven…and he always listened! "Guys? Guys, we gotta get out of here. I got it on good authority."

Bull and Conrad both looked at the sky. The storm had begun to move. "Evie, can you get Andrea to the beach?" Simon knew all Conrad could think of was racing up that hill and grabbing his wife in his arms, and covering her with kisses. That's what he would have done. Even where he stood on the ship, Simon ached to hold Evie. His fingers needed to feel her. His lips needed to touch hers. His— He cut off the thoughts before he couldn't walk straight. He could imagine how Conrad must be feeling after thinking his wife had died. He shot a quick mental thanks to his uncle, wherever the man was.

"No problema, mahn." Evie was relieved and her humor was returning with her breath. "Andrea, we have to go. The storm is moving fast now. Can you walk okay?"

Simon was monitoring the conversations as the group started to move. He glanced at the up-to-the-minute weather map. "Move faster, folks."

The strength of the emotional deluge was beginning to fade and with Evie's help, Simon watched Andrea struggled to her feet. "Broken ribs." Andrea held her midsection. The statement was clear and strong, if punctuated with a tight groan.

"And you ran up that hill like a gazelle? I have new respect for those photographic feet."

****

Andrea grinned. She remembered the joke! She remembered everything.

Just before she and Conrad had taken their vows, Evie sat with her in the rectory of the church, fussing over her dress and posing for the required informal action pictures of pre-wedding prep. Andrea thought the two-inch, sparkly heels she wore made her feet look huge. She'd told the photographer, no pictures of her feet!

"Let's get out of here. But I need Silly Bird. I want to take it with me. It saved my life." Andrea looked around for the bird, but it was nowhere to be found. "Damn. Just like the little alchy. It's probably in our cave drinking again."

Evie gave her friend a quizzical look.

"No, really! It did save my life and it is an alcoholic." She picked her way down the hill ahead of Evie who'd paid little attention to where she'd run as she chased Andrea up the hill. "It must have belonged to someone at some point, because it can talk. The cave had stuff in it, like someone had lived there for a while."

"Yeah, about seven years," Evie retorted.

They found Pete, still sitting on the ground, still a little winded. He jumped up and went to hug Andrea, but paused, watching her face for some sign of recognition. He got it, as she limped forward into his arms.

"Pete! What are you doing here?" Andrea hugged her husband's partner.

"A little bird said you needed a ride." He chuckled.

"Silly Bird? Silly Bird told you I was here?" Andrea was amazed.

"Ah, no. Just a saying. Why?" Pete was clearly puzzled and Andrea shook her head at the thought. Pete was puzzled? He'd get over it. She'd just spent days with no memory at all. Silly Bird had circled the boat?

"Later, guys. We need to move."

On their way to the beach, they did stop at Andrea's cave for just a moment. Silly Bird was nowhere to be found. Andrea grabbed the last, unopened bottle of rum.

On the beach, Andrea could make out her husband. Conrad paced in front of the dinghy. Her heart soared, even though her legs moved like she was stuck in mud. The wind had come up and the lagoon wasn't quite as calm as it had been when they arrived. With one extra person, the dinghy would be precariously loaded. With the waves increasing, they would need to make two trips to the boat.

"Come on, folks! I've seen *the Perfect Storm*. I don't want to be in the remake." Conrad rushed toward the path to the cave as the sweaty, grimy crew came into view.

Evie held up her hands to ward off Conrad's enthusiastic approach. "Broken ribs. Hug carefully."

Andrea passed Evie and jumped into her husband's arms despite her wounds and broken ribs. Wincing between kisses, she plastered his face and found his lips. Wrapping her legs around him, she let the tears roll amid kisses and stabs of pain.

"I thought I'd lost you, babe." Conrad murmured into her hair. It smelled of salt, smoke, and sweat, but it was all Andrea. "I'll never let you out of my sight again." He squeezed a little too hard and Andrea squeaked in pain. It was enough to make him settle her to the ground, but still, she held him close not wanting to let the contact go for a while.

"Sorry. Does it hurt much?" For the first time he took a good look at his injured wife. "Holy shit! I should have killed that fucker after all."

Conrad touched Andrea's head wound, her split lip. The same lip that had just covered his face with kisses! It was open and bleeding now. "Damn!"

Andrea daubed at her lip with the filthy cuff of the shirt she wore. The only thing she wore!

"Come on, guys." Evie pointed at the sky that was darkening as they spoke. "Let's move."

Bull moved the dinghy back to the edge of the water. "Leave me and Mr. Newcastle here. Get the ladies onboard first." It was more an observation than an order, but Conrad was in complete agreement. Andrea wanted off her island as soon as possible.

"Thanks, Bull. I'll be back for you in a couple minutes. Hang tight."

"No other way." Bull fist bumped Conrad and

shoved the loaded boat into the lagoon. "Be right here."
****

Bull and Pete sat on the beach and watched as the dinghy sped to the Miss Bliss and discharged its passengers. "Ya know, I used to really resent Andrea's relationship with my buddy. I never realized how strong their connection was. Makes me think I'm missing something in my own life." Pete dug holes in the sand with his feet. "Know what I mean?"

"Nope." Bull's deep chuckle stalled in the thick air. "Women are all trouble. They wrap theyselves around you like a snake, and one day, wham! Bite a guy's head right off."

Pete stared at Bull for a second, then playfully punched the man in the shoulder, laughing at his statement.

Bull chuckled at Pete's punch, then returned the favor.

Pete went face down in the sand as Conrad, returning for them, came ashore with the dinghy.

Chapter 23

Back aboard the Miss Bliss, Captain Bligh sat at his wheel, yelling at the crew above the noise of the wind and lightning. As Conrad and Bull loaded the dinghy on board her mother ship, the storm hit. Now the ship battled wind, current, and pelting rain, heading back to Padre Island. "Damn the torpedoes, full speed ahead! Hang on to your shorts!" He thrust the throttle to the wall and gunned the engines. "Balls to the walls, boys."

Pete leaned toward Evie. "Does this guy speak anything other than old movie?"

"I don't think so." Evie grabbed for the handhold as the ship heaved and rocked. Conrad and Andrea were below. He was helping her clean and dress her wounds and whatever else they were doing. Bull stood in the bridge doorway, his umpteenth cup of joe sloshing in someone's cup. Simon, Evie, and Pete wedged themselves into the bench behind the nav station and held on as the boat raised and dropped with the waves that flowed through the reef's channel.

A huge wave crashed over the bow and Pete swallowed hard. "Oh God!"

"Oh no, no, no. Not on my computer!" Simon pulled his laptop off his lap and held it in the air as Evie reached for the small garbage can.

She shoved Pete's face into the receptacle just in

time. What little that remained in Pete's stomach departed, covering the tuna sandwich wrapper and a host of unidentifiable green and black goo-covered paper towels. Some kind of spicy sauce floated in the bottom of the pail.

"Uhg." Pete heaved again, but nothing came out.

Cecil pulled a drawer beneath his knees open and tossed Evie a half-empty package of soda crackers. "Dry heaves. No good for anyone."

Pete heaved again.

"You happen to have any sea sickness pills onboard, Captain?" Evie felt so bad for Pete, she would have swum back to the island for Dramamine.

"Don't know. Check the head. Might find something." Captain Cecil held onto the wheel as they breached the reef and sailed out into the open ocean, and the really big stuff!

As the ship rode the waves and lurched along into the wind, Evie searched both bathroom cabinets on board. She didn't find anything that would help Pete, but she did find some 7-Up, a whole mess of freeze-dried, prepackaged meals, a can of lard, a half-eaten Buddy-burger and Silly Bird, wedged in a corner on a shelf, snoring away as if he owned the place. His claw held tight to the neck of a full rum bottle.

"Andrea! Your bird is onboard!" Evie called out in surprise.

Conrad poked his head out of the second stateroom. He'd already heard the rambling tale from his wife, and knew exactly how much she would miss the friend who'd helped her survive on the island. "Will ya look at that!"

Andrea's head next appeared, much cleaner and

bandaged. She grinned at Evie. "I knew he'd follow the rum." She gazed lovingly at her husband. "We really need to teach our little child not to drink so much."

Conrad kissed her head with a chuckle. "Nah, I think I need a new drinking buddy after all of this."

Laughing at the couple, obviously back to their normal selves, but a little worse for the wear, Evie returned to the bridge.

Pete still sat with his head in the garbage pail. Simon had moved away from the retching guy next to him. Captain Cecil was singing "Ninety-nine Bottles of Beer on the Wall" as he fought the wheel, occasionally pausing to spit green slime into the half-full tuna can. Bull rode the waves, blocking himself in the doorway that held him tight.

"This be a whole shitload of fun." Bull had put his cup down and laughed outrageously as another wave lifted the bow of the boat into the air on the crest, then sent it smashing down again into the wave's trough. Evie held onto the railing as she watched Bull's head hit the roof of the bridge at the crest, then his knees buckled as the floor fell from beneath his feet. His huge hands gripped the doorframe as his laughter rang out through the cabin. "This be an E-ticket ride, man!"

Pete's voice echoed from the trashcan. "I don't like amusement park rides for a reason."

Evie took the garbage can and wedged it between Pete's feet, popped the soda can and handed it to him. "Sip this. It helps." She held out a few crackers.

Pete raised the can to his mouth just as the boat lurched and bucked an oncoming wave. The soda went everywhere, but in his mouth.

"Eighty-five bottles of beer on the wall, eighty-five

bottles of beer! Take one down. Spill it around. Eighty-four bottles of beer on the wall." Captain Cecil held to the spinning wheel and continued singing.

"I'm gonna kill that man." Pete mumbled as he dabbed at his shirt and face with a paper towel and tried a sip again. This time it went down his throat. "If we get out of this alive."

"Argh, me matey! This is nuttin' compared to some of the weather Miss Bliss and I seen together. She's a busty old ship and she'll get us home. Mark my words." Cecil went back to singing and Evie carefully, hand hold, by hand hold, worked her way to the bench near Simon.

Pete managed a few more sips of pop and it did seem to make him feel a bit better. He tackled a cracker in tiny pieces and Evie could tell his nausea was abating. However, he still vowed to never set foot on a small boat again. Often and out loud.

****

Below deck, Conrad settled into the corner of the couch and pulled Andrea into his arms. "Is it all back?" Conrad had not let go of Andrea since they boarded the ship. A handhold, a hug, an arm around her waist, tenderly cleaning and dressing her wounds, now she lay against his chest, secure and relaxed.

"I think so. I know who I am. I know who you are. I recognized Evie after a while." She cuddled against her husband's warmth. His strong arms held her as the boat rocked and pitched. She didn't seem to care. She was with Conrad and his world was just fine.

"So Dembeck was the one who beat you, then shot you when you escaped?" Conrad wanted the German beaten to a pulp, cut into little pieces and fed to the fish.

"You did good, babe. Just like before." He kissed the top of her head, about the only place that wasn't cut, scraped, shot, or bruised.

"Yeah, about that *before* part. I only survived because of the State Department training and all my experiences in the Middle East with you. I kept thinking I should take pictures." She sat up and looked into the face of her beloved husband. "Even when I was floating in the middle of the ocean, I looked at the clouds and thought, this might make a fantastic shot!" Conrad studied her as she explained. "It kept me alive." She lay back against him. He wanted her to know how her disappearance had affected him, but the emotions were still raw, and he paused, just holding his precious woman.

"I got that." Conrad shifted a little. "Andrea, do you remember you disappeared on the night of our fifth anniversary?"

"Of course. It was only two days ago, right?"

"Uh huh. Two days and ten years of my life! I don't know what I'd have done, if I lost you."

His confession wasn't news to Andrea's ears, and he hoped she felt the same way about him. What would life be without your soul mate and the major part of your heart?

She closed her eyes and smiled. "Find me. That's what you always did, and still do."

Conrad fed her a chunk of protein bar from his Go-bag. He still hadn't given up the habit of having a backpack ready to go at a moment's notice. All good spec-ops guys did. But he wasn't spec-ops anymore. He was a civilian contractor with a wife and home now. He had an office, secretary, fancy car, big house, bigger mortgage, lifetime membership to a prestigious gym and a partner that depended on him. Soon, he would have tickets to the Policeman's Ball and another charity clambering for the excessive amounts of money he made from lucrative government contracts. Somewhere, he heard the prison door slammed shut and the lock click securely into place.

Andrea's soft voice interrupted his thoughts. "Ya know, we should put some Spam in that bag of yours." Andrea's comment pulled him out of his head.

"Spam? That greasy stuff in a can?" He pulled her up onto his lap. "You know they put chicken lips in that stuff, right?"

Andrea held her sides and chuckled, kissing his rough, two-day old whiskers. "It's not bad cooked over a campfire. On a stick. With a rum chaser."

"Now the rum chaser I can get into, but Spam? Really?" Where was all this coming from, Conrad wondered. And why did she want him to add to his Go-bag. She hated the idea that he was always prepared to bug out.

"Someday I'll tell you about me, Silly Bird, rum and chicken lips on a stick." She pressed her sore lips to his and he found something much better than Spam.

Conrad's tongue searched for hers and the heat sizzled, like chicken lips on a stick. He didn't even notice the boat had settled its pitching and now ran calm and level.

****

Above the lovers, Captain Cecil was down to thirty-three bottles of beer on the wall. Pete was outside the cabin, his face into the wind, breathing deeply. Simon was back to coding on his laptop, and Evie had crawled up to the fly-bridge and sat watching the horizon. She could almost make out a brown speck and some tall buildings. South Padre Island. It would be a couple of hours, but they'd weathered the storm and were on their way home.

Bull had finally emptied the ship's entire pot of coffee, given up who's ever cup he was drinking out of, and stretched out on a palette rack. She could hear the snores from her perch above the deck. How did he drink three hundred gallons of coffee in less than twelve hours and drop off to sleep in a wink? Evie shook her head and closed her eyes. God was in his heaven and all was right with the world, she thought.

Of course! A childish giggle came to her across the waves.

"Amee?" Evie sat up. It was close to sunset and through the shimmery rays on the horizon, she caught a glimpse of a young blonde woman in a red dress, holding the hand of a tall handsome sailor. They looked perfect together, and so in love. "Uncle Grady?"

The man in the image nodded. The woman gave a little wave.

Evie hesitantly waved back. Her eyes filled with tears at the overwhelmingly beautiful sight. Heaven was beyond description and Evie was blessed to have each little glimpse of the afterlife and her little ghost, now an angel.

You got to get that boy to commit, baby girl. He needs you. He just don't know it yet. I know your heart. You love him and he loves you. Don't make the mistake I did all those years ago, Evie.

Amee nodded in agreement with her love as the scene faded with the sun.

Evie sat back to watch the land grow ever larger as the Miss Bliss headed home. "Holy cow!"

Chapter 24

It was dark by the time the Miss Bliss made her dock. The heat of the day was beginning to dissipate, and the ocean had calmed to the point of glassy water. Captain Cecil expertly moored the boat in its slip and tied her up with a little clumsy help from Simon. Bull snored like a logger through the entire event, and only woke when Simon tripped over the sleeping man, in an attempt to throw the rope ashore.

"Ah, boss, I was sleepin' so good." Bull sat up. "We back?"

"Yes, and remind me to get you a palette rack for your bedroom when we get back to California." Simon snickered, watching Bull stretch and try to stand after laying flat on the boards for several hours on a rocking boat. "I think you have nail imprints on your back."

Bull shook himself.

Captain Cecil had radioed ahead, and Carl Morehead stood ready on the dock.

"Ahoy, Miss Bliss. Permission to come aboard?" He stepped onto the ship and slapped Pete on the back. "You survived! Proud of you, Pete."

"Just barely and never again." Pete stepped up onto the dock and presented the nearest piling with a loud smooch. "I am a landlubber and proud of it."

A little quieter, Carl asked, "How's Rad and Andi?"

"All things considered, okay. She needs to see a doctor, but she's alive and all lovey-dovey. Amazing what a woman'll do for the man who saves her life, twice."

"More than that, if I recall." He gave a hand to Evie, stepping off the ship. "Major Gastineau, successful mission, I take it."

"Roger that. And it's Evie now." She turned to grab Simon's briefcase as Carl steadied the geek when he tried to jump the foot between the dock and boat. Bull was right behind his boss and caught Simon as he lost his balance.

"Steady there, boss. I can't let you drown until I get my palette rack." Bull chuckled.

The stress of finding Andrea and getting back to South Padre Island alive had vanished, and the team was back in humor order. Even Pete looked a lighter shade of green.

Andrea came up the stairs from below deck, cradling a sleeping bird, who still clutched a bottle of rum in its claw. Conrad followed. He wore a huge smile and some serious five o'clock shadow.

"Got a car for y'all and a medic for the lady." Carl had effectively anticipated their return. "He'll do a check on the way to the hospital. Pete, can you drive?" Carl threw the Navigator keys to Pete.

Evie intercepted the keys with a quick snatch. "He's had a little too much fun today. I'll drive."

Conrad and Andrea piled into the spacious van with the medic, Carl and his driver. Evie, Simon, Bull and Pete took the Navigator.

"See y'all back at the ranch!" Pete hollered out the window. "Roll 'em, roll 'em, roll 'em." Pete directed

Evie with song. The car filled with laughter as the occupants began various versions of the Rawhide theme on their way back to Pete's warehouse apartment. Bull's was the most imaginative, but definitely unrepeatable.

As the gate rose and the Navigator drove into the parking garage, Simon studied the building. "Hey, my *relationshipee*, maybe I should scout around the Oakland area for a building like this. It's got plenty of room for the two of us, and more."

Evie saw him wink at her in the rearview mirror. She blinked. It was the first time Simon talked about them in terms of a permanent thing, other than the job he offered her upon separation from the service, and that was business. But living together wasn't commitment. Uncle Grady had said the word. Evie knew better than to challenge heavenly direction. And personally, she'd never considered living with a guy as a commitment. It was a stall tactic at best, and she had more respect for herself than to settle for the second-best scenario.

Pete, unusually direct, simply spoke for the elephant in the room. "Just propose, get hitched and get over it, Simon. Or isn't there a digital code for that?" He didn't mean it to come out so sarcastically, but they'd all just faced death together, and he'd vomited in front of them all. Many times. They were family now. Sarcasm was a family tradition.

Simon was uncharacteristically silent after Pete's comment.

Bull shifted to peer at his boss and Evie got an eyeful in the rearview mirror. Her boyfriend looked like he'd just bit into a sour grape.

Sheepishly Pete apologized. "Sorry. I didn't mean that to come out so harsh, but I've been sick. Barf and 7-up will do that to ya."

Evie parked next to the elevator in the handicapped parking spot. There would be no handicapped vehicles in Pete's parking lot this evening. Or ever, probably.

Figuring the best part of valor was retreat, Evie nodded toward the elevator. Pete bailed out followed by Bull. They got into the elevator and held the gate for a few seconds. When realization dawned that they would be elevating alone, Bull closed the gate and, he and Pete disappeared upward.

"Hope they make it to the top." Simon sat quietly in the back seat of the SUV.

"Yeah." Evie sat quietly in the front seat. She knew Pete's comment about marriage had Simon thinking hard. He had a lot of personal baggage when it came to commitment and the "m" word. His childhood had colored his view of family and fidelity.

"So, shall we go?" Simon gathered his things.

"I guess." Evie was tired and...deflating rapidly. After the complete excitement and satisfaction of finding Andrea alive, the sheer relief of surviving the storm, and then her heavenly interlude, she'd had way more than her share of the emotional rollercoaster. She dragged her bag out of the trunk and followed Simon to the elevator.

Neither one spoke. No physical touch, nod, or even recognition. The elevator had returned after letting its first two passengers off on the tenth floor. It creaked, groaned, and took them to Pete's apartment in one piece. Finding Andrea alive was the first miracle of her visit. Getting to the tenth floor in Pete's elevator was the second miracle of the day.

Evie dragged her bag off the elevator and dropped it at the end of the couch, then promptly flopped down on the cream leather. In seconds she was asleep.

****

Bull was already preparing a feast from the contents of the fridge, humming "Ninety-Nine Bottles of Beer on the Wall." Pete was in the shower and Simon sat in a chair, watching Evie sleep. Even after a tough day, the woman was incredibly beautiful and sensuous.

He considered Pete's rather direct statement.

His life was in order, the way it should have been. Why change the game now?

He had a fantastic life and all the money in the world. A seven point six-million-dollar bonus awaited deposit, out in California.

He had a great career.

He had security. He glanced at Bull, who was flipping vegetables in a wok, while meat sizzled in a fry pan, an ever-present cup of coffee next to the stove. And good friends.

He had a penthouse.

He had his own jet.

He had Evie.

Or did he?

He got up and took a beer from the fridge. Returning to his seat, he watched the woman who'd survived months of torture in a Taliban prison, plotted an escape and saved the lives of two soldiers in the mix. She'd found Uncle Grady's Amee, and made it possible for them to be together in the end. And now she headed up his company's Security division. She was a vision in satin and heels, and had the common sense and humor he needed to stay grounded. Something other than his manhood stirred...

He needed?

A voice in the back of his head answered that question. *You need her, son. And she needs you. But more than that, search your heart. The answer lies there, not in the bank, or your big, high-falootin' job. In the end, all that counts is love. Take my word for it.*

"You always were right, Uncle Grady." Simon mumbled into his bottle as he finished his beer.

He did love Evie.

He did!

But then his mother had loved, too. And look what happened to her. Look what happened to him.

"Chow in five, boss." Bull called from the kitchen area.

Pete came out of the bathroom, a thick white terrycloth robe wrapped around his slender frame. His hair dripped, but he looked happy and at ease. "Plates are in the glass cupboard. Drinks in the fridge." He sat at the big table that formed a bar off the cooking and food prep area like a big T. It was a massive butcher block, some eight feet long and five feet wide. Polished to a smooth finish, the lines of wood were beautifully displayed. In the center, an artistically carved myrtlewood bowl held a sand pattern with a peace sign drawn in the middle. A miniature rake lay to one side. Pete absently cleared the sand pattern with a shake of the bowl. He drew an elementary boat outline, then replaced the rake.

Evie pulled herself off the couch, shook her hair out, and joined Pete and Simon at the table.

The microwave beeped and Bull took a huge bowl of rice from the oven. "Strip steak, stir fry veggies and rice." He slid the rice bowl across the counter to the head of the table, and dumped the delicious looking stir-fry into another bowl. The pile of steak filled a platter and they were ready to eat.

"There's enough here to feed an army, Bull. It looks great. And smells heavenly!" Evie sat on a padded stool across from Simon and Pete.

"Chef Cheddar, at your service." Bull heaped his plate full of rice and steak. "Simon's uncle taught me how to make some great dishes out of mostly nothin'. He was a wiz at making a little, go a long ways." Bull proceeded to stuff his mouth with big scoops of food. "Yum yum, that be good eats."

Pete was once again amazed at the skills of Simon's bodyguard, butler, childhood friend, and now, it seemed, chef. Pete wondered if Simon appreciated everything he had. Since his blurted statement, Simon and Evie had been unusually quiet, and now neither one looked at each other, except for sideways glances. "Ever think about opening a restaurant for enormous people?" Pete watched Bull refill his plate as he himself tackled a truly tasty chunk of steak.

"Nope. Eat myself out of the profit!" Everyone chuckled at that and the atmosphere took a step toward pleasantry.

Pete's phone vibrated in a circle. "It's Conrad." He picked up the phone and answered the dancing ring. "Conrad? You're on speaker."

"Yeah. Everybody okay at your place?" He didn't wait for the answer. "Andrea's in X-ray right now. The doc here in the ER says she is going to be fine with rest and hydration. He's sure she's got a couple broken ribs, but they will mend in time."

"That's fantastic news, Rad. Bull fixed dinner, and I got a shower. Our world is looking up." Pete's shiny face gleamed after a shave and moisturizer. "Will she stay in the hospital, or come home?"

"No point in staying here. We'll be home in an hour or so. She'll sleep better in her own bed. So will I. As long as she's there." Simon could hear Conrad's voice break a little.

"Great! You guys want to be alone for the night? Or should I drop your company off at the house?" Pete mouthed and signaled to the folks at his dinner table. *Wanna stay or go?*

"I got beds. You got the floor. Would you mind dropping them at the house after dinner?"

"Not at all. As soon as we finish this mountain of food." Pete laughed.

Simon chimed in. "Bull is a great cook. We'll save you a few hundred pounds."

Conrad wasn't up for humor yet, but he was sounding better by the minute. "Thanks, Pete, guys."

"No problema, buddy. Take care of our gal. See ya soon." Pete hung up.

Simon repeated what he'd heard. "The doctor says Andrea's going to be fine. She's getting an x-ray and probably has a few broken ribs, but they'll heal in time. Right?" Her face had looked a great deal like his mother's, before the funeral home folks worked their magic. Unfortunately, his little-boy-self had seen everything and the picture of both sorely wounded women was stuck in his mind.

Bull growled around a mouthful of veggies. After

swallowing, he asked, "Think we can make bail for Henry-fuckin'Mikamoto, boss?"

"Make bail?" Simon's head popped up. "Whatever for? He's a murderer and a slimeball, Bull."

"Yep. But I'd sure like him to feel a little of what he did to Conrad's wife." Bull chuckled and stabbed a slab of meat. "Maybe a lot of what he did to her. I've yet to really meet the lady, but no woman deserves to be beat like that." A dark shadow crossed Bull's face.

"I could have a word with Officer Billings…" Pete smiled brightly.

"God, no!" Simon was well aware of Bull's more violent past and his sister's boyfriend history. Once, when they were still in high school, Crissy had come to pick Bull up at Uncle Grady's house. She had a black eye and a colorful set of bruises on her arm that looked like fingerprints. She waved off Uncle Grady's concern, but the dark look in her eyes told a different story. The next week, everyone at school was talking about this guy who'd up and disappeared from the hood. He was a player and a dealer, so no one thought much about it, but Crissy wore a big smile and her bruises healed quickly. After that, Bull kept pretty close tabs on his sister and her dating habits. The talk got around and no one touched Crissy again. She up and married a Baptist preacher a few years back, and had a passel of kids now. And no more bruises.

Evie chuckled. "It's not that he doesn't deserve it." She was picking up speed with her fork. "This tastes like manna from heaven. It's amazing, Bull."

Bull just nodded, his mouth full of rice and veggies.

****

"Thanks, Doc." Conrad shook the doctor's hand as he helped Andrea into the back of Morehead's van. "I'll take good care of her. I promise."

Andrea had been fitted with an elastic wrap around her middle. Her wounds had been cleaned again, and pronounced clear of infection. She was tired and ready for her own bed. "Thank you." She took Morehead's hand and Conrad lifted her into the seat. "And thank you, Carl." She settled as best she could into the seat while Carl fastened her seat belt carefully, keeping the harness part away from her ribs.

Andrea and Conrad were well acquainted with Carl and his family. Andrea had known him as a journalist embedded with his unit, before joining Conrad and his small group of spec ops guys. After they were married, she'd photographed Carl's wedding and each of his six newborn children as they came along, including the latest set of twins. Rebecca was happy with her family and Carl was a good husband and father. Conrad had a lot of respect for a man who ran his own business, had six kids at home and still dropped everything to help a fellow army buddy in need.

Conrad slid in next to Andrea and took her least bruised hand. "Okay, babe?" He looked intently for any painful reaction to the move.

"I'm fine." She smiled at her husband, the scary guy in sunglasses who had carried a gun in her mind. "Now."

"We'll get you home and to bed. Doc says in a few days you should be pretty good, except for the ribs." He kissed his wife on the ear. "Guess we'll have to postpone our fifth wedding anniversary celebration for a while."

"Oh my God, I completely forgot!" Andrea frowned.

"Completely understandable." Carl's remark came from the seat behind them.

Conrad aimed for Andrea's ear and one more kiss, but she turned her head and took his lips in hers. The kiss lasted longer than was comfortable with strangers around, but Conrad wasn't willing to let go. He had his wife back and he never wanted to let go. He had to be touching her, holding her, kissing her for the rest of his life. Despite the air-conditioned van, Conrad's body flared with heat, as their kiss deepened.

Carl cleared his throat and Conrad unwillingly sat back in his seat, a dreamy smile plastered across his face.

Andrea chuckled, then winced.

It was time to bite the bullet. Conrad leaned in close to his wife. "I had a surprise for you. For our anniversary."

Andrea smiled and pushed into his shoulder, her eyes closed, but a smile played across her lips. "And what was that?"

"I've been consumed with business these past few months…"

"Years…" Andrea whispered.

"Years. And it's about time I got my priorities straight."

"Priorities?" Her mumbled words told Conrad she was settling into sleep, but he continued. He'd started. If he didn't keep going and say what needed to be said, he might just chicken out. This was too important to be left unsaid for one more minute.

"You, my love. You are my priority. And I forgot

that for a while. But I got my head straight when I thought I might have lost you. Actually, lost me."

"Umm, found me..." Andrea smiled again. She was drifting and heard the words but couldn't quite focus on their meaning. He'd always found her, and her camera.

"Yes, found you and me...in the process." He kissed her hair and smelled the beautiful scent of his wife. "And I'll never lose track of us again. I have a plan to change our lives."

Andrea yawned and snuggled closer.

"I'm backing out of GST. At least for a while."

Andrea sat up then winced. "What?"

"I think it's time to concentrate on us for a while and leave off working twenty-four-seven. Pete'll take care of the company and I can watch my favorite gal chase photos. She may need someone to save her camera every once in a while." Conrad's lips eliminated any protest Andrea may have been thinking.

Chapter 25

Three days later, everyone had pretty much caught up on sleep, cleanliness, and caloric consumption. Andrea and Evie sat in lounge chairs beside the McIntyre's backyard pool, relaxing in the morning sunshine. Sweet tea in a pitcher sweated rivulets as the two women chatted amicably.

"Evie, I can't understand how you survived all those months. I know what happened, cause Conrad told me some of the stuff, but my God!" Andrea rubbed her bandaged ribs and sipped the iced tea.

"I wanted to live. That was the bottom line. Each day I woke up and just wanted to live." Evie rubbed a long scar on her shoulder. "You do what you have to."

Silly Bird sat on his perch, pecking at a suet bar of seeds and lard in the shade. Now that he had regular food, he seemed to settle down a bit, but he still begged for rum! "The whole time I was in the cell and the ocean, I kept hearing a voice that told me what to do. I thought for a while I was going crazy, but…" She took another sip of tea and lay back. "I guess I just wanted to live, too. Or maybe I was a little crazy. I don't know."

Evie tried to hide her smile. She knew whose voice Andrea had heard, but Conrad's wife would never believe it if she told her. Evie sent a thought of thanks to Amee and Grady. *Wherever you two are, thanks for helping Andrea survive.*

The ice in the pitcher broke apart and tinkled into the tea. A wave of warmth passed across Evie's soul, as the virtual hug enveloped her being. She smiled again.

"You're welcome," came the reply.

As the women relaxed in the Texas sunshine and talked, Evie knew Simon was inside at the dining room table, catching up on business. His bonus had hit the bank, and he was doing a happy dance every time he sent an email. His partner had been furious that Simon missed the debut party in his honor, but Simon was actually relieved he didn't have to make the required appearance in front of screaming fans. He had some strange fears about crowds and people reaching for him, and Evie, of all people, completely understood. She didn't much like crowds either. The occasional touch from a stranger still caused her to jump or pull away.

"So, you and Simon? Is it a permanent thing, or just a fling with the boss?" Andrea was curious. She'd been watching the distant couple for several days.

"Oh Andi, I don't know. Sometimes I feel like I don't want to be without him. Then other times I just want to throttle the guy and throw his computer in the toilet." Evie looked over the fence. A curl of white smoke followed Mrs. Chamber's location as she worked the imaginary flowerbeds near the fence, eavesdropping on their conversation.

"Morning, Mrs. Chambers." Evie called, out of pure entertainment.

Mrs. Chamber's head popped up above the fence. "Good morning, girls." Her cigarette hung off the corner of her lips. "Mrs. McIntyre, did you have an accident?" The nosy woman just had to ask.

Rather than explain the entire chain of events, Andi

kept it simple. "Yes, Mrs. Chambers. Thanks for asking." Andrea rubbed her middle and waved. "Doing fine now, though."

That ended the conversation and Mrs. Chambers went back to poking at the bottom of the fence, probably one ear cocked for any gossip she could pass on at the community club card game that evening.

"Evie, relationships are the hardest thing you'll ever tackle. Conrad and I started out so incredibly happy and in love, then I don't know either, what happened." She took a gulp of tea as an ice cube let loose and fell forward. "Ya know, I was a combat journalist, then I was a new wife and Conrad started his company with Pete. Things just progressed and took a left turn somewhere." She looked at her friend and lowered her voice. "We were supposed to celebrate our fifth wedding anniversary the night I got kidnapped, and I was miserable."

It wasn't news to Evie. When she'd separated from the military, both Pete and Conrad had come for the ceremony. Conrad had babbled something about quitting his job and taking Andrea on a worldwide photo safari, because he thought their marriage was in trouble. Pete was flirting with some perky new lieutenant from the Pentagon and out of earshot. "Well, figure it out and fix it, or escape." Evie figured a little reality therapy might be just what was needed.

"I'd never leave Conrad. He's my soul mate. I knew it the first time he pulled me out of a shell hole and covered my head with his helmet!" Andrea giggled. "Silly boy, he got a concussion for his gallantry and I got the *New York Times* Best Picture of the Year." She sobered. "Those were the days."

"They can be again." Conrad stepped from the sliding glass doors. How much of their conversation had he been listening to? He sat on the end of the chaise lounge and gingerly placed a bound folder of papers in his wife's lap. "Read 'em and celebrate." He took a drink of his wife's sweet tea.

"What's this?" Andrea stared at the folder and Evie was a little stunned. A new contract that would take him away more often? Something to occupy all of his time, while his wife continued her race up virtual mountains and through fake flowery fields? Andrea had told her about their conversation in the limo on the way back from the hospital. Hadn't he told his wife he was taking some time off? Or was that the drugs and Andi's wishful thinking...Evie could see the tension crawl back into her healing friend.

"Happy anniversary, honey." He kissed her head and strolled back into the house, as casual as all get out.

Andrea didn't move. She couldn't open the cover. She'd seen enough of those blue bound contracts before. She once told Evie how she hated reading through Conrad's contracts because all she could see was a clock ticking away, away from her. "Here." She handed it over to Evie. "You're secretly cleared and all that stuff. You read it. I can't handle this right now." Tears were forming at the corners of Andrea's eyes.

Evie took the folder. She opened the cover and peered at the first page. If this was a contract, it sure started out in a strange manner. *"Dear Andrea, my wife."* She skimmed the document. *"In the last five years, I have concentrated on building a life that would be comfortable, and a company that would provide enough cash flow to cover anything we wanted to do. It was my primary mission. I now realize, the baby Pete and I developed has become an adult and I have sorely neglected my home duties. GST is ready to operate, on its own. I know that. I also have come to understand that money isn't everything. What's most important is you, babe. So, Pete and I've drawn up the following papers to separate me from the company over..."* Evie stopped. "Maybe you should read this yourself." She closed the folder and handed it out to Andrea.

Andrea blinked several times. She was totally confused at Evie's serious tone. "No. If he wants a divorce, I want to hear it from someone else." Andrea choked out through her tears. Obviously, she had tuned out Evie's words and now thought the worst.

"Nope. No can do. For your eyes only." Evie pushed the folder farther toward Andrea.

Andrea grabbed the folder out of Evie's hands. "What?" She sped read through the letter and flipped through the twenty accompanying pages. "Oh, my God. Oh, my God!" Andrea leveraged herself out of the lounge chair as best she could and ran through the doors. "Conrad! Conrad? Where are you?"

Evie picked up the folder and followed Andrea. She didn't need to read the words. She suspected what the folder contained by the short passage she'd already read.

Conrad and Simon sat at the dining room table in deep conversation. At the loud commotion, Conrad stood and caught his injured wife as she ran into his arms. Her lips found his. Despite the pain it must have caused, her arms wound around his neck and she plastered herself against her husband.

Evie followed and dropped the blue folder on the

table. It was time to let her army buddy and his wife work a few things out. That was, if they could get their lips apart for two seconds to actually speak. "Come on, Simon, let's see if Morehead's team has found any more bugs, upstairs." She nodded her head toward the stairs. "Now, already."

Simon looked at her, then looked at the kissing couple. He got up and followed Evie up the stairs. At the top, he paused and looked back. Conrad had pulled Andrea into his lap on a chair as they continued to smooch. "What was that all about?"

"I think Andrea just got the best anniversary present Conrad could ever have given her." Evie was a little teary-eyed at the prospect.

"What was that, if you don't mind me asking?" Simon followed Evie down the hall where Morehead's crew was running bug-detecting devices over the walls and furniture.

"Him." Evie took Simon's hand and pulled him into their guest room. "She got her husband back."

The bug checkers had finished their room. Evie kicked the door shut and pulled Simon toward the rumpled bed.

"I don't get it." Simon was a little confused as he pulled back and watched her suspiciously.

"Oh, you will." She pulled Simon down and joined him on the bed. "You definitely will!"

From somewhere, a soft giggle crept through the room and out into the sunshine. *"They'll be fine, Grady me matey!"*

Chapter 26

By the end of the week, Andrea was doing much better and Conrad was running around the house making plans for their first adventure.

Pete and Conrad had resolved things with the South Padre Island Police, including a full explanation for Officer Billings' ears only, and a sizeable contribution to the Widows and Orphans Fund. They also had tickets for everyone in their company to attend the Policemen's Ball!

Bull was cooking surprising delicious delights every evening and baking cookies for Mrs. Chambers. He was in heaven in the McIntyre kitchen, with all of its gadgets and accouterments.

Evie had taken Simon to the water park and decided it was the place to be on hot Texas days free from the constraints of job and publicity. They enjoyed the anonymity and the amusement park like two little kids. Evie learned Simon had never been to a real amusement park. She loved watching Simon be a little boy again and learn to enjoy life a little. To his complete amazement, and her complete surprise, he loved the rides and floating the moving river around the park.

Pete had been to the office a couple days in a row, smoothing feathers and figuring out how the new workload would be divvied up. Conrad would still consult on the design elements and have a say as to the contracts. He'd work part-time as his new life permitted, but Pete would shoulder the brunt of the work, with his very efficient administrative assistant. Conrad's secretary, Rita, was promoted to Project Manager and Head Communicator with Conrad, wherever he might be in the world, at any particular moment. Pete seemed to come to terms with his partner's need to be with his wife and Rita was capable of setting up a communication system that could track the guy anywhere in the world if they needed him in an emergency. By their short conversations, Evie was happy that Pete was slowly developing a new appreciation for what a marriage could be. He no longer considered Andrea an interloper, but a valuable asset. And Conrad's level of happiness had doubled in the last few days.

Evie was the lone observer when Pete, remorseful about his part in the surveillance camera scam, made a grand and eloquent attempt to apologize and explain everything to Brittney, the athletic store clerk. He'd really felt bad about what they'd done and didn't like using her and abusing her trust. To his surprise, Brittney turned out to be a pretty observant, smart cookie. She was just completing her degree in business and she actually suggested a dinner invitation in lieu of formal charges. Pete knew a good deal when he saw one, and jumped at the opportunity. After a twenty-minute conversation-flirtation-apology-date suggestion, Evie got the idea that Pete may have found a new friend with potential. Brittney might make a good addition to Pete's life and possibly his company, if things panned out as she thought they might. The flirtatious conversation between the two was so cute, Evie had to step away to maintain any sense of decorum. She damped down the giggles and pretended to shop while the two exchanged their gooey, drippy, sexy banter.

Andrea was in seventh heaven as the world bustled around her lounge chair. Her ribs were still quite painful, but the cuts and bruises were fading fast. Bull's cooking was filling the hole three days without food had produced. Evie invited Callista and Wilmer to come for a visit. Wilmer told Andrea about some 'soft' exercises that would help her stiffness and Calli brought essential oils to rub on her traumatized skin and foot. Andrea hadn't had so much attention since being crowned Homecoming Queen back in high school and was loving it. Evie congratulated herself on her people-judgment skills. Wilmer and Callista were stand-up folks and after learning of his brother's part in Andrea's kidnapping, he vowed to cut off all contact with his useless brother. They told everyone about their plans for the future and Evie noticed how interested Pete and Brittney seemed to be. The world was moving on and the entire drama of the past week was fading with her friend's bruises.

****

All good things have to come to an end eventually, and it was time for Evie and Simon to get back to the real world.

Bull planned a sumptuous Sunday night dinner, complete with prime rib, corn on the cob, three-bean salad and homemade cornbread. Pete had invited Brittney to the dinner, and Simon's pilot tore himself away from his Confederate Air Force buddies to join the party. As they all sat down to the feast, Simon was unusually quiet.

He'd been doing a lot of thinking. Pete's comment at the beginning of the week had made quite an impact, and the happiness that had surrounded him in the last few days, was forming a picture he didn't want to let go of.

"Chow's on. Come and get it!" Bull called from behind the stove. He stood, slicing a giant hunk of rock salt-crusted prime rib. "Let me know how hungry you are, and how done you want it." He wore a new Chef's hat with the words *Chef Cheddar* embroidered on the rim. It was a gift from Pete, via Brittney's suggestion. She was pretty much a fixture by Pete's side now.

As everyone took their seats, Simon spoke up. "Hang on a minute, Bull. I have something I need to know."

Bull grinned. He'd figured it out already.

"When are we going to do this again?" Then Simon quickly rephrased his question. "Not the kidnapping part, the get-together and food." He took a big hunk of prime rib and shoved it in his mouth. He'd never had a big family. Actually, it had only been Uncle Grady and himself, even before his mother had passed away. Now, he was really enjoying the closeness of these new friends and the way they considered him 'family by choice'. It awakened feelings in him that he truly liked and valued, and didn't want to lose when they flew off to his old life.

Everyone spoke at once with different dates and locations.

Simon turned to Evie. Her smile was huge, and he chuckled. "Now look what you did, Mister. Opened a can of worms that will never go back!"

That called for a toast and Conrad stood. He raised his wine glass, and everyone followed suit with whatever they were drinking. "To my family and friends, the same, one and all!"

After dinner, Simon and Pete were clearing the dishes and cleaning up the kitchen. Bull was asleep on a recliner chair, his enormous legs stretched out into the living room as he snored softly. Full belly and satisfied with his dinner, he'd retired right after the dessert was done, and promptly dropped off to sleep.

Pete waved toward Bull. "He's quite the chef, that one. But I bet he eats most of his work!"

They both chuckled. "He deserves it. He grew up on the streets of Oakland. The only good meals he got were at our place." Simon commented. "Don't know how he got so big."

"No kidding." Pete was quiet for a moment, watching Evie and Britney chatting with Andrea. "So, you gonna ask her?" He nodded toward Evie.

Simon choked. On nothing at all.

"Don't let her get away, Simon. She's your other half, if you don't know it already. Anyone with an ounce of brain could tell in just one glance."

Somehow Evie knew they were talking about her and looked toward the two men in the kitchen. She raised an eyebrow then winked with a grin.

"See..." Pete chuckled. "So, what's it gonna be, brother? Make the biggest mistake of your life and lose that gorgeous woman? Or pull up your big boy pants and ask her to share your life?"

Simon was flabbergasted. In the first place, no one had ever called him brother before. In the second place, he'd not been aware that Pete was so observant.

"We're all betting you do the ring thing." Pete punched him softly in the shoulder and put the plates in the cupboard, then went to join his friends in the living room.

Simon stood in the kitchen, contemplating Pete's words. He concentrated on scrubbing the clean broiler pan in the deep sink. His mind was literally swirling. Like his head had in the junior high toilet, when one school bully had caught him alone in the boy's bathroom. Nothing mattered except getting away. But he was an adult now, and running was not an option. Besides, how could he run from something he wanted more than life itself.

"Good you figured that out, boy." Uncle Grady's voice drifted through the open window above the sink. *"I taught you well. Just listen to your heart, or me. I lost my love and had to wait a lifetime to get her back. Hate for you to learn the hard way, like I did."*

Simon heard Amee giggle and maybe a pair of lips kissing a cheek somewhere in heaven. His uncle was right. He had everything he wanted right in front of him. Now all he needed was the courage to grab for the brass ring. Like it always did when he contemplated emotions, a picture of his mother materialized before his eyes, her beautiful smiling face and tight white lace mini dress. She held the hand of the man she said I do' to, the first time. Then the dress faded to rags and her smile was gone, wilted into sunken cheeks and black eyes. The man was gone too, but his handiwork remained, as well as the baby boy they'd created. He'd never known his father and Uncle Grady never, ever made a point of it. He just stepped in and became the man Simon needed in his life.

Simon squeezed his eyes shut. He'd seen the same thing over and over. Too many times to count. The last time, there were only the empty, closed eyes of a shriveled addict, beaten and worn out. No more life left to live on. And he was alone…

"You're never alone, boy, if you truly love." Uncle Grady's tone held such love, it passed over him like a soft, warm wave of complete and tender acceptance. It was the kind of love he'd always wanted from a mother who couldn't break the curse of drugs and alcohol, and men who used and discarded her.

"Simon," Conrad called from the living room, "Now I got a question for you."

Pulled from his own depressing memories, Simon froze. He prayed, please no talk about the ring thing!

Conrad had a map of Brazil on the coffee table and a book of Amazonian animal classification in his lap. "What do you think about a family reunion in Rio de Janeiro?" He pointed to the map on the table.

Simon took a deep breath, dried his hands and joined the group. "Rio?"

Brittney perched on the arm of Pete's overstuffed chair. "Brazil, where the nuts come from!"

Pete gave her a silly look.

"It's a line from Charlie's Aunt. Didn't you ever see the oldie-but-goodie? Young man, you have missed so much!" She wagged her finger at Pete. "Jack Benny? Ann Baxter? Oh my God, you have to see it."

Simon and Conrad were with Pete, but they laughed anyway. Apparently, Pete's new friend was an old movie buff. Bull had come to life with the laughter and added, "I'll make the popcorn."

Chapter 27

In the morning, Bull had produced stacks of buttermilk pancakes, all kinds of sweet toppings, and a mountain of crisp bacon for breakfast. Fresh squeezed orange juice and black coffee was available to wash the sumptuous meal down. The old movie Brittney found in her Netflix catalog, had been hilarious, and the perfect light touch to a very emotional evening.

Pete had swung by the airport before tackling the traffic to the office, just to get one more round of hugs and say a quick good bye. He told Evie and Simon that Brittney was shopping for an Internet tutorial for them to learn Portuguese for their next rendezvous in Rio!

As Conrad and Andrea helped Evie, Simon, and Bull loaded their belongings, both old and new, Simon remained uncharacteristically quiet. Evie was beginning to worry about her boyfriend and boss, as she got ready to board their plane. She tucked the giant stuffed panda into a seat and belted it in. She won the stuffed bear on the sharp shooting carnival game at the water park, and Simon had proudly carried it around all day. He kept pointing out to perfect strangers that wandered by, the fact that his girlfriend had won it for him. How silly, but fun. He was so proud of her rifle prowess!

"Rad, have you noticed that Simon is acting a little different?" Evie whispered to Conrad as she hugged him goodbye.

"The guy's got a lot on his mind. He and Pete had a chat about boy and girl things." Conrad tried not to snicker. "More like Pete did a birds and bees lecture."

"Ah hah. I get it now." Evie smiled and hugged Andrea.

"Have a safe flight, Evielynne. See you in Rio." The last statement brought giggles to both women and a happy smile to Conrad. "This new life is going to be something. I'll keep you posted." The women had bonded over the week and now were fast friends, as well as family.

"Let me know how goes it with Pete and Brittney. If I'm not mistaken, there was something happening between them." Evie spoke quietly.

Andrea glanced toward Simon, standing next to Bull and Zack, their pilot. "The love bug, I think it's going around." She giggled.

Simon seemed to be supervising the loading, even though he didn't know a thing about planes or flying. But it was a good excuse to avoid emotional goodbyes that Evie knew her man detested. Just before boarding, he came toward the small group standing next to Conrad's SUV. He put out his hand to shake with Conrad, but it was a useless maneuver. Conrad grabbed the geek in a full bear hug. Complete with a noisy bro-kiss on the cheek! "Love ya man. Rio. September, right?" Before he let Simon go, Conrad whispered noisily enough for Evie to hear, "Good place for a wedding, right?"

Simon almost fainted.

Evie took his arm as Andrea hugged Simon a little less gregariously. "Thank you for everything, Simon. If it hadn't been for you…" She had to stop before the tears began to flow.

"It was wonderful getting to know Evie's friends, or extended family." He stumbled over the words. He was not good at accepting compliments or gratitude, but he was beginning to relax with physical contact in their little group. Evie was proud of him and hoped it was a new beginning for them both.

Andrea held her arms around him and he didn't squirm. "You are family. Remember that. You're stuck with us now." She placed a sweet kiss on his cheek and moved to stand next to her husband.

Simon just stood there with a glazed look on his face so Evie spoke for him. "Yep, family we are, and I am really looking forward to Rio!"

"Boss, we're ready any time you are." Bull trotted up, shook hands with Conrad and kissed Andrea carefully. "Nice to meet all of ya. I'll cook for you anytime!" He laughed and pulled Simon toward the plane. "Come on, Simon. Time to go."

A laughing Evie followed, waving happily as she boarded the plane.

****

Andrea stood in the arms of her husband. "Think they'll be all right, Rad?"

"Oh, I think Simon is in for a run for his money, and he won't even know it. But I also think he is head over heels in love with our gal. And she with him."

"When did you become Dr. Oz?" Andrea kissed her husband as he helped her into the car.

"How could you miss it? Clear as day." Conrad got into the driver side and started the engine. "Now all he has to do is realize it."

They sat in the SUV listening to some country

western love song, holding hands, as the private jet taxied out onto the tarmac.

****

Inside, Evie and Simon sat in the front two seats. Behind them was Giant Panda and giant Bull. He was already snoring. The side effects of ten pounds of pancakes with butter and syrup, and about the same amount of crispy bacon.

Simon closed his eyes. He needed to shut out the world for a few minutes. He needed to think.

Evie recognized the behavior and let him have his space. Whatever was bothering him, he would work out. If it was their relationship, she couldn't help him anyway. But she had faith that things would somehow work out. Like Uncle Grady's reunion with his ghostly love, Andrea's rescue, and Conrad's decision to work on their marriage, Simon would come around. Or not.

****

Simon sat, still but not relaxed. Pete's words still bothered him. But so did his past.

"Your past ain't what makes the future, boy. Unless you let it." The words Uncle Grady spoke at his mother's funeral came back to him, full force. Could he let go of the memories that haunted him? Could he leave the mental picture of his mother, beaten and dead, behind? How could he be sure, even if he did ask Evie to marry him, that he wouldn't add hurt to her already wounded body and soul? That would kill him.

"Only you can decide what you will, and will not, do. Your mama had the drugs tellin' her. She didn't make her choices, her addiction did. You ain't got that problem, boy. All you got was a bad break that tainted your soul. Now let it go, son. Forgive and forget. Toss

the bad stuff out. Let Evie fill up that place where the bad stuff was, and you'll find the kind of love me, and my Amee have. That's all I got to say on that."

Simon smiled to himself. Uncle Grady always used that statement just before he headed into the second lecture.

"She's worth it, boy. And that's really all I got to say." Again, Simon heard a heavenly giggle, like sweet chimes from above. Amee was laughing at his uncle!

He opened his eyes to see Evie looking at his smile.

"What's so funny, Simon?" Evie was curious.

"Oh, I was just thinking about Grady and Amee. They can be very helpful, when they want, ya know." He chuckled.

Evie smiled at his statement. "They sure helped us with Andrea. I don't think we would have found her, had it not been for Amee talking to me." She spoke a little prayer of thanks to her guardian angel that only Simon could hear. "We wouldn't even have known she was alive."

"So I was thinking…" Simon turned sideways in his seat. "And so was everyone else back at Conrad's place." He grimaced a little, then took a deep breath. "Evie, will you marry me?"

It was out.

"Marry you?" Evie blinked in surprise. She had expected some kind of move toward the next step in their relationship, but marriage? Now that was a bolt out of the blue. "Like, be your wife?"

Now that the question was out, Simon experienced a whole new set of feelings kick in. He chuckled. "Yeah, ya know, like Andrea. A wife."

"Your wife?" Evie was still having trouble believing her ears.

"Maybe you should send her an email, boss." Bull mumbled from the rear seat.

Simon didn't know what to expect, but he had sort of visualized Evie melting into his arms, all teary with a resounding yes! And she just sat there, looking at him. Granted, she did look surprised, but...

"What's it gonna be, baby sister?" Bull held Giant Panda's arms up in question.

Evie slid out of her seat across the aisle and hugged Simon. "Yes. Yes, Simon, I will marry you." She settled next to him, cuddling into his arms with a huge grin.

"Ah, I don't have a ring or anything." Now he was stumbling. This whole thing had just popped out of his mouth so suddenly.

From behind him, Bull pressed a beautiful, folded gold filigree cigar band into his hand. "Been holdin' onto that for some time now. Thought it might come in handy."

Simon took the cigar band and slipped it on Evie's fourth finger. It fit like it was made for her, and he thought he saw it twinkle just a tad as he slipped it on.

"Just like the Unsinkable Molly Brown. I love it." Evie held up her hand to the sunlight streaming through the windows of the Phenom 300.

"Who is Molly Brown and why is she unsinkable?" Simon had never seen the classic old movies.

"Next family reunion, I'm gonna have to introduce her to you, via Netflix. I'm sure it is one of Brittney's favorites." Evie kissed her fiancé soundly and snuggled back in for the long flight home.

Home was going to take on a new meaning after this flight, she thought to herself.

"It sure will. I am so happy for you!" A chiming giggle sounded throughout the plane.

"Guess we got the vote of approval." Simon kissed her head and closed his eyes.

Bull was grinning like an idiot. Simon and Evie were *finally* engaged.

God was in his heaven and all was really right with the world!

Chapter 28

Rose slammed her apartment door. The painting next to the door rattled and fell to the floor.

"Don't break it. You're just a renter." The sarcastic comment came from a man slouched on the couch across the room. "So, your little scheme didn't pan out, sis?" He took the channel changer and began surfing through the programs. "Nothing you do ever works out, does it? The Tools of God, right! More like the blunder of the century."

"Shut up, you imbecile. It's not over 'til it's over." She threw her purse against the floor and stomped into the small galley kitchen. "I don't care what I have to do to bring back our family honor. This is only round one. And just what are you doing to get our family business back on its feet? Huh? You haven't gotten off that couch for three days, and Zede has about had it with you." She shot her brother a dirty look, then frowned at her kitchen. Dishes covered the counter and a half-eaten bowl of cereal sat in the sink. "Why don't you get your lazy ass up and get a job? The guys that belong to the Tools of God do real work. They don't sit around hoping something will happen, or depending on a woman to do the heavy work."

She threw the cereal bowl at him and stomped into her bedroom.

A word from the author...

I am originally from the Pacific Northwest, but knew Alaska would be my heart's home as soon as I stepped off that plane and saw the mountains, way back in the early 1980s. Soon I was truly in love with all the things that make living in Alaska so appealing: fishing, flying, skiing, hunting and long winter nights.

A pilot and avid outdoorswoman, many of my stories involve aviation, the military world, strong female characters, and the cultures and legends of my wild, untamed Alaska. In the last few years, underwater photography and glass art have barged their way into my busy days and writing time.

Initially, I began spinning romantic stories to add spice to a long-distance relationship with my husband, who was often stationed in remote locations around the state and the world. Then the stories made their way to paper. Now my family includes all kinds of interesting characters that invade my daily conversations and cause a raised eyebrow or two in public places.

I enjoy weaving intricate plots with current or historical events, and cultural legends and myths. When I'm not writing, I can be found teaching women's self-defense seminars and martial arts, scuba diving in tropical locales, flying to meet my husband for a quick rendezvous in some romantic out-of-the-way spot, playing with graphic design...or just kicking back with my characters and developing their lives and stories.

You can always stay in touch with me on my webpage (www.miriammatthews.com) or on Facebook (www.facebook.com/miriam.matthews.773).

http://www.miriammatthews.com

Thank you for purchasing
this publication of The Wild Rose Press, Inc.

For questions or more information
contact us at
info@thewildrosepress.com.

The Wild Rose Press, Inc.
www.thewildrosepress.com

To visit with authors of
The Wild Rose Press, Inc.
join our yahoo loop at
http://groups.yahoo.com/group/thewildrosepress/

CPSIA information can be obtained
at www.ICGtesting.com
Printed in the USA
LVHW081449111120
671411LV00020B/88

9 781509 228232